DEAD AS
A SCONE

DEAD AS A SCONE

BY RON AND JANET BENREY

BARBOUR
PUBLISHING

The author is represented by Joyce Hart, Hartline Marketing, 123 Queenston Drive, Pittsburgh, Pennsylvania 15235.

Our mission is to publish and distribute inspirational products offering exceptional value and biblical encouragement to the masses.

Member of the
Evangelical Christian
Publishers Association

Printed in the United States of America.
5 4 3 2 1

We dedicate this book to our many friends at
New Spirit Community Church
in Howard County, Maryland.

Acknowledgments

We wish to thank:

- Diane Talbot, Public Relations Manager of Tunbridge Wells Borough Council, and Anne Mc-Carthy, spokesperson for the West Kent Police, who generously contributed their time to assist us with our research.
- Dr. Irini A. Stamatoudi, a specialist in intellectual property and cultural property law, who provided key insights into the United Kingdom's Limitations Act.
- Dr. Ian Beavis, Technical Officer of Tunbridge Wells Museum—a real museum where one can see a fine collection of antique Tunbridge Ware.
- Daniel Bech, his wife Katharina Mahler, and the other contributors to "Historical and Interesting Views of Tunbridge Wells." Their extraordinary collection of digital photos, maps, and old publications brought Royal Tunbridge Wells to us in Maryland.
- Joyce Hart, our longtime literary agent, and Shannon Hill, our new editor at Barbour Publishing. They made it great fun to write this book.

About Royal Tunbridge Wells

This book is a novel, but Royal Tunbridge Wells is quite real. We have tried to faithfully describe many of the town's well-known locales. As it happens, Janet grew up on the very patch of land where we located the "Royal Tunbridge Wells Tea Museum." The museum is fictional—although it has become fully authentic to us.

RON AND JANET BENREY
Columbia, Maryland
July 2004

The Royal Tunbridge Wells Tea Museum

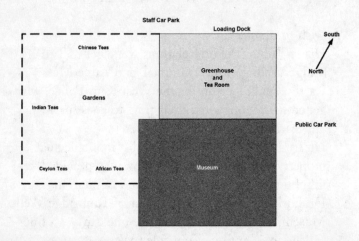

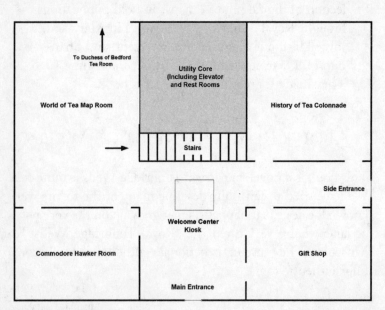

Ground Floor (Main Building)

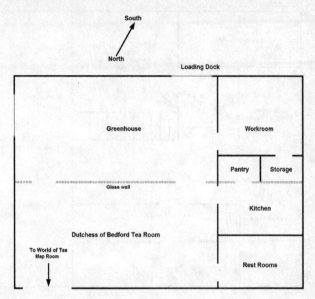

Ground Floor (Extension)

South

North

Loading Dock

Greenhouse

Workroom

Pantry

Storage

Glass wall

Kitchen

Dutchess of Bedford Tea Room

To World of Tea
Map Room

Rest Rooms

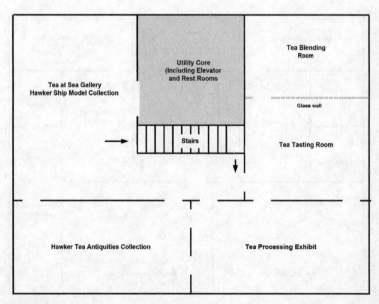

Tea Blending
Room

Utility Core
(Including Elevator
and Rest Rooms)

Tea at Sea Gallery
Hawker Ship Model Collection

Glass wall

Stairs

Tea Tasting Room

Hawker Tea Antiquities Collection

Tea Processing Exhibit

First Floor

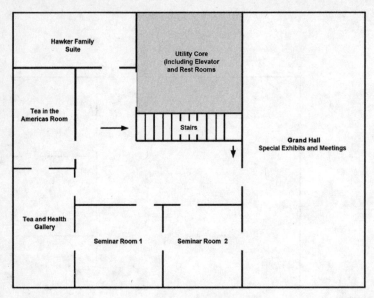

Second Floor

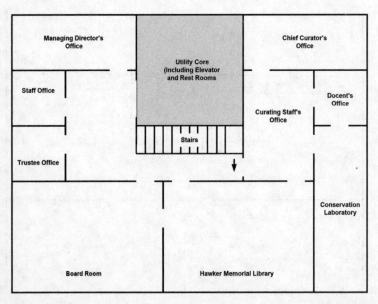

Third Floor

ONE

What does the old dear have up her sleeve? Nigel Owen asked himself as he considered the odd request just proposed to him. Nigel looked across his desk at the plump, rosy-cheeked, elegantly coiffed woman sitting in his visitor's chair. Elspeth Hawker was eighty-four years old but appeared—and sounded—fifteen years younger. This morning, her usually placid face seemed filled with a curious determination.

"Let me understand you, Dame Elspeth," Nigel said. "You want to speak at the end of our trustees' meeting this afternoon, but you don't want me to announce your intentions to the other trustees until the very last moment—is that correct?"

She nodded slowly. "Indeed. You will not mention me until the rest of our program is finished."

"Is it someone's birthday?" Nigel asked. "Do you plan to reveal that one of the trustees won an award?"

"No. It's nothing like that." She gazed down at the tops of her hands. "I know that I am imposing on our friendship,

11

Nigel, but I ask your indulgence as a personal favor."

"Won't you at least tell me what you plan to talk about?" Nigel asked.

"If I do, will you promise to add me to the agenda without any further questions?"

He nodded. "Absolutely!"

Elspeth hesitated for several seconds. "I recently made a painful discovery," she finally said. "We have a thief in our midst—an exceedingly clever thief, I might add. I feel it my duty to explain the circumstances to the other trustees."

The pen Nigel had been holding slipped from his hand. "Dame Elspeth! You surely are not suggesting that one of the trustees of the Royal Tunbridge Wells Tea Museum is a criminal."

"I have led a sheltered, pampered life—so perhaps I am overly surprised at the willingness of people to repay evil with evil."

"Evil? I don't understand what you mean."

Nigel noted that Elspeth no longer was looking his way. She seemed to be staring at the wall behind his head. "When a thief is caught, he must pay back double," she said softly.

"Double?" Nigel felt wholly bewildered at Elspeth's rapid changes of subject.

Elspeth peered at him once again with her alert blue eyes. "That rule is from the Bible, you know. Exodus 22:7."

"No, I didn't know. But, getting back to your—*ah*—explanation to the trustees."

Elspeth refused to be steered. "Paying back double is the right thing to do under normal circumstances. But this is a museum. Our circumstances are special. Paying back single will have to suffice. I must explain that to the other trustees."

Nigel pressed. "*Who* is this thief? *What* was stolen? *What* do you intend to say to the other trustees? I am quite at a loss."

"You see, this is why I don't want a formal place on the program. The other trustees are certain to ask me the very same questions." She sighed. "It is all so complicated. I prefer to tell my wretched tale only once today."

Nigel changed tack.

"Dame Elspeth, as acting director of this museum, I have to rely on the absolute integrity of our trustees. You have broached the topic of thievery—I really must ask you to share your suspicions with me."

"And so I shall, at the end of our meeting this afternoon." She reached across the desk and patted Nigel's hand. "The other trustees think me a foolish old woman. Permit me to behave like one today. What is the harm in that?"

Nigel thought a moment. *Probably no harm at all.* His momentary surge of concern vanished as he realized that Elspeth's "thief in our midst" could not be anything more than a colorful exaggeration. Serious thievery from the Royal Tunbridge Wells Tea Museum was impossible. An impenetrable electronic security system protected the artifacts on display, and the museum's state-of-the-art financial software would rapidly detect any significant embezzling of money.

Nigel felt himself smile. Dame Elspeth must have uncovered a case of minor pilferage from the gift shop or the Duchess of Bedford Tearoom. If she wanted to present her discovery to the trustees—well, she certainly was entitled to have her way. Hawker money, after all, built and stocked the museum. Moreover, her out-of-the-blue "explanation" would liven up what promised to be an especially dull trustees' meeting.

He glanced at the printed meeting schedule on his desktop. There was no significant business to discuss, no burning issues. The museum was chugging along uneventfully, thanks in large measure to his fine management skills. The "high spot" today would be a lecture by Dr. Felicity Adams, the museum's new chief curator, about the different approaches to professional tea tasting in different tea-growing regions of the world.

I can't wait, Nigel thought grimly. He gave a tiny shudder.

"Consider it done, Dame Elspeth," Nigel said grandly. "Only you and I know that you will speak the final words this afternoon."

Nigel fought to stay awake by cataloging the various inducements to sleep that weighed down his eyelids.

For starters, the trustees of the Royal Tunbridge Wells Tea Museum had enjoyed a lavish afternoon "cream tea" at three thirty—a high-carbohydrate festival of assorted scones, clotted cream, and ten different kinds of jams, preserves, and conserves.

Immediately thereafter, Felicity Adams had begun a soporific lecture on the art and science of tasting tea. Flick Adams, as she preferred to be called, had spoken in her monotonous American voice for more than sixty minutes so far, and there was no telling how much longer her mind-numbing oration might drag on.

To numb one's mind even further, the museum's boardroom was overheated. The outside temperature on that sunny Wednesday afternoon in mid-October had risen to a pleasant fifteen degrees Celsius—almost sixty degrees Fahrenheit—but the museum's archaic central heating plant obliviously continued to pump torrents of hot water through the radiators. Alas, it was impossible to open a window because someone had shut the drapes, presumably to make Flick's tedious images of tea-tasting rooms in Asia, Europe, and Africa easier to see on the screen.

Who cares about the proper way to "cup" a Darjeeling?

Nigel swallowed a yawn and looked around the conference table. To his astonishment, the museum's eight trustees appeared spellbound by Flick's presentation. Their rapt expressions looked sincere; their total attention to her words struck him as authentic. They actually seemed *interested* in the trivial fact that a tea taster tastes tea that is five times stronger than the brew most people drink.

Well, seven of the eight seem interested.

Diagonally across the immaculately polished mahogany table from Nigel, Dame Elspeth Hawker had dozed off. She sat slumped in her chair, snoring delicately, her head resting comfortably against the leather wing. Nigel smiled at the sight of the snoozing octogenarian. *She's earned the right not to listen. If I were eighty-four years old—and filthy rich, to boot— I'd be fast asleep, too. Especially if I had eaten* three *raisin scones slathered with Danish lingonberry preserves and topped with dollops of thick cream.*

A delightful notion took shape in Nigel's mind. Perhaps he could use the dozing grande dame as an excuse to have the kitchen brew a decent pot of strong coffee. After all, one of his chief responsibilities as acting director of the museum was to orchestrate successful monthly meetings of the trustees. Dame Elspeth needed to be fully awake and alert when Flick finally sat down—and so did her seven colleagues.

Nigel surveyed the seven other trustees again and felt modestly virtuous that he had kept his word to Elspeth. None of them knew that Elspeth would close the meeting with the tale of an "exceedingly clever thief." Strong coffee all around might be just the ticket.

Nigel let the delicious idea percolate awhile. Even the lowliest coffee would be preferable to the three kinds of estate-grown tea—one from China, one from India, one from Ceylon—that he had served to the trustees from elegant Coalport teapots. Tradition demanded that the director play "mother" at trustee meetings, but his heart had not been in it. A hot *cuppa* at "teatime" was pleasant enough, Nigel agreed, but certainly not in the same league as a steaming mug of freshly brewed coffee.

How had tea managed to become the so-called national drink of Great Britain, anyway? The great irony was that tea was first offered in the coffeehouses of England during the middle of the seventeenth century. Even today, Brits consumed colossal quantities of coffee—except, of course, at the Royal Tunbridge Wells Tea Museum.

Feeling genuine regret, Nigel decided that his scheme to switch beverage was doomed to failure. "The trustees are blasted tea aficionados," he muttered under his breath. "The merest hint of coffee will put the lot of them off their feed." With the exception of Dame Elspeth, the eight men and women who presided over the Royal Tunbridge Wells Tea Museum were quite similar: fiftyish, give or take a few years, superbly successful in their careers, and—this last trait puzzled Nigel endlessly—gaga about tea. How could highly educated people be so *passionate* about shriveled leaves soaked in boiling water?

Nigel concealed a sigh. *Ah, well—some mysteries have no explanations.* Besides, it made little difference whether or not he understood the trustees' motivations. The simple fact was if they loved tea, Nigel would pretend that he loved tea just as much.

For the past six months, Nigel had gone the extra mile to please the trustees. His yearlong stint as acting director was half-finished, and Nigel counted on one of the eight to pave the way for his next position—preferably a permanent rather than temporary post.

Nine months ago, Nigel Owen had been declared redundant when a behemoth Dutch conglomerate purchased the London-based insurance company he had worked at for ten years. Senior management jobs were tight—even for someone with his sterling education, broad experience, and still relatively tender age of thirty-eight. He had been fortunate to land the acting directorship at the museum. What he needed now was an influential person to offer a helping hand. And say what he might about their loopy affection for tea, the museum's trustees included some exceedingly influential people.

Nigel's tidy mind had meticulously organized them in order of their likely ability to advance his career: The unmistakable leader in career clout was Archibald Meicklejohn, the chair of the trustees. A trim, balding, always impeccably dressed banker from the City, London's financial centre, he sat on several corporate boards of directors, hobnobbed with the prime minister, and owned the rather spectacular Bentley that currently reposed in the museum's staff car park. Nigel liked to imagine Archibald calling one evening to ask, "What salary and perks would you require to join my staff as my personal financial advisor?"

Next in line was Sir Simon Clowes, a distinguished cardiologist whose large hands, craggy face, and thick graying hair made him look more like a veteran mountain climber than a successful doctor with offices in London and Tunbridge Wells. Sir Simon was well situated to tout Nigel's skills to the executives of healthcare organizations. Nigel could easily picture himself as an administrator at a major hospital or possibly a financial manager at an international pharmaceutical firm. Sir Simon could start the ball rolling with a simple e-mail to one of his cronies.

Nigel's most exotic fantasy involved Iona Saxby, an Oxford-based solicitor who looked as if she had been drawn by Leonardo DaVinci: statuesque, stylish, with a magnificently enigmatic face that could camouflage her every emotion. What would happen, Nigel mused, should Iona invite him to become business director of her high-powered law firm? He would accept the offer—after suitably playing hard to get, of course—and spend the rest of his career as a shadowy power broker, a puller of legal strings, feared and respected throughout the realm.

The other trustees were less easy to sort out.

The Reverend William de Rudd, vicar of St. Stephen's Church in Tunbridge Wells, was reportedly a school chum of the current archbishop of Canterbury. The ever jovial, decidedly rotund clergyman reputedly had prominent friends across England, but not in circles of interest to Nigel Owen.

Matthew Eaton was a renowned landscape architect headquartered up the road in East Grinstead. A large man, he made himself look even bulkier by invariably wearing Harris Tweed suits and sport coats. His clients included Her Majesty the Queen, and it was widely assumed that "Sir Matthew" would show up on the nation's Honours list next year. Well and good for him—but how could a glorified gardener give Nigel a leg up?

A similar question might be asked about Dorothy McAndrews—a PhD art historian turned antiques dealer, who owned a string of fifteen antique shops scattered throughout Kent and Sussex. Easily the most glamorous of the trustees, with a classic Celtic combination of red hair, greenish eyes, and fair, porcelain-like skin, she appeared regularly on the telly, on the BBC show that traveled around

Britain appraising antiques. However, her ability to help Nigel land a better job seemed rather thin.

Marjorie Halifax was the politician among the trustees. She served as a councilwoman on the Tunbridge Wells Borough Council and was widely considered an expert on Kentish tourism. Marjorie was one of those women who, though short, seemed tall. Her loud voice and extravagant gestures more than made up for her petite stature. Marjorie had scads of influence locally—but Nigel's daydreams extended beyond the precincts of Tunbridge Wells. Or should he say *Royal* Tunbridge Wells? Nigel never felt certain—and apparently neither did the locals. In 1909, King Edward VII had bestowed the right to add the somewhat pretentious prefix "Royal" to Tunbridge Wells—but many residents chose not to do so. Royal or not, Nigel thought the small city too tame, too bucolic, and longed to return to London.

Finally, there was Dame Elspeth herself, granddaughter of Commodore Desmond Hawker. *The* Desmond Hawker— the fabled, somewhat notorious, nineteenth-century tea merchant who used much of the huge fortune he amassed to endow the great foundation that bore his name. It had been Dame Elspeth's half sister—Mary Hawker Evans—who, some forty years earlier, wheedled and coaxed the Hawker Foundation to establish a tea museum to house the family's many tea-related antiquities, celebrate the importance of tea in Great Britain, and, "While we're at it, honor Commodore Desmond's memory. And wouldn't it be lovely to locate the museum in Commodore Desmond's favorite English town: Royal Tunbridge Wells, on the border of Kent and Sussex?"

The Royal Tunbridge Wells Tea Museum Charitable Trust had been duly created on 1 March 1964. Soon thereafter, the trust erected an impressive, four-story Georgian-style building on Eridge Road, opposite the Tunbridge Wells Common, a short walk from the Pantiles, the charming colonnaded walkway one sees in all the tourist brochures about Royal Tunbridge Wells. With its five major galleries—tea blending and tasting rooms; meeting facilities; tea parlor; and garden, complete with a greenhouse holding the largest collection of tea plants in England—the museum met every requirement on Mary Hawker Evans's wish list.

Several letters to the editor of the *Kent and Sussex Courier* called the vast building a white elephant, questioned the wisdom of honoring a man of checkered reputation, and expressed caustic doubt that sensible vacationers would choose to visit the Royal Tunbridge Wells Tea Museum. But visit they did—in droves. Tea lovers from Tennessee, Taiwan, and Tasmania made pilgrimages of thousands of miles to see the clipper ship models in the Tea at Sea Gallery, the famed collection of gimcracks and crockery in the Tea Antiquities Gallery, and the huge diorama in the History of Tea Colonnade. The museum quickly became one of the most popular attractions in the south of England and, surprisingly to everyone involved, a source of considerable academic scholarship about tea.

Tea economists, tea historians, tea chemists, and tea geographers from around the world discovered that Desmond Hawker and his descendants had assembled a truly world-class collection of tea-related documents, memorabilia, and relics. As they also flocked to Royal Tunbridge Wells, they dramatically changed the character of the museum's workforce. The Hawker Foundation had assumed that the museum's curator would be little more than a watchman who tended the various exhibits. But today, the Royal Tunbridge Wells Tea Museum had a staff of four professional curators—experts in document restoration, wood preservation, art history, and cartography—

led by a chief curator, the long-winded Felicity Adams, PhD.

A dissonance of different laughs, followed by a burst of robust applause as the lights came on in the room, brought Nigel back to the present. Praise the Lord! Flick had held her lecture to only an hour and ten minutes. She must have ended with a joke about tea tasting, if such a thing were even possible.

The new chief curator had been appointed the previous summer. The trustees had debated for nearly a year before they finally chose Felicity Adams from among a field of ten candidates. Nigel had been present for their final discussion; the choice had not been unanimous. Matthew Eaton had been reluctant to appoint an American to "a distinctly British position"; Dorothy McAndrews wanted a "museum person" rather than a "tea person"; and Iona Saxby had worried that "Dr. Adams, age thirty-six, was a tad too young to be taken seriously by her much older peers at other museums."

In the end, Flick's credentials had carried the day. She held a doctorate in food chemistry from the prestigious University of Michigan, had been a senior tea taster at a leading tea purveyor, and had written three successful books for laypeople about tea—including the unexpectedly popular *How to Host an English Tea.* She possessed, Nigel thought, all of the characteristics a successful chief curator required: arrogance, self-importance, dreariness, and a fanatic love of tea.

Time to take charge of the meeting.

"Thank you for sharing your expertise, Dr. Adams," he said. "It's really quite amazing how *much* there is to know about tea."

The soft-spoken Rev. de Rudd murmured a barely audible "Hear! Hear!" The drum-throated Archibald Meicklejohn roared, "Entirely amazing! And I am sure we all agree—*fascinating!*" The ever-political Marjorie Halifax added, "I concur! Fascinating is the only possible word!"

Nigel knew, of course, that Flick Adams understood his understated sarcasm. She smiled warmly and said, "Thanks, everyone. It's a pleasure to talk to people who are thoroughly knowledgeable about tea." She stared directly at him. "Many laypeople are *so* ignorant."

"Yes, well, let's move on," Nigel said.

"Move on?" Archibald Meicklejohn spoke up. "Our meeting ended with Dr. Adams's brilliant presentation."

"Not quite," Nigel said. "We have one more item of new business. Dame Elspeth wants to discuss a matter of considerable importance."

"No one told me!" Archibald said, somewhat testily. "As chair of the trustees, I am certainly entitled to know of changes to our agenda."

"Dame Elspeth visited my office before the meeting." Nigel added a little white lie: "It seemed too late to notify you. I apologize for not doing so."

Nigel looked across the table and saw that Dame Elspeth was still asleep, though no longer snoring. There was something unnatural about the pallor of her skin. And—was it possible?—she had slipped farther down in her chair.

Before Nigel could make sense of his four observations, Iona Saxby, who was seated alongside the elderly woman, let loose a robust shriek: "Good heavens! Dame Elspeth is ill!" Regrettably, the startled attorney also gave the Dame's swivel chair an accidental shove. The shriek and the shove worked together in perfect unison; as every eye in the room turned toward the oldest trustee, she slid off the slick leather upholstery and fell to the floor with a lifeless thump.

Dr. Clowes moved to her side in an instant, but Nigel had not the slightest doubt that Dame Elspeth Hawker was dead.

And neither, apparently, did the six trustees who stayed anchored in their seats. Nigel watched their frozen smiles, their eyes darting to and fro nervously, occasionally joining beams with his.

After several seconds of mental wheel-spinning, Nigel's good sense kicked in and he reached for his cell phone. "I'll call for an ambulance."

"There is no need for haste," the doctor said, rising. "Dame Elspeth is quite dead. She seems to have slipped away several minutes ago."

Nigel snapped the cell phone shut.

"However," Flick Adams said, "there is every need to call the police."

It was only then that Nigel noticed Flick had switched the lights back on and was standing directly over Dame Elspeth.

"Why the police?" he asked her.

"Elspeth Hawker has been poisoned. Look at her."

Dr. Clowes stiffened. "I have looked at Dame Elspeth! What possible line of thinking leads you to suggest—"

Flick didn't wait for Dr. Clowes to finish. "Check out the color of her face," she said. "Look at her eyes. Feel how cold her skin is. She has the classic symptoms of sudden death from a barbiturate overdose."

Nigel heard a definite crack in Flick's voice. She was clearly upset and fighting to control herself.

Dr. Clowes harrumphed loudly. "One cannot make such a determination after death without a battery of tests. In any case, may I remind you, *Dr.* Adams, you are not a medical doctor!"

"True—but I probably know more about forensic toxicology than you do. There are definite indications that can't be ignored."

Somewhere in the back of his intellect, Nigel vaguely

grasped that a noisy argument between Sir Simon Clowes and Felicity Adams had begun. He didn't hear their verbal thrusts and parries, however, because the spasm of alarm that abruptly gripped the front of his intellect overpowered his senses. He worked frantically to connect the logical dots that swarmed like gnats in his brain:

Dame Elspeth was dead. That much was certain. Flick Adams *might* be right about an overdose of barbiturates. If so, that would indeed mean Elspeth had been murdered.

Why was she murdered? Possibly to silence her before she could announce to the other trustees the identity of the "exceedingly clever thief" she had discovered.

If so, the thief might well assume that Dame Elspeth shared her concerns with Nigel Owen when she asked him to modify the meeting's agenda.

Dame Elspeth's final question echoed through his mind: "What is the harm in that?"

The blooming harm, you foolish old woman, is that I may now be in significant danger, too.

Nigel poured through his memory again. Had Elspeth said anything else that might point to the person she had in mind? Not a word!

A woman's voice shouted, "Nonsense!"

A man's voice bellowed, "Poppycock!"

With a start, Nigel realized that the noisy argument in front of him had become explosive. He looked up in time to see—and hear—Sir Simon Clowes roar, "I will not hear another utterance of your inane twaddle! Dame Elspeth's heart failed. There is no doubt in my mind my diagnosis is correct. Not a whit of misgiving. Not a trice. Not a smidgen."

Nigel felt his own heart leap for joy. A heart attack meant no poison. And no poisoner. And no danger to himself. Of course, there was still the matter of Dame Elspeth's suspicions to deal with. . . .

Or was there?

The old woman's fuzzy meanderings in his office hardly made sense. She had refused to flesh out her vague claim with specifics. He would be foolish to repeat her words to anyone. Far better to forget them lest they cast a pall on Dame Elspeth's memory.

Nigel rapped the table with his knuckles. "Excuse me," he said. "I urge us all to listen to Sir Simon's wise counsel. I also intend to send out for coffee. Would anyone else like a cup?"

Two

Felicity Katherine Adams —*Flick* to her friends—yanked three more tissues from the box on her desk, blew her nose for what seemed the umpteenth time, and wondered when it would finally stop dripping.

Blast them all—their closed minds and calloused hearts.

She crumpled the tissues into a tight ball and decided that if ever there was a proper occasion for unabated sniveling, this was it. How could she *not* cry after losing a wonderful friend *and* smashing into a stone wall of obstinate stupidity? No one else in the boardroom recognized the obvious facts. Not one of them would pay attention to simple truth.

Starting today, they have new names: the fool, the oaf, and the six toadies.

The chief curator's office filled the southwest corner on the top floor of the Royal Tunbridge Wells Tea Museum and provided an uninspiring view of the public and private car parks. Flick moved to the window behind her desk and stared at the ambulance parked directly below. The boxy white Renault van seemed to glow in the white floodlights that illuminated the area behind the museum. It reminded Flick of the bread truck that made predawn deliveries on her street in York, Pennsylvania, during her childhood.

The *fool*—Sir Simon Clowes—stood next to the ambulance's still-open rear door, signing paperwork for the ambulance technician, who seemed to savor the physician's every word. The technician was a tall, athletic woman in her late twenties wearing a yellow jumpsuit. Her deferential body language signaled that she knew of Dr. Clowes and his impeccable reputation. She hadn't even bothered to check for signs of life in the boardroom before hefting poor Elspeth onto the gurney. The doctor's golden judgment had been sufficient to convince her.

Flick felt a twinge of guilt. Perhaps she should have chosen more tactful words during her argument with Sir Simon. Calling one of England's leading cardiologists a "feeble-minded quack" might have been an overreaction. She peered at her hazy reflection in the window glass and watched herself shrug. What other label fit a doctor who ignored all the classic symptoms of barbiturate poisoning, *then* refused to listen to reason—again and again?

He was dead wrong! I've forgotten more forensic toxicology than he ever learned.

That's what made the situation really galling. A physician of Sir Simon's age had studied little, if any, forensic chemistry or forensic toxicology; whereas Flick had taken every class she could find on these subjects and had seriously considered switching her major to one of the forensic sciences. In the end, though, simple squeamishness drove her career choice: Flick loved the intellectual challenge of being a scientific detective but hated the grim reality of handling bits and pieces of a corpse. Her favorite forensic toxicology professor decided that the problem was Flick's spirited imagination. "You simply can't put enough emotional distance between you and dead crime victims," he had said. The happier work of food chemistry won her over.

Flick looked down at the car park again. The *oaf*—Nigel Owen—stood near the front of the ambulance, talking to the driver. He had been less than useless when the lights came on in the boardroom, frozen in place like a statue, staring wide-eyed, pasty-faced, and slack-jawed while Flick fought her losing battle with Simon Clowes. Nigel might have chimed in, perhaps suggesting a second opinion or at the very least agreeing to call the police. But no! The oaf had sided with one of the trustees against his chief curator—a miserable, disloyal thing even for a stand-in museum director to do.

How can a tea museum be managed successfully by a man who hates tea?

Soon after she met Nigel, Flick decided that he had been hired as acting director chiefly because he looked the part. Tall, lanky, ruddy-faced, with a shock of reddish-blond hair— the typical hail-fellow-well-met wing commander character she'd seen encouraging his men in old World War II movies.

In fact, Nigel's adventurous Battle of Britain image vanished the moment he opened his mouth. The man had the mind, heart, and imagination of a bean counter. He consistently showed himself more concerned about finances and policy than about the quality of the experience visitors enjoyed at the museum.

"We have met the *real* Nigel Owen," Flick muttered. "A stuffy, pretentious pain in the rump who expects to have everything his own way. And he usually gets it, because the trustees follow his every lead. Like now, for example."

The six other surviving trustees—the *six toadies*—were gathered a few paces behind Nigel, chatting quietly. They had agreed instantly when he urged them to "listen to Sir Simon's wise counsel." How could Flick have expected otherwise? The trustees were easily swayed by cachet and reputation. Nigel held an MBA degree from the prestigious INSEAD in Fontainebleau, France. Consequently, the toadies apparently assumed he must be an intelligent, efficient, practical manager. Therefore, they acted with complete reliance on his judgment—even when he made rotten suggestions, like this afternoon.

Well, to be perfectly fair, they always do what you ask, too.

Flick resolved to find a new epithet. "Toadies" seemed too negative a description of the museum's trustees. They were basically good people who had been exceptionally supportive during her brief tenure as chief curator. No, she shouldn't blame them for being led astray by Sir Simon Clowes. After all, most people expect a licensed physician to know what he's talking about.

A noise from the car park caught Flick's attention. The ambulance technician had slammed the van's rear door shut. She shuddered at the finality of the ugly thump. Dame Elspeth Hawker had begun her final journey. There would be no further medical scrutiny, no postmortem examination of her body, no toxicology tests, all because Dr. Clowes claimed—no, insisted!—that an old woman had suffered a "massive coronary failure."

The law is on his side. There's no way I can undo what he's done.

Once again, Flick felt the chaotic combination of grief, anger, and powerlessness that had compelled her to take refuge in her office an hour earlier. Thank goodness for a full box of tissues. She didn't cope well with situational stone walls. But then, none of the Adamses did. A doggedness to succeed threaded Flick's family tree like steel rods through re-inforced concrete.

John and Pauline Adams, her parents, owned and stub-bornly operated the White Rose of York, an eighteenth-century English inn in York, Pennsylvania, complete with an authentic pub. The White Rose had remained true to its founders' dream despite a fire, three recessions, and two takeover attempts by large hotel chains.

Her uncle, now a homicide detective in the York Police Department, had managed to foil an armed robbery after he'd been badly wounded. The bullet fragment still lodged in his back fifteen years later testified to his tenacity.

Flick's older brother was an entrepreneur who launched a successful publishing empire on a shoestring budget. Her cousins included a female astronaut and a color-blind artist.

In short: Count on an Adams *not* to take no for an answer. It was the personality trait she was most proud of—a quality that helped her earn her PhD at the tender age of twenty-four.

The ambulance's diesel engine rumbled to life. Flick could not be positive from so far away, but it looked like Sir Simon had a smile on his face as he watched the ambulance negotiate the museum's private driveway that circled around the rear of the building and served the loading dock and the employees' car park.

"What's going through that devious mind of yours?" she said softly.

Flick wished she could ask him a point-blank question: Why would a competent doctor choose to sweep the facts of El-speth's poisoning under the museum's Bokhara rug? Surely he must know that the unexplained drop in Elspeth's body tem-perature while she sat in a warm room was an absolute giveaway. Her body had lost heat *before* she died because the barbiturates coursing through her bloodstream triggered hypothermia.

Sir Simon's vehement rebuff to Flick's straightforward observation of this fact made no sense at all. . .*or did it*?

Flick moved her head to get a better view of Sir Simon. He was shaking Nigel's hand—and this time there definitely was a smile on his face. "Maybe he thinks that Dame Elspeth killed herself," she murmured. "That would explain everything. He lied to protect the family from a scandal in the British tabloids."

Could Elspeth have intentionally taken an overdose?

"Impossible!" Flick shouted at her reflection.

Suicide was unthinkable. Everyone around Dame Elspeth could see how excited she was to be alive. Her growing interest in the museum, her enthusiasm at trustee meetings, and her newfound happiness spoke volumes about the state of her mind.

For seventy years, Elspeth had lived under the larger-than-life shadow cast by her older half sister, Mary Hawker Evans. Mary had been the undisputed leader of the family—a calculating matriarch who ruled her children and her timid sibling like a tsarina. Elspeth had never married or pursued a career, being content to lead a reclusive life confined mostly to her own house and garden. But fourteen years ago, when Mary died, the real Elspeth emerged like a butterfly from a chrysalis.

When Elspeth became the sole owner of the finest antiquities on display, her interest in the Royal Tunbridge Wells Tea Museum blossomed. She explored every corner of the museum, becoming reacquainted with her grandfather's many treasures—more than three thousand cataloged items in all—including an unparalleled collection of tea-related paintings, maps, and photographs; unique models of clipper ships; cases full of ships' logs and captains' correspondence; the famed

"All the Teas of China" Tunbridge Ware tea caddy collection; thousands of pieces of rare chinaware and porcelain; a king's ransom of silver tea sets and Russian samovars; a salon full of tea-processing machinery; and detailed records from Desmond Hawker's two tea-importing businesses.

Elspeth grew to be one of the hardest working trustees. She had led the search committee that recruited Flick Adams as chief curator and then spent many hours helping Flick understand the museum's considerable holdings. Together they had explored the basement archives, perused the thousands of books in the Desmond Hawker Library, and become fast friends. . . .

She quickly blew her nose before she could begin to cry again.

Don't try to do two things at once! Grieve for Elspeth later, after the rest of them understand what really happened in the boardroom.

It was ridiculous to imagine Elspeth Hawker taking her own life. And almost as absurd to claim she suddenly—and silently—succumbed to heart failure. No, the truth was plain as a Scottish scone. Elspeth had been murdered, even though no one besides Flick accepted the possibility.

Correction!

One other individual at the museum knew the truth. The person who had fed Elspeth a lethal dose of barbiturates during the tea break.

Flick looked again at her reflection and asked, "How many people were in the building when Elspeth was poisoned?"

Not many at all.

The museum had begun to follow its shortened winter schedule on October 15: Open to the public from 11:00 a.m. to 4:00 p.m.; closed all day Sunday and Wednesday. Because there were no visitors that Wednesday, the two docents and the three security guards were off as a matter of course. The curators and most of the office staff had left early in the afternoon, when the trustees' monthly meeting had begun.

Flick began to count noses. Nigel Owen was in the building. Plus the seven other trustees. Plus three members of the museum's staff who were on hand to support the meeting: Polly Reid, the administrative assistant who worked for both Flick and Nigel Owen; Giselle Logan, the hostess of the Duchess of Bedford Tearoom; and Conan Davies, the chief of security. A total of twelve people, including herself.

I didn't do it, so we're down to eleven.

And Polly Reid left before the tea break. Ten.

And Giselle merely wheeled the tea trolley into the room. It was Nigel who distributed the goodies. Nine.

And Vicar de Rudd arrived at the meeting near the end of the tea break—too late to tamper with anything that Elspeth consumed. Eight.

A determined knock made her turn. Her office door swung open before Flick could move toward it—or even say come in.

"There you are! The elusive Dr. Adams!" said Marjorie Halifax. "You have been avoiding us, haven't you?"

It made no sense to deny the obvious. Flick responded with a guilty nod.

"The trustees took a vote," Marjorie went on. "We decided unanimously that you shall accompany the four of us who will dine tonight at the Swan Hotel in the Pantiles."

Flick checked her watch. It was almost six thirty, but she had lost her appetite.

"I can't face dinner tonight. I'm too upset to eat."

"No arguments! The matter is out of your hands." Marjorie punctuated her edict with her imperious little trademark laugh followed by a toss of her expensively styled blond hair.

Flick countered with a profound sigh. Marjorie instantly switched to her benevolent politician countenance. "I know you are grieving, Dr. Adams. We all are. That is precisely why we need you along. During the past three months, you got to know Elspeth better than any of us. How can we reminisce this evening without you?"

An abrupt thought stunned Flick: *What if Marjorie Halifax poisoned Elspeth? Did a murderer just invite me to dinner?*

Flick tried to maintain an even expression, but Marjorie apparently noticed a change.

"You look about to faint. Do you need to sit down?"

"I feel fine." Flick segued to a different subject. "You said that only four trustees plan to eat at the Swan tonight?"

"Vicar De Rudd has gone round to Lion's Peak to comfort Elspeth's niece and nephew. He will undoubtedly dine with them. Archibald Meicklejohn is working with Nigel Owen to prepare a press statement about Elspeth. They may drop by later, although I doubt it—their scrivening is bound to consume most of the evening. Lastly and mercifully, Sir Simon has a previous engagement, so you needn't fear crossing swords with him again. That leaves Iona Saxby, Dorothy McAndrews, Matthew Eaton, me—and you. Dinner for five makes a cozy but interesting table." She smiled broadly. "Do say you will join us."

Flick matched Marjorie's smile. "I won't be the best of company, but sure, I'll tag along. It will be an excellent opportunity to apologize for the brouhaha I started this afternoon."

"Oh, my dear, no one blames you for caring about Elspeth deeply or reacting the way you did to her unexpected demise. Frankly, Sir Simon should have explained that he was Elspeth's personal physician. Has been for years. I expect she had a dodgy ticker."

"Are you sure about that? I mean the physician part."

"Absolutely. He's also my physician. And the vicar's." She made a face. "I suppose Sir Simon assumed that you knew. All the other trustees do."

"I'm glad you told me."

"Good! Now, how long will you need to restore your charming face? I represent a hungry bunch."

"Five minutes?" It was as much a question as an answer.

"Done! We shall await you on the ground floor."

Flick used most of the five minutes to think.

Maybe she had been too hasty in conjuring up a stone wall? Maybe there *was* a way to undo what Sir Simon had done. Marjorie Halifax had been right. Flick had learned a lot about Elspeth Hawker. Possibly enough to figure out why someone would want to murder a harmless, eighty-four-year-old spinster. In her forensics classes, she had shown great skill at deducing valid conclusions from limited facts. Why not apply those skills now?

For example: If Dr. Clowes wanted to kill a patient, he wouldn't need to do it publicly. Therefore, someone else was probably responsible.

Seven suspects left on the list.

Another example: If Dr. Clowes's diagnosis was a surprise to Flick, it must have amazed the poisoner. He—or she—couldn't have expected a doctor to ignore the signs of barbiturate poisoning and jump to a faulty conclusion. Therefore, whoever had poisoned Elspeth must have invented a devious way to feed her the drugs.

A third example: Sir Simon adamantly stuck to his guns despite Flick's noisy protests. Therefore, he has a reason for wanting Elspeth's death to be considered natural.

Not bad! Not bad at all.

All was silent when Flick left her fourth-floor office—or should she say *third* floor? Flick had figured out English money and had mastered driving on the left rather than the right, but floor numbers in England still caught her off guard. She often had to remind herself that one flight up is the *first* floor in England, not the second. Her office on the museum's fourth story was on the third floor.

From the outside, the Royal Tunbridge Wells Tea Museum resembled a large Georgian manor house, but inside it was more like an office building, with a utility core toward the rear that housed the main staircase, the elevator, the fire exits, and the rest rooms. The useful space on each floor wrapped around the core like a large U.

The top floor U was divided into three areas:

The right "stroke" was the curators' wing, encompassing Flick's office, the curating staff room (divided into cubicles), the Conservation Laboratory, and a small office for the docents.

The bottom "stroke"—running along the front of the museum—contained the Hawker Memorial Library and the boardroom.

The left "stroke" accommodated the administrative staff offices. The director's office was a mirror image of the chief curator's, except that it overlooked the museum's gardens and the greenhouse. *Life is unfair,* Flick thought the first time she saw the spectacular view that Nigel Owen neither appreciated nor understood. The Hawker Foundation's money had done the impossible. Hot water flowing through subterranean pipes gently heated the screened, open-air garden, so that tropical tea shrubs could grow outdoors in England. Not exceptionally fine tea, mind you, but then the garden's purpose was to educate visitors, few of whom had seen a live tea bush.

Flick sprinted down the main staircase, a lovely marble-stepped affair with dark oak banisters and risers. The four trustees were waiting near the Welcome Centre kiosk on the ground floor. Marjorie Halifax flashed another of her high-voltage politician smiles, and Matthew Eaton extended his arms to hug Flick; but neither Iona Saxby nor Dorothy McAndrews acted especially eager to dine with her. Iona, wearing a sprawling blue hat that matched her eyes, gave Flick a decidedly dyspeptic glance and straightaway made for the bronze front doors. Dorothy offered a lukewarm smile from afar, seemingly wanting to keep her distance.

They're probably annoyed that the only man at our table decided to squire me.

Flick waved good night to Conan Davies, who stood patiently like a sentinel near the doors, waiting for an opportunity to lock up and set the alarm system. Conan, a large man of few words, returned a wink.

The night air felt chilly. Flick tightened the belt on her Burberry and tried to ignore the cars speeding by on Eridge Road. Marjorie and the others didn't seem to notice, but Flick found them alarmingly close—even with tall, solid Matthew Eaton walking next to her on the sidewalk. Happily, she knew the Pantiles and the Swan were only a five-minute walk away.

When Flick had first visited England at the age of eleven, some twenty-five years ago, the country's narrow lanes, high hedgerows, and twisty curves had enchanted her. Back then, the English favored small cars, appropriate to the width of their roads. But now, like Americans, they drove full-sized sport-utility vehicles and minivans. These big vehicles seemed to overflow the still-narrow roads and overpower the woefully inadequate in-town car parks. She marveled that local drivers managed to whiz past each other without colliding and then park their big Mercedes SUVs and Range Rovers in "stalls" that were laid out decades ago for compact Austins and Morris Minors.

Matthew Eaton gently tapped her arm. "If I may ask a possibly impertinent question, Dr. Adams. . .how did a woman born and raised in faraway Pennsylvania acquire two *veddy, veddy* English monikers?"

"Both of my parents are determined Anglophiles," she said. "My mother chose *Felicity* and my father immediately added the appropriate English nickname, *Flick*."

"Well done!"

"I agree. I've always thought that Flick Adams has an interesting ring to it."

Somewhere in the distance a siren warbled. Flick immediately thought about Elspeth Hawker. *If I were a real detective investigating her murder, what questions would I ask my suspects?*

Flick caught her breath. "Good heavens!" she muttered softly. "I have to treat them all like secret suspects. I hope I can manage that."

"Did you say something?" Matthew asked.

"No! I didn't!" she answered, much louder than she meant to.

It's time to start lying to my friends and superiors.

Flick looked up at Matthew's bewildered face and smiled.

THREE

"What makes the job especially difficult, you see, is that Dame Elspeth Hawker offers no obvious media handles."

The earnest public relations practitioner paused to let his gloomy pronouncement sink in. Nigel Owen duly jotted the words "no media handles" on his yellow pad. He even added an underline to emphasize the severity of the problem, although he had no idea what kind of handles Elspeth might have possessed or why her lack of them would cause such despair.

Nigel set down his pen and nodded in agreement. It simply wouldn't do to display his ignorance of communications jargon in front of Archibald Meicklejohn. It had been Nigel, after all, who suggested that they get assistance crafting the statement about Elspeth's death. "This sort of writing needs a deft professional touch," he had said to Archibald. In fact, Nigel saw no reason to invest hours of his own time learning enough about the Hawker clan to write Elspeth's obituary. Six months from now, the Hawkers would be a fading memory.

The corpulent, fiftyish PR man heaved a melancholy sigh and went on. "Elspeth seems to have spent her long life growing tea roses and taking the odd trip to Bath. No occupation. No husband or children. No hobbies. No observable idiosyncrasies. *Nothing!* Not a single media handle I can see."

Nigel thought about asking for clarification, but as he weighed the pros and cons, Archibald beat him to the punch. "Stuart, what pray tell is a *media handle*? And how might Elspeth Hawker be so equipped?"

Nigel relaxed. *Good! The spotlight is on Stuart, where it belongs.*

Stuart Battlebridge was a principal in the firm of Gordon & Battlebridge, the agency that provided public relations support for the Royal Tunbridge Wells Tea Museum. Nigel admired the brochures and news releases that G&B developed, but he thought the firm worked a tad too hard to stay on the cutting edge of societal trends. To wit: The only beverages on offer were bottled waters and decaffeinated soft drinks. The photos on the walls showcased endangered species. The staff wore business casual clothing every day; Stuart's khaki slacks and wool Aran sweater presented a decided contrast to Nigel's and Archibald's three-piece suits. And Stuart's office, where the three of them now chatted, featured an eclectic hodgepodge of furniture that supposedly connoted creativity. Nigel sat on a plain wooden rocker, Archibald in a leather upholstered club chair, and Stuart on the edge of his glass and metal desk.

Nigel leaned back in his chair as Stuart prefaced his explanation with a toothy smile. "We want our public relations efforts for the museum to pay dividends," Stuart said. "Recall what happened fourteen years ago when we announced the demise of Mary Hawker Evans. She was such a fascinating character that our news release read like a novel. It generated no less than seven major feature articles."

Archibald pressed his inquiry: "And a *handle* is?"

"An idea that a reporter can pick up and run with. For example, Mary Hawker Evans was an accomplished yachts-woman who once sailed to India using nineteenth-century tea-route charts that are now on display in the museum's map room. The details we provided the press grew into a story about the museum's superb map collection."

Archibald abruptly grunted an acknowledgment, then said, "In other words, Elspeth led a boring life of no possible interest to reporters."

Stuart shrugged. "One doesn't make bread without flour or feature articles without handles."

The mention of bread made Nigel realize that he felt peck-ish. At the trustees' meeting, he had nibbled the edges of a scone chiefly to camouflage how much he disliked them. But that had been hours earlier. He glanced out the window. The offices of Gordon & Battlebridge were on Monson Road, a short street in Tunbridge Wells's town centre known for its varied shops and businesses. A few doors away was a bakery that did lovely French pastries and brewed an excellent cup of coffee. Perhaps he could persuade Stuart to send out for a snack.

Regrettably, Nigel waited a moment too long to ask.

"Aren't you forgetting something?" Archibald said. "The Hawkers are one of England's great mercantile families. Certainly there are historical details that will intrigue the press."

Stuart let loose another sigh. "I know the Hawker saga by heart. Stop me when I say something that strikes you as interesting:

"The Hawker dynasty was created by Commodore

Desmond Hawker, the founder of the Hawker & Son Tea Merchants." Stuart's droning delivery reminded Nigel of a history teacher he hadn't thought of for twenty-five years. "One is advised not to look *too* closely at the business methods Desmond used to grow his fortune. Rumors abound of aggressive tactics and close-to-the-edge practices. Some say the man was a scoundrel. As we all know, back in the nineteenth century, *scoundrel* was often synonymous with *successful*.

"Desmond was born in 1810, during the heart of the Napoleonic War, and lived to the ripe old age of ninety-four. The Hawkers tend to be hale and hearty folk, with several octogenarians and nonagenarians in the fold. Mary Hawker Evans made it to an even ninety years.

"Desmond married late in life. His one son, Basil Hawker—born in 1865, died in 1950—is best described as a superb businessman but a bland, unimaginative individual."

Nigel noted that Stuart looked his way when he said "bland, unimaginative individual." The ungrateful rotter was willing to bite the hand that fed him.

Stuart droned on: "Sir Basil cleverly sold off the Hawker business assets to other companies at a significant profit before the Great Depression. He invested wisely and consolidated the family's fortune. So, by 1930, the Hawker family was out of the tea business and enjoying a mostly quiet life of genteel leisure in Lion's Peak, the oversized manor house that Desmond had built circa 1875 on the road to Pembury, some two miles northeast of where we sit."

Stuart pointed to the window behind Nigel to indicate the general direction before he continued. "As an aside, the commodore lured Decimus Burton out of retirement to design Lion's Peak. Legend has it that Decimus thought Desmond a *nouveaux riches* lout, which explains why most students of architecture feel that the house is one of Burton's lesser accomplishments to be seen in Tunbridge Wells. Lion's Peak, however, made up in durability for what it lacked in aesthetic appeal. A serious fire, apparently set by a local lunatic, destroyed almost a third of the house in 1924 or 1925. Sir Basil was able to quickly rebuild and restore the old monstrosity."

Stuart shifted his position on the edge of the desk, presumably to a more comfortable one. "Returning to Sir Basil Hawker's personal life," he said. "Well, he had two wives during his eighty-five years. Sarah, wife number one, died while giving birth to Mary Hawker, way back in 1897. Gwyneth, his second wife, produced two children: Edmund and Elspeth, in 1918 and 1920, respectively. Gwyneth, incidentally, was killed by a V1 Buzz Bomb explosion during World War II.

"Mary Hawker married Rupert Evans in 1921, was widowed in 1947, and took charge of the family when Sir Basil died in 1950. She encouraged the establishment of the Royal Tunbridge Wells Tea Museum.

"Meanwhile, Edmund Hawker—Mary's half brother—lived his life as a *bon-vivant* wastrel and died at the mere age of seventy in 1988. However, he did manage to marry and father the next generation of Hawkers: Harriet and Alfred.

"Elspeth Hawker chose a different path. She lived most of her life in self-imposed solitude. That changed when Mary Hawker Evans died in 1990. Elspeth surprised all and sundry by taking on the mantle of family leadership. She was by all accounts a benevolent despot, with few interests outside the museum." Stuart added, "And today she died."

Nigel didn't respond. He looked at Archibald in time to see the banker shake his head and say, "I see your point—dull as dishwater."

The room fell silent, giving Nigel a chance to brood over

Archibald's conclusion. *If Stuart doesn't write the silly obit, you'll get stuck with the job.*

"Hold on a moment," Nigel said. "I've had a thought. Elspeth Hawker wasn't a sailor, so perhaps we can try a different tack. She spent the golden years of her life studying the museum's collection of antiquities. One of our docents told me that Elspeth knew more about our dusty old clobber than our professional curators did."

Stuart sprang to his feet. "I like it! The self-taught amateur who outpaces her professional colleagues. That has definite possibilities." He moved to a whiteboard affixed to the wall behind his desk, picked up a red marker, and wrote in bold letters, *AMATEUR OUTDOES THE EXPERTS!*

"What else did she do?" Stuart asked Nigel excitedly.

Nigel stared at his hands. *What else did Elspeth do?* He couldn't think of a single thing, other than she claimed to have discovered "an exceedingly clever thief."

You can't talk about that.

Happily, the muse of epitaphs provided Stuart Battlebridge with an answer to his own question. "I know!" He spun back to his whiteboard. "We can say that Elspeth died while working to improve the museum she esteemed above all else." He wrote, *DIED IN HARNESS!*

"Isn't that a bit. . .well, grisly?" Archibald asked.

"Not at all!" Stuart answered over his shoulder. "I presume that they carried Elspeth out feet first? If so, she fulfilled the requirements of the hackneyed old cliché."

"Possibly," Archibald admitted. "But let's not exceed the bounds of good taste."

Nigel listened in amazement as Stuart, oblivious to interruption, continued on a roll: "English reporters love tales of captains going down with their ships. We will point out that

Elspeth went down *at* her museum." He wrote *A LIFE OF GREAT PERSONAL SACRIFICE!* on the board and simultaneously asked, "Does anyone remember what she ate and drank before her death?"

"Indeed I do!" Nigel said, joining in the spirit of the moment. "As usual, Elspeth ate raisin scones with her favorite Danish lingonberry preserves and clotted cream. She drank several cups of estate Darjeeling."

"Magnificent!" Stuart roared. "Dame Elspeth Hawker died sipping tea and munching scones while standing at the helm of the Royal Tunbridge Wells Tea Museum."

"I beg your pardon!" Archibald tried to get Stuart's attention. Nigel bit back a smile as Archibald added somewhat testily, "As the *chair* of the trustees, I stand at the helm of the museum."

Stuart refused to be corrected—or slowed down. He wrote with extravagant strokes: *FALLEN MUSEUM LEADER EXPIRES AFTER ENJOYING HER LAST AFTERNOON TEA!* "Of course," he said, "we must employ poetic license. A wholesome Scottish marmalade has more editorial appeal than some obscure Danish jelly. And a modest workingman's cuppa, perhaps a hearty Earl Grey, seems more appropriate for Dame Elspeth than a tarted-up Darjeeling."

Nigel felt a buzzing on his hip: a call coming in on his cell phone. *What now?* Only a handful of people had his number. Nigel moved the phone to his ear and shielded the microphone with his hand. "Nigel Owen."

"Good evening, Nigel," spoke a well-modulated voice. "William de Rudd here."

"Ah! Vicar!" Nigel said guardedly. Why would the vicar of St. Stephen's Church be calling at this hour?

"The Hawker family needs your help. Both Alfred and

Harriet are distraught over their aunt's unexpected death."

"Are they?" Nigel tried to hide his skepticism. He had met the younger Hawkers twice. They both seemed hard as nails—hardly the sort to grieve over Elspeth. Nonetheless, they were the lawful heirs to the Hawker estate and now deserved the deference that the museum had paid to their two aunts. "What sort of help do they require?"

"Alfred and Harriet have no experience planning a funeral. I assured them that your staff would provide all necessary assistance in their time of crisis."

Nigel swallowed a groan. His "staff" consisted of one administrative assistant he shared with Flick. He would have to do most of the work himself.

"When would they like. . .ah. . .*us* to begin?"

"The Hawkers expect a visit from you tomorrow morning."

Nigel snapped the phone shut with more force than necessary. The sharp *snap* echoed around the office, but neither Archibald nor Stuart, now standing together near the whiteboard, seemed to notice. It took Nigel a moment to realize they were negotiating how Elspeth should be described in the obituary. Stuart favored "legendary grande dame of the Royal Tunbridge Wells Tea Museum"; Archibald preferred the less flashy "oldest trustee of well-known museum in Kent."

"Tell the truth, Elspeth," Nigel muttered, as he peered skyward, "did you have any idea when you woke up this morning how much tumult you would create today?"

Flick lifted her half pint of English cider as Matthew Eaton said, "We raise our glasses to Dame Elspeth Hawker—a lovely lady and a fine friend. She had a good innings, then passed swiftly in old age. One can hardly ask for more than that."

There were murmurs of agreement and a throaty "Here! Here!" from Iona Saxby, seated in the chair next to Flick. Iona punctuated her exclamation with a sensuous toss of her head that brushed the wide brim of her blue hat against Flick's cheek.

Don't flinch at Iona's oversized hat. Don't be annoyed that they're toasting a murder victim. Act like one of the bunch.

Flick drank some cider and reminded herself that her mission this evening was to probe Elspeth's relationships with the trustees. The trick was to be an effective observer—part of the proceedings but also separate.

Flick looked to her left and her right. Matthew's toast had left the other trustees in a reflective mood. They sipped their drinks quietly, perhaps thinking about Dame Elspeth— or possibly their decidedly un-English surroundings. No oaken beams, no low ceilings and small windows, no fireplace roaring in the corner.

Hammonds Restaurant in the Swan Hotel billed itself as an "American-style bistro"—a curious sort of eating place, Flick thought, to be associated with a hotel that traced its wholly English roots back to the seventeenth century. The party of five was on the balcony, seated at a corner table that of-fered a bird's-eye view of the modern interior. The window be-hind Flick faced Eridge Road, but she could look completely across Hammonds's spacious dining room and central palm court and out the front windows into the heart of the Pantiles.

A nifty place to live.

The first document that Flick read when she became chief curator was a site report prepared in 1960 by a consultant to the Hawker Foundation. "If you choose to locate a museum in the city of Tunbridge Wells," the author recommended, "a most sensible location is on Eridge Road, south of the town centre, near the Pantiles, a well-established destination for visitors."

Flick wasn't surprised that the Hawker Foundation accepted this recommendation and purchased land less than a third of a mile away from the southern end of the Pantiles. She made a similar decision on her initial visit to Tunbridge Wells and rented a second-story apartment on the Pantiles's Lower Walk, opposite and down a short flight of steps from the famous colonnade.

She had written to her parents, "I have 'let a flat,' as the English say, in the old commercial centre of Tunbridge Wells. The Pantiles is a seventeenth-century pedestrian-only shopping street (what the Brits call a 'precinct') that could be the ancestor of a modern American strip mall. It is about two of our city blocks long. One side has a row of colonnaded shops—mostly selling antiques, clothing, jewelry, and food—with four- and five-story buildings above them.

"The place was named the 'Pantiles' when the walkways were paved with baked clay pantiles circa 1700. At the northern end is a spring, discovered in 1606, that yields iron-rich water. The stuff is supposed to be good for you, but I find it too bitter to drink. In any case, people traveled from far and wide to 'take the waters,' and shops grew up around the 'dipping house.'"

A waiter interrupted Flick's recollecting. She surprised herself by ordering steak salad. "An excellent choice!" Marjorie Halifax said loudly. "A proper meal is just the ticket for you tonight." She looked at Flick over the top of her menu. "And there is no need to apologize again. As I told you in your office, we *all* understand your deep feelings for Dame Elspeth. Isn't that right?"

There were four nods of agreement accentuated by the clinks of knives and forks against water glasses.

Flick did her best to look remorseful. "Thank you for allowing my love for Dame Elspeth to get in the way of my common sense."

Don't stop now! Get them on your side.

"Challenging Dr. Clowes in public was inappropriate and unwise," Flick said evenly. "I won't make the same mistake again."

"Pity!" Iona said. "I have never seen Sir Simon more exercised than he was this afternoon. I admit it was fun to watch you push all his buttons at once. Our Harley Street specialist can be rather pompous at times."

Dorothy McAndrews, sitting across the table, brushed her long red hair away from her eyes and intoned in her gravely voice, "Well, I for one found your distress perfectly understandable, Dr. Adams. You are new to England, and Dame Elspeth became your friend and confidante, dare I even say it, a mother figure."

Flick hesitated. The notion that Elspeth had become her substitute mother was laughable—but Dorothy seemed eager to have her insight acknowledged. "Perhaps you're right," Flick said. "Elspeth was exceptionally kind to me. I'm grateful that she took me under her wing and introduced me to many of the antiquities in our collection."

Dorothy frowned. "Not to speak ill of the dead, but take everything she told you with a grain of salt. I see Elspeth Hawker as more of a dilettante than an expert, not even in the same league as the knowledgeable customers who frequent my antique shops. Her grasp of the museum's holdings was a mile wide but only an inch deep—if you take my meaning."

Flick forced herself to take a long, slow sip of cider. *Don't argue with her. Don't tell her she's wrong. Just listen!*

"I will not comment as to whether Dame Elspeth was a

dilettante," Marjorie said, "but her vistas were certainly limited. On several occasions I tried to interest her in local politics. As one of Tunbridge Wells's leading citizens, she should have played a more active role in local governance. She insisted that she was too busy, either rummaging around in the basement of the museum or else tending to the roses in her garden."

"I believe that 'dilettante' is a perfect word to describe Dame Elspeth," Iona said. "History will record her as a rather capricious woman who lacked the earnestness—the *gravitas*—of her late half sister. The time she wasted with the items on display would have been better spent helping her fellow trustees with our management duties." Iona added, "That won't be a problem with the next generation of Hawkers. Alfred Hawker and Harriet Hawker Peckham are extremely interested in the future of the museum."

"Like owls are interested in the future of field mice, I shouldn't wonder," Dorothy said. "After meeting thousands of customers, one gets to know the signs of avarice. I see them all over Harriet's face whenever she visits the museum."

Matthew Eaton chuckled. "Feel free to speak your mind, Dorothy. Tell us what you really think about our newest trustee."

"You can't be serious!" Dorothy said, all at once wide-eyed.

Iona reached over the table to pat Dorothy's hand. "There always has been and always will be a member of the Hawker family on the museum's board. I agree that Harriet is the most appropriate Hawker to succeed Dame Elspeth."

Dorothy hefted her glass. "God save the Royal Tunbridge Wells Tea Museum."

Flick joined in the laughter, considering all the while how she might turn the subject of the conversation back to Elspeth. She decided to ask a direct question.

"I've been told, Mr. Eaton," she said, "that you are quite

skilled at growing roses. Did Dame Elspeth ever ask your help for her garden?"

"She did not!" His tone carried more than a hint of annoyance. "I volunteered my horticultural expertise more than once, but she never took me up on my offer."

"Consider yourself lucky!" said Dorothy McAndrews. "Since I became a trustee last year, I received *dozens* of requests from Dame Elspeth. Did I have a book she might borrow on nineteenth-century paintings? Did I employ an appraiser who specialized in fine china? Was anyone on my staff an authority on Tunbridge Ware?" Dorothy paused a moment. "In fact, she nearly drove me mad with calls about Tunbridge Ware."

Flick noticed a sly smile appear on Dorothy's face as she said, "I suspect that Elspeth regaled our new chief curator with long lectures on her favorite wooden antiques."

Too many to count!

For about two hundred fifty years, local artisans in Tunbridge Wells produced useful wooden articles decorated with ingenious wooden mosaics. There were small boxes of every imaginable size and purpose, tea caddies, bowls, salad spoons, bookends, earrings, music stands, flower stands, spinning wheels, small tables, writing desks, cribbage boards, chess and backgammon boards—the list stretched on and on. During the eighteenth and nineteenth centuries, almost every shop in the Pantiles had some Tunbridge Ware for sale. The tea museum had an impressive collection of tea-related Tunbridge Ware, so Flick had a reason to become acquainted with its history. Elspeth knew the story of every antique thingamabob, toy, and doodad by heart. She also took Flick on "field trips," as Elspeth called them, to see the large Tunbridge Ware collection at the Tunbridge Wells Museum and Art Gallery in the Civic Centre on Mount Pleasant Road. Elspeth had taught Flick all that she needed to know—and then some. And in the process, Flick had come to love one particular set of Tunbridge Ware tea caddies.

Before Flick could answer Dorothy's question, Iona said, "I surrender. Please talk about *anything* but Tunbridge Ware. I can't stand the awful stuff."

Flick bit back a smile as she realized what had happened. Dorothy had turned the conversation to Tunbridge Ware to pay back Iona for her patronizing hand pat a few minutes earlier.

"I agree with Iona," Matthew said gallantly. "Let us make a pact. Henceforth, for the remainder of this evening we will not bring up any of Dame Elspeth's eccentricities or foibles. As my first schoolmaster might have said, we shall talk about the good things in her long life or nothing at all."

Flick hoped that no one at the table heard her groan.

FOUR

Much to Nigel Owen's relief—and thanks to his splendid planning—the funeral of Elspeth Olivia Hawker, dame commander of the British Empire, went off without a hitch on Saturday morning.

Elspeth's interment in the family mausoleum at Lion's Peak took place promptly at nine o'clock. This had been a private ceremony, limited to family members, the trustees, and the handful of museum employees who had come to know Elspeth well. Vicar William de Rudd officiated.

Nigel had hired five classic Daimler DS420 limousines to convey the private mourners to the second gathering—a public service of thanksgiving at St. Stephen's Church. It commenced at ten o'clock sharp and was also celebrated by Vicar de Rudd. The significantly larger crowd in the church included three reporters and two news photographers, expertly shepherded by Stuart Battlebridge. Nigel had grown up in the Church of England, and although he had stopped attending regularly, he felt comfortable with the liturgy. He selected the three hymns sung by the choir: "Guide Me, O Thou Great Je-hovah," "Alleluia! Sing to Jesus!" and "Lord of the Living." Marjorie Halifax presented the tribute. She spoke, Nigel thought, as if she had known Elspeth her entire life.

The third, blessedly final, component was a reception for family and friends in the Duchess of Bedford Tearoom on the ground floor of the Royal Tunbridge Wells Tea Museum. It began at eleven, with Nigel as one of the ushers. He took up po-sition next to a sign explaining that in 1840 the Duchess of Bed-ford, one of Queen Victoria's ladies-in-waiting, had invented the English afternoon tea—a meal of tea, thin sandwiches, and small cakes—to overcome the "sinking feeling" she felt in the late afternoon. Nigel managed to nod solemnly as mourners passed by, but he did not feel in a mood to chitchat. When Iona Saxby said, "This is a distressing day for us all," he muttered under his breath, "You should have been here yesterday."

The previous two days of Nigel's life had been a pandemo-nium of telephone calls, faxes, and e-mails. He had, as he antic-ipated, done all of the organizing for the funeral. He had even foreseen the challenge of dealing with the two Hawker heirs.

On Thursday morning, he had driven out to Lion's Peak to visit Alfred Hawker and Harriet Hawker Peckham—who apparently had taken up joint residence in the family manse upon receiving news of Elspeth's death. As Nigel recalled, Harriet owned a bungalow in Rusthall, a self-contained vil-lage about a mile west of the Tunbridge Wells town centre. Alfred rented an in-town flat on Claremont Road.

The Hawker house on Pembury Road was an oversized sandstone "villa" that seemed. . .well, *lumpy* was the first word that came to Nigel's mind. The interior—at least the foyer, hallway, and sitting room that he saw—were filled with Art Deco furniture. Nigel decided that the pile must have been decorated by Basil Hawker during the 1930s and left unchanged since.

As usual, the junior Hawkers appeared underfed.

Harriet, a thin reed of a woman, greeted Nigel with a limp hand and a skeptical smile. She was in her midfifties but seemed older. Alfred, as scrawny as his sister, was younger by a few years. Both siblings shared watery brown eyes, long narrow noses, and thin, dark hair streaked with gray. Nigel followed the pair into the sitting room. They sat together on a small brocade-covered sofa. He chose a round-sided, scalloped back chair that proved to be less comfortable than it appeared at a distance.

"Please accept my sincerest condolences for your loss," Nigel said.

"Thank you," Alfred said. "Aunt Elspeth was our—"

Harriet cut her brother off in midsentence. "We can't offer you refreshments this morning, Mr. Owen, because we're alone in the house and fending for ourselves. Dame Elspeth's housemaid abandoned her post and fled to her sister's home in Brighton."

Nigel nodded noncommittally. The "housemaid" in question was more of a live-in companion than a servant. Katherine Quarles, a robust, rosy-cheeked woman in her early seventies, often accompanied Elspeth to the museum. Nigel knew she had been with Elspeth for nearly fifty years. He made a mental note to find out if she needed transport to the funeral.

Harriet continued. "It will be best to get right to the matters at hand."

Nigel reached into his breast pocket. He had thought ahead and prepared a tentative list of people who might want to attend Elspeth's funeral. Harriet scanned the two sheets of paper, occasionally scowling, occasionally shaking her head.

"There must be a hundred names here," she said with a final grimace.

"One hundred and nine," Nigel admitted.

Harriet frowned. "It is certainly true that our famous ancestor, Desmond Hawker, was flamboyant by nature. Dame Elspeth, however, lived a highly private life. She would hardly approve of entertaining a crowd of strangers. We believe that a small, discreet funeral attended by only her inner circle would be most in keeping with her wishes." She glanced at Alfred. "Isn't that right?"

Alfred's head bobbled up and down like a wind-up doll.

Nigel managed another vague nod, although he felt like laughing in Harriet's face. Harriet's fabled stinginess, not Elspeth's "wishes," had driven her response. He had expected and prepared for just such a prospect.

"I believe you are right, Mrs. Peckham," Nigel said, through gritted teeth. "Therefore let me offer a suggestion. We begin the day with private interment here at Lion's Peak, then follow with a public memorial service and a reception at the museum."

Alfred looked puzzled. "Doesn't holding an interment first put the cart before the horse, so to speak?"

"Not really," Nigel said. "Vicar de Rudd assures me that interment-first funerals have become quite common."

"An excellent idea, Mr. Owen," Harriet said, her voice bubbling with contentment. "I take it that the museum plans to sponsor the reception."

"Oh yes, Mrs. Peckham. We will provide refreshments for the mourners."

"Flowers, too?"

"I will contact the florist this morning." Nigel comforted himself with the thought that since Harriet was a widow, Alfred a bachelor, and neither had children, the pair certainly must be the last of the Hawkers.

"And a good job, too," Nigel muttered as he left Lion's Peak.

He telephoned Vicar de Rudd as he drove back to the museum.

"I know that Alfred and Harriet can be *difficult*," the vicar had said, "but remember that this is a time of great pain for them. We must make allowances."

"Speaking of allowances—Harriet asked me to make a request of you. She would like bells to toll before the service of thanksgiving."

The cell phone fell silent. "Bells?" the vicar said at last. "I regret that we don't have a bell tower at St. Stephen's."

"When I attempted to explain that well-known fact, Harriet said, 'Don't be silly. All churches have bells.' "

"But. . .*but*. . .that makes no sense at all."

"A perfect description of Harriet Hawker Peckham!" Nigel said triumphantly.

Now, two mornings later, he saw lights at the end of two tunnels. Minutes from now, Elspeth's funeral would be history. And in a mere six months, he would be free of the whole Hawker clan.

I'll be back in glorious London where I belong.

The notion made him smile.

"A penny for your thoughts," said a woman's voice.

"Sorry?" He turned.

Flick Adams, an amused smile on her face, handed him a tall, cool glass. "You seem relaxed for the first time in days. I thought you might like something to drink." She added, "I figured you would want lemonade rather than tea."

"Thank you. Lemonade is perfect."

"I also wanted to offer my compliments."

"For what?"

"For taking charge of Elspeth's funeral. You did a magnificent job."

"Ah. . . yes. . .well. . ."

"I'll let you get back to your duties. I've been told that it's bad form to interrupt a Brit when he's standing guard."

Nigel sipped his lemonade and watched Flick walk back to the Duchess of Bedford Tearoom. He noticed with some surprise that she appeared remarkably fetching this morning in her tailored black dress. When he first met Flick, Nigel concluded that she didn't fit the mold of chief curator. A proper curator should be a gangly, stoop-shouldered scientist—the usual boffin with horn-rimmed glasses. But Felicity Adams was a lovely brunette with fine features who looked younger than her thirty-six years. The label "corn-fed beauty" had straightaway come to mind.

"Excuse me, sir. Are you Mr. Nigel Owen? The acting director of the museum?"

The second voice that disrupted Nigel's pondering was masculine—and not the least bit pleasing.

"I am he," Nigel owned up to the roundish, potbellied, middle-aged man who had surprisingly appeared before him.

"My name is Bleasdale," the man said. "I am a solicitor, currently in the employ of Harriet Hawker Peckham and Alfred Hawker."

Nigel gestured with his glass. "You will find your clients inside yonder tearoom."

"Actually, I came to see you."

"Me?"

"You."

"In that event, how can I be of help, Mr. Bleasdale?"

"It is a simple matter," Bleasdale replied. "I want to make an appointment to meet with you. At your convenience, naturally, but no later than the close of business on Monday, next."

"May I inquire as to the nature of our meeting?"

"Again—a simple matter. When the last will and testament of the late Dame Elspeth Hawker goes to probate, Mrs. Peckham and Mr. Hawker will be recognized as coexecutors of the estate and also as legal owners of all family property. Upon receiving the grant of representation from the probate registry, they plan to retrieve the various artifacts and antiquities on loan to this museum. I have been asked to act on their behalf to make arrangements for the expeditious return of said property."

It took awhile for Nigel's mind to make sense of the barrage of legal jargon. "Are you talking about the *museum's* antiquities?" he said finally. "The clobber on display in this building?"

Bleasdale arched his ample brows. "*Your* valuables are yours to keep. The Hawkers seek only the return of *their* property. Specifically, the several thousand items originally lent to the museum by Mary Hawker Evans. Paintings, antiques, bric-a-brac, knickknacks, books, maps, curios, and the like."

"May I ask why they want the items returned?" Nigel asked, although the answer was patently obvious.

"To sell them, of course. Dame Elspeth's estate must pay mammoth inheritance taxes to our friends at Inland Revenue. Forty percent of her estate will need to be sold. It comes down to a simple choice for Harriet and Alfred. Sell this collection or sell Lion's Peak." He handed Nigel a business card. "As you might imagine, my clients would prefer the museum to purchase the pieces from the estate. We can discuss all that on Monday. Is two o'clock good for you?"

"As good as any other time," Nigel said somberly. The enormity of "several thousand items" had begun to hit home.

Bleasdale glanced circumspectly to his left and right. "Perhaps I shouldn't reveal this, but you will soon learn that Dame Elspeth left the museum a tidy cash bequest. It will make a good start on the purchase price."

For one merry moment, Nigel thought about emptying his half-full glass of lemonade atop the solicitor's pomaded head. In the end, discretion and British reserve won the day. Nigel held his tongue—and his cold drink—as Bleasdale waddled away.

Flick Adams ignored her thumping heart and, with as much professional detachment as she could muster, asked, "How much time do we have?"

Nigel Owen, sitting behind his desk, gave a feeble wave. "Months at most, I should say. Certainly no longer than a half year."

"Aren't there procedural ways to delay the process? Things a devious lawyer can do?"

"Not when one is dealing with death duties." Nigel shrugged. "The Inland Revenue expects payment promptly—on most assets within six months of a death. After that they tack on interest charges, which further reduce the value of the estate. Bleasdale may resemble the Michelin Man, but his chubby face glows with the boundless confidence of a solicitor who is wholly prepared to deal with legal maneuvering that will cost his clients money. In short, bid farewell to the Hawker antiquities."

Flick was standing in the corner of Nigel's office, next to the window with the spectacular view of the museum's gardens. She counted nine visitors strolling among the tea bushes—not a large crowd for a Saturday. But then, the museum had not opened to the public until one, after the mourners had left the reception. As a further discouragement to local tourism, the afternoon had turned bleak and chilly.

Appropriate weather to talk about impending doom.

"If we had more time," Flick said, "we could launch a fundraising campaign to purchase the antiquities. We could go after donations and grants and approach other foundations for support. The Hawkers weren't the only family in the tea trade."

Nigel replied with a halfhearted grunt that made Flick spin around and peer at him. *Does the oaf really care? After all, he'll leave just about when the museum gets cleaned out.*

She guiltily banished the disagreeable thoughts. Nigel hadn't acted anything like an oaf in recent days. He had gone beyond the call of duty to put together an excellent send-off for Elspeth. Moreover, he seemed as upset as she felt over the threat to the museum. Happily, Nigel hadn't noticed her fleeting glare at him.

"Your predecessor served for, what, fifteen years as chief curator?" he said.

"Malcolm Dunlevy held the post for closer to twenty years."

"Why didn't he purchase the items owned by the Hawker family?"

"I'm sure he never saw the need," Flick said. "The Hawker Foundation built the museum as a showcase for the Hawker collection. Over the years, Mary Hawker Evans donated many items to the museum. Upon her death, she bequeathed us a number of valuable antiquities, and her will made arrangements to pay the inheritance taxes on the other items. Malcolm probably assumed that Elspeth had done the same. I certainly did— up until a half hour ago." She added, "I wonder how much of the Hawker collection we'll be able to purchase."

"I don't suppose we will have a definitive answer until Bleasdale sends in the appraisers and we learn how large a bequest Elspeth gave the museum." Nigel sprang upright in his chair. "Oh bother!"

"What's wrong?"

"Your question reminded me that I don't know our collection as well as I ought. In truth, I have no idea what we own and what the Hawkers own."

"There's a register of the family's property in my office."

"Brilliant! Would you be willing to show me around the museum this afternoon? I don't want to be at a hopeless disadvantage when I meet with Bleasdale on Monday."

"Sure—I'd rather visit the exhibits than mope. We can start in the Hawker Memorial Library and then work our way down."

Flick retrieved the register—a one-inch-thick binder stuffed with computer-generated inventory logs—from the bookcase in her office. She also swapped the three-inch-heel pumps she had worn to the funeral for a pair of comfortable walking shoes. She found Nigel waiting for her in the library, holding a legal pad and staring at the tall bookshelves that lined the walls.

"Another penny for your thoughts," she said.

"I'm forever amazed that so many books have been written about tea," he said.

"There are many different aspects of tea to write about. Agriculture, manufacturing, economics, history, geography, marketing, shipping, chemistry, food preparation, etiquette, chinaware, silverware. . ."

"I take your point," Nigel said. "How many books do we have?"

"Roughly three thousand, including about six hundred nineteenth-century tomes from Commodore Hawker's personal library. They are on loan to us."

"Do you have a sense of their value?"

"Oh, the commodore's books are old and unusual, but I doubt there are many collectors who covet specialized volumes about tea. I'd guess an average price tag of say fifty pounds each."

"Perhaps thirty thousand pounds in all—between fifty and fifty-five thousand dollars."

Flick nodded.

Nigel made notes on his pad, then said, "I rarely see ordinary museum guests perusing these shelves."

"True. The library is mostly used by visiting academics and students—and, of course, my staff of curators."

"Does anything else on this floor belong to the Hawkers?"

"No," Flick answered. "The museum owns all of the paraphernalia in the Conservation Laboratory and our office equipment."

"In that case—onward and downward."

Flick followed Nigel down the staircase to the second floor. Directly across from the bottom of the flight of steps was the doorway to the Tea in the Americas Room. She peeked inside. No museum guests.

"I love this exhibit," Flick said. "The two most important items belong to the Hawker family." She pointed at two large oil paintings hung on opposite walls. "They are both by Lilly Martin Spencer, an American painter who worked in the nineteenth century. One is the renowned Boston Tea Party of 1773. . .the other of the well-known Edenton Ladies Tea Party."

"Where might one find Edenton?" Nigel asked.

"It's a small coastal town in North Carolina. During the autumn of 1774, fifty-one Edenton ladies held a public meeting and resolved not to drink East Indian tea until the Crown eliminated the import tax. They also refused to wear any clothing from England."

"The rebels!" Nigel said with a wink. "But I agree that the paintings are lovely."

"I can't begin to estimate their worth."

"Several hundred thousand pounds at a minimum, one would think."

"And then there are many related artifacts on display. English newspaper articles about the 'outrages' in the colonies. Other illustrations and cartoons. Tea chests of the late colonial era. An original parliamentary copy of the Tea Act of 1773. *Rats!*"

Nigel looked up from his writing. "Say again?"

"I can't get used to the idea that all of this may disappear. The Hawkers own everything—except the tea bag exhibit."

"Ah! I've wanted to ask you about that ever since my first look-see through the museum. It seems odd to me that a Yank invented the tea bag."

Flick smiled. "Legend says that it happened in New York City, back in 1908. A tea merchant named Thomas Sullivan supposedly became annoyed with the cost of the little tin boxes he used to send samples to customers. So he switched to small silk bags. One of the recipients brewed a pot of tea by simply pouring hot water over the bag—and the rest is history."

"From your tone, I assume the legend isn't true."

Flick pointed at a framed document. "That's a copy of the U.S. patent issued in 1903 for a 'tea leaf holder' made out of fabric. Tom Sullivan seems to have received the credit for an invention actually made by two gentlemen named Lawson and McLaren."

"Where next?" Nigel asked.

"We're done with this floor. The only other permanent exhibit room is the Tea and Health Gallery—we own all of the displays."

"And a *fascinating* read they are."

"There's no need to be sarcastic. Studies have shown that tea is good for your teeth because it's a natural source of fluoride, and it's also brimming with flavonoids, antioxidants that have all sorts of healthful properties."

"Coffee is good for the health, too. On many occasions it has kept me from falling asleep behind the wheel of my BMW."

"Very droll." Flick strode into the second-floor lobby, Nigel close behind.

"The small silver lining in this cloud," he said, "is that we can immediately reclaim the square footage set aside for the Hawker family suite." He pointed to a door labeled PRIVATE. "To begin with, I doubt Alfred or Harriet plans to spend any time in the museum. To end with, I see no need for us to provide the greedy rotters any office space in this institution."

Flick caught her breath. *He's talking about Elspeth's room.*

Directly under Nigel's office was an equivalent space on the second floor set aside as an office for the Hawkers. It had a large desk, a comfortable sofa, a private loo, even a small kitchen area. Mary Hawker Evans had occupied it sparingly—chiefly on days when the trustees met—but Elspeth had used it almost daily. "My *pied-à-terre* in Tunbridge Wells," she often said. "My home away from home."

"Someone will have to pack up Dame Elspeth's kit," Nigel said.

"I'll put it on my list of things to do." Flick sighed. She had intended to browse through the Hawker Suite as part of her efforts to gather additional facts about Elspeth's relationships with museum people before her death, but her private investigation, if that was the right term for it, had run out of steam. Her plan had been both simple and vague: Engage trustees and museum employees in conversations about Elspeth and listen carefully to everything they said. Well, she had heard nothing the least bit irregular at her dinner with four of the trustees, or in a subsequent chat with Archibald Meicklejohn about her desire to add a professional tea taster to the museum's staff, or in routine meetings with the curators and docents. Every passing day seemed to soften her conviction that Elspeth had been fed an overdose of barbiturates.

So much for your delusions of detective grandeur.

"Let's head downstairs," she said to Nigel.

"Before we do," he replied, "what about the paintings in the Grand Hall?"

"Rats! I forgot all about them."

The Grand Hall, the largest room in the museum, filled the western side of the second floor and was used both for scholarly conferences and special exhibits. Flick loved the décor: Chinese silk draperies, wooden moldings painted in yellow and blue, and comfortable gilded "salon chairs" upholstered in matching blue damask. The dozen oil paintings in the room—each done by a different member of Britain's Royal Academy of Arts in the late nineteenth century—depicted various personalities associated with the history of tea, commencing with the possibly mythical Chinese emperor Shen Nung, who purportedly discovered that tea was good to drink in 2737 BC, and running down through the ages to Commodore Desmond Hawker and Sir Thomas Lipton.

"The paintings are probably worth *millions,*" she said.

"I agree," he answered as he scribbled.

She pirouetted in place. "I can't have forgotten anything else. The two other rooms on this floor are classrooms we use for seminars."

"To the staircase!"

Flick trod down the steps behind Nigel, dreading the

coming few minutes. "Better sharpen your pencil," she said. "The first floor is overflowing with Hawker property."

The lobby on the first floor was part of the Tea at Sea Gallery, the museum's second most popular exhibit. Only the History of Tea Colonnade on the ground floor drew more visitors. The seven guests in the gallery were wearing headsets and apparently listening to the room's audio tour guide system.

"Everything here is on loan from the Hawkers," Flick said. "The forty models of tea clipper ships. The binnacles and compasses. The ships' logs. The antique charts. The ships' wheels. The figureheads. The photographs and paintings. The chronometers and navigation tools. The nautical relics. Everything." She opened the binder and flipped through a sheaf of pages. "There must be six hundred cataloged items."

"Each of the clipper ship models will fetch a pretty penny," Nigel said. "I'll guess ten thousand quid apiece. That's four hundred thousand, right there. I'll be generous and estimate two and a half million for everything in the room." He glanced at Flick. "What do you think?"

She shrugged.

"Is that a 'too high' shrug or a 'too low' shrug?" he asked.

"Your numbers are beginning to make me feel queasy."

"Then I withdraw my question. Press on!"

Flick peeked into the gallery at the front of the first floor that held the Hawker collection of tea-related antiquities. As she anticipated, there were five guests widely scattered around the room, looking at individual objects on display. Guests seemed to choose favorite items and linger around them.

Nigel came up behind her and said, "Every time I pass this gallery, I am reminded of an antique store. It offers the same kind of cluttered ambience. A happy jumble of porcelain, silver, and wood."

"I see it as more of a treasure trove. Each antiquity is a gem. Unique. Irreplaceable. Priceless."

"Priceless in a symbolic sense," Nigel said with a soft laugh. "Appraisers always manage to come up with literal prices."

Flick nodded glumly. "And there are scads of wealthy collectors around who can pay them—although it would be tragic to hide these objects in private collections." She gestured inconspicuously. "That woman in the green sweater and brown slacks is standing next to the earliest surviving examples of Yixing, purple-clay teapots. They were fired in China, in the thirteenth century, during the Sung Dynasty." She gestured again. "The man wearing blue jeans is looking at a gold and silver eighteenth-century samovar that belonged to the royal family of Russia. Again, the earliest surviving example. And the woman in gray is browsing through our collection of Japanese tea ceremony utensils. We have some of the finest Edo-period porcelains in Europe. They date back to the early sixteenth century."

"I need a guesstimate of value," Nigel said. "How about a few million?"

Flick chuckled.

"What is so funny?" Nigel said.

"Which do you suppose is my favorite tea antiquity?"

"I have no idea, though I doubt it's the tsar's tea machine."

"I used to covet the portable silver tea service that Napoleon toted around on his campaigns." She pointed to a small mahogany trunk, propped open at an angle to show its intricate shelves, fittings, and utensils. "But then Elspeth turned me on to 'All the Teas in China,' the matched collection of Tunbridge Ware tea caddies, back in the corner."

"The pretty wooden boxes?"

"Eighteen oversized tea caddies covered with mosaics

depicting different tea-growing regions in China. Each caddy is one of a kind, with a distinctive profile, but all eighteen are perfectly matched in color. They represent the pinnacle of Tunbridge Ware artistry—made in 1867 and 1868 by the great Robert Russell himself. Elspeth guessed the set would fetch a half million pounds at auction."

"Blimey! That much lolly for kitchen canisters?"

"Yep. And most of the items on display in this gallery are worth far more."

"Ten million for the lot?" Nigel said hopefully.

"*Several* tens of millions is more like it." Flick rubbed her eyes. "I have a rip-roaring headache."

"Only one more level to go," Nigel said. "I presume that we own everything else on this floor—the contents of the Tea Blending Room, the Tea Tasting Room, and the Tea Processing Salon."

"Down to the last tasting cup."

This time Flick was first to the stairway. The sooner they completed the impromptu inventory, the sooner this miserable day would be over. She skipped down the steps, almost colliding with two museum guests on their way up. Nigel caught up with her in The World of Tea Map Room. They moved to an out-of-the-way corner, in the shadow of a ten-foot-high map of the Indian subcontinent.

Flick perused the register, did a quick mental calculation, and said, "All the antique maps belong to the Hawkers. And most of the paintings and lithographs."

"I'll put down another half million," Nigel said.

"Sure. Why not?" *What difference does it make? We'll never raise enough money to buy it all.*

"That leaves the Commodore Hawker Room and the History of Tea Colonnade," Nigel said.

Flick looked up. "Nothing in the Commodore Hawker Room is on the block. Mary Hawker Evans donated her grandfather's office furniture when she died, along with his company documents and private papers. Most of the latter are stored in the basement archives."

"Excellent!" Nigel jotted on his pad.

"However, about half of the colonnade antiquities belong to the Hawkers. Many of them are unique, too. A broadsheet advertising the first English teahouse. Royal menus for afternoon teas. Centuries-old tea chests." Flick hesitated. "You know what? This is a silly exercise in futility."

Nigel gazed at his notes. Flick tugged at the pad.

"Don't waste your time adding up the total," she said. "We'll never assemble the funds to buy our exhibits back. No museum our size has access to those kinds of resources."

"Sad but true. However, as I look at this list, I can see a bit of a bright side."

"Which is?"

"The museum's academic efforts will survive the loss. We own most of Desmond Hawker's letters, papers, and memorabilia. These are the materials that support your various tea-related studies."

"In other words, shut our doors as a museum and become some kind of tea research institute."

"Temporarily, perhaps," Nigel said with a shrug of his shoulders. "A determined fund-raising campaign will enable the museum to eventually replace much of the crockery, silver, and woodenware."

"We'll keep a basement full of old papers and lose our finest antiquities. Is that your idea of a fair trade?"

"I admit it's not a perfect solution, but one must make the best of one's circumstances."

"Wow! Didn't you forget to say, 'Stiff upper lip, old chap'?"

"There's no need to be snippy."

"Here!" Flick lobbed the register of on-loan items to Nigel. She thrust out her jaw and threw back her shoulders, hoping that her demeanor would further signal her displeasure. "You'll need this on Monday, when you and the Hawkers' lawyer plan the destruction of my museum."

He caught the binder against his chest and said softly, "Flick, I'm only trying to help."

"The way you can help is by figuring out a way to save our collections. We need good ideas, not dumb solutions. You have a reputation for being smart. Prove it!"

Flick watched Nigel's face go pale. He walked away, shaking his head.

Why did you do that?

"You're mad at the Hawkers and the British tax system," she murmured, "but you took it out on poor Nigel. Stupid! Stupid! Stupid!"

FIVE

At 1:35 on Monday afternoon, Nigel said, "Thank you, Iona. I appreciate your wise advice," and hung up his telephone. He lifted the business card that lay on his desk—"B. Bleasdale, Solicitor"—and ran his fingernail over the raised lettering.

"Iona says you're a clever boots," he said to the card. "Near the top of your class, not a lawyer to be trifled with. She also told me that the B stands for Barrington, a forename you detest." Nigel pronounced the lawyer's full name slowly, enunciating the five syllables separately. *"Bar–ring–ton Bleas–dale.* Poor blighter. Your mother must have been a fan of Jane Austen. No wonder you grew into an overachiever at law."

Nigel had spent the morning arranging an emergency meeting of the board of trustees for Wednesday afternoon to deal with the collections crisis. The trustees were none too eager to gather again at the museum so soon after Elspeth's funeral, but all eventually agreed. And then he called Iona Saxby back to talk about the legal options available to the museum.

Iona had listened patiently to his summation of the facts, then said, "You don't need me to tell you how often this happens in England, Nigel. A wealthy person dies, inheritance taxes must be paid, and family treasures travel to the auction block."

"I'm sure that Elspeth would have wanted the antiquities kept on display."

"If so, she had every opportunity to write a proper will that bequeathed them to the museum or at the very least to do some shrewd tax planning. Failing that, we have no alternative but to disgorge the antiquities upon the family's demand. Harriet and Alfred will be empowered to decide which of the estate's assets to sell. According to their solicitor, they already have reached a decision."

"Is there nothing the law can do?"

"This is a matter where common sense is more important than law. Every child understands the principle that a borrowed item must be returned upon the request of the rightful owner. The Hawker family lent their property to the museum in good faith for purposes of exhibition, and they now ask for it back. The fact that one generation of Hawkers did the lending and another generation the asking back is essentially immaterial. I wish I had something more to offer you, Nigel, but the crux of the issue is clear-cut: Harriet Hawker Peckham and Alfred Hawker own the antiquities and we do not."

Nigel replied with a forlorn grunt. "Now you sound like Solicitor Bleasdale."

"Frankly, I am astonished that Bleasdale saw a need to become personally involved in this matter. Reclaiming lent property is the sort of trivial chore I pass to my paralegal. One doesn't send a three-star chef to fry up a plate of fish and chips."

Iona's out-of-the-blue culinary metaphor left Nigel feeling hungry. He had worked through lunch, and Bleasdale wasn't due for another fifteen minutes. That left ample time to zip down to the Duchess of Bedford Tearoom for a sandwich and a cup of coffee. Pity they didn't do fish and chips.

Nigel had risen halfway out of his chair when his telephone rang. The caller-ID panel proclaimed "WELCOME CENTRE KIOSK."

Rats. The eager beaver lawyer came early.

Nigel immediately began to formulate a plan B. He would send down for refreshments for both Bleasdale and himself. He snatched up the receiver.

"Owen here."

"It's me, sir. I'm at the welcome desk."

Nigel easily recognized Conan Davies's gravelly voice. But why would the museum's chief of security stand duty at the Welcome Centre kiosk? And what were those odd sounds he could hear in the background?

Davies continued. "There's a gentleman here to see you. A Mr. Bleasdale."

Nigel thought he heard a dog bark, but he must have been mistaken. Only guide dogs and working dogs accompanying handicapped guests could enter the museum—and they almost never barked.

"Send Mr. Bleasdale right up," Nigel said.

The noises in the background became even louder. Nigel distinguished chirping, a squeak, and what might have been mewing.

"It would be better for you to come down here, sir. We have an issue with the animals."

Animals? "Did you say animals, Conan?"

"A small dog, sir. And a big bird. And two stout cats."

"None of the above is allowed in the museum, Conan. You know that—you wrote our rule book."

"We need you down here, sir." Nigel heard a sense of urgency in Conan's words, coupled with a plea for help.

"Oh, very well. I'm on my way."

The last flight of steps offered Nigel an all-inclusive view of the Welcome Centre kiosk, but what he saw made no sense at all.

Margo McKendrick, the museum's unflappable greeter, a petite woman of sixty, stood outside her kiosk staring with furrowed brow at the three objects sitting on her normally pristine marble countertop: two medium-sized plastic airline pet containers and one oversized birdcage that measured at least four feet tall. Inside the cage perched a large gray bird that Nigel recognized as a member of the parrot family. It had a charcoal beak and red tail.

Conan Davies, wearing an equally displeased expression, held a dog lead in his right hand. The small dog attached to the other end resembled a fox: perhaps fifteen inches tall, compactly built, with a thick reddish coat and patches of white on its neck, legs, and puffy cheeks. It had small pointed ears, triangular eyes, a rather impudent arched tail held high, and a smile on its face.

That dog is definitely grinning at me, Nigel thought. *Why not? Solicitor Bleasdale is grinning at me, too.*

"Good afternoon, Mr. Owen," Bleasdale said. "Because we were scheduled to meet today, I chose to kill two birds with one stone, although"—he tipped his head toward the parrot—"that comes across as a clumsy metaphor given the circumstances. I have brought Dame Elspeth's pets to the museum. The Hawker heirs thought you would want them immediately."

"Me want her pets? Why would they—or you—think that?"

Nigel watched the contentment on Bleasdale's countenance turn to puzzlement that morphed into concern and finally became resignation.

"Oh dear!" the solicitor said. "My clients assumed, incorrectly it appears, that the acting director of this museum would have full knowledge of the contractual arrangements made between the institution and Dame Elspeth Hawker."

The small dog made a yodel-like bark that trailed off into a high-pitched lamenting whimper. Had it recognized the name of its late owner? Nigel wondered.

"*What* contractual arrangements?" he asked.

"I have never acted for Dame Elspeth, but I can repeat what my clients told me. Approximately one year ago, Dame Elspeth became concerned that her cherished pets might outlive her, as they in fact have done. And so she made an agreement with your predecessor. The museum agreed to take charge of the animals upon her death and maintain them until their natural demise. The Hawker heirs understand that Dame Elspeth agreed to a generous stipend as consideration for the museum's commitment. They feel that the time is ripe for you to keep your end of the bargain."

Nigel peered into one of the pet crates. Two enormous orange eyes peered back at him. He turned to Conan Davies and said, "Does any of this sound familiar?"

The big man nodded. "I'm afraid it does, sir. As I recall, Nathanial Swithin, the former director, did make such an agreement. Dame Elspeth felt—well, not to put too fine a point on it—*reluctant* to have the younger Hawkers take charge of her pets should she no longer be able to care for them."

Nigel looked down. The foxy face was studying him with rapt attention. "What sort of dog is that?" he asked.

"A Shiba Inu," Bleasdale said, "an ancient Japanese breed known for its intelligence, inquisitiveness, love of human interaction, infrequent barking, robust independent streak, and a compelling instinct to chase and kill small animals. Because of the latter, Harriet Hawker Peckham recommends that you never take the dog outdoors without its lead." He added, "His name is Cha-Cha."

Nigel's curiosity overpowered his reluctance to continue this inane conversation. "Why would Elspeth name a Japanese dog after a Latin dance?"

"Begging your pardon, sir," Margo said. "*Cha* is the name for tea in much of the world, including Japan. It strikes me that Dame Elspeth chose a tea-related name for her dog."

"And for her other pets as well," Bleasdale said amiably. "The cats—both female British Shorthairs—are named Lapsang and Souchong. And the bird, an African Grey parrot, is named Earl."

"Very clever, indeed," Conan said. "Earl the grey. Get it, sir? *Earl grey*. Like the tea."

Nigel smiled. He relished good puns, but this wasn't the time to admit it. "Despite their witty names, Mr. Bleasdale, the museum can't accept these animals. What would we do with them?"

"I suggest daily feeding and watering for the lot," Bleasdale said, "plus in the case of the dog, occasional walks—perhaps on the Common, across the road."

"You understood perfectly well what I meant. This is a museum, not a kennel."

"To the contrary, Mr. Owen. Your predecessor entered into a binding contract that Elspeth Hawker's heirs intend to enforce. I am certain that you have a signed memorandum of contract somewhere in your files, but I will save you the trouble of looking. Alfred Hawker located a copy of the document among Dame Elspeth's papers. I brought it with me." He tapped his breast pocket. "The Royal Tunbridge Wells Tea Museum is now the official caregiver to these orphaned creatures."

Nigel sensed triumph in the solicitor's proclamation. Before he could invent an appropriate reply, Margo McKendrick said, "Sir, a busload of guests just arrived in the car park. You might want to continue your discussions away from the general public."

Nigel made a command decision. "Bird, cats, dog, solicitor, security chief—everyone up to the Hawker Suite!"

Conan Davies, birdcage in arms, led the entourage. Bleasdale, amidships, toted a pet carrier in each hand. Nigel, holding firmly on Cha-Cha's lead, brought up the rear. The dog trotted with untroubled self-confidence into the museum's snug service elevator.

This is not the first time you have ridden upstairs, Nigel realized. He recalled the lumpy canvas bag that Elspeth Hawker often carried into the museum. *Your mistress was a smuggler.*

The door slid shut, and a shrill cockney voice filled the elevator: "Can I have a cuppa? It's better than a cracker."

"The blooming parrot talks!" Conan bellowed. Nigel saw the cage begin to fall and helped Conan reposition it in his arms.

"Indeed your new *rara avis* talks," Bleasdale said. "In fact, African Greys are reputed to be the smartest of all birds and can be compared in intelligence to a five-year-old human child, although they usually display the emotional development of a typical two-year-old." He chuckled. "By the way, Earl is only ten years old, a mere pup by parrot standards. The museum can expect to care for him for, oh, sixty more years."

"Put a sock in it, *Barrington*," Nigel said.

Nigel saw that his gibe had its intended effect: Bleasdale's smug simper faded. But before anyone—or anything—could speak another word, the elevator door opened on the second floor. Nigel, who had been last getting into the elevator, instantly became first getting out, propelled by a startlingly strong tug on the lead he had wrapped around his wrist. Cha-Cha, who from Nigel's perspective looked like a miniature Siberian husky towing a sled, yanked him straight to the door of the Hawker Suite then sat down on its haunches.

Blasted undisciplined hound.

Nigel worked the push-button combination lock and turned the knob. The small dog zoomed through the partially ajar door. Nigel's hand flew through the opening, but the rest of him took a second or two to catch up.

"Cha-Cha!" Flick said cheerfully. "I didn't expect to see you today."

The dog bounded over and licked her face—an easy task because Flick was sitting on the floor near the window that overlooked the tea garden, surrounded by piles of papers, books, metal business tins, and open corrugated cartons.

Of course! She's packing up Elspeth's belongings.

Nigel gingerly stepped between a carton of file folders and a framed photograph of Harriet and Alfred sitting side by side in a garden. Judging from the ratio of unpacked clobber to taped-and-labeled boxes, Flick had half the job completed. She seemed in a much-improved mood today.

Hurray! The last thing he needed today was a fresh temper tantrum from Felicity Adams.

"Pardon, sir," Conan Davies said from the doorway. "Where should I set the birdcage?"

Nigel quickly scanned the room. "Why not the small round conference table to the left of the chief curator?"

Bleasdale, glaring all the while, followed Conan inside and stacked the two cat crates on the floor, beneath the cage.

"These felines are not used to confinement," Bleasdale said

stiffly. "I suggest you release them at your earliest convenience."

Nigel saw furry blue faces pressing against the screens. *Blimey! Blue cats with orange eyes.* He tried to think. He had been foolish to bait a visiting solicitor a few minutes before important negotiations began in earnest. Perhaps he could mend the fence he had thoroughly demolished.

"Mr. Bleasdale," he said, "I congratulate you on your in-depth knowledge of these animals. Would you know how well the cats and the dog get along?"

"Splendidly," Bleasdale replied, a decidedly frosty tone in his voice. "Your museum may not own its antiquities, but it now possesses a happy little family."

Nigel forced himself to smile at the solicitor's malevolent taunt.

It is going to be a long afternoon.

Flick surveyed the crowd of men and animals that had mysteriously gathered around her. Nigel Owen appeared perturbed, Conan Davies befuddled, Earl stoical, Lapsang and Souchong annoyed, and Cha-Cha—well, he had acted uncommonly friendly for a Shiba Inu. She quickly sorted out the one creature she hadn't met before. The heavyset man in the custom-tailored suit must be Bleasdale, the solicitor.

What were they all doing here?

Why was Bleasdale glaring daggers at Nigel?

And how was she going to get up? The rather tight skirt she had on would rise to her hips if she tried to stand.

Bleasdale answered her third question by offering his hand. "You are Dr. Adams, are you not?" He pulled her to her feet, introduced himself, and gave a slight bow. "I saw your photograph in the museum's annual report. Very becoming." He waved gracefully at the clutter on the floor. "By any chance, are you assembling Dame Elspeth's miscellany for shipment to the family?"

"Yes, I am." Flick hoped that she looked less amused than she felt. She had imagined Bleasdale as a foppish seventeenth-century courtier, dispensing English chivalry with a trowel.

"Excellent! I shall be delighted to take any boxes you have completed back to the family," Bleasdale said. "My firm's mini-van is parked in the rear. It was the easiest means of transporting Elspeth's pets to the museum."

The pets! No wonder Nigel looks upset.

She had meant to confer with Nigel about Elspeth's contract with the museum. Elspeth had often talked to her about it—and had even expressed a wish or two about her pets' long-term living arrangements.

First things first.

Flick pointed at three sealed and stacked boxes. "Those are ready to go."

Conan spoke up. "Shall I arrange to have them taken to the loading dock and placed in Mr. Bleasdale's minivan?"

"Please do," Flick and Nigel said simultaneously. His voice was much louder—a clear signal that any orders given this afternoon should come from him.

Flick moved away from the piles of paper, sat on the edge of the table, and crossed her arms.

It's all yours, pal.

"Where's my tea?" Earl squawked unexpectedly. "You promised me a crumpet."

Flick sprang to her feet. Bleasdale laughed out loud. "Surprisingly, the bird does enjoy a crumpet on occasion," he said to her, "complete with bitter orange marmalade, I've been told. Which reminds me: There are several pet-related accessories in my van." He began to count on his chubby fingers. "Two cat litter boxes, three water bowls, three food bowls, two cases of cat food, two fifteen-kilo packages of dog kibble, a thirty-kilo sack of parrot food, and a box full of sundry treats and toys."

Nigel rolled his eyes. "Conan, please inform Giselle Logan that we need to commandeer a shelf in her pantry."

"Aye, sir. I'll move these boxes downstairs and see to the pet supplies." The big man lifted the stack of cartons as if they were empty.

"Take extra care with the one on top," Flick said. "I packed Elspeth's personal items inside it."

The thought brought a new round of tears to her eyes. Earlier that day, while disassembling the well-equipped "survival kit" in Elspeth's desk, Flick had gone through five tissues and a paper towel. Elspeth had carefully organized three drawers on one side of her desk to hold a roll-up toiletries pouch, a makeup box, two extra pairs of eyeglasses, a first-aid box, a sewing box, three teacups and saucers, a small electric teakettle, a packet of tea bags, a bottle of vitamin tablets, two bottles of ink for her fountain pen, an extra fountain pen, a pair of sensible shoes, several packages of stockings, a supply of dog food and doggie treats, a Bible, and an ancient copy of the *Book of Common Prayer*, with her name inscribed in a neat, childish hand. Elspeth had even managed to squeeze in a silvery roll of duct tape.

Flick blew her nose in a sixth tissue and said, "If no one objects, I will let the cats out of their crates."

Nigel surprised her. "Not quite yet." He addressed the solicitor: "Mr. Bleasdale, why don't we meet here rather than in my office? What more fitting venue than the Hawker Suite to talk about the Hawker collection. Besides, I think it will be useful for Dr. Adams, our chief curator, to observe the discussion."

Bleasdale nodded at Nigel, then beamed at Flick. She smiled back, not sure how else to react.

What is Nigel playing at? On Saturday, he had made it abundantly clear that he alone would meet the Hawkers' lawyer. And the word "observe" seemed to indicate that he didn't want Flick to actually participate.

A likely answer gelled in her mind. *Bleasdale is miffed at Nigel for some reason, but he seems to like me. Therefore, Nigel asked me to stay. . . . Men can be such jerks.*

"Shall we sit down?" Nigel gestured grandly toward the small sofa adjacent to the round conference table. He dragged over an austere wooden side chair for himself, leaving the more comfortable upholstered seating for Flick and Bleasdale. Bleasdale sat down facing Nigel and promptly crossed his arms; Flick nestled into the far end of the sofa, where she could watch both men without pivoting her head. Cha-Cha, still pinioned to Nigel's wrist with the lead, curled up at Nigel's feet.

"This morning," Nigel began, "I read the museum's original contract with Mary Hawker Evans. It calls for any items lent to us by the Hawker family to be returned upon ninety days' notice. Is that your understanding of the terms, Mr. Bleasdale?"

The solicitor replied with a begrudging nod and a stiff "Correct."

"I presume that the ninety-day period will be measured from the date the museum receives such notice from the executor of Dame Elspeth's estate."

"Also correct. Alfred Hawker and Harriet Hawker Peckham are the coexecutors. I shall advise them in their duties."

"When do you expect the Probate Registry to issue the grant of representation to the Hawker heirs?"

Flick did a quick Britain–to–United States translation. In Pennsylvania, the register of wills granted letters testamentary to the executor of the estate. Otherwise the process of settling an estate sounded pretty much the same. A court dealing in wills and estates would give the Hawkers the authority to demand the return of the items on display.

"Oh, one suspects it will happen quickly," Bleasdale said. "Dame Elspeth died testate, and her will was prepared by an excellent solicitor. I am confident that her estate is fully in order."

"Then our antiquities could be gone in as little as five or six months," Nigel said gloomily.

"Not necessarily." Bleasdale leaned forward, as if he were sharing a secret with Nigel. "I suspect that our impromptu meeting on Saturday left you with the impression that the Hawkers are unreasonable folk. In fact, Harriet and Alfred fully understand that their best course of action is to work out a flexible arrangement with you that will enable the museum to acquire the Hawker collection."

Flick found herself staring at Bleasdale. As if a switch had been thrown, his voice had become silky, free of any annoyance. The anger on his face was gone, replaced by a new expression bursting with empathy and concern. His hands lying open in his lap made him appear fully at ease.

The man is an emotional quick-change artist.

Nigel didn't seem to perceive Bleasdale's abrupt transformation. "Really?" he said in a surprised tone. "What sort of arrangement will allow us to complete such an acquisition?"

Bleasdale leaned even closer to Nigel. "Creative financing."

"No one is that creative," Nigel said with a sour laugh. "Our preliminary estimates of the value of the collection"—he glanced at Flick—"place the cost far beyond our resources."

"As I said before—not necessarily." Bleasdale spoke barely louder than a whisper. Flick had to strain to hear him. "If one were to find a levelheaded antiquities appraiser who understands true market value and who works quickly, a valuation satisfactory to Inland Revenue, the Hawkers, and the museum could be arrived at in perhaps three weeks. That is step one. Step two is to arrange a short-term loan to finance the inheritance taxes, a commonplace thing to do. Are you with me so far?"

Nigel nodded. "Appraise the collection and pay the taxes."

"Now, for step three. The museum borrows the money to buy the antiquities. The collection itself will serve as collateral for a long-term loan—say payable over a comfortable ten years."

"What about the down payment?"

"The Hawkers will accept a promissory note for the amount of the cash bequest you will receive from the estate."

Flick's mind raced. *Could it work?* Museums never would volunteer their antiquities as collateral for financial transactions, but this was a different situation. The Royal Tunbridge Wells Tea Museum didn't own the Hawker collection. The loan would help the museum purchase it in the first place. Ten years would be more than enough time to raise the necessary funds. *It might work!*

Flick waited for Nigel to ask another question, but he looked lost in thought. She jumped into the conversation. "Mr. Bleasdale, is this a theory or a real course of action?"

"The Hawkers have approved my choice of a qualified appraiser. The estate must complete step one and step two whether or not the museum decides to buy the collection. However. . ." —Bleasdale grinned from ear to ear—"I have also taken the liberty of approaching a financial institution in London that specializes in long-term loans collateralized by artwork and antiques. The ducks are in a row and ready to quack."

Nigel snapped out of his musing. "You have given us much to think about, Mr. Bleasdale."

"Think rapidly, Mr. Owen. If we begin immediately, the whole transaction can be completed within days of the grant of representation. Speed is of value to both sides."

Bleasdale bowed again to Flick. "I am confident we will meet again soon, Dr. Adams."

Flick took Cha-Cha off Nigel's hands—literally—so that he could escort Bleasdale downstairs. She shut the door behind them and unlatched the cat crates. "If I remember what Elspeth told me," she said softly, "cats of your size prefer not to be picked up."

Flick was sitting on the floor once again, playing with the cats, when Nigel returned.

"They look like blue plush toys," he said. "*Big* plush toys at that." He turned the side chair around and sat down.

"The British Shorthair is a fairly docile breed. Quite friendly and not at all destructive."

"Which is Lapsang and which is Souchong?"

Oh dear!

"As I recall," Flick said, "Lapsang is the larger of the two." It was a guess, but who would argue with her? Certainly not the cats.

"Where's the pooch?" Nigel asked

"Look to your left. He came over when you came in. He's definitely taken a fancy to you."

Nigel reached down and scratched behind Cha-Cha's ears. "What's your opinion of Bleasdale?" he asked.

"Answer a question for me first. Why was he mad at you?"

"We had a slight *contretemps* in the lift. He behaved

pompously and I overreacted. Why do you ask?"

"Because I'm skeptical about his remarkable change in demeanor. He turned off his anger like a faucet. It takes a great actor to do that. Or a consummate liar."

Nigel made a face. "You're playing detective again. Last week, you contrived the case of the conniving cardiologist. Today, you invented the incident of the insincere solicitor."

Flick's back stiffened. *Count to ten. Don't let him make you mad.*

"I watched Bleasdale closely," she said evenly.

"As did I, and it happens that I am an excellent poker player." He added, "I withdraw my question. You obviously presume he is up to no good."

"I don't *presume* anything. I don't know what Bleasdale is up to."

"I happen to think his scheme has merit."

"I do, too. I just wish a lawyer less skilled at body language had proposed it."

"Do you realize how silly that sounds?"

Count to ten again.

"Let's talk about something else," she said.

"I have the perfect topic," Nigel said. "Animals. Specifically, what are we to do with them?"

"Elspeth hoped that her cats would have the run of the museum."

"I'm afraid that's impossible. Some people will be allergic to them during the day, and they might set off our burglar alarms at night."

"Both good points," she agreed. "In that case, I volunteer the curators' wing on the third floor. They can live among our lab equipment—assuming, of course, that none of the curators have cat allergies. The combined square footage of the Conservation Laboratory and offices is comparable to a good-sized house. Best of all, they'll have plenty of company all day."

"Fine with me. What about the bird?"

"I propose to place him in the Duchess of Bedford Tearoom. We can put a large Victorian cage in the corner and make Earl a part of the ambience. Parrots and teahouses go together nicely."

"That might work. . . ." Nigel eyed Earl suspiciously. "Assuming his vocabulary doesn't include any profanity."

"I sincerely doubt that Elspeth Hawker taught her parrot how to curse."

"Then let's give it a try. That leaves the—*the*—I forgot what kind of dog this is."

"A Shiba Inu. Elspeth told me it means 'small dog' in Japanese."

"Very apropos. Who cares for him?"

"The curators have the cats. It seems only fair that the administrative staff adopt the dog."

Nigel frowned. "What happens at night and on weekends? We can't simply lock the hound in my office when the museum is closed."

"Another good point. I guess you and I can take turns bringing Cha-Cha home. A 'joint custody' agreement, so to speak."

"*Me?*"

"*Us.* At least until we can work out a better arrangement."

"I am not at all certain that pets are allowed in my flat."

Flick pointed to a large canvas tote bag. "I was going to send that back to the Hawkers, but perhaps we'd better keep it."

"How can a self-respecting dog *not* hate being carried about in a sack like contraband goods?"

"He's used to it. Elspeth began to bring him to the museum

when he was a puppy."

"You knew about this?"

Flick felt herself blush. " 'Fraid so. Elspeth was quite attached to Cha-Cha. She took him with her everywhere."

Cha-Cha raised his head and made a soft yip.

"He seems to know when people talk about him," Nigel said.

"I believe that's his 'I need to go out' bark."

"Oh."

"I hung his lead on the coatrack."

Nigel sighed. "Perhaps I'll get lucky while strolling through the Common. I'll think of a way to foist this animal on someone else."

It was the word *foist* that set Flick to thinking when Nigel and Cha-Cha left. Elspeth cared too much for her pets to risk foisting them on strangers. If she had been warned about a "dodgy ticker," to quote Marjorie Halifax, Elspeth immediately would have made detailed provisions for the pets.

"But she didn't, did she?" Flick said to Lapsang—or possibly Souchong—who had rolled over to have its tummy rubbed. As Flick crouched down to oblige, her cat's-eye view of the office revealed an object attached beneath the wooden side chair that Nigel had just vacated.

She crawled closer to the chair and saw that two crossed strips of duct tape held a small metal box to the underside of the seat. She peeled the tape loose. The box was an old tobacco tin—*Brophy's Finest Pipe Tobacco*—that opened on one end. She snapped the hinged flap aside and saw a small leather-bound notebook wedged into the can. It took several tugs—and lots of rocking—to pull the notebook out.

Flick had just sorted hundreds of samples of Elspeth's clear, large handwriting; without doubt, Elspeth had written the words, numbers, and symbols on the first nineteen pages. She moved to Elspeth's desk, sat down, and turned on the lamp. She realized vaguely that both cats had followed her across the room and were taking turns rubbing against her ankle, but she was too engrossed to care.

It's some sort of diary or logbook.

The lined pages were covered with abbreviations: *Mos.—Ptn.—Pat.—Mos. Constsy.—T.W.—R.R.—Col. Mkgs.—Devs. —Reg.* And numbers: *50%—75%—100%.* And occasional complete words, such as *Hunan, Anhui,* and *Yunnan.* Most of the entries had been neatly inscribed with a fountain pen, but on the top right corner of every page, Elspeth had used a red marker to write a large *F.* Each page also had an obvious date neatly printed near the top. The dates spanned a nine-month period that culminated less than a month earlier.

She flipped the pages back and forth for nearly ten minutes. The notebook must have something to do with tea. Hunan, Anhui, and Yunnan were all tea-growing regions in China. Perhaps these are Elspeth's tea-tasting notes?

Don't be silly!

Flick took a deep breath and urged herself to think methodically. "There really are two questions to answer," she murmured aloud. "What does the content mean? And why would Elspeth work so hard to hide it?"

Wrong!

"You know the notebook was hidden," she said in full voice. "That's the starting point. What kind of diary would Elspeth want to hide?"

Flick stared at the pages. She turned them slowly.

What am I looking at? What does F *stand for?*

A chill as strong as an electric shock ran down Flick's spine.

F *stands for Fake! Or Fraud! Or Forgery!*

Like tumblers falling in place inside a lock, the abbreviations began to make sense. "T.W." for Tunbridge Ware. "Mos." for mosaic. "Ptn." for pattern and "Pat." for patina.

Figure out the rest later.

More tumblers dropped into slots. Each page represented a different antiquity—most of them pieces of Tunbridge Ware. The abbreviations described the specific characteristics of each item.

The notebook documented Elspeth's home-brew evaluations of nineteen different antiquities on display. Elspeth had identified a group of forgeries in the museum—including many of her favorite Tunbridge Ware items.

The lock opened. Someone had replaced the originals with fakes. Someone who realized Dame Elspeth had discovered the deception.

The someone who poisoned Elspeth.

Flick addressed Souchong—or possibly Lapsang. "I knew it had to be murder," she said. "No one believed me, but now I have a solid piece of evidence." She laughed. "And you know what? The notebook means that Nigel Owen is off my list of suspects. The antiquity thefts began long before he arrived at the museum."

Six suspects left. Five trustees and Conan Davies.

Almost without meaning to, Flick flipped through the pages of the notebook. All of the pages in the middle were blank, but Elspeth had written eight names on the very last page:

Archibald Meicklejohn?
Marjorie Halifax?
Dorothy McAndrews?
~~Sir Simon Clowes~~

Matthew Eaton?

~~William de Rudd~~

Iona Saxby?

Conan Davies?

Flick gave a slight gasp as she realized that Elspeth had assembled a list of thievery suspects. She, too, had started with the seven other trustees and Conan Davies.

"Two of the names are scratched out," Flick murmured. "The same two I eliminated."

Six left. One of them murdered Elspeth Hawker.

Six

A tray of unadorned biscuits rather than a cart full of jam-covered scones provided sustenance at the emergency meeting of the trustees of the Tunbridge Wells Tea Museum on Wednesday afternoon. Nigel had expected a jibe or two about the simplified menu, which included only one kind of tea, and he wasn't disappointed.

"I see you've put us on half rations, Nigel," Vicar William de Rudd said. "A symbol, I suppose, of the hardships the museum will face in the years ahead."

"Either that," Marjorie Halifax said, "or a reminder that the museum now has four new mouths to feed." She fought to hold a large blue cat on her lap, plainly a losing battle. "Thank goodness you served us a good cuppa. This really is a charming Formosa Oolong."

"I admit that the tea is first-rate," Matthew Eaton said. "Delightful peachy overtones. However, store-bought British biscuits simply won't do. The only reason I attend these interminable meetings is to eat scones baked by Alain Rousseau."

Dorothy McAndrews, sitting next to Matthew and wearing an almost identically patterned Harris Tweed jacket, chimed in, "It hardly seems fair that a French chef does brilliant Scottish scones, but there you are."

"You should consider yourselves blessed to eat plain biscuits today," Sir Simon Clowes said. "Alain's scones taste good because they are overloaded with butter. Most of us at this table have reached the age when we require heart-healthy diets. I say that both as friend and physician."

"It's not the scones I miss," Iona Saxby said, "but those lovely homemade conserves that Alain puts up. And the clotted cream, of course."

Sir Simon groaned. "You must realize that clotted cream is an extraordinarily potent source of cholesterol and that Alain's cloyingly sweet jams and jellies are almost pure sugar."

Iona, undeterred, shook her head in mock sadness. "You really have shown us your wretched side, Nigel, by cutting back on our tea break. At heart you are a parsimonious bean counter."

"Amen!" Archibald Meicklejohn bellowed from his place at the head of the table. "Tightfisted financial leadership is precisely what the Royal Tunbridge Wells Tea Museum requires in the months ahead. The more parsimonious the better."

Nigel dutifully smiled at the comments made in jest and acknowledged the doctor's earnest pleas with pensive nods. At least the trustees had loosened up during the past hour. They had arrived at three o'clock in a suitably dismal mood, each clutching a printout of the e-mail Nigel had sent the previous afternoon. The grim document tallied the major antiquities currently owned by the Hawkers and estimated their total market value at more than forty million pounds.

Nigel had surprised the trustees by beginning the special meeting on a lighter note. "You may wonder why I invited a dog, two cats, and a parrot to join us today. Well, on Monday I received the astonishing news that the museum inherited this menagerie and is duty bound to provide lifetime care."

"Don't tell me that he went ahead and did it!" Iona wailed. "Despite my urgings, despite my warnings."

Nigel lifted three sheets of paper stapled together. "I presume that you are talking about this purportedly ironbound contract, entered into between Dame Elspeth Hawker and Nathanial Swithin."

"Bother!" Iona said. "On occasion, Nathanial can be a nincompoop."

"One shouldn't blame Nate," Marjorie said. "Dame Elspeth could be exceptionally persuasive."

"Especially when wielding her chequebook," Sir Simon added.

"A lifetime of care for these animals represents a significant financial commitment by the museum," Archibald said. "I presume that we were properly compensated. If not, perhaps we can find a way to breach the contract."

"A total breach may not be necessary," Iona said. "A court might conclude that we have honored the agreement if we find suitable homes for Dame Elspeth's pets."

"That certainly seems fair," Sir Simon said.

"Not to me!" Dorothy said. "I feel duty bound to speak on behalf of those in the room who cannot speak for themselves —specifically, Cha-Cha, Lapsang, Souchong, and Earl. This board has a moral obligation to honor the *spirit* of the agreement made between Nathanial Swithin and Elspeth Hawker. We must provide compassionate care, as Dame Elspeth envisioned we would."

"I wholly agree," the Reverend de Rudd said.

"Who speaks for the *other* living things in this museum?" Matthew's swivel chair clanked as he rocked forward. "Unrestrained cat clawing, bird perching, and dog sprinkling will do irreparable harm to the tea bushes and other plants in the tea garden."

"Not a problem, Matthew," Nigel said. "We won't allow the animals to run loose in the building or gardens. Our chief curator has come up with an ingenious scheme that divides the responsibilities for pet care among our administrative staff, our curators, and our tearoom. It seems to be working perfectly."

Nigel tilted his head toward Flick, who despite his obvious invitation to join in merely offered an affirmative grunt.

That is not the Felicity Adams I know. Where is her eager smile? Nigel wondered. *Or the rush of enthusiastic words about her latest accomplishment?*

Flick had seemed lost in thought since the meeting with Solicitor Bleasdale on Monday. She had spent most of the past forty-eight hours in the Tea Antiquities Gallery. Every time Nigel had walked by the entrance archway, there was Flick examining one of the Hawker-owned items on display.

Figure out Flick later. There is work to be done now.

Nigel had planned the day's agenda with thorough attention to detail. After six months, he knew the trustees well enough to orchestrate a meeting that would actually lead to a decision.

Nigel led off with a concise summary of the facts. He reviewed his white paper and described his conversations with Bleasdale about the Hawkers' intentions to reclaim the antiquities. The trustees, all of them wealthy, understood both the nature of British inheritance taxes and the family's need to sell off more than a third of Dame Elspeth's estate. Most nodded grimly when Nigel explained how he and Flick had made ad hoc guesstimates of the collection's current value.

"I fear that your total is too low," Dorothy said, "perhaps by as much as twenty million pounds. The market for the choicest items has never been better. Oh how I wish that Dame Elspeth had bequeathed the collection to the museum."

"I repeatedly urged her to do so," Iona said. "Talk to your solicitor, I begged. Talk to your financial advisor, I pleaded. But she seemed—*reluctant*, I suppose is the right word. One can never fully comprehend another person's motives."

"I don't think Dame Elspeth truly accepted the notion that the antiquities belonged to her," Vicar de Rudd said. "Perhaps a year ago she talked to me about wanting to revise the small signs on the exhibits throughout the museum. As I recall, she felt that the phrase "From the collection of Dame Elspeth Hawker" should be changed to "Owned Anonymously.""

"What pray tell does that signify?" Archibald said.

"I assumed that Dame Elspeth was speaking from humility. Her tone suggested that she did not feel worthy to possess such riches."

"Moving right along," Nigel said, "the signs on our exhibits are the least of our worries. We have to face the fact that the majority of antiquities currently on display in the museum will likely vanish during the coming six months."

He paused for a barrage of sighs, groans, and growls from the trustees—plus another "Bother!" from Iona.

"I believe that we have three options available to us," Nigel went on. "Option one is to accept the inevitable. We bite the bullet and change the mission of the museum, perhaps becoming an academic institution that is primarily research oriented."

"No!" Dr. Clowes smacked the table with his palm. "That is not what Mary Hawker Evans had in mind forty-odd years ago. This museum was built to be a proper *museum*."

"Well spoken, Sir Simon," Marjorie said. "Also remember that in our role as a proper museum, we have developed into a leading tourist destination in Tunbridge Wells. If we give up our collection—if we tinker with our mission—we will destroy the soul of this institution."

"Exactly!" Dorothy said. "Somehow we must prevent our antiquities from being dispersed around the world. The collection on display in this building is a national treasure."

Archibald glanced at Flick. "Does our chief curator have anything to add?"

Flick replied softly, "Quite simply, I would consider it a failure of our leadership and a colossal tragedy if we did nothing to stop the loss of the antiquities on display."

"Here! Here!" Iona said.

"Yes indeed!" the reverend agreed.

Archibald turned toward Nigel. "The consensus of the trustees is that option one is not an option. We will not go gentle into that good night."

Nigel surveyed the table and saw a unanimous volley of nods.

He cleared his throat and began again. "Option two would be to engage in a delaying action. We don't have to return the antiquities until ninety days—three full months—after a demand is made by the court-appointed executors of Elspeth's estate. If we refuse to cooperate with the appraisers sent to value the collection, we can probably delay the grant of representation by the Probate Registry by three months more. Those six months might be enough time to raise sufficient funds to purchase a reasonable number of antiquities—say 20 percent of the collection.

"On the upside, we will emerge with a sufficient number

of major antiquities to remain a museum that welcomes the general public. The downside, alas, is that we will alienate the Hawker heirs and may incite them to take legal action against us."

"How can we function with only 20 percent of our exhibits?" Marjorie asked.

"I've given that some thought," Nigel said. "We will try to fill our empty galleries with traveling exhibits borrowed from universities and other museums."

"This is a tea museum," Iona said. "Where can we find a sufficient number of suitable exhibits?"

Nigel could feel the awkward smile on his face. "I said 'try to fill,' Iona. It won't be easy."

Steady on! You sound like a dunce.

Nigel hated to make silly-sounding statements at trustee meetings. Everything he said, everything *everyone* said, flowed into four small microphones strategically placed on the conference table. The microphones sent their signals to a voice-operated tape recorder in Polly Reid's office. It had been Nigel's idea to record trustee meetings and then have Polly produce a written transcript. "A complete transcript is more useful than meeting minutes," Nigel had said to her, "and there's no need for you to waste time sitting through our tedious meetings."

Flick unexpectedly saved the day. "We'll need to be creative about borrowed exhibits. For example, the Victoria and Albert Museum in London owns a collection of antique teddy bears that they lend out on a regular basis. I can envision a Teddy Bears' Tea Party exhibit aimed at children, designed to teach them about tea."

Once again, Archibald took charge: "Option two certainly is not as bad as option one, Nigel, but it is not wholly desirable, either."

Nigel looked around the table. The nods and expressions signaled that the other trustees agreed with the chair. Nigel gave Flick a thank-you wink.

Good. Now they are primed to hear the real plan.

He took a deep breath. "Option three was actually proposed by the Hawkers' solicitor. Mr. Bleasdale believes he can put together a so-called 'creative financing' package—structured around a ten-year chattel mortgage—that will enable us to acquire the entire Hawker collection in one fell swoop." Nigel described the details, then concluded: "The downside to this option is that the museum will be encumbered by a large loan for the next decade. We will have to do almost continuous fundraising and development work. However, we will be able to sell off some of the less desirable assets in the collection to reduce our outstanding debt. This is precisely what companies do after they borrow money to acquire other businesses."

"I like it!" Matthew Eaton said. "The museum should have acquired the collection decades ago."

"Without doubt!" Marjorie Halifax said. "And as for the ten-year loan—well, most people I know have twenty-five-year mortgages to pay for their houses."

Nigel took another deep breath. "I must report, however, that one comment made by Mr. Bleasdale has me concerned. His suggestion that we find a 'levelheaded antiquities appraiser' set off alarm bells in my mind. We certainly don't want any part of a scheme to defraud the Inland Revenue."

"Balderdash!" Iona Saxby said. "Not that Bleasdale is likely to do a fiddle with the valuations, but if he should, it is his problem—and the estate's. The museum will not be at risk."

"I like it even more!" Matthew Eaton said. "It seems the perfect solution."

"Raising five or six million pounds a year will be difficult but doable," Dorothy McAndrews said. "We are an inventive board."

"Inventive indeed!" echoed Sir Simon Clowes.

"I am vastly encouraged," said the Reverend William de Rudd. He aimed a warm smile at Nigel.

Archibald Meicklejohn raised his hand. "I am encouraged, too. However, I am also awed by the very notion of a ten-year loan for upwards of forty million pounds. During my banking career, I have seen many overly optimistic organizations dragged to their doom by similar commitments. This is an option we must consider carefully."

"As we shall," Nigel said. "I suggest that we recess for our tea break first and return refreshed to our deliberations."

And so at four o'clock, the trustees drank one kind of tea and ate store-bought biscuits.

The simplified tea break came to a natural end at four thirty, when the trustees had finished grousing about the menu, visiting the loo, and chatting together in duos and trios away from the table. Lapsang and Souchong had retreated to opposite corners of the boardroom. And Cha-Cha, who did seem to enjoy spending time with Nigel, had curled up against his left foot. Nigel felt a twinge of regret that Flick would take Cha-Cha home tonight, especially since the owners of his flat—a two-bedroom apartment up on Lime Hill Road, near the Tunbridge Wells town centre—had not objected to small pets.

Archibald spoke first after the break. "The more I think about the matter, Nigel, the more I am convinced that you and Dr. Adams must ultimately recommend whether to choose option two or option three."

"Sorry?" Nigel knew he was gawking at the chair of the trustees, but Archibald's statement had come as a complete surprise.

"I came to the very same conclusion," Sir Simon said. "After all, as a graduate of INSEAD, you have superlative financial credentials. And as for Dr. Adams—well, she knows the collection better than any of us. I for one am fully prepared to rely on your sound judgment."

Matthew weighed in. "A grand suggestion, Archibald." He turned to Nigel. "The director and the chief curator are our field generals, a perfect team to shepherd us through this crisis."

Nigel realized his mistake. By allowing the trustees time to think and chat among themselves, he had made it possible for Archibald to conjure up the idea of shifting responsibility to Flick and him.

Blimey! I've been had.

A "short-timer" acting director and a spanking new chief curator made ideal scapegoats. Should the tea museum be "dragged to its doom," the fault would lie with their recommendation.

I'm trapped. And so is Flick.

He looked over at her, sitting rigid in her chair, her eyes darting around the room as if she were looking for an excuse to leave the meeting.

You must have reached the same conclusion, Madame Curator. You know that your career is on the line, too.

The trustees discussed option three as planned, but they carefully prefaced most of their comments with "assuming that Mr. Owen and Dr. Adams recommend acquiring the collection" or "if they recommend we commit to a ten-year loan."

The last item of business was a mock motion by Matthew Eaton. "I move that the acting director be instructed to restore our scones, cakes, preserves, conserves, and clotted cream at the next trustee meeting." All the other trustees except Sir Simon shouted, "Second!"

Archibald adjourned the meeting at five. Flick abruptly grabbed Cha-Cha's lead and hurried out of the room.

"What do you suppose prompted such a quick departure?"

Nigel looked up at Iona Saxby grinning down at him.

She went on. "That was a rhetorical question, Nigel. You don't have to answer it."

Nigel managed a feeble "Okay."

Iona kept talking. "I'd like a private word with you." She sat down in the empty chair next to him. "You do realize that the full responsibility for making a good decision has been placed on your shoulders."

"Well, yes. It had occurred to me."

She touched his upper arm. "You seem to have very strong shoulders."

"Ah. . ." Nigel looked around. They were alone in the boardroom.

"Does the name Augustus Hoskins ring a bell?" Iona said softly.

Nigel nodded. "He is a museum development consultant."

"A legend in fund-raising and growth planning, who by a fortunate coincidence is also a friend of a friend of mine. I rang Hoskins's office in London during our tea break. He has agreed to drive down to Tunbridge Wells tomorrow and meet with you. He's expecting your call to arrange the details." Iona tucked a folded piece of paper into his jacket's breast pocket. "Have a heart-to-heart with him before you stick your neck out too far. You need good people in your corner at a time like this."

"Thank you, Iona."

She reached for his hand and gave it a gentle squeeze. "I find it a great shame that you can't fully rely on your staff."

"My staff? But Polly is a wonderful assistant." Nigel tried to tug his hand free; Iona held on tight.

"I was speaking of Felicity Adams. She is your subordinate, is she not?"

He hesitated a moment. "I suppose she is."

"Keep a close eye on her. She seems a loose cannon—an American bull in a china shop."

"In what way, Iona?"

"Dr. Adams can be dangerously unpredictable. Her bizarre performance at the last trustee meeting proves the point. So does her talk of teddy bears and exhibits for children when the very future of the museum is uncertain."

"I see." He managed to liberate his hand.

"Enough about business. Why don't you join me for dinner this evening?" Iona fluttered her eyelashes.

Nigel felt his stomach lurch. "I can't this evening. A previous commitment. In. . .*East Grinstead.* Can't be broken. Perhaps next time?"

Iona ran her index finger along the knot of his necktie. "I will definitely hold you to your promise."

Nigel smiled as best he could.

Who knows? I might be hit by a bus before the next trustees' meeting.

Flick tramped northeast on Eridge Road, mindful of the nearby cars, all but ignoring the gentle rain that pattered on her umbrella. Cha-Cha trotted jauntily alongside. Ten minutes past five in Tunbridge Wells translated to ten minutes past noon in Ann Arbor, Michigan. Dr. Cory Unger, her favorite forensic toxicology professor, almost certainly would be in his office. Cory was a workaholic who never ate lunch, never exercised, looked as skinny as a power pole, and probably would live to be one hundred. She needed to talk to him—immediately.

Cha-Cha deftly avoided a puddle that Flick splashed through head-on. Adjusting to England's celebrated damp climate had been easier than she had expected, probably because everyone else at the museum seemed to consider frequent rain a given. However, Flick did find the local weather forecasts amusing. The most common prediction was "a wet day with sunny intervals."

She stepped into another puddle, this one deep enough to splatter her legs. She hardly noticed; her mind was focused on Alain Rousseau's preserves and conserves. The instant Sir Simon had described them as cloyingly sweet, Flick understood how Elspeth Hawker had been poisoned. She immediately thought back to the afternoon Elspeth died. Nigel Owen had moved the tea trolley alongside the conference table and served each trustee an assortment of preserves in personal-sized jam pots. The exception had been Elspeth. She had received a single large jam pot filled with her beloved Danish lingonberry preserves. It seemed a perfect explanation—the *only* explanation. Barbiturates taste bitter, so hide a lethal dose in something chock full of sugar.

Cha-Cha began to tug on his lead when they reached the southern entrance to the Pantiles. He seemed to remember the way to Flick's apartment on the Lower Walk. Perhaps he also wanted to get out of the rain. A smattering of French caught her ear as a man and woman passed in the opposite direction. They were walking hand in hand. Probably a couple from France on their honeymoon. A stray dog trotted by, paused a moment to glance sideways at Cha-Cha, then hurried on.

A fairly steep, unexpectedly long staircase led to Flick's first-floor apartment. The building dated back to the mid–nineteenth century, an age of thick walls and high ceilings.

She dashed up the steps and unlocked her front door. Whoever had refurbished the old pile had laid out the flats with Continental-style floor plans. A hallway led first past the parlor, then the kitchen, then the bedroom. The bathroom was at the far end of the hallway.

Flick had deliberately chosen a small, one-bedroom apartment; it would be easy to furnish with a fifty-fifty mix of furniture shipped from the United States and rented in England. The telephone was in the bedroom, which also served as her home office.

Flick switched her computer on and waited impatiently for it to boot. With luck, she might find Cory Unger's telephone number in the e-mail program's address book.

"Bingo!" she murmured. She dialed the number in Michigan.

"This is Professor Unger. Good afternoon."

"Actually, it's almost evening over here in England, Cory," she replied.

"My, my! It's our illustrious—and squeamish—expatriate food chemist. Find any suspicious tea stains lately?"

"Funny you should ask that. I think I witnessed a murder last Wednesday. An old woman named Elspeth Hawker was poisoned while I gave a presentation on tea tasting."

The line went quiet. Flick could hear the professor breathing. He finally said, "You sound like you're serious."

"I am serious. Do you have two minutes to talk?"

The two minutes stretched into more than twenty as Flick described everything she had observed at the trustee meeting. She wrapped up by saying, "My theory is that her jam pot was chock full of a convenient barbiturate."

"Secobarbital sodium," he said.

"What?"

"Assuming she was fed a barbiturate, secobarbital sodium—trade name Seconal—would be the compound of choice under the circumstances. It is highly soluble in water and works much more quickly than most other barbiturates. It rapidly produces drowsiness, sedation, and in the case of overdose, a coma that leads to death. Your old dear would have had to ingest at least two grams—although if I were the poisoner, I'd go for a minimum of three or four grams."

"That doesn't sound like much."

"A teaspoon of salt weighs about six grams, a teaspoon of granulated sugar around four. Say secobarbital is in the same neighborhood. Three or four teaspoons of the drug mixed into a good-sized pot of lingonberry preserves should do the trick, if the victim ate enough of the stuff."

"It's possible then?"

"It's possible," Cory agreed.

"Then let's backtrack. What did you mean, 'assuming she was fed a barbiturate'?"

The line went quiet again. "Don't take this the wrong way, Flick, but the British physicians I've met have been mighty good at what they do. The Brits don't give knighthoods to feebleminded quacks."

"So everyone assures me. However, I'm mighty good at what I do, too, and I'm certain of what I saw."

"In that case, have you also considered that other drugs can mimic a heart attack?"

"Like digitalis and digitoxin?"

"Two good choices. An overdose of a cardiac glycoside can stop a heart cold. And a lethal quantity of digitalis is only three times the usual medicinal dose."

"Elspeth Hawker simply fell asleep and died. She presented no other symptoms. If I remember your lectures, an overdose of digitalis or digitoxin will make you nauseous, even cause blurred vision."

Cory grunted.

"I take that to mean I'm right."

He grunted again.

"Only one thing still bothers me," Flick said. "Can lingonberry preserves really mask the bitter taste of a barbiturate?"

The professor laughed. "I can't even tell you what a lingonberry looks like, Flick. I guess if you want a useful answer, you'll have to run an experiment."

"You know, that's not a bad idea."

"Whoa! It's a terrible idea. Do I have to remind you that I was kidding?"

"I won't use secobarbital, Cory. I promise. I have a more benign substance in mind."

Flick said her good-byes, put down the phone, and went looking for Cha-Cha. She found him curled up in the middle of the sofa in the parlor.

"You're lucky that sofa is a rental," she said.

Cha-Cha raised his head and stared at her quizzically.

"I don't suppose you would like another walk in the rain? I have to find a jar of lingonberry preserves."

Cha-Cha lowered his head without further comment.

Flick walked through the Pantiles, exited the northern end, and made for London Road—a thoroughfare sensible locals called the A26. She walked less than a half mile to where the road made a sharp left turn to the northwest and continued straight to the large Safeway superstore that seemed likely to stock lingonberry preserves. The store was crowded. Flick guessed that most of her fellow shoppers were professional folk who, like her, did their shopping in the evening.

Vaccinium vitisidaea. Without trying to, Flick remembered

the Latin name she had studied years earlier and other details, too. Lingonberry—a small, red, round berry with a tart, acidity taste. Also called the "mountain cranberry." A staple on tables throughout Scandinavia.

And apparently in southern England, too. Flick found three different brands of lingonberry preserves on the shelf but decided instead to buy a bottle of German-made lingonberry syrup sweetened with sugar.

The perfect form of lingonberry for my experiment.

On her walk home, Flick lingered a moment in front of the "Bath House" at the northern end of the Pantiles. It had been built in 1804 so that well-heeled visitors to Tunbridge Wells could soak in the mineral-rich waters. The original chalybeate, or iron-bearing, spring was still accessible down a short flight of steps in the Bath House's ornate, colonnaded façade.

Flick understood the chemistry of the water—how dissolved iron and manganese salts created its notorious metallic taste—but she enjoyed the local legend more than a cold scientific explanation. It seems that around the year 980, the devil quenched his burning nose in that very spring, thus imparting the metallic tang. Satan had foolishly tried to tempt Dunstan, the archbishop of Canterbury, by dressing up as a beautiful woman. The future saint spotted cloven hooves beneath the woman's dress and clamped red-hot tongs on her nose. This happened in the Sussex village of Mayfield. The devil, suffering great pain, leapt all the way to Tunbridge Wells in search of an available source of cooling water.

Flick had visited the spring during the previous summer and filled two dozen small bottles to accompany the Christmas cards she would send to friends and family in the United States. They were lined up on the bottom shelf of her refrigerator like a platoon of toy soldiers. She could still remember the bitter taste the water had left in her mouth.

Bitter like poison. A perfect stand-in for barbiturates in my experiment.

Flick's experiment was simplicity itself. She poured the contents of four small bottles of spring water into a tall glass, added a teaspoonful of lingonberry syrup, and tasted—then added more syrup and tasted again.

The bitter, metallic taste slowly receded but never completely disappeared.

Flick felt a nose poke her ankle. She looked down at Cha-Cha's hopeful face.

"Ah ha!" she said. "There's nothing like the sound of food being prepared to catch a dog's ear. Well, thank you for joining me in the kitchen, Cha-Cha. I appreciate your company. A second observer is always useful in scientific research."

She transferred a few spoonfuls of the water-and-syrup mix to a saucer, then set it down on the floor. The dog sniffed at the brew, took a tentative taste, then backed away in obvious annoyance.

"Don't look at me that way," Flick said. "A true scientist is willing to suffer when necessary to advance the cause of science. It is not my fault that you, like all canines, have a remarkably sensitive nose and a surprisingly small supply of taste buds. That means you reacted mostly to the strange odor of the mineral water. Or maybe you don't like lingonberries."

Flick gave Cha-Cha a doggy treat, instantly improving his disposition.

"Your mistress, however, relied chiefly on her sense of taste to spot dangerous-to-eat foods, and as we get older, our sense of taste can fade."

Cha-Cha begged for another treat. Flick let him eat it out of her hand.

"So let's imagine Elspeth Hawker at the meeting last Wednesday, happily chatting with the other trustees, cheerfully spooning big dollops of lingonberry preserves on her scones. I'll bet that she ignored the slight residual bitterness. She probably assumed that Alain Rousseau had changed his recipe or that he got hold of a batch of unripe lingonberries."

She reached down and stroked the dog's plush back.

"I'd say that our experiment is a success. We now know the method of murder. And Elspeth's little black book provides the motive. Oh—that reminds me! I didn't get a chance to tell you that I tracked down eighteen of the nineteen objects Elspeth identified as fakes. They are all on display in the Tea Antiquities Gallery. I'm not an expert on forgeries, but I'm pretty sure she was right. They don't look quite right to me."

Cha-Cha made a soft yipping sound.

"I agree with your assessment. We know the method and the motive—but what do we do next? Who can we tell?"

Who will believe us?

SEVEN

Nigel stepped out of the pharmacy at the northern end of the Pantiles. "We have time to talk this out before we meet with Augustus Hoskins," he said to Flick. "We're not due at the restaurant for another fifteen minutes."

"Fine with me. Where?"

"That bench looks comfortable."

Nigel and Flick had walked through the Pantiles so that he could buy a packet of antacid tablets. The bench he chose was on the Upper Walk, across from the colonnade, under a large linden tree. Two teenaged boys were sitting on an adjacent bench, talking, smoking, and occasionally laughing loudly.

"What do you think happened yesterday?" he asked Flick evenly.

"To repeat what I've already said twice, I think that the trustees tasked us to make a vital recommendation."

Nigel's immediate thought was that he disliked hearing "task" used as a verb, but he didn't want to argue with Flick's

112

choice of words. There were far bigger issues to deal with.

"The trustees took the easy way out," he said. "They dropped a crisis into our laps."

"That's where it belongs. We manage the museum; it's our job to solve tough problems. Anyway, this is a simple decision to make. We go with the creative financing option and buy our collection."

Nigel heaved a heavy sigh—heavy enough, he hoped, to signal his growing frustration. He opened a roll of antacids and put one in his mouth. His stomach had been churning most of the morning.

"You are missing my point," he said. "*Of course*, the museum will buy the collection. The problem is that the trustees have put you and me on the spot. We will take the blame should anything go wrong."

"What can go wrong? It seems a straightforward transaction. The collection will serve as collateral for the loan. If the museum can't make the payments for some reason, we'll simply sell off the antiquities. We'd be no worse off than we are today."

"That depends," Nigel said.

"On what?"

"Think back to the dismal possibility articulated by Archibald Meicklejohn."

"You mean about organizations being dragged to their doom by similar commitments?"

Nigel nodded. "Think what might happen if Britain experienced a serious economic recession during the coming few years. Fund-raising would slow down at the same time paintings, maps, crockery, and whatever become less valuable. We might not be able to sell off enough of the collection to cover the outstanding balance."

He enjoyed watching a look of recognition spread across

Flick's face. "Ouch!" she said with obvious sincerity.

"Ouch indeed! Therein lies the downward spiral that leads to doom. In the worst case, the museum would go bankrupt."

"But how could anyone pin the blame on us?"

"Clearly you misled the trustees about the long-term value of the antiquities, while I encouraged them to approve an excessively risky transaction." Nigel grimaced. "As least, that's what the trustees will tell their friends, colleagues, newspaper reporters, government boards of inquiry—anyone who asks why a successful museum went under. When two plump, defenseless scapegoats come along, no smart executive will miss the opportunity to make full use of them."

Flick took a few seconds to respond. "Wow. I owe you an apology."

"For what?"

"I assumed you were being paranoid—seeing bogeymen under your desk."

Nigel offered the roll of antacids. "Would you like a piece of museum-director's candy?"

Flick laughed. "No. But now I understand why you wanted me to come to lunch. We seem to be in this together."

"Like peas in the proverbial pod, although should the bottom fall out, my reputation will suffer far more than yours. The trustees are bound to take pity on the sitting chief curator, whereas I will be an irresistible target: the *former* acting director. I can imagine Archibald claiming that my temporary status encouraged me to be reckless."

"Then maybe we should be cautious and recommend one of the other options."

Nigel shook his head. "As you said earlier, there is only one choice to make. Doing nothing would be absurd, and dragging our heels accomplishes nothing. We *must* buy the antiquities. Or else the museum will go the way of the Wolseley Six Saloon."

"I've never heard of a Wolseley Six Saloon."

"I'm not surprised! My dad bought one of the last Sixes to be built—in *1975*. I learned to drive in that car."

"What's our plan for today?" Flick asked.

"The fellow we are meeting for lunch at Barn and Rafters in Lonsdale Gardens. . ." Nigel glanced at his watch. "We had better move along." He stood up. "The chappie's name is Augustus Hoskins, a world-class whiz at raising money for museums. He is so good, in fact, that two of his fund-raising campaigns have been turned into case histories for business-school textbooks. His nickname in the museum biz is 'the Great Hope.' We will pick his brain. Perhaps there is an option four?"

"Do I have to curtsy when I meet him?"

"A discreet kiss to his ring undoubtedly will be sufficient."

They left the Pantiles, looped around the Church of King Charles the Martyr on the corner of Neville and London Roads, and walked through Chapel Place to reach High Street. Nigel had to slow his pace so that Flick could stay with him.

"I assumed when you invited me to lunch that we would drive," Flick said. "Otherwise I'd have left my look-good pumps in my office and worn my comfortable walking shoes."

"It's scarcely more than a kilometer stroll from the museum to Lonsdale Gardens. Besides, walking in Tunbridge Wells is easier than parking."

"Frankly, I'm amazed at how much walking I do these days, despite the many hills. My friends back home don't believe me. They can't imagine that I have survived three whole months without buying a car."

"Remind me of where you are from."

"York. A small city in southeastern Pennsylvania."

"We have a York in England. Ours is somewhat older, though, and I'll wager more historic."

"Older maybe; my York dates back only to 1741. But more historic—*piffle!* The words 'United States of America' were first spoken in York. That was in 1777, when the Continental Congress met in York to adopt the Articles of Confederation, America's original constitution. York was the first U.S. capital."

Nigel held up his hands in a gesture of surrender. "I stand corrected."

They crossed to Mount Pleasant Road and trod uphill next to Central Railway Station. A train had just arrived. Several people ran past them into the station, clearly trying to catch the train.

"How large is your York?" Nigel asked.

"Slightly smaller than Tunbridge Wells—but otherwise quite comparable. I feel right at home here."

"You and Hoskins should get along like old mates. He grew up in the Wells."

"That's a coincidence."

"My very words to him yesterday." He hesitated. "Flick— there is something I need to say before we meet Augustus. I am afraid that I must be blunt with you. We don't want to give Hoskins the impression that anything criminal has gone on at the museum."

"By any chance are you thinking about the intentional poisoning of Dame Elspeth Hawker, followed by the negligent ignoring of obvious barbiturate overdose symptoms by one of England's leading physicians?"

Nigel stopped in his tracks and peered at Flick's face. She was grinning at him.

"Ah!" he said. "You are pulling my leg."

Nigel began walking again. Perhaps he deserved a mocking response from Flick. He had raised the issue chiefly because Iona Saxby's "loose cannon" comment of the day before had hit home. On the other hand, Flick seemed to have backed away from her belief that Elspeth had been murdered. On the other, other hand, Americans could be outrageously unpredictable.

Hope for the best, prepare for the worst, expect the unexpected.

He mulled the old cliché that had popped into his mind. It seemed wholly apropos for dealing both with tea museums and Felicity Adams.

Ahead on the left were the two stone pillars that marked the entrance to Lonsdale Gardens. They passed through and walked left again, toward Barn and Rafters.

"Have you been here before?" he asked.

"Yes. The Barn Pub on several occasions and once for dinner upstairs at the Rafters."

"Curiously, the place is new to me. We are here at Hoskins's suggestion."

"Do you know what he looks like?"

"No. But I doubt that a sixtyish museum consultant will be hard to spot."

Nigel opened the door and murmured, "Oh dear!"

"What's wrong?" Flick asked.

"I never have understood why so many English pubs revel in murky interiors crisscrossed by oaken rafters and filled with bucolic furniture that might have been owned by Nell Gwynne."

"Maybe because guests like me enjoy it. Look around— you are the only person in the place wearing a sour face."

"Bah humbug!"

"You may have to shut your eyes when we go upstairs. There are more red walls, high yellow ceilings, hewn beams, sprays of dried plants, and—"

"Let me guess," he interrupted. "And an artsy assortment of jumble-sale relics hung decorously around the room."

She smiled. "As I recall, there are paintings on the walls and a bookshelf or two."

"Lead on. Even though you have ruined my appetite."

They climbed the wooden staircase. At the top, Flick whispered, "That's got to be him. The distinguished-looking gentlemen sitting alone at the table for four near the railing."

"Mr. Hoskins?" Nigel asked cautiously.

"In the flesh!" He thrust out his hand. "You must be Nigel Owen."

Augustus had the look, Nigel thought, of a modernized Pickwickian: portly, jowly, bespectacled, ruddy-cheeked, a fringe of hair encircling a gleaming bald pate—and below that an intelligent face that quickly gained one's confidence. He wore a charcoal gray three-piece suit punctuated by an orange tie.

Hoskins smiled at Flick. "Dr. Adams, I presume." He shook her hand, then pointed at the two chairs on the opposite side of his table. "Sit. Please."

The waitress approached. Hoskins asked for a dry sherry. Nigel and Flick ordered small ciders.

"Would you be surprised to learn," Augustus began when they were alone, "that forty-odd years ago I danced the Twist in this very room?" He didn't wait for Nigel or Flick to reply. "It is perfectly true. This used to be a dance hall, with one large continuous floor. The ersatz skylight in the floor that provides a view of the pub below is a recent addition." He paused to look around the restaurant. "Think of it! They held dances here while less than a mile away workmen were pouring the concrete basement of your splendid museum. I was only a callow youth back then, but even I had heard of the mighty Hawker Foundation and their reputation for doing things right. So imagine my astonishment yesterday afternoon when the lovely and talented Iona Saxby told me that your exhibitory knickers are in a twist."

"It feels more like a double bowline knot than a simple twist," Nigel said. "We do not own the principle antiquities on display in our galleries. The Hawker heirs have announced their intention to reclaim—and sell—their entire collection. We estimate its worth to be at least forty million pounds. The proceeds should be sufficient to pay the inheritance taxes on Elspeth Hawker's estate, which is the reason they intend to sell the antiquities."

"Blasted death duties! Britain makes it easy for a rich man to enter the kingdom of heaven. Inland Revenue takes away half of his wealth when he dies." Hoskins's wry smile gave way to a serious glower. "And yet, one assumes that Dame Elspeth would have recognized the problem as she grew older and found a solution before her passing. The fact that she did not utterly bewilders me—it is completely out of character with her previous support of the museum."

Nigel nodded. Iona Saxby had made a similar comment. Elspeth Hawker loved the museum, yet she had ignored an absolutely fundamental question: What would happen to the Hawker antiquities when she died? Perhaps Elspeth was one of those people who refuse to contemplate her own demise? Or was there another reason?

What difference does it make? Nigel reminded himself that Elspeth's motives died with her. His job was to look ahead, not backwards, and to find a way to acquire the Hawker collection.

Augustus leaned his elbows on the table. "You must know that the Royal Tunbridge Wells Tea Museum has been the envy of other English museum directors for four decades. Generous initial funding from a major foundation. A one-of-a-kind collection on display. The devoted patronage of a wealthy family. Nary a need to chat with Augustus Hoskins about raising money." He chortled again. "What more could a museum ask?"

"I agree," Nigel said. "The tea museum led a blessed existence for forty years, but our joyful days came to an abrupt end last Wednesday. We can no longer rely on the Hawker family. Our antiquities are in jeopardy. The Hawker Foundation has ceased providing direct support. And we need as much help as you can give us. The fact is, we are being driven to make an important financial decision under pressure—a decision that may have severe repercussions in years to come."

"An ever-so-common complaint these days." Hoskins sat back in his chair, signaling that the waitress had arrived to serve their drinks. When she left, he said to Nigel, "Please continue with the details of your repercussive financial dilemma."

Nigel took ten minutes to recount his meetings with Barrington Bleasdale and summarize the three obvious options. Hoskins proved an excellent listener, saying nothing but offering a sympathetic frown and a steady stream of interested nods. Nigel finished by saying, "Flick and I would appreciate your advice in two areas. First, have we ignored a potential solution? Second, if we choose to purchase the collection, is there a way we can decrease risk inherent in a long-term loan?"

Hoskins steepled his fingers. "Your first question has a simple answer. Yes—there is another option. Find a new patron to replace the Hawkers, a tea fancier with the financial resources and cultural inclinations of Cosimo de' Medici. The modest museum he started in Florence during the early Renaissance is now the Uffizi Gallery." Hoskins began to chuckle. "Every museum director I know goes on such a quest. Unfortunately, an approach that worked in fifteenth-century Italy almost never succeeds in twenty-first-century Great Britain."

Hoskins turned to Flick. "Before I tackle Nigel's second question, I would like to know your opinion. As chief curator, how do you feel about acquiring your collection with long-term financing?"

Nigel realized that Flick was looking at him—apparently to get his go-ahead before she answered. *She's not a loose cannon!* He grinned at her and nodded his approval.

Flick began. "I fully endorse the general principle that a museum holds its assets in trust for the public. I would never consider mortgaging our antiquities to raise funds for another purpose—say to build a new building. But here the shoe is on the other foot. We're engaging in financial wizardry to purchase our collection. I feel comfortable about doing that."

"In that event," Augustus said, "your challenge is to retire the debt as quickly as possible." He looked at Nigel. "To reduce risk, you must find other sources of funding from people and organizations that support your mission. It won't be easy. I sometimes feel we are living in a philanthropic ice age. Nonetheless, with perseverance, one can make progress despite treacherous glaciers and blowing snow."

Flick chimed in. "We have the means to generate some additional revenues ourselves. We might create a line of replica artifacts, start a magazine for tea fanciers, publish a series of tea-related cookbooks, and even launch a chain of Duchess of Bedford Tearooms."

"All intriguing ideas," Hoskins said, "but alas, most will require significant investments before they begin to pay dividends."

She gave a sheepish shrug. "I know—it takes money to make money. Well, if absolutely necessary, we can begin to charge visitors a modest admission fee, although that would undo our forty-year tradition as a free museum."

"Perhaps it won't come to that. Let me ponder your problem for a day or two and see if the 'Great Hope' can live up to his overblown reputation." Augustus smiled benevolently. "If I may make an unrelated observation—you two seem ideally suited to work together. In my experience, the museum director and chief curator are often at each other's throats."

Nigel avoided Flick's gaze and suspected that she was trying to avoid his.

The awkward moment passed when Augustus waived at the waitress. "Let's order lunch," he said. "On me, of course. I intend to have a substantial meal, and I don't care to place a new financial burden on the museum."

He began to chuckle again. Flick joined in.

Nigel merely smiled. He didn't find the quip funny. These days, nothing about the Royal Tunbridge Wells Tea Museum seemed laughable.

Flick knocked on Nigel's doorframe. He looked up from the mass of paper on his desk. "I meant to ask you a question earlier," she said, "but it skipped my mind. At lunch you told Augustus Hoskins that the Hawker Foundation has ceased providing direct support to us. How come? After all, they created the museum in the first place."

Nigel rummaged in the sea of clutter, found a brochure, and folded back the cover. "I have here the current annual report published by the Hawker Foundation. Take a good look at this photograph."

Flick sat down in the visitor's chair next to Nigel's desk. The photo was an expensively done portrait of a distinguished man of perhaps fifty-five. He had salt-and-pepper hair, piercing eyes, beaky nose, square chin, and a no-nonsense expression.

"A nicely chiseled face," she said. "Who is he?"

"Jeremy Strain, the managing director. When he took charge of the foundation two years ago, he appeared on one of the BBC current affairs shows. He explained that henceforth the function of *his* foundation would be to do measurable good in the world and not to teach the Tunbridge Wells gentry how to brew a cup of English Breakfast tea."

"He said that?"

"Indeed! He also said that this museum never would have been built had he been managing director forty years ago."

"Oh my."

"How would you like to ask him for some ready money?"

"It might be tough—but if I were you, I'd definitely give it a go."

"Excellent! My teleconference with Strain begins in about ten minutes. You can be me. You do the asking."

Flick scrambled to her feet, feeling exceedingly foolish. "Forgive me. I didn't mean to imply that you couldn't—"

"Sit back down," Nigel said. "I am utterly serious. I groveled before Strain on two other occasions, to no avail. Perhaps we should try a new groveler?"

"Not a good idea!" She could hear the near panic in her own voice. "I don't know anything about British foundations. Even more important, I'm not very good at asking for money in person." Flick let herself sigh. "The truth is, when it comes to face-to-face fund-raising, I'm as useful as a chocolate teapot."

The look on Nigel's face began to alternate between skeptical and surprised. He seemed unsure how to respond to Flick's confession. She broke the silence. "I know it sounds silly, but I couldn't sell Girl Scout cookies when I was a kid.

And I've never been able to ask for a raise."

"Hmmm."

"However, I have no problem groveling on paper. I can write fabulous grant proposals."

"I see," he said, although it was obvious to Flick that he didn't.

"And I'll be happy to provide you with moral support." She dropped into the chair again. "As long as *you* do all the talking."

Nigel nodded slowly. "All right. I'll explain to Strain that I asked you to sit in—as my technical advisor."

"Perfect! Tell me what I need to know about the Hawker Foundation."

Nigel shrugged. "There isn't much to know. Desmond Hawker established it in 1902. He apparently got the idea from John Nobel, who bequeathed his dynamite money in 1900 to fund the Nobel Foundation. The difference was that Desmond created his charitable trust while he was still alive. He defined the purpose of the Hawker Foundation to 'promote the betterment of humanity by supporting advancements in education, healthcare, and religion.' " He hesitated. "Past grants to our museum presumably fell under 'education.' "

"What do you mean *presumably*? Museums educate people. We certainly do."

"Jeremy Strain doesn't see it that way. He thinks 'advancement' is another word for pure research and development that has broad application. Hang on!" Nigel reached into a desk drawer. He brought out a file folder. "Gordon & Battlebridge, our public relations agency, subscribes to a clipping service. They send me every magazine and newspaper article they come across that mentions Strain. I will read from a short piece that ran in *The Economist* last spring. I quote, 'When asked about his philosophy for guiding the venerable Hawker Foundation, Jeremy Strain said, "I run a charitable trust, not a betting shop. Our grants are investments, not gambles. I expect the projects we support to bear fruit that benefits the world at large." ' " Nigel switched clippings. "Here is the Strain quotation I like best: 'I want the organizations we support to believe that prying money from the Hawker Foundation is akin to squeezing water from a rock. If they succeed, they should believe that a miracle has taken place.' "

"I can understand how he feels," Flick said. "I might even agree that his goals are laudable. But why did he take a potshot at the museum on the BBC?"

Nigel flipped through the stack of clips. "Another reporter asked much the same question. Here is Strain's answer:

> *I have nothing against the Royal Tunbridge Wells Tea Museum as an institution. It has a large following and apparently serves a useful function. However, the Hawker Foundation spent a considerable sum of money to establish the museum for one reason only: the extraordinary persuasive powers of Mary Hawker Evans. The foundation made a great error, in my opinion, when it elected Mrs. Evans, the granddaughter of Desmond Hawker, to its board. She arrived with an agenda: to build an edifice honoring her illustrious ancestor. She eventually succeeded by unmercifully lobbying, browbeating, and bullying the other board members. We are an independent trust entirely divorced from the Hawker family. Mrs. Evans apparently forgot that critical fact.*

"Gosh. He's grousing about something that happened

more than forty years ago, long before he took charge of the foundation."

"When it comes to money, Strain seems to have a strong sense of history." Nigel closed the folder and dropped it atop the other clutter on his desk.

"What's with all this paper?" Flick asked.

"You see before you everything in our files pertaining to our relationship with the Hawker Foundation. I had hoped to find something that might improve my sales pitch. No joy!" He shook his head dolefully. "We asked for and received occasional grants under Strain's predecessors, all of them to enhance our facilities. The last one was three years ago to pay for our upgraded security system. I find no precedent for a grant to acquire antiquities. All our funding to do that came from the Hawker family."

Flick took another look at Jeremy Strain's picture. Definitely a hard-nosed manager. She had known foundation executives like him before in the United States. Tough administrators who enjoyed saying no to requests for funding. And yet, they often lavished money on their own pet projects. Did Strain have a favorite kind of investment, an area of research that would unlock the financial floodgates at the Hawker Foundation?

"Well, well," Nigel said excitedly. "More moral support has arrived."

Flick glimpsed a white-fringed tail out of the corner of her eye. She looked sideways in time to see Cha-Cha jump up on Nigel's sofa and smile at him. The dog didn't appear to notice that Flick was in the room, too.

Nigel went on, "He seems to understand that he will spend this evening with me."

Flick grunted. Cha-Cha did have the disquieting knack

of switching allegiance between its two caregivers without a second thought.

Shiba Inus are supposed to be loyal. Didn't you read the owner's guide?

"By the way," Nigel asked, "how are the cats doing?"

"Swimmingly. Lapsang and Souchong have taken over the curators' wing."

Although I still haven't figured out which is which.

Nigel's telephone rang. He held up two fingers in a "V for Victory" sign—the sort Winston Churchill used to make—then picked up the receiver.

"Nigel Owen here." He listened a moment, then said, "Good afternoon, Jeremy. If you don't mind, I shall place you on speakerphone. I have Dr. Felicity Adams, our new chief curator, here with me in my office."

Nigel pressed a button on his telephone.

"Hello, Dr. Adams," Jeremy said. "You must be the clever American food chemist I have heard so much about."

Flick loved Strain's voice. It was smooth and elegant, with the sort of cultured British accent that signaled a privileged upbringing and the best of English schools. But his comment stiffened her spine. Why did so many people in England refer to her as an "American"? And how had Strain been able to make it sound like an insult? For a mad split second, she wanted to respond, "And you must be the tightfisted limey jerk I have heard so much about."

She drove the lovely, nasty thought out of her mind. "That's me!" she said cheerfully. "But please call me Felicity or Flick."

"Felicity it is. Flick is too close to the French slang for policeman."

He laughed. Nigel joined in. She managed a halfhearted snigger.

That's pronounced fleek, *you bozos, not Flick.*

Nigel quickly got down to business. "Jeremy, the e-mail I sent you last week summed up our situation. The foundation has been generous to us in the past. We ask you to be generous again in this period of transition. We want to apply for a grant to help us purchase our antiquities on display."

"This is going to be a short conversation, Nigel. Even if the foundation were willing to provide funds for such an insipid purpose—which we most definitely are *not*—the present circumstances of your collection would argue strongly against such an investment."

"I don't grasp what you mean, Jeremy."

"I have been given to understand that there are doubts as to who owns the collection."

"What doubts? The Hawker family has always owned the antiquities."

Jeremy said nothing for several seconds. "Approximately nine months ago, Elspeth Hawker visited me and expressed concerns about the ownership of the collection. I had assumed that she also shared them with you."

Flick exchanged glances with Nigel. He looked as confused as she suddenly felt. She had read Elspeth's little black notebook cover to cover and deciphered every abbreviation. Elspeth had been troubled by forgeries, not issues of ownership.

"Excuse me, Jeremy," Flick said. "Might Elspeth have been talking about the *authenticity* of some items?"

"One surely knows the difference between ownership and authenticity." Strain provided an audible sniff. "Elspeth wanted any information we might have in our old files about the provenance of the collection. I asked her why. After a few hems and haws, she told me a vague family legend about Desmond Hawker. Please don't ask me to repeat any of it; I took no interest in the details. The gist, however, was that Desmond may have acquired the antiquities under less-than-honorable circumstances."

"I have never heard of such a legend," Nigel said. "Moreover, the items have been on display for the past forty years. If anyone had challenged the Hawkers' right to them, certainly we would have learned by now."

"One can, of course, suppose that Elspeth suffered from senile dementia—although she seemed largely sane to me. Nonetheless, if it were my money, I'd not spend a farthing on a single teapot without convincing proof that the Hawkers own the entire collection."

"Point well taken," Nigel said. "I will ask for a full provenance."

Strain made a soft *harrumph*. "Then I presume we have nothing more to talk about today."

An idea seemed to emerge full-blown in Flick's mind. Almost without thinking, she said, "Jeremy, can I ask you for some advice?"

"Advice?" Jeremy sounded puzzled. "Surely not with museum curating."

"A related topic. Nigel and I are planning to increase the research work we do at the museum."

Nigel mouthed, "Research? What kind of research?"

Jeremy said, "Research? What kind of research?"

"As you probably know," Flick said, "the museum has long supported tea-related scholarly studies. For example, a group of Oxford and Cambridge academics are holding a research conference here on Monday."

"Oxford and Cambridge? The *universities*?"

"Yes. But we want to expand the actual research we do in tea-related food chemistry, agriculture, and processing. We have a plan to grow our nonmuseum activities in the years ahead. Perhaps some of the institutions you support can provide us with useful tips about choosing projects that make the most sense for our staff and capabilities."

"Is there. . .much call for tea-related research?"

"Quite a lot. Tea is the second most popular drink in the world. Water is the first."

"I see. Well, let me think about how we might be able to help you. Certainly I can provide information, but we don't want to rule out other kinds of support, do we?"

Nigel thanked Jeremy for his time, hung up the phone, and said to Flick, "Have I just witnessed a miracle? I could almost hear the wheels turning in Jeremy's head, trying to figure out the best way to invest in your nonexistent research projects."

"We need to generate additional revenues. Doing research is a definite candidate."

"What happened to your chronic incapability to ask for money?"

"It's still in full bloom." Flick smiled. "I never actually talked about money with Strain. You will have to do that, when the time comes."

"Too true! You said nothing about money. But you did tell him a shameless fib. Our so-called research conference on Monday consists of twenty-odd lecturers in English literature who will gather in one of our seminar rooms to talk about"— Nigel managed to find a sheet of paper underneath the mass on his desk—"to talk about 'the Societal Metaphors and Allegories Inherent in the Mad Hatter's Tea Party.' "

"The organizers teach at Oxford and Cambridge, don't they?"

"Yes, but you made their meeting sound like a conclave of the Royal Academy."

Flick began to laugh along with Nigel but quickly fell silent.

Nigel peered at her. "Why the sudden change in mood?" he said. "I'm only yanking your chain. Jeremy deserves to be led astray."

"It's not you," she said. "I started to remember what he said about the ownership of our antiquities. Could Elspeth be right?"

"I don't see how. My best guess is that he didn't pay attention to her and misunderstood what she said."

Flick nodded in agreement, despite the niggle boring into the back of her mind. *Elspeth—you visited Jeremy Strain because you felt you had to. I think you discovered another serious problem at the Royal Tunbridge Wells Tea Museum.*

EIGHT

Cha-Cha strained against his lead, yanking Nigel toward Eridge Road and the museum. The compact dog could exert a pull all out of proportion to the size of his body, but Nigel enjoyed being dragged through the Common.

Nigel often walked to and from the museum because most evenings he left his BMW in the museum's car park. His flat had street permit parking, which meant that Nigel paid an annual fee for the right to search for a typically non-existent parking space on Lime Hill Road. The fastest route on foot from his flat was an easy two-kilometer jaunt through Tunbridge Wells. That Friday morning, he had intentionally taken the slightly longer scenic route through the Common—to give Cha-Cha a nice walk.

It was a glorious October morning, cool but sunny. The trees were beginning to lose their leaves, allowing patches of early-autumn sunlight to filter through the treetops and illuminate the pathways. All in all, the sort of morning one could ignore, at least for a half hour, the nasty responsibilities piling up at one's office.

How much longer could he delay the inevitable? *Tempus* clearly *fugit*. Bleasdale the solicitor had been remarkably patient, but he would expect the museum's answer soon. But that required the trustees to reach their decision first. And that could not occur until Nigel and Felicity Adams made their recommendation.

The ball is definitely in our court.

The path exited the Common across from the back side of the Pantiles. From there one could see the roof of the Royal Tunbridge Wells Tea Museum perhaps four hundred yards away on Eridge Road.

Nigel checked his watch as he waited for a break in traffic so that he could cross London Road. It had just reached nine o'clock. Flick definitely would be in her office. Pity that she had such a short commute to the museum. A brisk walk every morning might make her less impulsive. When she acted thoughtfully rather than going off half-cocked, she could be a valuable colleague.

Yesterday is a perfect example.

Flick had been wholly supportive during their meeting with Augustus Hoskins, and she had done a first-class job of handling Jeremy Strain. She had even looked into Strain's odd comments about the provenance of the Hawker collection. Flick had visited her basement archives and found three newspaper articles written when the museum was established. All confirmed that the Hawker antiquities had been in the family since the late nineteenth century.

So much for Dame Elspeth's alleged ownership concerns.

Nigel walked along Eridge Road feeling genuine regret that his commute was nearly over. Cha-Cha seemed to feel the same way, because he had stopped pulling on his lead. Nigel decided to use the museum's rear service entrance, next to the private car park. He climbed the steps alongside the truck-loading bay, walked through the greenhouse, and then into the Duchess of Bedford Tearoom. Cha-Cha had proved well enough behaved during the past week to be allowed the run of the museum during off-hours. Nigel unhooked the lead and watched the dog trot off through the thicket of wrought-iron table legs. Cha-Cha liked to start each day with a visit to his old friend Earl, who seemed splendidly at home in his corner of the tearoom. Earl still lived in his boxy, chromed wire cage, but soon that would change. Flick had ordered a wrought-iron cage that stood almost seven feet tall.

Nigel heard a gentle clatter of crockery behind him. He looked around as Giselle Logan, the tearoom's hostess, exited the kitchen pushing a tea trolley laden with cups, saucers, a pot of tea, a carafe of coffee, and a plate of biscuits.

"Ah, Nigel," she said, "you *have* arrived."

His heart thumped. Giselle was a willowy brunette, twenty-five, with a degree in hospitality management, a luscious voice, and an exotic Eurasian beauty that Nigel found mesmerizing. He had no doubt that she would climb the ranks of her profession to oversee a major restaurant chain or hotel. He felt equally confident that she intended to stay married to her husband, a local dentist.

Giselle answered his unasked question. "This is for the meeting going on in your office. Dr. Adams requested tea for six. She also has been trying to find you."

Nigel searched his mind. Had he bollixed up his schedule for the day? Had he stupidly forgotten a meeting with five other people?

Giselle steered the tea trolley toward the service elevator.

Nigel made for the stairs—the fastest way to his office—and climbed them two at a time.

Flick was waiting for him in the third-floor lobby area.

"What's going on?" he asked breathlessly.

"James Bond wants to see you."

"Who?"

"A Brit spy. He showed up this morning and said he was from"—she looked at a slip of paper—"Em-Eye-Five."

"*MI5!* That's Britain's Security Service. Criminy! What does an MI5 spook want with me?"

"With *us*. His name is Nicholas Mitchell. He flashed his ID card to Margo McKendrick at the Welcome Centre kiosk. She couldn't find you, so she called me down to chat with him. He asked to see"—Flick began to count on her fingers—"the head of the museum, the person in charge of security, the person responsible for the exhibits on display, and the people who show visitors around the museum." She added, "He does look a lot like James Bond."

"You've got the organizations mixed up. The fictional James Bond works for MI6, our Secret Intelligence Service. MI5 is our domestic security agency, a lot like your Federal Bureau of Investigation. MI5 does counterintelligence work inside Britain."

"The *spook*, as you call him, didn't explain the difference. Anyway, he's in your office discussing the pros and cons of the museum's burglar alarm with Conan Davies and our two docents."

Nigel peered around his doorframe. Conan Davies, perched against a windowsill, his long legs stretched out in front of him, was holding forth about biometric access control devices. The man listening attentively to Conan looked like many of the other young English civil servants Nigel had met. Medium height. Cheerful face. Uncontrolled shock of ash-blond hair. Gray-pinstriped three-piece suit. Blue shirt. Maroon-striped school tie. Nigel guessed his age to be thirty.

Mirabelle Hubbard and Trevor Dangerfield, the museum's two docents, sat together on his sofa looking like an old married couple. In some ways they were closer: The pair had worked together at the museum since it opened in 1962. Mirabelle was a rosy-cheeked widow in her midseventies, with elaborately coiffed gray hair. She had been Nathanial Swithin's secretary throughout his long stint as director. Trevor, closer to eighty, still resembled the tall, wiry, former Royal Marines sergeant who had been hired as the museum's first security guard.

Nigel took a deep breath and strode into the office. Flick moved around him and performed the introductions. "Agent Nicholas Mitchell, may I present Nigel Owen, the acting director of the museum." She turned to Nigel. "Agent Mitchell has requested that we call him Nicholas."

Nigel shook Nicholas's hand.

He doesn't look anything like James Bond. He's much too short.

Giselle rolled the tea trolley into the office and vanished discreetly. Nigel sat down behind his desk, Nicholas and Flick each took a visitor's chair, Conan returned to his windowsill. Mirabelle moved to the cart and began to pour.

"First, let me thank you for seeing me without an appointment," Nicholas said. "I suspect you are curious as to why an agent from MI5 has come to see you."

Nigel smiled. "The question did cross my mind."

"I am part of a task force that is investigating the smuggling of missing artifacts from the Iraqi National Museum in Baghdad."

"I read of that program," Conan said. "It's a joint effort with the Yanks."

Nicholas nodded. "As you know, the museum was looted about the time that Baghdad fell in April 2003. Thousands of artifacts from the Sumerian, Babylonian, Assyrian, and Islamic cultures disappeared."

"I thought that the Americans retrieved most of the artifacts," Nigel said.

"Most but not all. Regrettably, hundreds of worthwhile pieces are still missing, including a few irreplaceable masterpieces. We believe these items were smuggled out of Iraq to Asia and Europe. It's probable that some have made their way to England."

Mirabelle gave Nicholas and Flick cups of tea and Nigel a cup of coffee. She had placed two biscuits on each saucer.

"Retrieving antiques seems more like a job for Scotland Yard than MI5," Conan said to Nicholas.

"We're involved because it is likely that the moneys earned by selling the antiquities will be used to finance terrorism."

Conan grunted, apparently satisfied by the answer.

Nicholas pushed a thick document bound with green plastic covers across Nigel's desk. "Here is a catalog of the still-missing items. I brought this copy for you and your staff."

Nigel flipped through a few of the pages, looking at photographs and descriptions of an engraved stone slab, a pitcher-like vessel made of clay, a small carved marble head of a man, a small statue of a bearded man praying, a carved stone bowl inlaid with shell mosaics, a burial helmet made of gold, and a golden dagger—also for ceremonial use. All were more than four thousand years old.

He slid the catalog to Flick. She browsed for a moment and then said, "With respect, Nicholas, including us on your list of museums doesn't make much sense. Unless the Baghdad museum had Ishtar's teapot on display, we are not likely to acquire any purloined artifacts. Our mission as a museum does not extend into Babylonian daggers and Sumerian statues."

"Neither does our acquisitions budget," Nigel said. "I can assure you that our funds to buy antiquities are fully committed." He exchanged a half smile with Flick. "These objects must cost the earth."

"Millions upon millions," Nicholas said. "However, a reputable museum would never buy any of these items. And not even a dubious institution would put them on display. They are too well known"—he spoke to Flick—"too *hot*, as you Americans might say. However. . ." Nicholas opened the catalog to the photograph of the dagger. "If you are a wealthy but unscrupulous collector and someone offers you a natty golden dagger that looks like this one, how would you verify that it is real? After all, you don't want to spend millions on a fake stolen relic."

"I see where you are going with this," Conan said. "Everyone knows that museums are careful when they purchase antiquities. We often call in experts to authenticate an artifact."

"Precisely. Our unscrupulous dagger collector might well get it into his head to visit his local museum and chat up the docents." Nicholas switched to a put-on London accent. 'I was wondering, Mirabelle, if you might know the name of the chap who told you that solid-gold teaspoon was worth all the lolly you paid for it.' "

Nigel gestured with a biscuit. "I can imagine that question being asked at the Victoria and Albert, but we are a small, specialized museum."

Mirabelle jumped in. "Oh sir, it happens a lot."

"It does?"

"I wish I had a bob for every harebrained question I hear," Trevor agreed. "It's all because of that barmy antiques show on the telly. Half the ladies in Tunbridge Wells think they have an attic full of valuables. Some visitors even bring their jumble with them, expecting that our curators do on-the-spot valuations."

"How do you respond when asked?" Nicholas said.

"I usually point them to Mrs. McAndrews's antique shop in the High Street. She is one of our trustees; I might as well send the appraising business her way."

"Well, from now on please ask what kind of antique they want valued. If the explanation sounds at all suspicious—or if someone describes a piece that Abraham or Sarah might have purchased in ancient Ur—please call me at once."

Nicholas handed out business cards.

Nigel stood up. "Thank you for bringing the problem to our attention. We certainly will cooperate in every way we can."

"I appreciate that, Nigel," Nicholas said, giving a quick grin. "However, I'm not quite finished."

Nigel sat down. "Carry on then."

"As you doubtless know, several museums in Europe have been exploited to store stolen antiquities."

Nigel did not know, but he had no intentions of adding to his embarrassment by making a public admission of ignorance. He replied with an ambiguous nod.

Nicholas continued. "Any museum that has storerooms or an archive is potentially vulnerable."

"We have both," Conan admitted.

"For the scheme to work, the thief must have a confederate working inside the museum, ideally one of the curators. The partner in crime simply creates a false accession record and places the stolen artifact in the museum's vault."

"Why go to the trouble of doing that?" Mirabelle asked.

"Where better to store a stolen artifact than inside a museum? You have an elaborate security system, proper storage conditions, and none of the legal requirements of a bank's safe-deposit box."

"I'm afraid you've lost me," Mirabelle said. "At the end of the day, what has the thief accomplished?"

"The best way to answer your question is with a hypothetical example. Imagine that a shifty individual in Tunbridge Wells did manage to acquire Ishtar's teapot."

Mirabelle began to laugh. "Sorry, sir, but I can't picture a stony idol pouring tea."

Nigel glanced at Nicholas. The MI5 agent seemed perfectly content to play along with Mirabelle's joke.

"I do understand," Nicholas said. "How about King Tut's teacup?"

"That might work," Mirabelle said. "Ask Trevor. He's an old Egyptian hand."

"Well, now. . ." Trevor stroked his chin. "I believe that Tutankhamen reigned in the fourteenth century BC."

"Which would make him even older than you."

Trevor threw a crumpled napkin at Mirabelle. "There is a painting in the Grand Hall that shows tea being discovered in China about fourteen hundred years before King Tut lived. So it is possible, one could even say probable, that caravans carried tea from China to Egypt." He smiled at Nicholas. "Press on with your example."

"Good!" Nicholas lifted his teacup to eye level. "If I had stolen King Tut's teacup, I would be consumed with worry. What if my house burned down? Or what if one of my bent friends wanted to steal it from me?"

"Now I understand," Mirabelle said. "You want to *hide* it in the museum."

"Exactly! So I convince Felicity Adams to stash my cup in a bin full of other teacups that are not on display. King Tut's teacup becomes one more unseen item in the museum's collection."

Conan raised a hand. "I see a hitch. All our antiquities are numbered and entered into our computer. We do a thorough inventory every year; I might discover the extra item."

"Your accessions are computerized?"

"One of the virtues of being a rather small museum. Many of our larger cousins are still making the transition from accession ledgers to computer databases. We did it four years ago."

"I suppose," Flick said, "an easy way around that problem is simply to give the teacup its own official accession number."

Conan countered, "But then anyone browsing through our catalog would find 'King Tut's Teacup' listed among the other crockery."

"Not if I entered it in the database as 'Sam the Scribe's Teacup.'"

"Well done!" Nicholas clapped. "By giving the stolen antiquity a false identity, one can hide it in plain sight, much like Edgar Allen Poe's 'Purloined Letter.'"

Trevor shook his head. "And here I thought a museum was a peaceful, crime-free zone."

"Quite the contrary," Conan said. "Even a small museum like ours is a treasure house. Valuable antiquities attract inventive thieves."

"And also the occasional murderer," Nicholas added.

"*Really?*" Mirabelle half-shouted.

"Alas, yes. There have been killings in museums related to antiquity theft."

Nigel winced. Of all the gratuitous comments an MI5 man might have made, Nicholas had accidentally chosen the one most likely to goose Felicity Adams into high gear. Nigel glanced warily at Flick and waited for her to say something illogical.

Much to his relief, Flick didn't say anything. Instead, she stood up and carried her teacup to the tea trolley.

Nicholas spoke to Nigel. "On behalf of Her Majesty's Government, let me thank you for sharing your valuable time. I'll be off."

Flick spun around. "Before you go, Nicholas, why not take a quick tour of the museum and our archives? We don't open to the public until noon, so this is an ideal time."

Nigel was caught off guard. *Why give a spook a guided tour?* He quickly recovered. "Yes, please do," he said heartily. "In fact, I will join you."

Nicholas smiled at them. "I'd like a tour very much."

Nigel followed Flick and Nicholas out of his office. When he reached the door, he looked back and saw Mirabelle serving more tea and biscuits to Trevor and Conan.

Give tea fanciers an inch and they have a tea party.

As Nigel expected she would, Flick followed the itinerary she had once described as her "Fifty-Cent Visiting Fireman Tour" of the museum. It began on the third floor with a quick walk through the Hawker Library and a longer visit to the Conservation Laboratory. One of the cats came over to investigate. She sniffed Nicholas's shoe, then ran away.

She must think he smells like James Bond, Nigel thought. He passed a pleasant few seconds pondering why the arch villain in several of the movies owned a cat, but James himself did not.

Nicholas dutifully examined the microscopes, the fume hood, the drying chamber, and the photographic documentation station with its lights and digital camera.

"We photograph everything placed on display from lots of different angles," Flick explained. "Should an antiquity ever be damaged, the restorers will have a set of photographs to work from."

They traveled to the second floor, where Flick seemed to take longer than usual gushing about her favorites in the Tea in the Americas Room and delivering her "Did-you-know-that-tea-is-good-for-you?" lecture in the Tea and Health Gallery.

Does anybody drink tea because it's a health food? Nigel felt moved to ask, but he promptly quelled the temptation. Inviting Flick to embellish her presentation would merely extend his agony.

He felt his cell phone vibrate on his hip.

"Nigel Owen."

"Can you come down to the ground floor, sir?" Margo McKendrick said. "There's been a—an *incident* with the dog. As I understand the problem, he caught a squirrel in the greenhouse and is now in the tearoom eating it for breakfast."

Nigel interrupted Flick's lengthy discussion of the power of fluoride-rich tea to prevent caries in teeth. "Is it standard operating procedure for a Shiba Inu to kill and eat squirrels?"

" 'Fraid so," Flick replied. "Apparently they have a powerful instinct to hunt rodents. Why do you ask?"

"You carry on with the tour. I have a clean-up chore to supervise."

Nigel left feeling invigorated. Dealing with a half-eaten squirrel seemed far less boring than following Flick Adams around the museum.

Flick made a snap decision. Cha-Cha had given her a few unexpected minutes alone with Nicholas Mitchell—an opportunity she would be silly to ignore. If she worked quickly, she could steer their conversation in the direction she wanted. With luck, she might gain enough information about British law enforcement to kick-start a real investigation into Elspeth Hawker's murder.

She would have to bypass the local police, somehow reach higher-ups in British law enforcement who would be willing to listen to her ideas—who wouldn't automatically accept Sir Simon Clowes's diagnosis as gospel.

I need a name. A person to call.

As she guided Nicholas down the staircase to the first floor, Flick said, "I don't know much about MI5, I'm afraid."

"We have been responsible for British internal security since 1909."

"Nigel told me that MI5 is roughly equivalent to America's FBI."

"We do many of the same things, but there are major differences. Our principal duty is to defend against covert threats to the United Kingdom, including espionage, terrorism, and proliferation of weapons of mass destruction. About ten years ago our charter was expanded to include serious crime—drugs, smuggling—"

"Antiquities theft," Flick said with a smile. "And the occasional related murder."

"Yes, but MI5 is not a police department. We investigate serious crime in close consultation with other law-enforcement agencies." Nicholas stopped. "Let me tell you something that many Brits don't realize. MI5 doesn't have the power to arrest people. We have to call in a local plod to do the actual arresting."

"Plod?"

"Rozzer. Old Bill. Bobby. Copper."

"A policeman, you mean?"

Nicholas seemed puzzled at Flick's response. "Didn't your mum ever read to you from one of Enid Blyton's books?"

She shook her head. "Nope."

"No wonder you haven't heard of Britain's most famous policeman, the redoubtable Police Constable Plod of Toy Town. A strict but fair local copper who is a great friend to little, wooden Noddy and is absolutely wizard at tracking down and arresting robbers." He laughed. "Of course, the local plod I work with most often is a female plainclothes officer from Scotland Yard's Special Branch. She looks nothing like PC Plod."

Flick led Nicholas into the Tea Processing Salon.

"What is the purpose of that peculiar-looking apparatus?" he asked.

"It's a CTC—a cut, tear, and curl machine—typically used to process tea leaves that are destined for tea bags. It can transform the whole top of a tea plant, stems, twigs, and all, into small pieces."

"What if I don't want stems and twigs in my cuppa?"

"The alternative is the traditional 'orthodox' method. It's a simple five-step manufacturing process." Flick pointed at a wall-mounted exhibit. "First, you handpick the topmost leaves and buds on the tea plant. Second, you allow the leaves to wither. Third, you squeeze them between metal rollers to blend the naturally occurring chemicals. Four, you let the rolled leaves oxidize in the open air for a while. Finally, you heat the leaves to stop further oxidation and dehydrate them. *Voila!* Tea the way it's been made for thousands of years."

"The orthodox technique sounds more expensive."

Flick nodded. "A tea picker needs to collect three hundred leaves to make one pound of tea. All that hand labor adds to the cost. Orthodox processing is usually reserved for the best grades of tea—the kind sold loose rather than in tea bags." She added, "I have a question for you."

"Fire away."

"Does MI5 ever work with the police in Tunbridge Wells?"

"Ah, the celebrated Kent County constabulary, now known officially as the Kent police. Well, naturally I am forbidden to give you specific details, but anyone perusing a map of Kent will find Dover, one of the country's major ports, and Folkstone, the English end of the Channel Tunnel, and Manston, which has a recently developed international airport."

"In other words, one might safely reach the conclusion that MI5 has a well-established relationship with the Kent police."

"Indeed one might."

Flick guided Nicholas through the first-floor lobby into the Tea at Sea Gallery.

"These models are exquisite," he said. "The tea clippers were beautiful ships."

"And built purposely for speed. Their sleek lines and large sails represent the pinnacle of merchant sailing ship technology. A well-found tea clipper could go as fast as twenty knots if the wind was right." She pointed to a painting on the far wall. "There's *Taeping* arriving in London on the sixth of September 1866, with *Ariel* a short distance behind her. Both clippers left from Foochow, China, on the twenty-ninth of May. They traveled sixteen thousand miles in about a hundred days—a journey that used to take a full year in a traditional sailing ship."

"Why did a ship meant to carry tea leaves have to be fast?"

"The usual answer: money. The first ships that arrived with the new tea crop from China could command much higher prices for their cargoes."

"May I conduct an experiment?" Nicholas asked. He touched the hull of the closest model, a clipper named the *Fiery Cross*. He smiled at Flick and said, "Nothing happened."

"What did you think might happen?"

"Bells. Flashing lights. Screaming security guards." He

gave a careless wave. "Conan Davies told me that individual items on display are not alarmed. Obviously he was right."

"I know how to disable our security system when I enter the museum after hours and then turn it back on again when I leave—but I don't understand the specific details of how the alarm works. That's on my list of things to learn when I have more free time. Are we good or bad?"

"Quite good actually." Nicholas looked around the room. "I can see three passive infrared motion detectors on the walls. Apparently there are a dozen on each floor. They switch on to provide secondary defense in depth when everyone has left the museum. As Conan explained to me, your primary alarm protects the perimeter of the museum proper—the main building and your tearoom. A network of magnetic switches on the windows and doors will detect any intruder imprudent enough to break in after hours. His trespass will trigger a silent alarm and bring the police here in minutes. Even your greenhouse has its own dedicated alarm system. In short, you have a top-of-the-line security system."

Flick looked away from Nicholas to hide the frisson of annoyance she felt. In all her thinking about Elspeth's discoveries, she had foolishly ignored the museum's elaborate intruder alarm.

Why didn't our "quite good" security system call the police when someone replaced several of the antiquities on display with fakes?

Not even Houdini could have made the exchanges during the day. The antiquities marked with big red *F*s in Elspeth's little black book were too large to smuggle under a coat or inside a bag. Each "swap" required a round-trip: bringing a counterfeit item in and taking a genuine item out. It had to have been done when the museum was closed, when the security system was armed and operating.

But that presented a new problem. Only a small group of museum staffers had personal access codes to arm and disarm the perimeter alarm: the acting director, the chief curator, the chief of security, and the four security guards. And the biometric sensor would recognize only their finger images. Only those individuals could disable the motion detectors that protected the museum.

Simply put, none of the five trustees on Elspeth's list could—in theory—enter the building by himself or herself after hours. How did the guilty trustee manage to bypass a sophisticated security system?

Figure it out later—after Nicholas leaves.

She surveyed the room. He had moved across the gallery to a display case full of nineteenth-century navigation instruments. The stars of the exhibit were two venerable ship chronometers built by Brockbank & Atkins, a London clockmaker, in the 1840s. A small overhead spotlight made their polished wooden boxes glow and the brass rims around their dials gleam like gold. Trevor Dangerfield and Mirabelle Hubbard took turns winding the clocks every day the museum was open. They still kept nearly perfect time.

Flick sidled up to Nicholas. "How about you?" she said.

"How about me—what?"

"Do you know much about the Kent police?"

He gazed at her quizzically. "I know the odd fact learned here and there. Why do you ask?"

Flick shrugged as innocently as she could. "Curiosity mostly. My uncle is a detective in York, Pennsylvania. I understand police procedure in the United States, but not in England."

"What might you be curious about?"

"Let's say there was an antiquities-related murder in this museum, the sort of murder you talked about earlier, except that it involved items that were stolen from this museum. Would our local police station in Tunbridge Wells conduct the investigation?"

"Almost certainly not. The Tunbridge Wells Police Station on Civic Way is a satellite used by local patrol officers. It doesn't have the resources required to conduct a full-scale homicide investigation. Kent's Major Crime Unit is based in Maidstone, at Kent Police Headquarters. The detectives probably would manage the case from an incident room established there."

Flick decided to gamble. "Do you have a contact in the Major Crime Unit? A detective who might be willing to answer any other questions I have?"

Nicholas frowned at Flick. "Where is this bizarre tête-à-tête leading, Dr. Adams?" His voice had become distant, almost bureaucratic. "Are you trying to tell me that an antiquities-related murder has been committed at this museum?"

"Possibly."

"*Possibly?* The question I asked you calls for a yes or no answer."

Flick sighed. *I've done it now.* She knew at once that she had gone too far.

"Yes," she said. "Everyone assures me that I'm wrong, but I have lingering concerns about the recent death of one of our trustees."

"You can't mean Dame Elspeth Hawker?"

Flick nodded.

Mitchell puffed out his cheeks. "This morning I prepared for my visit by reading a précis of recent news about the museum. My understanding is that Dame Elspeth suffered a fatal heart attack during a trustee meeting while in the presence of an experienced physician."

"All true—except for the heart attack. I believe she was poisoned, probably by one of the other trustees."

"Poisoned? How?"

"An overdose of Seconal placed in a pot full of preserves."

"Why would someone want to kill an old lady?"

"To hide the theft of antiquities—"

Nicholas held up his hands. "*Stop!* I was mistaken to ask and I don't want to know. This discussion is sheer lunacy on my part." He took a step back from Flick. "I take it that no one else at the museum thinks Elspeth Hawker was murdered?"

Flick shook her head.

"And that you haven't spoken to the Kent police?"

Another shake.

"Then why in the name of heaven tell me?"

"Because you are an expert in antiquities theft and you work for the British equivalent of the FBI. You're an ideal person to tell."

"Naturally you have persuasive evidence to bolster your belief."

Flick hesitated. Nicholas had asked a simple question. Given the skeptical edge to his voice, he expected a simple answer. But did she have one? The sum total of her "persuasive evidence" was a hurried observation she had made, an informal experiment she had conducted, and a notebook full of cryptic writing she had found. Thought about the right way, they came together to reveal the method and the motive for murder. But if Nicholas thought about them the wrong way—with a mind's eye predisposed to disbelieve her—she would seem a complete fool.

Keep Elspeth's notebook a secret.

"You can probably use another cup of tea," she said. "Let me offer you one in our tearoom. That will give me a proper opportunity to describe the evidence I've gathered."

"I think not." Nicholas looked for the exit. "It's best that I leave. If you have evidence, share it with the Kent police." He turned away without offering his hand.

Flick called after him, "I'll walk downstairs with you."

"No need," he said over his shoulder. "I can see myself out."

Flick reached her office and the window across from her desk in time to see Nicholas walk to the visitors' car park and climb into his car. To her surprise, he didn't start the engine. Instead, he began to write on a large yellow pad. She watched him fill two pages before he put the pad down.

Oh boy. What did I just do?

NINE

Nigel put down his telephone and stared glumly at the notation he had just been compelled to scribble on his desk calendar: *Informal Trustee Meeting, Saturday 2:00 p.m.* The designer who had drawn the calendar knew that most sensible folk choose not to work on Saturdays and that the few who do rarely schedule silly meetings on Saturday afternoons. Consequently, he or she had made the Saturday box much smaller than the other days of the week.

Obviously you have never met Marjorie Halifax.

Not that Nigel rejected outright the notion of working on weekends. He begrudgingly reported to his office on Saturdays, on the theory that the acting director should be at the helm whenever the Royal Tunbridge Wells Tea Museum was open to the public. No, what bothered Nigel most was that he had allowed Marjorie to bully him into organizing a largely unnecessary meeting when he had more productive things to do.

Nigel had planned to spend that particular Saturday reading

the boxful of information on grants and fund-raising campaigns that Augustus Hoskins had sent along with a brief note:

Here are examples of other small museums that have successfully raised the amount of money you require. You should be able to adapt their techniques and approaches to your situation. Furthermore, I pray that their successes will buoy your spirits. Bringing in forty million pounds over the next decade is doable, although your successor and Dr. Adams will have to sing for many a supper in the years to come.

Nigel felt the muscles in his neck start to tighten. He rolled his head slowly from side to side to ease the tension. He looked at Cha-Cha lying half-asleep on his sofa and said, "Marjorie Halifax is a bona fide pain in the neck."

He craned his neck to stretch the muscles. Years ago he'd taken yoga lessons to help him cope with stress. Deep-breathing exercises had helped him deal with far tougher bosses than Marjorie Halifax. He filled his lungs slowly, then exhaled slowly.

"There will be only four trustees at the meeting, Nigel," she had said. "There is no need to make a fuss over us. We can do without scones, although tea would be lovely. And if the boardroom is unavailable, we will happily congregate around your desk in your office."

"The boardroom is available," he said, struggling to retain a modicum of civility in his voice. "And I will arrange for tea to be served. Do you have an agenda in mind?"

"I hardly see a need for a formal agenda. We will gather to review the progress you have made in formulating your recommendation and also to provide whatever help we can." Her tone shifted to noble. "Please understand that we care about you, Nigel. We are happy to give up our Saturday afternoon for your benefit. We want you to succeed."

"Thank you, Marjorie. Who will be the four attendees?"

"Myself and three of the local trustees: Dorothy McAndrews, Matthew Eaton, and Vicar de Rudd. Sir Simon can't break loose from the hospital this afternoon. And I decided not to ask Archibald or Iona to make the trip to Tunbridge Wells. No need to burden them excessively."

But you have no compunctions against burdening me excessively.

"I presume that you want Dr. Adams to attend the meeting?" he said.

"Indeed we want our chief curator to be there," came the reply. "You and she have a joint responsibility to make a recommendation."

"Precisely! Dr. Adams and I intended to confer this afternoon to discuss our options. The meeting will delay us from doing that."

Marjorie sighed deeply. "Heavens, Nigel, why do you make it difficult for us to help you? The museum is facing the worst crisis in its history. I won't deny that the trustees need reassurance from you—and perhaps even some hand-holding. I shan't name names, but some of us are bewildered that a businessperson with your training and experience hasn't already made his recommendation. It seems obvious what we have to do if we are to keep the museum open."

Nigel noted Marjorie's use of "we" and gazed heavenward. The whole purpose of shifting the creative responsibility to Flick and him was to ensure that "we" could not be blamed if something went wrong. Marjorie knew it. So did the other trustees. Probably so did Cha-Cha.

"I had hoped to present a comprehensive proposal early next week," Nigel said, "one that includes a detailed funding plan. I am confident that the trustees will find that more useful than a bare recommendation to buy the Hawker collection."

"Excellent! You can tell us all about your intentions this afternoon."

"I relish the opportunity, Marjorie," he lied.

"Ta ta, Nigel."

Nigel sat lost in thought until Cha-Cha yipped.

"A bit nosy, are we?" he said. "Well, if you must know, that was Marjorie Halifax. As Elspeth may have told you, Marjorie serves on the Tunbridge Wells Borough Council and fancies herself a tourism guru. She snookered three of our trustees into cosponsoring a silly meeting to make certain that Tunbridge Wells doesn't lose a major visitors' attraction."

The dog's tail wagged slowly. He appeared to be enjoying their chat.

"You should also attend, because your future is up in the air, too. If we don't manage to acquire the collection, the local trustees will be so angry with the Hawkers that they will undoubtedly declare you *persona non grata* along with me."

The dog tilted his head as if puzzled.

"I'm sorry, Cha-Cha, but I don't know the Japanese equivalent of persona non grata. It's Latin for 'Get your sorry bum out of the building before sunset.'"

Cha-Cha dropped his tail with a thump.

"Ah, now you understand. Persona non grata means an end to sleeping on my sofa and no more tasty squirrels in the greenhouse."

Nigel's phone rang.

Maybe Marjorie came to her senses and cancelled the meeting.

His optimism was replaced by curiosity when he saw MARGO MCKENDRICK flash on the caller-ID panel. He wasn't expecting any visitors today.

"Hello, Margo."

"Good morning, sir."

"Are you having a good day?"

"I am, sir."

"Glad to hear it." *Because I am not.*

He pictured Margo sitting in the kiosk. Gracious, amiable, always considerate of other people. Not a devious bone in her body. Pity she hadn't become a trustee.

"Please don't tell me that Cha-Cha has deposited another eviscerated rodent on the teahouse floor?"

"Oh no, sir. There are two people here to see you. Detective Inspector Marc Pennyman and Detective Constable Sally Kerr. Both from the Kent police."

More coppers? First a visit from MI5, now an unannounced drop-in by the local constabulary, undoubtedly to deliver a new round of superfluous warnings about stolen Iraqi treasures. Didn't English law-enforcement personnel have anything better to do than waste the time of a busy museum keeper? *Specifically, this busy museum keeper.* The plods really needed to learn the difference between the British Museum and a blooming little tea museum in the hinterland of Kent County.

"Send them up." He added, "Point them to the stairs. Don't even tell them we have an elevator."

Nigel met the pair in the third-floor lobby. He dithered a moment, uncertain who to greet first: the taller, but subordinate, woman or the shorter, and higher-ranking, man.

The detective inspector solved the problem by extending his hand. "I'm DI Pennyman," he said, "and this is DC Kerr."

Pennyman was in his late thirties, balding, with a compact build and a cheerless countenance tinted red from the brisk climb up the stairs. Kerr, perhaps ten years younger, was somewhat gangly and angular, with short ash-blond hair and a seemingly cordial smile.

Bad cop, good cop? Nigel wondered. *And if so, why?*

He led them into his office. No sooner had the police officers crossed the threshold than Cha-Cha leapt off the sofa, skirted the edge of the room, and padded out the door—tail tightly curled and ears drooping.

Nigel bit back a snicker. *A dog that doesn't like coppers.*

He waved at the just-vacated sofa. "Please make yourselves comfortable." He moved a visitor's chair to face the sofa, and the three sat down.

"May I offer you a spot of tea?" Nigel said. "They tell me our tearoom brews the best in town."

"No, thank you," Pennyman said. "We are pressed for time; I will get right to the matter at hand."

Nigel sat up straight. This plod sounded as unhappy as he looked.

Pennyman continued. "I asked for you in the lobby as a courtesy because you are in charge of this institution. Our business is actually with one of your employees." He trained an inquiring expression on his colleague.

"Dr. Felicity Adams," Kerr said, then added, "Oh! Sir, your suit."

"Good heavens!" Nigel said when he saw that DI Pennyman was sitting in a *pool*—there was no other word to describe it—of dog hair approximately the same color as the sofa's rust-colored upholstery. "I didn't appreciate how much a Shiba Inu sheds." He raced back to his desk and retrieved a clothes brush from the bottom drawer. "My apologies."

Pennyman stood and brushed his jacket and pants legs.

"You want to see Dr. Adams," Nigel prompted.

"In fact, I am here to caution Dr. Adams." Pennyman handed the clothes brush to Kerr. "You have a go." He spoke to Nigel. "Yesterday she engaged in a rather unfortunate conversation with an MI5 agent named Nicholas Mitchell."

Flick, you didn't!

"Dr. Adams conveyed her suspicions about the alleged homicide of Dame Elspeth Hawker."

Flick, you did!

Nigel blurted out, "There's been no murder at our museum."

But hang around, chaps. Things might change.

"We know that, Mr. Owen." Pennyman straightened his jacket. "Where might we find Dr. Adams?"

"Follow me!"

They tramped purposefully through the lobby, around the staircase, and into the curating wing. The door to Flick's office stood open; Nigel could hear the *clickety-click* sound of skilled typing on a computer keyboard. He strode into the room without knocking, the two detectives close behind. Flick peered up at him—he fancied that was a look of annoyance on her face—and said, "Nigel! What a surprise."

He saw a flash of rusty red out of the corner of his eye. Once again Cha-Cha had fled from the minions of the law. Nigel made a mental note to discover how a Shiba Inu could spot the peelers.

"Dr. Adams"—Nigel wanted to sound formal as well as exasperated—"this is Detective Inspector Pennyman and Detective Constable Kerr, both with the Kent police. They have come to see you in an official capacity."

Nigel expected to see astonishment, shock, even consternation, but Flick merely rocked back in her swivel chair and nodded. The only emotion he could detect was. . .*satisfaction*?

Please don't make it worse, Flick!

Pennyman and Kerr chose visitors' chairs in front of

Flick's desk. Nigel took a side chair near the back wall. He hadn't been asked to stay, but then he hadn't been asked to leave, either.

Pennyman wasted no time on pleasantries. "Dr. Adams, we have information to the effect that you reported a homicide by means of poison to a security agent employed by Her Majesty's Government. Not a routine homicide, mind you. Rather, the intentional murder of a dame commander of the British Empire by one of the seven other trustees in attendance that day—each one a leading citizen in his or her own right. Is our information correct?"

"Mostly."

"I prefer *totally*." Pennyman's hands rested on his knees, his fingers drumming a tattoo that Nigel could hear ten feet away. "Do you have any idea the turmoil you caused at Kent Police Headquarters?"

Flick started to say something, but Pennyman kept talking. "Agent Mitchell felt duty bound to report your conclusions. His report traveled to his superior, who forwarded it immediately to the chief constable, who—as you Americans are apt to say—had a cow."

Flick started to smile then seemed to think better of it.

"The lights blazed late last night in Maidstone, Dr. Adams. I trust your ears burned with equal ferocity, because countless unpleasant things were said about you by many unhappy police officers."

"I didn't intend to inconvenience anyone, Detective Inspector, but in retrospect I'm delighted that my comments to Agent Mitchell prompted the Kent police to launch an investigation into Elspeth Hawker's unexplained death. I have a lot to tell you about her murder and the motive behind it. You will conclude, as I did, that Elspeth was poisoned because she discovered a major theft of antiquities from this museum."

Nigel's heart hammered. His discussion with Elspeth Hawker on the day she died replayed in his mind like a DVD on fast-forward. He had not mentioned Elspeth's suspicions to anyone, but somehow Flick had tumbled to the notion of an "exceedingly clever thief" loose in the museum. He had ignored the suggestion, more or less banished the idea to the far corners of his memory. But here it was again. Could both Elspeth and Flick be wrong?

Or are they both right?

Nigel realized that he was clenching and unclenching his hands nervously. Even though no one was watching him, he gripped the sides of his knees. *You can't just sit here like a dummy,* he told himself. *Quite possibly the police are pillorying Flick unfairly. Make a decision.*

He faced a simple question. Should he tell the police what Elspeth said to him? Flick was out on a limb by herself. A bit of corroboration certainly would give her some comfort.

And put you out on the limb, too.

Pennyman gave a harsh laugh. "There *was* an investigation, Dr. Adams. We concluded it last night. The Kent police are completely satisfied with the·death certificate signed by Dame Elspeth's personal physician. Sir Simon Clowes was less than ten feet away when she died. He determined that her death was caused by occlusive coronary artery thrombosis. Not an unusual medical condition in an eighty-four-year-old woman. I interviewed Sir Simon last night and would rather not repeat what he said about your diagnostic skills. Suffice it to say that a graduate degree in food chemistry from an American university"—he made "American" sound vaguely like an insult—"does not empower you to challenge the reasoned conclusion of a trained British cardiologist. In short, Dr.

Adams, there has been no homicide and we have no need to consider a motive."

He leaned across the edge of Flick's desk, pointed a finger at her, and said, "If you feel that the museum has suffered a theft, I invite you to file a report at the Tunbridge Wells police station. However, I urge you to think very carefully should you ever talk to the police again. You are perilously close to being arrested on a charge of wasting police time."

Pennyman nodded to Kerr. "Section 6 of the Criminal Law Act clearly states," she said, "that 'Where a person causes any wasteful employment of the Police by knowingly making to any person a false report intending to show that an offence has been committed, or to give rise to apprehension of the safety of any persons or property, or intending to show that he has information material to any Police enquiry, he should be liable.'"

Pennyman took over again. "Your extremely foolish behavior violated English law and diverted a dozen senior officers from other essential business, not to mention from their families. I have the power to impose an on-the-spot fine of eighty pounds and, if I choose, to arrest you. However"—he eased back in his chair—"I merely will caution you today that any further unsubstantiated cries of murder will bring a swift response from me."

Nigel held his breath. Flick and Pennyman stared at each other across her glass-topped desk. She broke the strained silence. "Thank you, Detective Inspector, I appreciate your candor. I know where I stand now. I apologize for any bother I caused the police. You will hear no more unsubstantiated cries of any kind from me."

Nigel began to breathe again.

"Splendid!" Pennyman and Kerr rose as if one. "Good-bye to you both."

Nigel acknowledged their departure with a feeble wave. He hoped that DC Kerr wouldn't spot the new veneer of dog hair on the back of her boss's suit until they reached their car. Cha-Cha must prefer the visitor's chair in this office.

He watched Flick staring into space, lost in thought—obviously thinking about *something*. She had been ready to tell her story to the police, but DI Pennyman had cut her off. Nigel felt guilty for not supporting Flick when he had the chance, but he also felt curious. For the first time since Elspeth Hawker died, he wondered. . .

What does Flick know that I don't?

"I have to stop acting like a nitwit," Flick murmured as she sat alone in the boardroom waiting for Nigel and the four local trustees to arrive. She felt irritated at the brainless decision she had made the day before. She knew better than to blindly trust an MI5 agent. How often had her uncle complained about the FBI? "Those Feds love to make local cops look stupid. That's why we never tell 'em anything they don't absolutely, positively need to know."

Then again, maybe the Kent police deserved to look stupid. DI Pennyman did come across as rather dense when he threatened to charge her with wasting police time.

"I charge you with letting a murderer go unpunished."

No one in authority seemed willing to listen to reason. *Correction!* That wasn't quite true. The real problem was that everyone gave Sir Simon Clowes more respect than he deserved. He was Elspeth's doctor. He was in the room when she died. He signed her death certificate. End of story.

But the story didn't end there. The real ending was yet to

be told. There were two distinct possibilities: Either Dr. Clowes made a stupid mistake or else he deliberately concealed the cause of death.

The first didn't feel right, and the second—well, why would a respected physician suppress the truth? His behavior made no sense unless he had poisoned Elspeth, but that didn't feel right, either. Her early opinion hadn't changed. As Elspeth's personal physician, he could have found a more convenient venue for murder than a trustees' meeting.

Flick wanted to cringe at the sheer absurdity of the situation. Elspeth might not receive the justice she deserved merely because her own doctor was sitting a few feet away as she unwittingly consumed a lethal dose of barbiturates.

She looked up when the door creaked open. Nigel came in, followed by Giselle Logan pushing a tea trolley. Nigel took the chair to Flick's right. "Margo McKendrick just called," he said. "Marjorie and the others are on their way up."

Flick acknowledged his presence with a small nod. *He doesn't even deserve that after storming into my office at the head of an invading army.*

"We both know that I have nothing to contribute to this worthless meeting," she said. "What are you going to tell them?"

"I don't have much choice." Nigel shrugged. "I will say what Marjorie Halifax wants to hear. That we will recommend that the museum take on debt up to its eyeballs and pay the appraised value for the Hawker collection."

"Sounds good to me. Once you placate Marjorie, I'm going home. I've had more than enough fun for one day."

Flick heard voices outside the door. The four local trustees swooped into the room—the lot of them dour-faced. Close behind marched Polly Reid, the administrative assistant whom Flick shared with Nigel.

Now what's going on?

Flick peered at Nigel; he also seemed bewildered by Polly's unexpected arrival.

Marjorie sat down opposite Flick. She began talking as she carried cups of tea to their seats. "Nigel, I have taken the liberty of asking Ms. Reid to arrange for Archibald Meicklejohn and Iona Saxby to telephone into our meeting. Unfortunately, Sir Simon remains unavailable."

"This is supposed to be an informal get-together," Nigel said.

"Unhappily, the circumstances have changed since we talked this morning, and so has the required agenda of our meeting. I feel that Archibald and Iona must participate."

Flick felt the color rising in her cheeks. *Oh boy! This has to be about me.*

Polly placed a speakerphone that resembled a large starfish on the table and positioned the device close to Marjorie and Flick. She dialed the phone and verified that both Archibald and Iona were on the line.

"Archibald here, from London," came his voice out of the speakerphone, followed by, "Hello, everyone, this is Iona in Oxford."

Marjorie began. "One hour ago, the chief constable of the Kent police informed me during a telephone call that our chief curator may—and these are his words—be mentally unstable. He assured me that the accusation she made to an agent of the Security Service was unsubstantiated to the point of being deranged and that I did not have to worry that one of my colleagues on the board of trustees is a cold-blooded poisoner."

Flick sighed. How could she even begin to defend herself?

Marjorie took a breath and resumed talking. "The chief

constable called me as a courtesy because of my position in local government. He also told me that while he has no intention of reporting the incident to the media, he won't be able to deny it should word of your accusation leak out. In that event, we certainly will face an onslaught from the tabloid press, replete with garish headlines. The chief constable thought that 'Dead as a Scone' was a definite possibility, although he himself favors 'Pantiles Peerage Poisoning Plot.' "

Vicar de Rudd and Dorothy McAndrews both chuckled. A laugh came from the speakerphone. Flick couldn't tell if Archibald or Iona was responsible.

Marjorie brought her hand down on the sprawling conference table with enough force to make the top quiver. "You gave us your word, Dr. Adams. You even apologized for making a fuss when Elspeth passed away. Now you have made a much bigger one, a potentially disastrous to-do, that can't possibly help our fund-raising efforts."

Flick looked around the table at the other trustees. Dorothy McAndrews's face wore a pinched moue, Matthew Eaton's a peeved scowl, and Vicar de Rudd's a pained grimace. The word *resignation* flitted through her mind. Did Marjorie expect her to "do the right thing" and commit professional suicide?

No way!

Flick fixed her gaze firmly on the decorative centerpiece of the conference table: a grouping of sixteenth-century Japanese artifacts and utensils designed for the traditional Japanese tea ceremony. *Chanoyu*, the common name of the ceremony, literally meant "hot water for tea." Whoever planned the centerpiece clearly had tongue in cheek. Chanoyu's main purpose was to create harmony among the partakers; actually having a cuppa was secondary. Consequently, a *chawan*, a communal bowl of tea, was shared by everyone in a highly stylized ceremony designed to encourage peace and serenity. Maybe it worked in Japan, but peace and serenity rarely made an appearance at meetings held in the museum's boardroom. Today's get-together had turned out to be especially noisy and chaotic.

And then the inexplicable happened. To Flick's astonishment, Nigel abruptly took charge.

"Thank you, Marjorie, for bringing us up to date," he said, "although I am growing weary of one-sided tirades against Dr. Adams."

Flick risked a sideways glance at Marjorie. Surprise radiated from her vaulted brows, wide eyes, and parted lips. In a few seconds, she had recovered sufficiently to say, "I beg your pardon!"

You took the words out of my mouth. Why had Nigel, of all people, decided to defend her? A few hours earlier, he had seemed an avid supporter of the police.

Nigel continued. "The presumption that underlies everything the chief constable said is that Felicity Adams *must* be wrong. Why are we all so quick to doubt what she says she observed?"

"Of course, she is wrong," Marjorie said. "The idea that Elspeth was poisoned by one of us is wholly unthinkable."

"I feel the same way," Nigel said. "And yet, we have to acknowledge that Dr. Adams is neither crazy nor stupid. We know that to be true, even if MI5 and the Kent police think otherwise."

Flick found it odd to hear herself talked about in the third person, but she kept staring at the iron *kama* kettle and brick *furo* stove in the *chanoyu* centerpiece. *Where is Nigel going with this?*

"This morning," Nigel said, "I witnessed a similar harangue delivered by a detective inspector on the chief constable's staff. I became aware of a curious thing as I listened to him scold Dr. Adams. None of us has ever asked her to explain *why* she adamantly insists that Dame Elspeth did not die a natural death. I, for one, would like to hear what she has to say."

The room fell silent. Matthew finally broke it. "Upon reflection, I agree with Nigel. We have been rather reticent to hear Dr. Adams out."

"I suppose we must give her the opportunity," Dorothy said stiffly.

"I concur," Iona said over the speakerphone.

Archibald spoke up. "Do I hear any disagreement from the trustees?" He paused to listen. "As there are no objections, now seems the perfect time—if Dr. Adams is willing."

Flick realized that everyone was watching her attentively. She nodded and managed a half smile. "Okay. Give me a moment to gather my thoughts."

"I know how to use that moment," the vicar said. "We traditionally open our meetings with prayer. Today we'll take a prayer break in the middle."

Flick exchanged a knowing smile with Nigel. Three months earlier, Flick had asked him about the custom. "Put a clergyman on the board of trustees," he had said, "and you get opening prayers—it's as simple as that. I don't take them seriously, of course."

Flick had laughed. "Me neither."

Vicar de Rudd cleared his throat. "Almighty God, source of all wisdom and understanding, we ask You to be present with us today as we secure the future of this fine institution. Teach us to seek first Your honor and glory. Give us wisdom and discernment. Help us to perceive what is right, and grant us both the courage to pursue it and the grace to accomplish it, through Jesus Christ our Lord."

Flick said a robust "Amen." Not that she believed the

vicar's prayer could make a difference, but wouldn't it be wonderful if the trustees miraculously received an extra helping of
wisdom and discernment?

Flick looked around the table. Five of the six people on
her list of suspects were in the room or listening on the telephone. Only Conan Davies, the least likely suspect, was ab-
sent. High odds, indeed, that she would explain her
conclusions to the person responsible for poisoning Elspeth
Hawker. Her presentation took shape in her mind. She would
talk about everything, except Elspeth's little black book.

That's my ace in the hole.

Flick began. "I was halfway through my talk on tea tasting
when I noticed that Elspeth had fallen asleep. I remember
thinking to myself, *How unusual.* She always managed to stay
awake during my presentations, no matter how dull. Thirty
minutes later, we discovered that Elspeth was dead. She expired
without a single warning of distress—quite literally died in her
sleep. Again, I remember thinking to myself, *That's also unusual.*

"I moved to Elspeth's side when Sir Simon did. Her pupils
looked dilated and her face had a bluish tint. Most telling of
all, despite the boardroom being unusually warm that afternoon, her skin felt icy cold. Those are obvious symptoms of
barbiturate poisoning. A likely candidate is secobarbital
sodium, a fast-acting drug. A sufficient overdose can kill in
less than two hours. I believe that Elspeth was poisoned during our tea break."

Dorothy raised a hand. "But we all ate the same food."

"Not quite. Elspeth had her personal pot of lingonberry preserves, which she alone consumed. Alain Rousseau's preserves
are sweet enough to camouflage the bitter taste of a barbiturate."

"Why?" Matthew asked. "Why would anyone want to kill
Dame Elspeth?"

"To silence her. Elspeth uncovered a systematic scheme to exchange bona fide antiquities in the Hawker collection with forgeries."

Iona's disembodied shout filled the room. "How do you know that?"

Flick hesitated. "She communicated her discoveries to me."

"What discoveries?" Dorothy snapped. "Elspeth wasn't qualified to determine the authenticity of anything."

"Possibly true. But she knew the Hawker antiquities well enough to recognize when an old familiar friend had been replaced with an imposter."

Flick couldn't be sure, but had she just glimpsed a look of recognition on Nigel's face? It seemed the expression of someone who just had an *Aha!* moment.

Dorothy resumed her attack. "That is pure speculation! Give me a list of these so-called forgeries. I will have them examined."

Archibald boomed over the speakerphone, "Not necessary, Dorothy. The entire Hawker collection will be appraised during the coming months. In fact, the valuation will prove—or disprove—the conclusions Dr. Adams has reached."

Flick said nothing. She had located the last of the nineteen items that had earned a big red F from Elspeth. Every one was a clever forgery that looked authentic and might not be detected by a team of appraisers working at high speed to value a large collection for probate.

Archibald went on. "I think we can safely defer any additional discussion about Dr. Adams's conduct until then."

Flick saw Marjorie roll her eyes. *She's disappointed. She acts like she expected the trustees to fire me.*

Silence reigned until Nigel filled the vacuum. "Since we seem to have completed our revised agenda, perhaps we also can accomplish the original purpose of this informal meeting. Dr. Adams and I expect to present a proposal for acquiring the Hawker collection from the estate. With the trustees' concurrence, I will express our interest to the Hawkers' solicitor, tell him we are working out the specifics of our offer, and invite him to schedule the appraisal as soon as practical."

Flick cast another glance at Marjorie. She was smiling. "Exactly what I had hoped to hear you say," she said.

"I agree," Archibald said. "However, when you talk to Bleasdale, impress upon him the need to sharpen his pencil. If we will purchase the whole collection, we expect the best possible price."

"And tell him that we want a say in choosing the firm that does the appraisals," Dorothy said. "There are some bad eggs out there. I know who they are."

Flick let herself relax. The trustees had turned their attention away from her and toward the details of acquiring the Hawker antiquities. Nigel, too, seemed more at ease as he dutifully scribbled their suggestions on a yellow pad. Consequently, only Flick noticed Giselle Logan slip into the boardroom and crook her finger. The panicked look on Giselle's face brought Flick to her feet.

Not another disaster!

"We have a predicament, Dr. Adams," Giselle said softly. "Alain Rousseau went home ill. His wife believes he has the flu and will be out of commission for several days. We won't have fresh-baked scones and other tea cakes for the academic conference on Monday."

"I thought we have a substitute chef on call."

"We do. But he can't arrive early enough on Monday morning to do all the extra baking. I'll have to find a bakery in Tunbridge Wells that does proper scones."

"Rats! I promised the conferees a deluxe cream tea, with all the trimmings fresh from the oven. A genuine Mad Hatter's Tea Party."

Flick was still brooding when Archibald said, "I believe we have done enough business for a Saturday afternoon." A few minutes later, she and Nigel were alone once more in the boardroom.

"You look like you lost a pound and found a penny," he said.

"This has been a truly rotten day. And now I have to worry about scones." She told Nigel about Alain Rousseau.

"Not a problem," Nigel said. "I'll take care of it." He added, "Do you realize that you are gawking at me?"

"I've hardly begun to gawk. How do you plan to 'take care of it'?"

"Leave it to me. The 'scone king' shall tend to the feeding of the ravenous academics."

"You sound as mad as the Mad Hatter."

He stood up and moved to the door. "Aren't you going home?"

She shook her head. "No. I feel like moping some more."

As the door closed behind him, Flick suddenly remembered that she hadn't thanked Nigel for doing battle with Marjorie Halifax.

"Even more important," she murmured, "I didn't ask him why he stuck his own neck out for me."

TEN

Nigel turned the key in the lock. Once he opened the museum's side door, he would have sixty seconds to reach the alarm system panel hidden in the Welcome Centre kiosk and enter his personal access code.

"Get ready, Cha-Cha." Nigel wrapped the dog's lead twice around his hand. "Run!"

Nigel yanked his key free, zipped across the threshold, slammed the door behind him, raced through the fifty-foot-long hallway, passed the History of Tea Colonnade on his right and the gift shop on his left, skidded around the back side of the kiosk, tugged open the control panel door, and punched buttons on the keypad: 9-0-7-9-7-3.

The red lamp on the panel flashed yellow.

"We made it, Cha-Cha. Now we have another whole minute to disable the motion detectors."

Nigel pressed his thumb against a rectangular glass plate. He heard a soft beep as a tiny TV camera behind the glass imaged his thumbprint. The yellow lamp turned to green. A female voice sounded from a small speaker: "Security system disarmed by Nigel Owen. Sunday. Ten twenty-six."

Yes indeed, madam. Nigel Owen single-handedly vanquished our wizard alarm.

Nigel contemplated the now-benign control panel with annoyance. He had never triggered the museum's security alarm by accident. He had never even come close to exhausting the two sixty-second grace periods. Yet this morning he felt curiously intimidated by the complex system with its hundreds of sensors. A false alarm would send the Kent police racing to the front door of the Royal Tunbridge Wells Tea Museum, and he had no desire to increase his aggravation by meeting a new copper.

Nigel felt annoyed enough, thank you very much, that he was about to spend most of his only real day off that week doing someone else's job. He also knew of no one to blame but himself. Neither Giselle nor Flick had asked him to solve the scone problem.

You volunteered all by your lonesome.

Why had he offered to help? Probably because vague pangs of remorse kept reminding him that he had intentionally ignored two opportunities to do right by Flick Adams. He might have eased Flick's sequential scoldings—first by DI Pennyman and then by the trustees—if he had repeated what Elspeth said on the day she died. As Iona Saxby had pointedly reminded him, Flick was part of his staff. He owed her a reasonable portion of loyalty and support.

Had he been held back by simple fear—the notion that he might put himself in danger if one of the trustees was really a murderer? Or had it been the concern that the more influential trustees would begin to think of him as a "loose cannon" along with Flick?

In either case, yesterday he had not seen his finest hour.

Nigel unclipped Cha-Cha's lead. "You're now free to roam about the museum while I check that the side door is locked." But the dog didn't seem in a mood to wander. He trotted alongside as Nigel—pondering the ingredients of scones and tea cakes—ambled back down the hallway.

Cha-Cha unexpectedly yipped twice. Startled, Nigel looked up. Flick Adams stood in the doorway, a key in her hand, a bemused grin on her face.

"Thank goodness I don't have to make a forty-yard dash to the kiosk," she said.

"I didn't expect to meet anyone else here today." He shut the side door securely and turned the deadbolt. "Especially you. You seemed well and truly knackered yesterday afternoon."

"I felt kinda guilty dumping the scone problem into your lap. The least I can do is to help you order what's necessary."

"Order? I don't follow you."

"You said that you would get the baked goods we need for the conference from the Scone King bakery."

Nigel laughed. "No, I said that the 'scone king' will feed the visiting academics." He paused for effect. "I am the scone king. I intend to do the baking myself."

"*You?*"

"Don't look so astonished. One has to support oneself at university. I worked as a journeyman baker in a baker's shop for three years and even entertained the idea of becoming a pastry chef." Nigel added, "If you really want to help today, join me in the kitchen. How are you at baking?"

"Great in theory. I wrote my master's thesis on the chemistry of yeast in flour-based carbohydrate matrices."

Nigel needed a moment to decipher Flick's technical jargon. "In simpler terms, that would be how yeast makes bread dough rise."

"Exactly. However, my practice needs work. I'm famous in Pennsylvania for my lumpy, misshapen bread."

"A scullery maid will be of greater use to me this afternoon than an assistant baker. I am sure you have all the skills required to lift, carry, stir, and wash."

"Why, how kind of you to say so, sir." She feigned a coy giggle. "Your word is my command."

Nigel led the way through the World of Tea Map Room and into the Duchess of Bedford Tearoom. They made for the door to the kitchen, on the right side of the tearoom, toward the rear. Earl Grey heard their footsteps and began to chirp; Cha-Cha responded with a delighted yip.

"I'll meet you in the kitchen," Nigel said to Flick. "A brief pet stop seems in order." He crossed the tearoom and removed the tablecloth from Earl's cage. The bird peered at him, then stretched out a leg.

"Get me a hot cuppa!" it squawked.

"What say a piece of apple instead? Will that do?"

Earl answered with a piercing wolf whistle. Cha-Cha yipped again.

"I take that as a yes," Nigel said.

He joined Flick in the kitchen, where she had turned on the lights. The polished black-and-white floor tiles and the shiny stainless-steel commercial appliances gleamed beneath several banks of overhead fluorescent lamps.

"As your first assignment," he said, "see if you can locate Alain Rousseau's recipe collection. Then we'll decide what sort of goodies to prepare."

"The stack of notebooks on Alain's desk looks promising." She began to read aloud the labels on the spines. "English Breakfasts. . .Lunches. . .Picnics. . .Appetizers. . .Entrees. . . Desserts. . .here we go"—she tugged a book free from the stack—*"English Afternoon and High Teas."*

To Nigel's astonishment, Flick began to frown as she flipped through the pages.

"What can be distressing about a book full of recipes?" he asked.

"It made me think of an argument I had with the owner of a tea shop in Pennsylvania, one of those pretentious places that spells shop *s-h-o-p-p-e*. We went at it hammer and tongs for a while."

"Heaven forfend! I can't imagine you disagreeing with anyone."

Flick stuck her tongue out at Nigel. "Our fight was over her menu. She described 'high tea' as an elegant afternoon repast enjoyed by the English social elite."

"Not so. High tea is a workingman's evening meal."

"She knew that. But many Americans assume that 'high' is short for 'high class.' The owner said, 'It's not my job to educate guests that high tea is really a supperlike meal served on a high kitchen table rather than on a low tea table.'" Flick heaved a sigh. "She didn't want to argue with paying customers."

"How shocking. The triumph of business expediency over the truth." Nigel shifted gears. "Speaking of paying customers—how many academics will descend on us tomorrow?"

"Twenty-two in all. They ordered our complete English cream tea. Four kinds of tea—one Chinese black, one Indian black, one oolong, one green—plus scones, savories, sandwiches, and cakes." Flick handed the notebook to Nigel. "I phoned Giselle this morning. The replacement chef will brew the tea, provide the savories—probably sausage rolls and a nice Welsh rarebit—and assemble the usual variety of tea sandwiches. Giselle assured me there are ample supplies of Alain's preserves in the pantry and gallons of clotted cream in the fridge. You are responsible for the scones and the cakes."

"I still am bewildered by what these learned men and women will chat about while eating my scones. The societal *something* concerning the Mad Hatter's Tea Party."

"The societal metaphors and allegories inherent in the Mad Hatter's Tea Party."

"How did you speak those words without retching?" Nigel rolled his eyes. "Tomorrow's conference may represent the worst example of pompous twaddle I have heard all year."

Flick laughed. "Professors of literature care about such things."

"I repeat—pompous twaddle!"

"Aren't you being a tad judgmental? After all, Lewis Carroll is widely recognized as one of England's great writers—a man who apparently satirized nineteenth-century England when he wrote *Alice's Adventures in Wonderland*. Besides, remember our chat with Jeremy Strain the other day. We want to encourage academics to use our facilities."

"Bah humbug! It pains me to serve my delightful scones at such a gathering. However"—he gave an exaggerated sigh—"I propose that we offer two kinds: plain and cinnamon raisin."

Nigel opened Alain's notebook but glanced obliquely at Flick. He had had an amusing idea. "You like to dazzle innocent bystanders with facts about food. Let me ask you a question a food chemist probably can't answer. Do you know where the name *scone* comes from?"

Flick cleared her throat. "There are several theories. Given the apparent Scottish origin of the scone, some hold the name memorializes the Abbey of Scone, where the kings of Scotland were crowned as they sat on the so-called stone of destiny. Others argue that *scone* comes from *schoonbrot*, Dutch for beautiful bread, and still others that it derives from *sgonn*, a Gaelic word that means shapeless blob.

"But whether pronounced 'scone' or 'scon'—as in northern England and Scotland—the product is technically a quick bread, a bread made without yeast."

Nigel found it difficult to scowl at Flick's wry grin. "You can be a world-class wally, Mizz Adams."

"What's a wally?"

"A prat."

"What's a prat?"

"Look in the mirror." He let himself smile. "Enough small talk. We have to decide what else I bake for tomorrow. Do you recall if the Mad Hatter served a particular kind of cake to Alice?"

"No cake at all. Alice ate a slice of bread and butter."

"We can do better than that." Nigel leafed through the notebook. Alain had neatly glued a typed recipe card in the middle of each page. Each recipe was sized to serve forty-eight people. There would be leftovers of everything Nigel baked, which certainly would please Alain's temporary replacement. "I propose," he eventually said, "that we make lemon curd tarts and chocolate pound cake."

"Sounds yummy. Can we also bake a batch of fairy cakes?"

"If you insist."

"With raspberry fondant icing?"

"Is there any other sort?"

"The scullery maid would like to ask the journeyman baker a practical question."

"I feel egalitarian today. Ask what you will."

"If we bake scones and cakes this afternoon, won't they be stale by tomorrow?"

"The pound cake, tarts, and fairy cakes will stay fresh overnight in the refrigerator. However, scones are best when served hot from the oven. We will do a classic baker's fiddle with them."

Nigel countered Flick's mystified expression with what he hoped was a shrewd smirk.

"We will prebake the scones today, up to the point when they take on a bit of color. Then we freeze them. The substitute chef can pop them back in the oven tomorrow, a half hour before tea is served. I guarantee they will taste wholly fresh baked." Nigel lobbed the notebook atop the vast marble-topped preparation table that stood in the middle of the kitchen. "Help me collect the ingredients."

The door to the pantry was next to a big commercial refrigerator. In traditional English fashion, the pantry had been set four feet into the ground so that it stayed cool during the summer but never froze during the winter. This had been possible because the tearoom and greenhouse were extensions to the museum proper and not built above a full basement like the main building. Flick stood in the open doorway while Nigel—a few steps below—passed up sacks, boxes, bottles, cans, jars, jugs, and the occasional tube.

"That's the lot," he finally said.

"When did you make a list of ingredients?"

"I have it all in my head."

"Show-off!"

"If your hands are free, join me down here."

"Is there something especially heavy you want me to lift?"

"Actually, you get to choose the three scone toppings that will accompany the clotted cream tomorrow."

Nigel stepped away from the stairs to make room for Flick. The pantry was a small rectangular room, its walls covered with floor-to-ceiling shelving. The shelves were made of marble, three feet deep and filled to overflowing. The centre aisle was too narrow for two people to stand together side by side. Nigel guided Flick to a shelf filled to capacity with jars of home-canned preserves.

"Aren't they pretty?" she said.

"Lovely. Pick three."

"Raspberry for sure." She peered at the various jars. "Sour cherry conserves sounds tasty. And. . .*oh my!*"

Nigel followed Flick's line of sight to a row of jars labeled "Lingonberry Preserves."

The "murder weapon" in Flick's theory.

He held up one of the jars to a hanging light fixture. "You aren't suggesting that these preserves contain barbiturates, are you?"

She shook her head. "I'm betting that Elspeth's poisoner put the drugs in her personal jam pot. That way, no one else was at risk."

"Ah." *Assuming, of course, that Elspeth was poisoned.* The jury was still out on that issue.

"By the way," Flick said, "I didn't get the chance to thank you yesterday. I'd probably be packing up my office today if you hadn't jumped in the way you did."

"Marjorie Halifax's bark is worse than her bite." Nigel returned the jar to the shelf. "She fancies herself the vice-chair of the trustees. She assumes that she will replace Archibald Meicklejohn when he moves on to greener pastures."

"Maybe so, but I really appreciate you standing up for me. You showed lots of courage."

Nigel felt a surge of embarrassment. He had been anything but courageous at the trustees' meeting or earlier with the Kent police. Fortunately, Flick didn't press the point or expect a response. Instead, she turned back to the preserves shelf and said, "We can't go wrong with good-old apricot preserves."

"Choose two aprons before you leave." Nigel pointed to a collection of chef's aprons hanging inside a tall, wardrobe-sized gap in the shelving on the right side of the pantry. "And grab an apple from the bin—I promised Earl the parrot a snack."

"That's an odd place to put a clothes closet." Flick gazed at a three-foot-wide gap. "Why waste prime real estate inside a crowded pantry?"

"One will never know. The carpenter who built these shelves is probably long dead."

"Unless. . ."

"Unless what?"

"Forget it. What's next?"

"Mixing, kneading, shaping, and baking. We'll make the scones first."

Once back in the kitchen, Nigel donned his apron and helped Flick tie hers. She seemed eager and ready to help. A good egg, after all.

We may have a lot more in common than I once thought.

He filled a large aluminum scoop to the twelve-cup mark with baking flour and emptied it into the dough mixer.

Perhaps I need to rethink an idea or two about Dr. Adams.

Flick pressed the button marked *1* with her elbow. The door slid shut, and the three plates she clutched in her hands and arms infused the small elevator with delectable aromas. She looked down with satisfaction at two fully baked scones, two lemon curd tarts, two iced fairy cakes, and a miniature chocolate pound cake.

I helped every step of the way.

Cha-Cha sat obediently at her feet, sniffing the air, occasionally yipping for a treat.

"Maybe later," she said, "if anything is left when the grown-ups are finished."

Flick felt astonished by what she had just seen. Nigel had described himself as a journeyman; in fact, he was a better baker than Alain Rousseau. His scones seemed lighter than Alain's, with a better texture. His cakes looked too pretty to eat. He had thrown dough around with seemingly wild abandon, had stamped out scones like a punch press, and had stuck "wings" on fairy cakes in dizzying succession. In only four hours, they had made forty-eight lemon curd tarts, two sheets of chocolate pound cake, forty-eight fairy cakes, and ninety-six prebaked scones—half plain, half cinnamon raisin.

"I'm slowing down in my old age," he had said. "You should have seen me at age twenty. A veritable baking machine."

Most of Nigel's apparent pomposity had vanished as they worked together and she got to know him better. He also had shown himself to have a good sense of humor and had even responded cheerfully to her "I know more than you do" answer to his question about scones. And then the biggest surprise of all: Nigel had done an utterly unexpected thing when they began to clean up the kitchen.

"Let's sample our handiwork when we are finished," Nigel had said. "I've made us our own private assortment of goodies."

"In that case, I suggest we adjourn to the Tea Tasting Room on the first floor. I'll brew a pot of tea for me and perk a pot of coffee for you. It seems silly to fire up the big kettle and the big coffeemaker for just the two of us."

"Upstairs. Yes. That's a fine idea." Nigel seemed to hesitate.

"However, perhaps I can do without the coffee."

Flick had been sponging down the preparation table. She froze midswipe. "You? No coffee?"

"It seems only fair that I learn more about the beverage that currently pays my rent and supports my lifestyle." He glanced at his watch. "It's not late, only fourteen thirty"—he smiled again—"two thirty, I mean. If you have no pressing plans, I'd like to sample a reasonable cross section of teas and find the one I like best."

"You're saying you want me to set up a personal tea tasting for you?"

His sudden nervous chortle intensified her surprise. "Well, yes—but with normal strength tea. I doubt that I'm ready for the extra-strong brew you tea tasters drink. And, of course, I won't promise that I will like any of them. I am, however, willing to try what you suggest."

"I'd be honored to help you find a tea you will really enjoy."

"Tell you what. You go upstairs and work your magic. I'll finish putting the bowls and pans away and join you in about fifteen minutes."

The elevator arrived at the first floor. Flick toted her cargo of samples through the Tea at Sea Gallery, around the staircase, and into the Tea Tasting Room. Visitors to the museum often commented on its most distinctive feature: a glass wall in the rear that overlooked the Tea Blending Room, the one exhibit that visitors had to watch from a distance.

The Tea Tasting Room was the least furnished room in the museum. There was a large, square slate-topped table in the middle of the floor, several tall storage cupboards and a refrigerator on the wall opposite the windows, and a long row of waist-high cabinets built next to the windows. The wood cabinets were painted white and looked like a cross between kitchen cabinetry and laboratory equipment. The slate countertop had a sink at each end, both equipped with filters that eliminated chlorine and other impurities. The only chairs in the room were eight tall stools arrayed around the central table.

Afternoon sunlight streamed through the westward-facing windows. Flick mused for the hundredth time that the Tea Tasting Room was on the wrong side of the museum. The color of brewed tea, an important evaluation factor, was best evaluated in uniform daylight away from bright sunshine. Cool northern light was ideal.

Flick tugged a cord to close the floor-to-ceiling translucent draperies that offered a partial solution, then went next door to the Tea Blending Room. She browsed among more than two hundred canisters on the shelves and made six selections. She would serve four representative teas to Nigel—and have a bit of fun with two other "unusual" teas. She put two tablespoons of each tea into a small paper cup. She decided not to label the six cups; it was easy to tell by appearance which tea was which.

Flick had an idea as she carried the paper cups back to the Tea Tasting Room. Maybe she should serve Nigel a cup of her favorite tea. The tea leaves were in her office, but she had more than enough time for a quick trip to the third floor. She made a snap decision: *I'll do it.*

A soft yip caught her attention.

Uh-oh. There's trouble waiting to happen.

Cha-Cha sat a few feet away from the central table eyeing the baked goods intently. He seemed especially interested in the miniature chocolate pound cake. Flick didn't think he could manage a leap to the top, but she also knew that Shiba Inus were the most catlike of dogs.

Better safe than sorry.

His lead was in her coat pocket. She clipped it to his collar. "You are coming along with me."

She jogged up the stairs, Cha-Cha trotting close behind.

The tea canister was atop the credenza behind her desk, on a tray that also held an electric kettle made of black plastic, a four-cup teapot, and three ceramic mugs. She had remembered to bring another paper cup with her. She dipped it inside the canister and scooped up a few tablespoons of tea.

Flick glanced at the electric kettle. Elspeth's little black book, wrapped in a black plastic bag, was hidden in the bottom. It was virtually invisible, even if someone were to lift the lid and look inside the tall, narrow appliance.

Should I show the notebook to Nigel?

She remembered his skeptical expression in the pantry. He still had his doubts that Elspeth had been poisoned. Would Elspeth's notebook help to convince him otherwise?

Probably not. And anyway, this isn't the right time to talk about murder.

Back in the Tea Tasting Room, Flick took three full-sized electric kettles from a cupboard, filled each to the brim, and plugged the trio into power points recessed in the top of the central table. She lined up seven clear glass teapots—Nigel might enjoy watching the tea leaves steep—and fourteen white tea-cups: a fresh cup for Nigel and her for each tea they sampled.

She thought about wheeling in the tall stainless-steel spittoon, but decided against it. When Flick participated in a real tea-tasting session, she rolled hefty sips of tea around in her mouth, then spit them out.

She surveyed the table. Was anything missing?

Rats! I forgot milk, sugar, teaspoons, and the most important utensils of all: tea strainers.

Flick was sitting at the table, beaming happily, when Nigel came in.

"Look at all this clobber," he said. "Tea tasting is as bad as baking." He peered at the row of paper cups. "What kind of teas are these?"

"I'll tell you as you drink them."

"Fair enough. Bring on the first candidate."

Flick emptied the first paper cup into the first teapot, then poured the boiling water.

"Hey, that's interesting," Nigel said. "The tea leaves move around as they brew."

"It's called the 'agony of the leaves.' The dried tea leaves relax and uncurl in the hot water. Some people prefer to say the 'ecstasy of the leaves.' "

"I am one of them." He gazed into the teapot. "That's a pretty color. A lovely deep red."

They watched in silence as the tea brewed.

"Three minutes," Flick said. "Your English Breakfast tea is ready, sir."

She filled a cup for Nigel, pouring the tea through the strainer to filter out the tea leaves that traveled through the spout, and then another for herself.

Nigel took several demure sips, then said, "Hmm. A pleasant bouquet that prepares one for the fruity tastes to come. A bit overambitious, but one is quickly amused at its presumption."

Flick snickered. "You sound like a wine taster. 'Fruity' is not necessarily a term of praise for tea. It can mean that the tea has an overripe taste and may have been oxidized too long when it was processed. If I were wearing my tea-taster hat right now, I would describe this as a hearty, full-bodied, full-flavored tea."

"What kind of tea bush makes English Breakfast tea?"

Flick struggled to keep a straight face. She had heard the question a thousand times before. "English Breakfast tea is actually a blend of different teas from India and Sri Lanka," she said evenly. "All true teas come from a single plant. Its Latin name is *Camellia sinensis*. It's a tropical evergreen, with glossy dark-green leaves. There are three major varieties—and lots of minor variations—of *Camellia sinensis* found in different parts of the world. Teas, of course, will also taste different depending on soil, climate, the amount of sunlight—all the usual growing factors."

Nigel nodded. He took another sip, then frowned. "Hang on a mo. My mother often drinks teas made of chamomile and rose hips."

Flick sighed. "It drives me bonkers when herbal infusions are called 'tea.' I wish we followed the French and called them *tisanes*." She shrugged. "I know it's a losing battle, so let's get back to English Breakfast tea. Did you know that adding a little milk may enhance a hearty tea? It actually can improve the taste. Some people even like sugar."

"I know about milk, but is it legal to put sugar in tea?"

"Lots of Americans do, the Chinese usually don't, the Brits are ambivalent, even though they came up with the idea first. George Orwell, the novelist who wrote *1984*, wrote a famous essay on tea that condemned the use of sugar."

Nigel added a bit of milk, stirred, and tasted. "Not bad, but I prefer mine black. What's next?"

"A charming Lapsang Souchong."

"Undoubtedly a pussycat of a tea." After Nigel stopped smirking, he asked, "Another blend?"

"Some are, but this one isn't. It's a single tea from one garden."

Flick poured boiling water over the tea leaves.

"What's that odor? Is something burning?" he asked.

"You can smell smoldering pine wood. Lapsang Souchong is *smoked* tea."

"Good heavens." Nigel sniffed at the pot. "How does it taste?"

"As smoky as it smells."

She filled two cups with tea.

"Strange," Nigel said after he tasted it.

"Lapsang Souchong is an acquired taste. Some people say it has the flavor of tar."

"I won't argue with them." He took another sip. "No, it's not my cup of tea."

"Then let's move on to a classic Russian Caravan."

As Flick poured boiling water, Nigel said, "This one definitely is a blend. I can see pieces of many different tea leaves."

"You're right. It contains several Chinese and Indian teas."

"I have a feeling I am going to like this one."

"Most people do. It's a hearty, flavorful tea."

"Brilliant!" Nigel said a few minutes later. "The best tea I've tried so far. There's an interesting hint of mystery lurking in the background."

Flick grinned mischievously. "That's because Russian Caravan contains a little Lapsang Souchong to remind you of evening campfires as the tea traveled across Asia on the backs of camels."

"Do you think scones were served at your typical caravansary?" He broke off a piece of scone and ate it. "Quite good, if I say so myself."

"I say so, too. All your baking is wonderful."

Flick began to brew the fourth pot of tea.

"More full-sized leaves," Nigel said, "and a really pretty color. I've always liked dark reds."

"Take a sniff."

Nigel wafted the rising vapors toward his nose. "The smell of old gym socks."

"This tea is called Pu'erh. The fermented tea leaves are aged—the best for more than fifty years."

"Hence the name: *Poo-uh*!"

"Try some. It has an earthy flavor."

"True," Nigel said as he risked a small sip. "It tastes like garden soil."

Flick laughed. "Another acquired taste."

"Yes, well, carry on while I eat a big piece of chocolate pound cake to get the 'earthy flavor' out of my mouth."

Flick prepared the next pot of tea.

"It's not red." Nigel had considerable surprise in his voice.

"Most Oolong teas brew up gold or amber."

Nigel took an enthusiastic sip. "It tastes like peaches."

"An excellent observation. Peaches with a suggestion of chestnut."

"I thought that a fruity taste was bad."

"A dominant fruity taste often signals a poorly made tea. But a specific hint of peaches in an Oolong tea is good."

"Ah. One of the mysteries of tea tasting."

"You got it!"

Flick readied the sixth teapot. "The next tea is a top-quality Indian Darjeeling, one of the most expensive teas you can buy. Brewing time is important with Darjeeling tea. Steeping the leaves too long can make the cup overly bitter and astringent."

"And we wouldn't want that, would we?" Nigel added a theatrical simper.

Flick began to giggle. "This is serious kitchen chemistry," she managed to say. "Darjeeling is considered the champaign of teas."

She filled clean cups.

"Very nice, indeed," Nigel said. "I can't quite describe the aroma."

"Floral with a hint of grapes and perhaps a touch of eucalyptus."

"You detected all that with one sniff? My compliments to your snout."

Flick giggled some more. Why had she believed that Nigel was a stuffy Englishman? He could be quite funny.

"Is it time for a drumroll?" he said. "I assume that you saved the best for last."

Flick nodded. "My personal favorite. An estate-grown Assam from India."

"It will have to be supergood to change my list," he said. "The Russian Caravan is solidly in first place."

She added boiling water to the seventh teapot and watched the swirling streaks of color slowly change the contents to a rich, dark amber.

"This Assam is a strong tea," she said, "with an exceptionally malty flavor and hints of chocolate."

"I can't wait."

Flick poured tea into Nigel's cup. She peered at him as he took a big sip. He made a grimace.

"Ugh," he said. "I'm surprised this is your favorite."

"You don't like it?"

"It might be okay with lots of milk and sugar, but it tastes too bitter to drink plain."

"Bitter?"

Flick filled her cup and sniffed the tea.

She glanced at Nigel. He was lifting his cup to his lips to take another sip.

"No!" she screamed. "Don't drink it! *Your tea is poisoned!*" She slapped the cup out of his hand.

ELEVEN

Nigel lurched toward the sofa in Flick's office and sank gratefully into the friendly leather cushions. The dose of syrup of ipecac he drank had worked as advertised. He had just spent five minutes in the bathroom—twenty seconds vomiting up the meager contents of his stomach and the rest of the time retching—all the while remembering vaguely that ipecac was no longer used routinely in Great Britain to expel swallowed poisons.

See what happens when you try to comfort a guilt-ridden American?

He lay down face-first on the sofa. The cool touch of old leather against his cheek felt refreshing. He could hear Flick talking on her telephone, but he couldn't make out what she was saying because she spoke in urgent whispers. Her tone signaled that she was still worried, still a bit panicky.

He would not soon forget the fusion of dread and remorse on Flick's face when she knocked the nasty-tasting cup of Assam tea out of his hands. Her cheeks had turned an odd

192

shade of gray, and her voice quavered as she shouted, "Your tea is poisoned!"

Your tea is poisoned!

Four words that had set his mind racing. He thought with incredible clarity during the next several seconds. Ideas dropped into place. Scales fell away from his eyes.

Flick had been right after all. One of the trustees of the Royal Tunbridge Wells Tea Museum was a poisoner.

Elspeth Hawker had been poisoned on purpose, while he had been poisoned by accident when he drank some of Flick's private tea. The poison clearly had been meant for Flick. She was the intended next victim.

"I've had a brainstorm!" he had said. "This was supposed to happen to you not me."

"I know that!" Flick made her response into a long, plaintive cry.

She had pulled him to his feet and dragged him to the elevator.

"Do you feel anything unusual?" She peered into his eyes from a distance of three inches. "Dizziness? Stomach pains? Changes in your heartbeat? Shortness of breath?"

"None of the above. I feel fine. Is that good or bad?"

Flick repeatedly punched the number 3 button with the heel of her hand. "Come on! Come on!"

The door had closed slowly. Nigel could hear the motor grinding far below as the old, slow hydraulic elevator lackadaisically lifted them to the top floor.

Once in her office, Flick had dashed to her credenza, nearly torn the lid off a tea canister, and poured the contents out on her desk with wild abandon. Nigel watched over her shoulder as she examined the broken tea leaves with a magnifying glass.

"Rats! Rats! Rats!" she bellowed. "How dim-witted can a

person be? Why didn't I spot the leaf fragments earlier?"

"What do you see?"

"Pieces of another kind of leaf mixed with the Assam tea leaves. Some chunks are light green; others are dark green."

"That doesn't sound like a barbiturate," he said.

"It's not," she said, her voice temporarily under control. "Barbiturate is a white powder. This must be some sort of plant poison."

"Are plant poisons dangerous?"

"Some of them are lethal." The jumpy voice returned. "In small doses."

"Ah."

She lowered her magnifying glass and spun around in her swivel chair so she could look up at Nigel. "I'm not sure what to do next," she said.

"Well, we could call 999 and ask for the local poison control centre."

"That's the one thing we can't do," she wailed. "The poison control people will call the Kent police, who will assume that I fed you the poison."

"Why would the police think that?"

"Because they have decided that I'm a loony American who will do anything to convince them I am right. If I fed a load of bunkum to an MI5 agent, why would I stop at poisoning you to make them take me seriously?"

"But that is not what happened. Someone else put green leaves in your tea."

"You know that and I know that, but the cops will blame me. They don't want to point fingers at the precious trustees. I'm the easy way out."

"Flick—you are merely speculating. We have a good police force in Kent."

"Right! Just like you have good cardiologists who ignore the obvious symptoms of barbiturate poisoning."

"Now you are mixing apples and oranges."

"My mind is made up. We can't call the poison control centre."

"Well, I for one would hate to see DI Pennyman cause you any additional distress. That being the case, perhaps you can start planning a suitable Church of England funeral for me. It needn't be as elaborate as the one I arranged for Elspeth, but I would prefer more smells and bells."

"That's not funny, Nigel!" She sprang to her feet and pushed Nigel down into a visitor's chair. "This is stupid. I know *exactly* what to do. What I need is in the Conservation Laboratory. Stay put."

"Where would I go to in my present hopeless condition?"

Flick ran out of the room without answering Nigel. In quick succession, he heard two drawers opening and closing, three cupboard doors slamming, and Flick shouting, "Why can't I find anything in this stupid laboratory when I really want it?" Several more rattles and thumps, then, "Oh, that's right! I put it in the first-aid kit."

She came rushing back and presented Nigel with a small bottle. "Hold your nose and drink the contents."

He read the label. "Syrup of ipecac?"

"It will make you throw up. We might as well empty your stomach."

"My stomach is empty. We didn't have lunch, remember? In fact, all I've eaten since breakfast is a bit of scone and a few sips of tea, most of them nonpoisoned."

"Drink the ipecac, Nigel." She folded his hand around the bottle. "Do it for me, if not for you. I don't want to force you."

"You wouldn't dare."

"That's a poor choice of words to use with an Adams."

Nigel wavered. Was ipecac called for in the present circumstances? He wasn't sure. But how could one ignore Flick's beseeching countenance? Or her threatening stance?

"Well, I suppose a swig or two won't hurt," he said.

"Good!" To Nigel's surprise, she reached down and gave him a hug. "I have to make a phone call."

She was still talking on her telephone when Nigel returned from the bathroom—his throat dry, a fetid taste in his mouth—and lay down on her sofa. He closed his eyes. Flick sounded anxious enough for both of them; he might as well try to relax. Maybe even take a little nap.

A gentle stirring alongside the sofa changed Nigel's mind. He opened his eyes and found himself staring at a small red snout that was alarmingly close to his own nose.

"What happened to your doggy grin?" Nigel managed to croak. "You look worried about me, too." Cha-Cha leapt onto the sofa and curled into a reassuring furry ball at Nigel's feet.

Flick abruptly spoke from across the room. "Good news, Nigel. We're making definite progress."

He raised his head. Her formerly fearful voice now surged with determination.

I don't like the sound of that.

"I refuse to drink any more ipecac," he said. "I would rather let those mysterious green leaves do me in."

"You aren't going to die."

"Easy for you to say."

"My friend Cory Unger assures me you won't." She smiled. "In fact, he wants to talk to you."

"And Cory is—"

"A professor of toxicology at the University of Michigan who knows all about common plant poisons."

Flick pressed a button on her telephone to switch on the speaker. She moved the phone close to the edge of her desk.

"Nigel, say hello to Cory."

"Hello, Cory."

Cory's voice responded, "How do you feel, Nigel?"

"A lot worse than before I drank the ipecac—a form of torture that has been abandoned in England."

Cory laughed. "The trouble with plant poisons is that they can sneak up on you. Did you ever hear the story of the man who jumped off the Eiffel Tower? Halfway down he said, 'So far so good.' Some plant poisons are like that. You feel fine for a while—then *blammo!*" He added, "Emesis is still a recommended treatment here in the States."

"Emesis?"

"Throwing up. Particularly for the kind of poison you ingested."

Flick interrupted. "You guys talk. I'm going back to the laboratory to get something else for Nigel."

"I can't wait," Nigel said under his breath as he maneuvered himself upright into a sitting position on the sofa. Then he spoke more loudly into the telephone, "Cory, what exactly did I drink?"

"From Flick's description, I'm pretty sure that the tea she brewed was laced with *Nerium oleander* leaves. Brits call the plant 'rose bay'; we call it 'oleander' on this side of the pond."

"A tall shrub with long, slender leaves and pink or white flowers."

"That's the one. Oleander is an evergreen that's quite common throughout Europe and the United States. Most owners don't realize that every part of the plant is poisonous—leaves, twigs, seeds, sap, the works."

"Poison as in sick or poison as in dead?"

"The latter. Oleander poisoning is a popular method of suicide in Sri Lanka." His voice grew somber. "How much tea did you drink?"

"A couple of sips at the most. It tasted foul."

"Oleandrin is very bitter," Cory said. "That's the primary cardiac glycoside that makes oleander deadly. A sufficient dose will cause cardiac arrhythmia and eventually death."

"Thank you for sharing."

To Nigel's annoyance, Cory took the mild sarcasm as an invitation to continue his lecture. "Oleandrin is very powerful; a little goes a long way. Purportedly, the water in a vase used to hold a spray of oleander blooms will turn into a lethal solution. The most unusual oleandrin victims I've heard about were a group of campers who got sick when they used oleander twigs to hold hot dogs over an open fire."

Nigel shook his head reproachfully, even though Cory couldn't see his gesture. American boffins were just like British boffins. Give them a chance to talk about science and off they went, gleefully forgetting whom they were talking to. *He* was the one who swallowed the blasted stuff; *he* was the one who had been poisoned. "Very encouraging," he said glumly. "How much longer do I have?"

"Don't sweat it, Nigel. Although a single oleander leaf contains enough oleandrin to poison a child, it takes a lot more to kill a healthy adult like you."

Nigel looked up as he heard Flick's footsteps. She came into the room carrying a drinking glass filled with something black.

"Crikey!" he said. "Now you want me to drink motor oil."

Flick handed the glass to Nigel. "This is activated charcoal mixed with water."

Cory's voice boomed out of the speaker, "Highly recommended, Nigel. Activated charcoal slurry is used routinely for gastrointestinal decontamination. It will sop up any poison still left in your system."

Nigel gazed into the glass. He could say no, but Cory seemed to know what he was talking about. And Flick, hovering next to the sofa, looked as if she might pour the potion down his throat if he refused.

"Do I have to drink it now?" Nigel winced at his own whininess.

"Bottoms up," Flick said. "Charcoal is odorless and tasteless."

"And utterly unappetizing." Nigel took a deep breath. "When I get my hands on the person who poisoned your tea. . ." He shut his eyes and glugged down the charcoal.

"That wasn't so bad, was it?" Flick asked hopefully.

"A tad like knocking back the contents of an ashtray," Nigel spoke to the telephone. "What happens now, Professor?"

"You lead a long and happy life," Cory replied. "I doubt that you consumed enough oleandrin to do real harm, and the charcoal should take care of the little that made its way past your stomach."

Nigel realized, with agreeable surprise, that the activated charcoal promptly had removed the miserable taste from his mouth. Moreover, it seemed hard at work settling his innards. He suddenly felt hungry. While Flick said her good-byes to Cory Unger, Nigel went to the candy dish she kept on her credenza and helped himself to a handful of gummy bears.

When she rang off, Nigel said, "I really do feel much better. Thank you for the charcoal—and even the ipecac."

Flick sat down on the sofa and gave a grudging nod. Nigel noted that her expression had changed. Instead of anxious, she now looked sorrowful.

"Knees up, Mother Adams!" he said cheerfully. "I am

perfectly okay. You heard the professor. No real damage done. Anyway, what happened is not your fault. You didn't try to kill me. You shouldn't blame yourself because we have a deranged, but considerate, poisoner loose in the museum."

Flick glanced at him. "Considerate? In what way?"

"Sabotaging your private stash of tea was akin to poisoning Elspeth's personal jam pot. As you observed yesterday, there was little chance that anyone else would sample the goods." He allowed a flicker of amusement to cross his face. "Of course, even the most carefully planned nefarious schemes sometimes go awry."

Flick heaved a sigh. "I think the poisoned tea may have been more of a warning rather than an actual attempt to kill me."

"A warning? The poison was real, was it not?"

"Absolutely real—that's what got me thinking. The 'deranged poisoner,' to use your apt description, knows that most poisons are bitter. And so, he—or she—used lingonberry preserves to camouflage the barbiturates that killed Elspeth. But the poisoner didn't do anything to mask the taste of the oleandrin."

Nigel pondered for a moment. "I take your point. Unsweetened tea makes a poor disguise for oleander leaves."

She nodded. "Especially when drunk by a fairly experienced tea taster. I was bound to realize that the Assam was tainted the instant I tasted the brewed tea. What's more, the bright green specks of leaf are easy to spot. I should have seen them when I scooped the dry tea out of the canister."

"Then why do it? Why poison your tea?"

Flick hugged her arms around herself. "To frighten me, I think. To encourage me to leave the museum. It would simplify the poisoner's life if I simply up and quit. Another body in the boardroom might raise suspicions." She half-smiled.

"Not even the Kent police would ignore two related deaths so close together in time."

Nigel pondered again. Flick was probably right. He, an inexperienced tea drinker, had eventually realized that something was amiss with the Assam. She would have diagnosed the added "flavor" instantly. And the notion of the poisoner trying to frighten Flick away made sense, too. It would probably seem an easy task to accomplish after the impromptu trustee meeting. A threat in the form of oleander leaves might well convince Flick that she was far out on a limb all by herself, that it was time to leave the museum.

"I say again," he said, "you shouldn't blame yourself. It's time to shed your unhappy face."

Flick looked away from Nigel. "There's a chance that I might have prevented what happened to you if I had told the police—and the trustees—everything I know. I held back a piece of important information. Something that might have changed people's minds. Something that might have sent the poisoner fleeing for places unknown."

"I see." Nigel looked away from Flick. Her admission had had the curious effect of making him wonder exactly the same thing. Had his decision to suppress the words Elspeth spoke in his office emboldened the murderer? The time was ripe to share his uncertain knowledge with Flick.

I will. As soon as she shares her secret with me.

Flick sighed deeply again. "Most people at the museum thought of Elspeth Hawker as a dotty old lady—an eccentric dilettante who had fun pretending to be an expert on the Hawker antiquities. The other day, Dorothy McAndrews described Elspeth's knowledge as a mile wide but only an inch deep." Temper flared on Flick's face. "That isn't true. Elspeth had a better eye than the professional antiquers who often wander through our galleries. She discovered an ongoing campaign of theft at the museum."

"You explained all that to the Kent police and to the trustees."

She nodded. "But I chose not to tell them that Elspeth had thoroughly documented her discoveries—and her suspicions—in a notebook she carefully hid in the Hawker Suite." Flick's expression became rueful. "I found the notebook. I used it to identify nineteen antiquities in the Hawker collection that have been replaced by excellent forgeries."

"Blimey!" Nigel said. Without thinking, he added, "An exceedingly clever thief, just like Elspeth thought."

Flick began to say something, then hesitated. "Who told you that about Elspeth? It's not something I ever said."

"We were talking about the good woman's notebook," Nigel said quickly. "Where is it?"

Flick gestured toward her credenza. "Sitting in the bottom of my electric teakettle."

Nigel laughed. "An excellent hiding place. Your tea has an amazing ability to defend itself."

"That's the second joke you've made today that isn't funny, Nigel."

"Actually, Flick, I find it quite funny."

Flick removed Elspeth's little black notebook from its protective plastic bag and handed it to Nigel.

"Elspeth wrote in a kind of code," she said. "But it's quite intuitive."

Flick was sitting behind her desk, Nigel in the visitor's chair alongside it. She practiced reading upside down while he skimmed the notebook's pages and asked occasional questions.

"I assume that *Mos.* means mosaic," he said, "and *Mkgs.* means markings, and *Ptn.* means pattern."

"Correct."

"Then what is *Pat.*?"

"Patina. The slight color change as wood and varnish get older."

"Of course. How foolish of me. *T.W.* must mean Tunbridge Wells?"

"Not quite," she said. "*T.W.* is Elspeth's abbreviation for Tunbridge Ware." She touched the open page. "Most important of all, a big red *F* means fake or forgery. There are fifteen *F*s in the book."

"How did she identify the objects as fakes?"

"Through a simple process of comparison. Look at page three." Flick paused while Nigel turned pages. "I've gotten to know that piece of Tunbridge Ware by heart. It's one of the tea caddies I showed you when we toured the museum the other day—part of the 'All the Teas in China' set of eighteen."

Nigel's eyebrows rose slightly as he studied the cryptic abbreviations. "Okay, *T.W.* stands for Tunbridge Ware. Hunan must be the tea-growing region in China the caddy memorializes. And *R.R.* is short for. . .*what*?"

"Robert Russell, one of the great makers of Tunbridge Ware."

"The words seem to make sense, but what do the odd numbers mean? I can't imagine what this notation signifies." Nigel pointed to the page on which Elspeth had written "*Pat.* 40% à 70%."

"The percentages are the keys to Elspeth's observations," Flick said. "She noted that the Hunan caddy's patina mysteriously deepened. It used to have a light patina, a level she called 40 percent. But the object on display now has a some-what richer patina. Elspeth awarded it a grade of 70 percent."

"Very clever—if she had a good eye for old wood."

"She identified other points of comparison, too."

"Such as this one," Nigel responded, pointing to a line that read, "*Mos. Constsy.* 100% à 80%."

"It took me a day to figure out that one. Elspeth was an am-ateur in one sense—she invented her own descriptive language. I believe that *Mos. Constsy.* refers to the visible consistency among the various mosaics on the caddy. The originals were masterpieces; a single craftsman used perfectly matched woods to make the mosaics. They depicted different images but were identical otherwise—sort of like different photographs taken with the same camera and same film by one photographer."

"Thus the consistency of the mosaics is 100 percent."

"But not anymore. Elspeth detected minute variations among the mosaics on the Hunan caddy. She rated the Hunan caddy's consistency at only 80 percent."

"Again, the question must be asked, Did she have that good an eye?"

"For the specific details she cared about—*yes!* These were pieces she loved, objects she looked at again and again. El-speth didn't use the language of a professional appraiser, and she may not have appreciated the most important features of each antiquity, but she was certainly able to notice minor dif-ferences in color, patina, or texture when they unexpectedly appeared. Those are the kinds of variations she recorded in her black book. It's not much different than a mother jotting down the little changes she notices in a child."

"I suppose that makes sense." He turned several pages, then pushed the book aside. "You say the forgeries are really good?"

"I've identified every item Elspeth identified as a sham. The entire 'All the Teas in China' collection—eighteen tea caddies—has been replaced with counterfeit Tunbridge Ware boxes. They are excellent fakes. I suspect they would fool most appraisers. But not Elspeth. The Hunan tea caddy makes a good illustration. When I examined the piece carefully, I realized that different woods had been used to depict the sky in several adjacent mosaics. They were close in grain and color, but not identical. Such a thing would not have been done when the set was created in the late 1860s. It's clearly a reproduction."

"What is the nineteenth forgery—a Tunbridge Ware sugar bowl?"

"No. The last item breaks the pattern. It's a miniature Japanese tea chest. It looks authentic from a distance, but when you get close, it isn't."

Nigel nodded sagely. "Now I understand the question you asked Jeremy Strain: Was Elspeth concerned about the authenticity of the Hawker antiquities when she visited him at the Hawker Foundation?"

"Don't remind me. The twit bit my head off." Flick switched to a stuffy English accent. "One surely knows the difference between ownership and authenticity."

"Well done, old chap." Nigel grinned his approval.

Flick leaned back in her chair. "You know, I still wonder what Elspeth had in mind when she waylaid Jeremy Strain. Desmond Hawker assembled the family's collection of antiquities in the nineteenth century. Any questions about how he acquired specific items must have been resolved more than a hundred years ago."

"Perhaps Elspeth really was a dotty old darling? Everyone associated with this museum seems a scone short of a tea party. Even our local antiquities thief." His expression grew serious. "Look, I'm certainly not an art expert, so maybe this is a nonsensical question. Why would anyone go to the trouble of faking wooden boxes?"

"Because they are exceptionally valuable wooden boxes. The full set is worth at least a half million pounds."

"But think of the vast expense involved in making those brilliant forgeries. One would have to replicate skills that disappeared more than a hundred years ago. From a business perspective, a simple matter of pounds and pence, it seems a poor investment. I can understand faking Rembrandts or Van Goghs—they generate astronomical profits—but not Tunbridge Ware tea caddies."

"Nonetheless, one of the trustees did just that." Flick slid the black notebook back in front of Nigel. "Look at the very last page."

He picked up the book and lifted the back cover. "Good heavens! Is this what I think it is?"

"Elspeth compiled a list of thievery suspects."

Nigel whistled softly. "Seven trustees plus Conan Davies. I'm delighted not to see my name on offer. Or yours."

"The thefts began before you or I arrived at the museum." Flick waited for Nigel to set down the notebook. "Notice that she drew lines through two names."

"Vicar de Rudd and Simon Clowes. She seems to have eliminated them as suspects."

"So have I. The vicar didn't have an opportunity to poison Elspeth, and the doctor had access to much more convenient means to kill her."

"Who am I to disagree?" Nigel said. "That leaves a total of six. Archibald Meicklejohn, megabanker; Marjorie Halifax, political powerhouse; Dorothy McAndrews, queen of antiques; Matthew Eaton, landscaper extraordinaire; Iona Saxby, superlawyer; and Conan Davies, security wizard." He made a grimace. "One of them, with malice aforethought, poisoned Elspeth's lingonberry preserves, doctòred your Assam tea, and stole a half million pounds' worth of antiquities."

"Any thoughts as to which one?"

Nigel gave a slight shrug. "Well, I cannot envision Conan nicking antique wooden boxes."

"Me neither. I keep him on the list for only one reason: He has an essential resource that the others don't. Conan knows the code to disable the museum's security system, and his thumbprint will turn off the motion detectors. He probably also knows how to erase the electronic logs that keep track of who enters or leaves after hours."

Nigel sat up straight. "I forgot about our alarm system."

"Same here," Flick said briskly, "until that merry MI5 man got me thinking. Somehow the trustee in question has managed to bypass it repeatedly."

"We really do have an *exceedingly* clever thief."

Flick fixed a frosty gaze on Nigel. She had thought the phrase odd when he spoke it earlier. Now he had said the same thing again in an even more ominous tone.

Nigel peered back at her. His mouth pulled into an awkward grin as he went on. "Those are not my words, by the way. I have a confession to make. Two hours before she died, Elspeth Hawker told me that we have an exceedingly clever thief in our midst."

Flick had been expecting some sort of surprise from Nigel, but not a bombshell that would take her breath away. Her mind filled with a muddle of unpleasant memories and unanswered questions that were swiftly overwhelmed by the compelling feeling that she had been betrayed. When she saw him shrink back in his chair, Flick realized she was glaring venomously at Nigel.

"Feel free to shout at me," he said. "Shouting will make you feel better."

"You bet I'll shout at you! Why didn't you say anything on the day Elspeth died? If someone is murdered a short time after they reveal a crime to you, don't you think that's a trifle suspicious?"

Nigel tried to say something, but Flick cut him off. "I know the answer, you ninny! You believed the doctor, not me."

"Of course, I believed Sir Simon," Nigel said calmly. "The man's credentials are impeccable. I also *wanted* to believe him. It seemed inconceivable that one of our trustees could be a murderer. I made a mistake. I apologize."

"Okay—forget about the day Elspeth died. Why didn't you back me up when the police interviewed me or when the trustees put me through the wringer?"

"I admit that I might have intervened—but to what effect? Would the police or the trustees have believed my late-breaking story?"

Flick gritted her teeth. She silently counted to ten before she said evenly, "Nigel, two accounts that support each other are far more convincing than one unsupported narrative." She added in a much louder voice, "Everybody knows that!"

Nigel seemed cowed, in no mood to argue. He merely clasped his hands together and allowed her to guide their conversation.

"Tell me what Elspeth said to you," she said. "Start from the beginning."

"That would be shortly before noon on the day of the fateful trustees' meeting. Elspeth came into my office. She announced her intention to speak after the formal agenda was over. She also requested that I say nothing to the other trustees."

"Why not?"

"The very question I asked Elspeth. She hemmed and hawed awhile, but then told me that she had discovered an exceedingly clever thief at work in the museum. She planned to reveal the details at the meeting. I suppose she wanted to keep the element of surprise."

Nigel seemed to hesitate.

"Keep going," Flick said with determination.

He sighed. "The rest of what she told me doesn't make any sense, although I have rehearsed it in my mind again and again. I asked her straight out: Is one of our trustees a criminal? Instead of answering, she sailed off on a weird tangent. She said she led a life of luxury and was surprised that people paid for evil with evil. Then she spouted a verse from the Bible I had never heard before. Something about justice being done to a criminal." He glanced unhappily at Flick. "End of a not-very-exciting story."

Flick looked out her window at a large flock of small black birds that swerved back and forth above the car park. Perhaps they were taking a vote on whether to fly south for the winter. Flick needed a moment to think, to decide which parts of Nigel's "story" she could believe. Her uncle the detective often said that senior executives make lousy witnesses because they never pay attention to the little details. Nigel Owen provided a fine example. Elspeth Hawker took her Christianity seriously. She often spoke verses from Proverbs or Psalms to Flick during their jaunts through the museum. But whenever Elspeth quoted the Bible, it was to illuminate a specific point, to convey a particular concept. Relevant verses came naturally to her because daily Bible reading had been a habit most of her life.

We need to know the verse she "spouted" to Nigel.

Flick looked back at Nigel. The melancholy expression

on his face seemed real enough.

"Am I forgiven?" he asked. "Before you answer, let me remind you that a mere twenty minutes ago you were begging my forgiveness for placing me at death's door with a cup of dodgy tea."

Flick managed not to laugh but couldn't help smiling. It was difficult to stay angry at Nigel Owen. He smiled back.

"Truce?" he asked.

"Truce," she said. "We have no choice but to forgive each other and work together. If we don't find out who murdered Elspeth Hawker, no one else will."

"I thought you might say that."

"Do you agree with me?"

"In theory—although I am a festival of opposing emotions."

"On the one hand. . . ," Flick offered.

"On the one hand, to coin a phrase—once poisoned, twice shy. If we move forward, we will put ourselves at risk, yet what can we really hope to accomplish? Our evidence is patchy and incomplete. We have your interpretation of Elspeth's death, a desktop covered with contaminated tea leaves, and a notebook full of questionable observations made by an old lady. Elspeth's notebook is tangible evidence, but what does it really signify? The Tunbridge Ware tea caddies have been on display for forty years. Even if an acknowledged expert declares them forgeries, we have no way of proving when the originals were actually replaced. You—and I—may accept Elspeth's opinions as valid. I doubt the rest of the world will."

"What about your other hand?" Flick asked.

"On the other hand, I am outraged that one of our overachieving trustees will likely get away with murder, not to mention a major antiquities theft, not to mention triggering a financial crisis at this museum, not to mention causing me to drink a bottle of ipecac."

Flick stared at Nigel. "Tell me that your 'other hand' wins."

"Hands down!"

"That's not funny, either."

Flick took advantage of the sudden lull in the conversation to rewrap Elspeth's black book and return it to the electric kettle.

When she had finished, Nigel said, "I'm hungry. In fact, I am starving. How about you?"

"Now that you mention it—"

"Don't laugh, but I am in the mood for a pizza."

Cha-Cha suddenly barked across the room.

"Pizza for three," Flick said.

"There's a pizzeria near the bottom of High Street, not far from the Pantiles. It is warm enough today that they might be serving alfresco. They make a brilliant *everything* pizza."

"I'll bring another bottle of ipecac."

"With a steaming cup of coffee, I should think," Nigel said, adding just a hint of a smirk. "I've had my fill of tea for a while."

Flick smirked back. *We'll see about that, Nigel.*

She was careful not to say it out loud.

TWELVE

Nigel stood on the steps outside the ornate front door of the Royal Tunbridge Wells Tea Museum and studied the stretch of Eridge Road that ran northeastward to the Pantiles. He pictured Flick Adams and Cha-Cha hurrying past the redbrick office building on Linden Park Road, striving to keep on schedule. If she had told him the truth the night before, then she should appear at the Neville Terrace roundabout within the next minute or so.

Let's see if she really is a slave to punctuality.

Flick had "confessed," if that was the right word, her addiction to being on time as they munched their way through a jumbo everything pizza that was nearly as large as the tiny table for two on the sidewalk in front of the pizzeria. Flick had gawked in mock horror as Nigel sprinkled a blizzard of hot pepper flakes on his first slice.

"I don't believe it," she had said. "Nigel Owen simply does not look like the sort of man who would enjoy red pepper. A splash of malt vinegar, perhaps, or a blob of Marmite, but nothing spicy enough to leave your tongue limp."

"Yum!" he said after he had finished half the slice. "That should give the activated charcoal something to think about."

"Once again you amaze me."

"Good! Now it's your turn. Tell me something peculiar about you that I don't know."

Flick took a bite of pizza and thought about it. "Well, one of my odder quirks is that I hate to be late for anything. I get to the airport at least two hours before every flight. I arrive at work at eight thirty sharp every morning. And when I'm invited to dinner, I usually show up five minutes early."

"Blimey, how many hostesses have you found in the shower?"

"I know it's silly, but I can't help it. It's my nature to be punctual."

Nigel nodded. "Which is why I find you at your seat in the boardroom, waiting for meetings to begin."

"And you always will."

After their alfresco supper, Nigel had strolled with Flick back to her apartment on the Pantiles's Lower Walk. She had taken Cha-Cha's lead, expressed regret yet again that her tea had nearly poisoned him, and agreed that first thing Monday morning she would give him a close-up tour of the sham Tunbridge Ware tea caddies.

"First thing in the morning" for Nigel was nine fifteen, occasionally nine thirty. But on that Monday, he had awakened outlandishly early and arrived at the museum at an unprecedented eight fifteen.

If eating peppers amazes her, this should knock her off her pins.

Nigel hoped that she would smile when she saw him that morning. There was something remarkably pleasing about

213

Flick's smile. And something delightful in the way her warm brown eyes seemed to glow more brightly. It would also be grand if she wore the same perfume she had on Sunday. He almost could remember the spicy scent of flowers as they walked side by side through the Pantiles.

Well, I'll be. . . There she is.

Nigel glanced at his watch. Flick had reached the roundabout at precisely 8:25. She was walking in her usual hurried stride, with Cha-Cha trotting alongside, his tail at a happy angle. Nigel scooted around the western corner of the museum before she could spot him. He ducked into the side entrance that the staffers used in the morning and waited patiently out of sight against the wall.

He pushed open the steel and glass door an instant before Flick reached for the handle.

"Eight thirty and all is well!" he said. "One can set one's clock by Felicity Adams."

Now, that's a pretty smile.

"Where did you come from?" she asked.

Her eyes are definitely gleaming.

"You are not the only early riser in Tunbridge Wells," he said dryly.

"And people say that the age of miracles is over."

Nigel stood aside to let Flick by. As she passed, he noticed that her heels were higher than usual, that her hair looked extra shiny, and that even a ubiquitous trench coat did a remarkable job of flattering her figure.

Flick let Cha-Cha off his lead. The Shiba Inu made a quick circle around Nigel, presumably to say hello, then took off for the Duchess of Bedford Tearoom. She handed Nigel the rewound lead and said, "I almost hate to give up Cha-Cha for the night. I like his company."

He watched her slip out of the trench coat. Instead of her usual skirt and blouse, she wore a stylish dress in a soft fabric that seemed to honor every curve of her body. Perhaps she intended to participate in the "Mad Hatter" research conference that afternoon.

The clatter of dog nails on marble tiles soon gave way to a friendly cacophony of squawks and yips in the distance.

"What a racket," Nigel said.

"Do you suppose they actually *like* each other?"

"I don't see why not. They lived together at Lion's Peak for several years." Nigel slipped the lead into his jacket pocket. "When I was a child, my cat Henry befriended a rabbit who lived in the woods behind our house. They were great pals."

"You had a cat named *Henry*?"

"A fine name for a fine cat." Nigel sniffed. "Anyway—every afternoon, a rather large brown and gray rabbit would appear at the hedge at the back of our garden. Henry would join the rabbit, and the pair went off for an hour or two."

"What was the rabbit's name?"

"Henry never told me."

"What did they do in the woods?"

"Commiserate about the sad decline of the English countryside, I should think."

They exchanged good mornings with the security guard sitting in the Welcome Centre kiosk in the middle of the ground floor, then climbed the stairs. As they neared the third floor, Flick asked, "What sort of cat was Henry?"

"Big, friendly, marmalade colored. Why do you ask?"

"Because no self-respecting American cat I know would make friends with a rabbit."

Nigel grinned. "Ah. Is that because Americans like to split hares?"

Flick groaned. "That's painful!"

"You can wreak revenge on me with a long, boring lecture about counterfeit Tunbridge Ware."

"You bet!" she said. "Give me ten minutes to read my e-mail and meet me in the Tea Antiquities Gallery."

Nigel went to his office. He checked his e-mail; nothing required his immediate response. Next, he played back the two voice messages stored in his telephone. The first was from Alain Rousseau's wife: The chef was on the mend, but wouldn't be back cooking before Thursday at the earliest. The second message was from Barrington Bleasdale: He would very much appreciate a "progress report" from the acting director.

Nigel shuddered as he put down the telephone. He had forgotten about the Hawker heirs and their pudgy solicitor. They would have to be told about the thefts *before* the collection was appraised. *How will they react*, he mused, *to finding themselves a half million pounds poorer?*

Definitely not well.

He walked downstairs to the first floor and found Flick waiting for him in the Tea Antiquities Gallery. She was kneeling on one knee, using a large magnifying lens to inspect a teak tea table inlaid with a map of India.

"Has Sherlock unearthed another fake?" he asked as he came up behind her.

"Completely real." She rose to her feet. "Although not especially valuable. Its sole claim to fame is that it was given to Desmond Hawker by an Indian maharaja as a token of his esteem." She gestured with the magnifying lens toward the far corner of the gallery. "There's our chief problem."

They moved to the octopus-like display rack that held the eighteen shoebox-sized tea caddies. Overhead, a sign proclaimed, ALL THE TEAS IN CHINA.

"Which one is the Hunan caddy?" he asked.

"The box in the middle of the display." Flick carefully lifted the Hunan caddy from the rack and set it down on the floor. She handed the magnifier to Nigel and said, "You look; I'll talk."

Nigel sat on the floor and examined the different mosaics on the top and sides of the box while Flick held forth on the thousands of individual pieces of wood in the mosaics. "In the nineteenth century," she said, "Tunbridge Ware makers routinely used 160 different woods to achieve the many different colors you can see in their mosaics."

Nigel thought the images fairly interesting. The mosaic on the top of the caddy was a landscape, presumably of Hunan, China. On one side, a scene of women picking tea leaves; on the other, a group of men drinking tea.

"Do you know how the original mosaics were made?" she asked.

"I haven't a clue."

"Thin strips of wood of different colors were glued together into a block. Then a slice of the block was cut to make a single 'line' of the mosaic. Many other blocks were required to complete the mosaic, each precisely assembled from different woods. It took enormous skill to plan the correct sequence of wood strips so that the finished mosaics would depict an image." She grimaced. "I don't know what technique was used to create these forgeries. Possibly some sort of computer-controlled machine."

Flick showed Nigel the minor variations in color, patina, or texture that Elspeth had identified. He found it difficult to concentrate on such trifling details. Flick, crouched on her knees next to him, was indeed wearing the same perfume as she had worn yesterday.

Think about the Tunbridge Ware.

217

"This box looks authentic to me," he said.

"I agree. It's a superb forgery." She added, "Although, take everything I say with a grain of salt. I'm not really an expert on Tunbridge Ware."

"You could have fooled me."

"I learned everything I know from Elspeth," she said with another smile.

Nigel's heart thumped. The combination of his proximity to Flick, her smile, and that incredible perfume was doing bizarre things to his composure. He jumped to his feet and said hoarsely, "How would one go about copying an authentic piece of Tunbridge Ware to make an imitation? The curators surely would have noticed if the original tea caddy had been missing for a while."

"A counterfeiter usually takes high-resolution photographs from many different angles, both inside and outside the object to be copied. The photos would be very much like the pictures we take in case we have to restore a damaged antiquity. A set of forty photographs probably would capture all the detail on a box of this size." Flick picked up the fake Hunan caddy and returned it to the display rack. "But to do that much picture taking, the thief would have to disable the museum's alarm system for the better part of an hour."

Nigel grunted. "We keep coming back to the security system. How did the thief get around it?"

They pondered in silence until Nigel said, "Where is the nineteenth fake?"

"Standing near the entrance to the gallery." Flick pointed at a squat cabinet with glass-paneled doors and several drawers. The piece sat atop a three-foot-high display pedestal that elevated its doors to the typical visitor's eye level.

Nigel moved to the object and read its descriptive sign

aloud. "Miniature Japanese *tansu* tea chest. Circa 1890. Made of cedar wood with turned cypress knobs. Twenty-four inches wide by thirty-five inches high by eleven inches deep. Collected by Desmond Hawker and donated by Mary Hawker Evans in 1968." He studied the chest a moment, then continued. "Interesting—but not the prettiest piece in the room."

"I agree, although Elspeth regarded the original as one of her favorites."

"Are we sure this is a fake? It looks real to me."

"Elspeth identified the mysterious disappearance of tool marks on the turned knobs and also changes in patina inside the cabinet."

Nigel peered through the glass-paneled doors and wondered if Elspeth could have been mistaken. To his admittedly unpracticed eye, the interior appeared wholly authentic. "How much was the original worth?"

"Eight thousand pounds at most. Frankly, I'm bewildered that a savvy antiquities thief would want to steal the original. There are many more valuable pieces in the gallery."

Nigel grunted again. "Counterfeiting this chest makes even less business sense than the tea caddies. The cost of replicating the original must have consumed all of the potential profits— maybe more."

He handed the magnifying lens to Flick. "I know I'm not the best of students. Thank you for being patient with me."

"Do you have time this morning to return the favor?"

"Absolutely. Would you like a scintillating lecture on the importance of operating profit as percentage of total annual turnover?"

Flick sniggered. The gallery abruptly seemed brighter to Nigel. He felt oddly self-conscious to be the object of her amusement.

"No, silly," she said. "What I had in mind is your help in searching the Hawker Suite. Maybe Elspeth hid something else of importance."

"I never asked you—where did you find the black notebook?"

"Taped to the underside of the old wooden side chair." Flick sighed. "I hope I didn't miss anything significant when I packed up her papers and belongings."

"I wouldn't think you did. Elspeth went to the trouble of hiding the notebook. She left her routine clobber—the possessions you retrieved from her desk and credenza—out in the open."

They climbed the stairs to the second floor.

Nigel went into the Hawker Suite first. The office was dark and smelled musty. He pulled back the draperies and opened a window. Flick stood in the doorway, slowly scanning the room, apparently engrossed by what she saw.

"A penny for your thoughts," he said.

"I'm trying to think like an eighty-four-year-old woman," she replied. "Where would she look for a hiding place?"

"It must have taken some effort to affix the notebook under the chair, but I can't envision Dame Elspeth crawling around on all fours. She was much more likely to do what you did, stash her secrets in a teakettle."

"Her electric kettle went back with the rest of her things—and yes, I did take the top off and look inside." She frowned. "I never thought about looking behind the drawers in her desk. She might have taped something to the desk frame."

Nigel strode to the desk and removed the empty drawers one at a time. "Nothing taped to the drawers themselves," he said, "and nothing inside the frame."

"You don't suppose there's a secret compartment behind

the built-in bookcase?"

Nigel laughed. "That is another cliché that Americans impose on Brits. You imagine that we have sliding panels and hidden passages in every building. However"—Nigel dutifully pounded the walls behind the empty shelves—"it sounds solid to me."

"I'm running out of ideas."

"I have one," Nigel said. "Let's look under the Oriental rug."

Nigel stood at one corner of the red, black, and gold carpet, Flick at the adjacent corner.

"One, two, three—lift!" he said. They rolled back the edge of the rug.

"Phew! A lot of dust, but no papers." Flick shook her head. "The other corners are pinned under furniture. No way Elspeth could have lifted them."

Flick dropped onto the small sofa in the suite. "I guess I found everything of Elspeth's the other day," she said.

Nigel moved toward her. "Now there is an easy-to-get-to hiding place we haven't searched. Under the sofa cushions."

Flick made a face. "Much too obvious. However. . ." She stood up and lifted the cushions. "Hey, there is something under here." She held up a flat black object that Nigel didn't recognize.

"It's a sleep mask," Flick said. "The sort of thing they hand out on airplanes at night."

"Why would Elspeth stash a sleep mask under a cush. . . ?" Nigel didn't need to finish his question. "Of course! Elspeth spent the occasional night in this office." He looked around the room. "There are no motion detectors on the ceiling, the suite has a private loo, she owned an electric kettle, and she had Cha-Cha to keep her company. Everything one needs for a cozy night at the museum."

"I agree it's possible. But what would be her purpose?"

"Don't ask me. You were her confidante." He gave an annoyed wave. "Perhaps she was trying to catch our exceedingly clever thief."

Nigel heard Flick gasp. He looked at her and felt a tremor of recognition pass between them. His offhand remark made perfect sense.

"You're right," Flick said in a breathy voice scarcely louder than a whisper. "In fact, she probably saw the thief at work. That's how she jumped from six suspects to one certainty. She came to the trustees' meeting ready to name the thief."

Nigel nodded. "I think you are bang on. She had a face full of determination when she stepped into my office."

Flick moved next to Nigel and stared into his eyes. "What did Elspeth say to you? I'm especially interested in the Bible verse she spoke. She knew her Bible backward and forward; she quoted the right verse for the occasion." She gripped his arm. "Nigel, it's important. Try to remember. The verse is one of the last things she said before she died."

"I told you yesterday," he said. "It was about justice being done to a criminal."

Flick seemed lost in thought. She scowled at him. "What kind of criminal? Elspeth used Bible verses in proper context. Could she have quoted a verse about a *thief*?"

"I suppose so. Does that make a difference?"

"A humongous difference!" Flick sounded positively merry. "Elspeth never used the computer in this office, but we will."

Nigel watched in silence while Flick sat down at the desk and turned on the computer that occupied one corner. "There are several sites on the Internet that let you search the Bible," she said. "All I have to do is find one."

He quietly shifted a visitor's chair so he could also see the monitor screen as Flick typed enthusiastically on the keyboard. After several unsuccessful tries, she said, "Bingo! Just what we're looking for. Now to enter T-H-I-E-F. . ."

Flick turned the monitor directly toward Nigel. "There are only twenty-three verses; start reading."

"Crikey!" he said. "It's the third one on the list. 'When a thief is caught he must pay back double.' " Nigel let himself grin. "I remember now. Elspeth spoke those words and then said, 'That rule is from the Bible.' But then she said that the rule shouldn't apply to a museum and she wanted to explain that to the other trustees."

Flick hesitated. "Gosh. That doesn't make much sense."

"Imagine how I felt listening to her illogical one-sided conversation. I couldn't fathom where she was going or why."

"Maybe the entire verse will give us more context."

Nigel peered at the screen and read aloud, "Exodus 22:7. 'If a man gives his neighbor silver or goods for safekeeping and they are stolen from the neighbor's house, the thief, if he is caught, must pay back double.' " He shrugged. "Still clear as mud."

"I have an idea. It's a long shot, but maybe it's worth a try. If Elspeth believed the verse important, maybe she discussed it with her pastor. Elspeth faithfully attended St. Stephen's."

Nigel barely managed not to roll his eyes. "Are you suggesting that we ask Vicar De Rudd?"

"Yes. He's a pleasant enough fellow, he's not on our list of suspects, and St. Stephen's Church is just on the other side of Tunbridge Wells."

Nigel barely managed not to groan. Visiting a long-winded vicar was low on his list of favorite things to do. "I suppose so," he said. "When?"

"I don't want to leave our academic conferees until the Mad Hatter's Tea Party is well underway. Giselle Logan can handle any crises at that point." She reflected a moment. "I'll meet you at, say, four thirty, in the car park."

"It's a date."

Nigel felt himself blush. He covered his awkward choice of words by quickly adding, "I shall call Vicar de Rudd and tell him we are coming."

"Wonderful!" Flick said. "See you later." Her smile had become brighter and more gracious than before.

How did she manage to do that?

Flick retied her trench coat's belt more tightly around her waist. Sunday afternoon had been gloriously warm and sunny; Monday afternoon finished bleak, damp, and chilly. "Welcome to England," she murmured as she let the museum's side door swing shut behind her.

She heard a roar to her left. Nigel's white BMW careened around the building and screeched to a stop. He jumped out, sprinted to the passenger door, and yanked the handle. "Allow me."

Flick climbed in and secured her seat belt. Nigel shut the door gently and dashed back around to the driver's seat.

"Thank you, Nigel," she said, hoping that her voice didn't carry too much surprise. Nigel was in fine fettle today—an agreeable extension of the unexpectedly good mood he had displayed the evening before at the pizzeria. Nigel had been a remarkably good sport, considering that she had accidentally poisoned him.

If Nigel was acting a bit silly today, so was she. There had been no reason for her to dress up this morning, even wearing her going-out shoes, other than the curious feeling that she should wear something special. Nigel probably didn't notice. After all, he dressed up every day in well-tailored suits that made him look distinguished and—she couldn't think of a better description—*hail-fellow-well-met*.

Nigel slid the gearshift into first, released the clutch, and made a U-turn in the car park. "How did the 'Mad Hatter' conference go?" he asked.

"Swimmingly! Your scones and tarts earned rave reviews at the tea party."

"Did our conferees successfully advance the state of societal metaphors?"

Flick chuckled. "I listened to one of the presentations. It examined why so many social activities in England begin with the serving of tea."

"And the reason is. . . ?"

"The tea party provides a uniquely English mechanism for people to interact and communicate. Thus, Alice felt free to communicate openly with the Mad Hatter and the White Rabbit and to exchange information in a peaceful, nonconfrontational setting."

"I've said it before—bah humbug!" Nigel tromped on the accelerator.

Flick did not enjoy driving or being driven through Tunbridge Wells's town centre. Nigel seemed to relish the challenge. He charged into the heavy flow of late-afternoon traffic crawling along Eridge Road.

"I chatted with the vicar, as promised," Nigel said, glancing at Flick. "He sounded happy that we wanted to visit him."

Flick needed all her willpower not to shout *"Don't talk! And keep your eyes on the road!"* It didn't help matters that the sun had set and the dazzling headlights of the oncoming traffic made her squint repeatedly.

Nigel zipped around a lorry lumbering in low gear and veered around several parked cars, coming perilously close to oncoming traffic.

Flick shut her eyes. Anyone driving like Nigel in York, Pennsylvania, would be sentenced to years in prison. In England everyone seemed to drive the same way.

"Were Elspeth and Vicar de Rudd good friends?" Nigel asked. "I never had the impression that they were. Of course, I have seen them together only at trustee meetings."

Nigel turned onto a two-lane road lined with tall trees that were busy dropping their leaves. The houses along the road were fewer and larger; many were hidden behind high hedgerows. In Pennsylvania, a road like this would be a quiet scenic lane. In Kent, it was a busy thoroughfare. Flick tightened her seat belt as Nigel revved the engine and the car shot forward.

"We're almost there," Nigel said. "Have you thought about what we are going to say to the vicar? He probably is tired of hearing you allege that one of his fellow trustees poisoned Elspeth."

"Very funny. However, *you* can tell him that Elspeth wanted to share a Bible verse with the other trustees but never got the chance. Say that you are curious about what she might have had in mind. Repeat the verse, but leave out the part about an exceedingly clever thief in our midst."

Nigel downshifted and passed a slow-moving bus. "Good! That's more or less the truth. I wasn't looking forward to lying to a vicar."

Flick squeaked out a laugh. "And here I thought you had lost your boyish faith."

"Oh, I still believe in God. I just don't do much about it."

"Same with me. I stopped going to church when I went off to college. Well, except for Christmas and Easter. I love the music."

"*Hmmm.* Me, too." He grinned at her. "Do you still remember the prayers you used to say when you were a kid?"

"I came close to praying yesterday when I thought you were poisoned."

"You were going to pray for me?"

Flick laughed. "Actually, I intended to pray for wisdom. For me."

The vicarage of St. Stephen's Church was on the north side of Pembury Road, opposite Dunorlan Park. Nigel steered the BMW into the vicarage driveway and parked next to the gray stone building. He seemed to anticipate her next question.

"It's made of some sort of limestone, I believe," he said. "If we get the chance, let's ask the vicar."

Nigel worked the large brass doorknocker.

"Don't you recognize what that is?" Flick asked excitedly. "It's a miniature tea clipper. How did it end up way out here?"

The door opened. Vicar de Rudd smiled and said, "Welcome to St. Stephen's."

Flick and Nigel followed the vicar—a man of her height but significantly larger girth—into a small parlor full of friendly looking overstuffed furniture. He guided them to two comfortable wing chairs and said, "I have a pot of tea brewing in the kitchen. How would everyone like a good cuppa?"

Flick said, "I'd love one." She expected Nigel to decline, but he nodded graciously. "Me, too."

"I'll be back in half a tick." The vicar suddenly stopped in the doorway. "Would anyone care for a biscuit? Elsie, my housekeeper, bakes the best shortbread in the realm."

"Please!" Flick said.

"Indeed!" added Nigel.

It wasn't long before Flick heard the vicar's footsteps on the wooden floor and the rattle of teacups on a tray. He set the tray on a small table and sat down opposite them. The vicar winked at Nigel. "If our museum *mother* doesn't object, I shall be mother at the vicarage."

Flick had heard the metaphor many times during her stay in England; one of these days she would have to ask for clarification. Was pouring tea while other members of the family looked on an inevitable responsibility of British motherhood? And why did the museum's trustees find great pleasure in repeatedly reminding Nigel that he was "mother" at their meetings?

Flick took a sip. She recognized the tea immediately. A good quality Ceylon, brewed strong enough to support a teaspoon.

"Very nice," she said. She took a bite of the shortbread biscuit.

What we call a butter cookie back in Pennsylvania.

Vicar de Rudd leaned back in his chair. "Now, to what do I owe the pleasure of this unexpected visit?"

Flick gave Nigel a "go ahead" nod. He cleared his throat and said, "Vicar, we have a bit of a biblical mystery that we hope you can solve."

She watched a grin creep across de Rudd's normally somber countenance. "You have come to the right place. I earn my daily bread helping people appreciate the Bible. Please go on."

"As you know," Nigel said, "Dame Elspeth visited me a few hours before she died."

The vicar nodded. "She wanted to speak briefly at the end of the trustee meeting. She asked you to arrange it."

"Yes. However, Dame Elspeth also said something curious to me—something that I have been wondering about ever since. She apparently planned to share a Bible verse with the trustees—a brief passage from Exodus. 'The thief, if he is caught, must pay back double.' Would you have any idea of the significance of that verse to Elspeth Hawker?"

Vicar de Rudd burst into laughter—a deep, rumbling belly laugh that Flick could not resist. She began to laugh along with the vicar, and so did Nigel. When everyone had stopped laughing, the vicar stood up and said, "Follow me, and all will be made clear."

Flashlight in hand, he led them out of the vicarage, along a narrow macadam pathway that wound through trees and brought them to the back of a shadowy stone structure that Flick could not make out in the dark.

"Wait here while I turn on the lights."

The vicar entered a rear door. A few seconds later, Flick had to shield her eyes with her hand as the area seemed to explode with light. Eight banks of floodlights—four in the ground, four hidden on the church—made St. Stephen's Church glow like a theme-park castle.

The vicar returned quickly, his face still beaming.

"Let me tell you about St. Stephen's," he said. "Our church accommodates two hundred worshippers. It was built late in the nineteenth century, but in the style of a fourteenth-century kirk. The primary building material is Kentish ragstone, a hard gray limestone from a local quarry. The vicarage also is made of ragstone. The dressings—the *trim*, if you prefer—are bathstone, a different kind of limestone that has a textured, open grain. The roof is made of tile. The cost to acquire the land and build the church was six thousand pounds."

Flick couldn't understand why this information was significant, but Vicar de Rudd seemed to be having such fun conveying it that she couldn't help smiling and nodding as he spoke.

The vicar led them to the front of the church and pushed open the front door. "Next, I direct your attention to the bronze tablet on the wall, just beyond the door." He used his flashlight to light up the tablet.

Flick read the inscription. *The Cornerstone of St. Stephen's Church Was Laid by Commodore Desmond Hawker on the Sixteenth Day of September, Anno Domini 1897. This Church Was Consecrated the Thirtieth Day of August, Anno Domini 1899.* And then at the bottom of the bronze plate: *St. Stephen's Church is the gift of a thief who made every effort to pay back double.*

She fought to keep the emotion she felt out of her voice. "Desmond Hawker paid for this church," she said calmly.

"And why not?" The vicar waved vaguely at Pembury Road. "We are scarcely a mile away from Lion's Peak. Desmond Hawker saw the need for a church close to his home, so he bought one. Six thousand pounds was nothing to a man of his means."

Flick thought she heard criticism in the vicar's tone. Did he disapprove of Desmond's wealth? Or did he dislike the outward haughtiness of a man who could decide one day to build a church where and when he wanted one—and even put a tea-clipper-shaped knocker on the vicarage door?

She took a step backward and nearly fell against Nigel, who had moved behind her to get closer to the tablet. He held her in his arms for a moment. When she looked up at him, she saw a startled-little-boy expression that made her smile.

The vicar went on. "The words that Elspeth spoke to Nigel are from Exodus 22:7. By all reckoning, that verse was Desmond Hawker's favorite Bible passage and became the equivalent of a family motto in his later years. I suspect that the verse became equally significant to Dame Elspeth as she approached the end of her life, although I can't begin to guess her reasons for sharing it with the board of trustees."

Flick reached out and touched the raised bronze letters on the tablet. "Why do you suppose Desmond considered that verse so important?"

The vicar began his reply with a slight shrug. "One need not look far to find an answer. As Desmond grew older, he undoubtedly came to understand the depth of the sins he had committed earlier during his life. He felt a strong need to repent and undo the damage he had done through a campaign of good works." The vicar sighed. "Hardly a unique story. Many powerful men have tried to buy their way into heaven."

Flick exchanged glances with Nigel. He didn't accept the vicar's "obvious" explanation, either. Desmond had called himself a thief, not merely a sinner. There had to be more behind Desmond's selection of that specific verse from Exodus and the way he modified it. Desmond's motives—whether he really had some scheme to put himself right with God—mattered less than his curious choice of words. If they could decipher what Desmond wanted to say, maybe they also could understand why Elspeth chose to speak similar words to describe a systematic theft at the museum.

Flick struggled to invent a reasonable pretext on the fly.

"Frankly, I am astonished," she said. "I thought I knew most of Desmond Hawker's life story, but you have introduced me to an entirely new chapter. St. Stephen's Church was obviously important to Desmond, yet we don't have a single mention of it at the museum. We must correct that oversight quickly."

The vicar stared at Flick, his eyebrows raised. "As chief curator, you know best, yet I can't imagine that visitors to a tea museum would care about a small country church that Desmond Hawker established. The world knows that the commodore performed the lion's share of his good works when he created the Hawker Foundation."

Flick ignored the vicar's mild rebuke. "Whom might I talk to if I want to learn more about Desmond Hawker's decision to build St. Stephen's?"

"The only person who might be able to answer such a question is Nathalie Stubbings. She was our church historian for many years. Nathalie is quite elderly now, of course, but still sharp-witted as ever. She lives with her son in London, in St. Johns Wood."

"Perhaps I will pay her a visit," Flick said, as if she had not yet decided. In fact, her racing mind had all but finished planning a trip to London.

THIRTEEN

Nigel perused the map the next morning. If they left Tunbridge Wells at eleven thirty, it should take no more than ninety minutes to reach Abercorn Place in St. Johns Wood, an upscale neighborhood close to the western boundary of London's congestion zone. The simple fact of Abercorn Place's location posed an interesting dilemma: Should he invest five pounds, pay the outrageous congestion tax, and drive through central London? Or would it be more sensible to take a more circuitous route and skirt the congestion zone entirely?

Have some fun. Enjoy your unnecessary afternoon away from the office.

Nigel rehashed the convoluted purpose of their journey. Because Flick thought it important to know why Elspeth had quoted a pithy Bible verse, she insisted on visiting the elderly woman who lived on Abercorn Place in the hope that she would explain why Desmond Hawker had chosen the same verse as a kind of personal motto. The instant Flick had reached the BMW, she used her cell phone to call Nathalie Stubbings. The pair had chatted for most of the trip from St. Stephen's vicarage back to Tunbridge Wells.

Flick had rung off with a huge smile on her face. "Mrs. Stubbings is eager to see us tomorrow afternoon. We are to call her Nathalie. She is a retired schoolteacher and a widow who lives with her son, Marcus. She's seventy-nine years old. She grew up in Brighton, not far from the Pavilion. She says it's been a dog's year since anyone has asked her about St. Stephen's Church. She often went to church with Elspeth Hawker. She considers Commodore Hawker a fascinating character and will be happy to tell us everything she knows about him."

"Even if she has to make everything up on the fly," Nigel had muttered.

"What?"

"Nothing," he had replied. Nigel's mother had a flock of elderly friends with little useful to say, who also loved to talk to strangers.

We're probably on a fool's errand.

Vicar de Rudd had provided the woman's address. "I have never been there," he had said, "but I have been told the flat is quite lovely. Keep in mind when you visit Nathalie Stubbings that she is—as we are encouraged to say these days—*mobility challenged*. She may offer more hospitality than she is able to provide. And go with my blessings. I may not understand your interest in these matters, but I pray that your questions are answered."

Nigel returned to his map. He couldn't remember the last time he had followed Regent Street through Piccadilly Circus. He thought of other familiar streets on the direct route: Portland Place, Marylebone Road, Baker Street, Park Place, and Wellington Road. After six months in Tunbridge Wells, he thought a drive through London seemed likely to recharge his batteries. And because Flick Adams was a dyed-in-the-wool Anglophile, the cross-London route undoubtedly would amuse her, too.

Nigel fired up his computer and entered his user name and personal identification number to pay the congestion tax online. Now the various TV cameras that watched license plates go by would know he had paid dearly for the privilege of driving through his favorite city.

That morning, Nigel had filled the BMW's petrol tank. Now, at nearly eleven thirty, he looked out his window at the steady drizzle. He definitely would need his raincoat today and also his umbrella, should he not find a car park close to Nathalie Stubbings's flat.

"Have you been to London before, Cha-Cha?" he asked. The dog, curled up on Nigel's sofa, immediately lifted his head. "You must be on your best behavior today or else I will stash you in Dame Elspeth's canvas bag for the duration of our trip. *Wakarimashita ka?*" Nigel had visited a "Learn Japanese" Web site and found the phrase for "Did you understand?" Cha-Cha let his head drop between his paws.

On his way out of the museum, Nigel stopped at the Duchess of Bedford Tearoom. Giselle Logan had arranged for the substitute chef to prepare two box lunches. "You have roast beef sandwiches, cookies, and cold tea," she said. "However, Flick picked up the boxes about five minutes ago. I think she's waiting for you outside."

Nigel looked at his wristwatch. Eleven twenty-nine. Thank goodness he wasn't late.

He found Flick standing under the awning just outside the side door. She smiled when she saw him and handed him a flask. "Strong coffee. I brewed it myself in the Conservation Laboratory."

"In that case," he said, "wait here; I'll get the car."

"Don't be silly. I won't melt in the rain."

Nigel watched Flick run toward the private car park. She really did look lovely in motion. He had to sprint to catch up with her. He worked the remote control to unlock the BMW's doors a moment before she reached the car.

He had been overly optimistic. The combination of heavy traffic and determined rain conspired to add twenty minutes to their forty-five-mile journey. As modest compensation, Nigel had found a car park only one long block away from Abercorn Place. At one twenty, a smiling, silver-haired woman scarcely five feet tall admitted them to Marcus Stubbings's fifth-floor flat. The woman walked with the aid of two aluminum canes.

"You must be Felicity," she said to Flick. "I am afraid that I have forgotten your colleague's name."

"Nathalie, this is Nigel Owen."

"Of course—Nigel! May I offer you both a cup of tea? You must be tired after your drive."

"Yes," Flick said, "but only if you let me help you make it."

"Too late. It is all made. But I will be happy to let you carry it to my room." Nathalie used her right cane as a pointer. Flick went off to the kitchen.

Nigel raised the lead in his hand. "I hope you don't mind, but we didn't want to leave the dog in the car."

Nathalie smiled. "Cha-Cha has been here before," she said.

Nigel didn't get a chance to pursue Nathalie's statement because she turned and moved haltingly across the flat's foyer toward a short hallway. Nigel followed slowly. She led him into a room that surely had been furnished one piece at a time, with a mélange of furniture from different eras. Nigel recognized a sofa table from the 1950s, a settee from a hundred years earlier, a rolltop desk from the 1920s, a canopied bed that Jane Eyre might have owned, a new telly on a stainless-steel stand, and a hodgepodge of chairs that spanned three centuries. The floor was covered by a large Oriental carpet, full of browns and reds, that had been worn bare in a few spots. Placed around the room were dozens of framed photographs, most black and white, many of a man who must have been Nathalie's late husband. One photo, in an antique silver frame, was of a woman Nigel had seen before. He needed several second looks to recognize a younger Elspeth Hawker. Probably at age sixty or so.

"Of course you knew Dame Elspeth from the Royal Tunbridge Wells Tea Museum," Nathalie said to Nigel. "She was quite striking twenty years ago, wasn't she?"

"Indeed. Did you know her well?"

"Oh my, yes. We were friends for many years. It nearly broke my heart when my doctor forbade me to travel to Elspeth's funeral."

Flick came in quietly, carrying a tray, her eyes gleaming. Nigel realized that she had heard Nathalie's answer and was eager to ask an obvious follow-up question.

We made the trip—I might as well do it.

Nigel said, "May I ask how you and Elspeth became friends?"

Nathalie sat down in a straight-back chair and hung her canes on hooks attached to the frame. Her expression had become reflective, but also, Nigel thought, rather content. Perhaps she hadn't expected such an easy opportunity to summon up more festive days.

"William—my husband—and I moved to Tunbridge Wells

in 1970. We bought a row house on Sherwood Road, quite close to St. Stephen's, and we attended more or less regularly. William died twenty years ago. I was a widow; Elspeth was a spinster who rarely left her house. We became fast friends. Compared to her fortune, I didn't have two pins to rub together, but that didn't make any difference to Elspeth—or to me."

Flick set the tea tray on a small table and moved it close to Nathalie. Nigel placed two of the assorted chairs opposite her, then he and Flick sat down.

Nathalie went on. "Four years ago, I moved to London. Naturally, I saw Elspeth less frequently—perhaps every other month. Blessedly, she paid a visit only a month before she died. And, of course, she brought Cha-Cha."

Nigel glanced down at the Shiba Inu, who had curled up next to his left foot. When Cha-Cha chose to behave, he could be the most obedient of dogs. When he looked back, he saw Nathalie filling her teacup by carefully pouring the tea over a teaspoon she had placed inside the cup. Flick put her teaspoon in the cup and did the same.

"You, too, Nigel," Nathalie said. "These teacups are older than I am."

Nigel leaned forward and looked in Flick's teacup. "I don't understand what we are doing."

"A silver teaspoon absorbs heat quickly," Flick said, "and prevents the stream of hot tea from shocking the porcelain. Without the spoon, the teacup might shatter."

"Ah. One learns something new every day."

"You should also remember to put the milk in your teacup before you add the tea," Nathalie said. "Your cuppa tastes better than if you do it the other way around."

Nigel resisted the urge to laugh in her face. "Milk first is superior to tea first?"

Flick jumped in. "A well-attested fact recently proved by scientific research. The milk heats more slowly and uniformly when the tea is added last. The chemistry of the brew is different."

Nigel sighed softly. Was there really a scientist who set such a low value on his time that he wasted it conducting such an experiment?

"I'd like to ask you what might seem a foolish question," Flick said to Nathalie. "When Elspeth paid her last visit, did she talk about the antiquities on display at the museum?"

Nathalie looked startled by Flick's question. Her brows arched and her lips parted in surprise.

"My goodness! You must be a mind reader," Nathalie said. "We spent most of the three hours she was here talking about the teacups and Tunbridge Ware. She wondered if my historical research about St. Stephen's had turned up any new information about the many antiques Desmond had acquired during his lifetime. I told Elspeth that the old rumors undoubtedly were just that: old rumors begun by unchristian people who were jealous of Desmond Hawker's success."

"Old rumors?" Flick pressed gently.

But Nathalie seemed determined to tell her story her way. "In truth, I've never cared much about crockery or bits of wood at the museum. I prefer the ship models and the paintings and the old maps. Curiously, though, my favorite exhibit is about the Portuguese Jesuit who first brought tea to Europe. Father Jasper de Cruz, in the year 1560—am I right?"

"On all counts," Flick said.

"Just think. . ." Nathalie had a faraway gleam in her eyes. "In those early days, a pound of tea cost more than a hundred pounds sterling." Nathalie lifted her teacup and took several satisfied sips.

Nigel could not fathom the connection between the price of tea and a Portuguese cleric, but it seemed better to sit back, listen quietly, and let Flick guide the conversation as best she could. This junket had been her idea.

She tried once again to corral Nathalie. "You mentioned old rumors. I've never heard any pertaining to the ownership of the Hawker collection."

"Oh, they go back many years—most have their roots in the nineteenth century. I heard all sorts when I gathered information to assemble a history of St. Stephen's on the occasion of its centennial." Nathalie's face brightened. "I hope Vicar de Rudd told you that I wrote the official history of St. Stephen's in 1999."

"He almost did," Flick said kindly. "He told us that you were the church historian, so naturally we assumed you wrote the official history."

The answer apparently satisfied Nathalie, because she went on. "Well, Commodore Hawker played a vital role in much of St. Stephen's early history. His generosity continued long after the church was built. And that made many of his contemporaries suspicious. They knew that the commodore could be a merciless competitor in business. Why then, they asked, did he choose to build and support a little church in the countryside northeast of Tunbridge Wells?"

Nigel let himself grin at Nathalie. "I admit that I have wondered the same thing."

"There are two quite preposterous answers that one often hears. The first is that the commodore used to attend St. Peter's Church on Bayhall Road, until he had an unpleasant fight with the vicar. By building St. Stephen's, so this assertion goes, he could choose his own clergyman." Nathalie grimaced. "Pure harebrained nonsense, but there you are! The second, more common answer is even sillier. I suspect you have heard that Desmond became guilt ridden by his years of playing fast and loose in commerce and built St. Stephen's to buy his way into heaven with good works."

Nathalie's statement unexpectedly had become a question. Nigel didn't know how to respond. He glanced at Flick; she looked equally uncomfortable.

"No need to answer," Nathalie said. "Your silence speaks eloquently. Vicar de Rudd is fond of that explanation. It is a point of contention between us." Nathalie paused to gather her thoughts. "You see, the chief problem is that many people refuse to separate Commodore Hawker's private life from his public life. They tell hurtful jokes about his so-called 'conversion on the road to Tunbridge Wells' because they won't accept the simple truth that Desmond Hawker became a genuine Christian toward the end of his life. He built St. Stephen's for one reason only: God laid on his heart the need for a new church in that part of Tunbridge Wells. The commodore's walk through life has much in common with that of John Newton, the slave trader who went on to become a minister and write the brilliant hymn 'Amazing Grace.'"

Nigel watched a flash of skepticism cross Flick's face. He had seen the same look in the vicarage. For some reason, she didn't buy into the notion of Desmond Hawker as a committed Christian.

Nathalie also must have twigged Flick's apparent disbelief. Her tone became earnest. "Like you, I once doubted the truth of Desmond Hawker's late-in-life conversion. It seemed easier to see him as merely a hypocrite in his later years. But that judgment ignores the power of the Holy Spirit to renew a man's heart."

Flick shrugged. "It seems so out of character with the

cold-blooded businessman I have come to know."

"Oh, I fully understand your unease. The Desmond Hawker on display in your museum was ruthless in his early years. He fought cruel battles against his enemies—other ruthless men. I have no doubt that he was the epitome of what Americans call a *robber baron*."

Flick nodded. "That's our man."

"Until the mid-1880s. Something happened—I don't know what. But it began a process of change that spanned five long years. We do know that Desmond Hawker considered himself a Christian during the influenza epidemic of 1890. Desmond's wife died of the disease, but he and his lone son survived. He wrote that his new faith gave him comfort in a time of great tragedy."

"He wrote about being a Christian?"

"Oh my, yes. Scores of letters he wrote to people in need and hundreds written to him by people he helped. They are reposing in the basement of your museum."

"You mean the Hawker archives?"

"Elspeth kindly arranged for me to have access to the commodore's papers when I prepared St. Stephen's history." Her face softened. "Perhaps I shouldn't say this, but I have often imagined Desmond the Christian blustering at the very idea of a Commodore Hawker Room at the museum. He refused many worldly honors after he became a Christian. He set up his foundation to quietly promote the betterment of mankind in ways that would not give him direct credit."

Nathalie paused to sip her tea. Nigel decided to ask a direct question.

"Nathalie," he said, "do you know why Desmond chose to describe himself as a thief?"

"You must be thinking of the *blinking* verse from Exodus

on the *blinking* bronze tablet." Nathalie put her hand to her mouth as she blushed beet red. "Forgive me my language. Elspeth often called it that. I am afraid I got into the same habit."

Nigel couldn't help grinning. "No need to apologize; I feel much the same—"

Flick interrupted. "Nathalie, are you saying that Elspeth didn't like that verse?"

Nigel felt angry for an instant—until he realized that Flick had grasped a vital point he had missed.

Nathalie's face clouded. "Elspeth came to loathe 'the gift of a thief who made every effort to pay back double.' She began to avert her eyes whenever she entered St. Stephen's."

"Do you know why?"

"Certainly. She blamed the verse for putting wrong ideas in Philip Oxley's head."

Nigel reacted first. "Who is Philip Oxley?" he said.

"A well-known historian. I believe he holds a chair at Oxford. He is purported to be an expert in the field of industrial history." Nathalie sniffed. "Disappointingly, Oxley fell for the old tittle-tattle that Commodore Hawker filched things from his former business partner"—she frowned—"I can never remember the man's name."

"Neville Brackenbury," Flick offered. "Desmond and Neville launched a tea importing business together. Desmond later bought out Neville's share of the partnership."

"Well, there were rumors in the nineteenth century that Desmond illegally acquired Neville's property."

"What kind of property? Neville's share of the tea business?"

"That, certainly—but also his private collection of paintings, maps, crockery, and Tunbridge Ware."

"Do you mean the Hawker antiquities that are now on display in the museum?"

"Yes. Some people claimed that the commodore somehow got them by robbing Neville."

Nigel felt his stomach tighten. He put forth the next question with considerable foreboding. "Nathalie, did Elspeth talk to you about the antiquities on display when she last visited you?"

Another nod. "Elspeth wondered if Philip Oxley might have been right to believe the rumors, after all. She wanted to reread the copy of the book she gave me."

"Book?" Flick shot straight up in her chair. "What book?"

"Philip Oxley's book, of course," Nathalie said. "He wrote a book about Desmond Hawker."

"The museum owns every book ever written about Desmond Hawker. I've never heard of one written by Philip Oxley."

"Of course, you haven't," Nathalie said grandly. "The book was never published. Mary Evans Hawker commissioned the work as a tribute to the commodore, but she decided not to put it into print. Elspeth was so furious when she read the manuscript that she refused to keep it in her house. She gave it to me with the hope that I could use the historical details that Oxley got right. That was more than fifteen years ago. I suppose a year before Mary Hawker Evans died."

"Do you still have your copy?"

Nathalie pointed to a bookshelf across the room. "The manuscript is about an inch thick. Look for green cardboard covers. Its title is *Transformation in the Tea Trade: How Desmond Hawker Turned Over a New Leaf.*"

Nigel found it immediately, neatly shelved next to an unabridged dictionary. He thumbed through the document. It seemed to be a copy of a professionally typed and edited manuscript, some two hundred pages long. In the middle of the document, simulating the photographs that would appear in a published volume, were four pages of photographic prints taped to sheets of blank paper. The first page had two photos of Desmond Hawker, the first taken in 1875, the second in 1896. They were indisputably of the same person but were remarkably different. Hawker had changed somehow as he grew older.

Flick interrupted Nigel's musings. "Nigel, I'd like to see the manuscript, too."

"Certainly." He passed it on.

Flick hastily examined the document, then asked Nathalie, "What did the Hawkers object to in the book?"

"As Elspeth often said, Oxley proved too creative for his own good. He invented relationships among events where none existed."

Nigel found himself baffled by Nathalie Stubbings's curious answer. Apparently, so did Flick, who took a deep breath, then asked, "What do you suppose Elspeth meant by 'relationships among events'?"

"The best example is in the last chapter of Oxley's manuscript," Nathalie said. "Oxley concluded that the big fire at Lion's Peak in 1925, the one that nearly killed Elspeth, was an act of revenge against the Hawker family. He assumed that the man who died after he set the fire was a descendant of Neville Brackenbury—and that he wanted to destroy the fruits of Desmond's thievery."

"Criminy!" Nigel said. "The tea trade is one tough business."

Flick tossed the manuscript into his lap. "Stop talking and read the last chapter."

"Yes, ma'am!"

Nigel began to turn pages.

It had been another of Flick's snap decisions. Nigel would review the manuscript while she continued to speak to Nathalie Stubbings. The woman's thoughts caromed erratically from topic to topic, but she possessed a wealth of information that might prove useful—if only Flick could guide the bouncing ball in Nathalie's mind.

Nathalie had poured herself another cup of tea. As she sipped, she seemed to be gazing off into the distance. Flick glanced in the same direction and discovered that Nathalie was staring at a picture frame across the small room. The old sepia-toned photo was of a girl in her teens.

"Is that also a photograph of Elspeth?" Flick asked.

Nathalie smiled. "She was fourteen at the time. It was taken at the seaside at Brighton on a Sunday afternoon in July 1934. I was probably on the same stretch of English Channel coastline on the same day at the same time."

Flick moved closer to the photograph. It showed a pretty young woman wearing a high-necked, long-sleeved white dress and off-white stockings. Elspeth stood near the water, grinning joyfully, holding her shoes in her hand. She had a large bow in her blond hair, which was cut short in the sort of bob that had been the fashion during the 1930s.

"She was lovely," Flick said. "Elspeth must have turned heads a few years later. Do you know why she never married?"

Natalie became pensive. "I often have wondered that very thing. The Elspeth I knew certainly seemed the kind of woman to make a success of home and family. Women a few years older than Elspeth were forced to become spinsters because a whole generation of young men died in the Great War of 1914–1918. Perhaps she also was swept up in the shortage

246

of eligible men—although it is hard for me to imagine that a wealthy, attractive young woman would find it difficult to attract a suitable match."

Flick looked over at Nigel, who appeared wholly absorbed by the manuscript. His head jiggled slightly as his eyes flashed down the page. She thought of something he had said the day before.

"Nathalie, what sort of relationship did Elspeth have with Vicar de Rudd? Were they good friends?"

Nathalie hesitated, plainly uncomfortable at the questions. Flick regretted that she had not asked them more obliquely.

"I hardly know how to answer you. When I lived in Tunbridge Wells, they were quite fond of each other. I suppose they drifted apart during the past year. Elspeth was quite circumspect when I saw her last. She mentioned something about the vicar chastising her for foolishly stirring up the past. She seemed. . . *exasperated* rather than angry when she spoke of him."

Flick imagined Elspeth approaching Vicar de Rudd and timidly seeking his advice about the "old rumors." Could the whispers about Desmond Hawker have been true? Might there be church records, old letters, diocesan documents—*anything*—that would help her find out, one way or another? The vicar didn't know how much importance she placed on learning the truth. And so, he urged her to let sleeping dogs lie. Or offered an equally banal cliché about leaving the past alone.

I'd get exasperated at de Rudd, too.

Nigel abruptly snapped the manuscript shut. "I can understand why the Hawker family decided not to publish this book," he said. "It is a miracle that one of them didn't shoot Philip Oxley when he presented his finished manuscript. He clearly had learned enough to cast doubt on the legend of Desmond Hawker."

Nathalie frowned. "Do you think it is true?"

Nigel sighed. " 'Fraid so. The chapter I read has a definite ring of truth. The manuscript also seems very well written by an author who knows how to begin a chapter with a fitting epigraph. 'The evil that men do lives after them; the good is oft interred with their bones.' "

Flick didn't try to restrain the rush of righteous anger she felt. "I don't care about miscellaneous quotations from Shakespeare!" she nearly shouted. "What did you read in the stupid chapter?"

Nigel laughed, but the amusement on his face drained away quickly as Flick stared him down. "An incredible story, actually," he said. "Oxley is somewhat sketchy on the details, but he asserts that Desmond Hawker ill-used Neville Brackenbury and was, in fact, responsible for his partner's personal bankruptcy in 1876. Rather than help save his friend, Desmond used the occasion to drive Brackenbury out of their partnership."

"In short," Flick said, "Oxley assumed that the old rumors were true."

Nigel nodded. "Time passed. Desmond Hawker thrived as a solo tea merchant, while Neville Brackenbury faltered and failed. He died in 1883, still in debt, leaving his wife and children destitute. They apparently migrated to Canada, where one might assume the story would end."

"However, it did not," she volunteered.

"Fast-forward to a Sunday morning in May 1925. Sir Basil Hawker; his wife, Gwyneth; and their two young children, Edmund and Elspeth, are at Lion's Peak asleep in their beds. You will recall that Gwyneth was Sir Basil's second wife. His first wife, Sarah, died almost thirty years earlier giving birth to Mary Hawker, who married Harry Evans in 1920."

"Is that significant?"

"Not in the least. What really matters is that at approximately six o'clock in the morning, a fast-moving fire began on the ground floor, toward the rear of the house, and rapidly engulfed one-third of the original structure—including the bedrooms. By a near miracle, three members of the family escaped without injury. Elspeth Hawker, age five, pulled loose from her mother, tried to rescue a caged songbird, and was burned—badly enough, it seems, to require a series of five surgeries over the next two years."

"Oh my, poor Elspeth."

"Enter the fire brigade. Because Decimus Burton had built Lion's Peak well, the firemen brought the blaze under control before it destroyed the house. When the gutted wing cooled enough to be examined, the authorities found an empty petrol can."

"An arson fire?" Flick asked.

"Yes. They also found the body of a man, presumably the arsonist. He obviously had miscalculated how quickly the fire would spread. He was too badly burned to be identified, and in any event, forensic identification was in its infancy in 1925."

"Case closed."

"Not so fast," Nigel said wryly. "The arsonist apparently wanted the reason for the fire to be known throughout Tunbridge Wells. On the Monday morning after the fire, an anonymous letter arrived at the *Kent and Sussex Courier*. It had been posted on Saturday. The letter itself was quite short. 'The person responsible for the destruction of Lion's Peak offers a lesser-known verse from scripture about thievery in response to a verse known to many in Tunbridge Wells.' Neatly copied below was a verse from. . ." Nigel began to thumb through the pages.

"The book of Zechariah," Nathalie said. "Specifically, chapter five. The writer of the letter used the King James Version.

Let me read you the passage in a modern translation." She reached for a black, leather-bound Bible on a small table near her chair. She opened it and began to read.

"I looked again—and there before me was a flying scroll! He asked me, 'What do you see?' I answered, 'I see a flying scroll, thirty feet long and fifteen feet wide.' And he said to me, 'This is the curse that is going out over the whole land; for according to what it says on one side, every thief will be banished, and according to what it says on the other, everyone who swears falsely will be banished. The Lord Almighty declares, 'I will send it out, and it will enter the house of the thief and the house of him who swears falsely by my name. It will remain in his house and destroy it, both its timbers and its stones.'"

Nathalie let the Bible drop into her lap. "Please continue with the story, Nigel. You tell it better than Philip Oxley did."

"There's more?" Flick asked.

"A minor media flurry in Tunbridge Wells," he said. "The editor of the *Courier* knew a good revenge story when he saw one. He also liked catchy headlines. For the next week or so, locals read and talked about 'the Flying Scroll Vendetta.'"

"Did the newspaper propose a reason for revenge?" Flick asked.

"Successive front pages floated several theories—from malevolent tea exporters in China to a lunatic cabal of Desmond's former competitors. The story petered out when the police lost interest in identifying the dead arsonist."

"And he never has been identified."

"Never," Nigel said grimly, "although Philip Oxley makes a fairly strong case for the arsonist being a long-lost relative of Neville Brackenbury."

Nathalie chimed in again. "That is true only if one believes that the commodore treated Neville badly. As you noted, the only evidence that Oxley could find to support his theory were vague reports of century-old rumors."

Nigel gave a seemingly reluctant nod. "I grant you that the direct evidence is sketchy, but Oxley cites many rumors of Desmond's wrongdoing. One begins to think that the presence of smoke indicates fire."

Flick turned to Nathalie. "What did Elspeth think when she reread the manuscript?"

"She left more confused than when she arrived. I urged her to take the manuscript with her, but she felt she had exhausted its possibilities."

Flick looked at the document resting in Nigel's upturned hands. "Nathalie, may I borrow the manuscript for a few days?"

A shadow of doubt crept across the woman's face. "I suppose so, although I would prefer that you don't make a copy for the museum library. I know Elspeth would disapprove."

Flick held up her right hand. "I promise!"

"Well, then, keep it as long as you like. The only reason I ever open the manuscript is to look at the photographs."

Flick paused a moment, not sure what photographs Nathalie meant. Nigel came to her rescue by opening the manuscript to the middle pages. He showed her the two photos of Desmond Hawker.

"The great man himself," Flick said. "Middle-aged and beyond."

"Much more than that," Nathalie said. "These are before-and-after photographs. Before he became a Christian. And after. See how he gained peace—the 'peace that surpasses understanding.' Being a committed Christian does that to people."

Flick looked closely at the photos. They were clearly different. She might trust the second man, but not the first. Was it merely a quirk of photography or something more?

Nathalie continued. "The first Desmond is worldly and sinful. The second is salt and light." Nathalie peered first at Flick, then at Nigel. "I hope you understand. It is the Christian's responsibility to be the salt of the earth and the light of the world—to do right and show the way by example."

Flick noticed out of the corner of her eye that Nigel was tapping his wristwatch. He had told her he wanted to be on the road back to Tunbridge Wells no later than two thirty in the afternoon. It had just turned three.

Exchanging good-byes with Nathalie took another ten minutes. She urged them to visit again; both Flick and Nigel promised they would. She found a treat for Cha-Cha, and she insisted on walking with them to the door. "Give my regards to Tunbridge Wells," she said. "I miss my little city."

Flick suddenly spun around. She moved back to the sepia-toned photograph she had looked at earlier and held it up for Nigel to view.

"Nigel, you haven't seen this fascinating photograph of Elspeth at age fourteen. It was taken on the beach at Brighton."

He peered at it for a few seconds. "Yes, quite lovely."

As they rode down in the lift, she said, "Did anything about the photo strike you as odd?"

"Other than your bizarre interest in it?" He shook his head. "It seemed a routine aging snap of a teenaged girl."

"Did you note what Elspeth was wearing?"

"Some sort of formal white dress—with long sleeves."

"Exactly!"

"Sorry. I haven't a clue what you are getting at."

"I think I've just figured out why Sir Simon Clowes lied to everyone."

OURTEEN

Could Flick be right?

Nigel gazed through the windscreen at the road, driving carefully but not paying attention as his favorite haunts in central London flashed by. His mind was trying to come to terms with Flick's latest brainstorm.

A week ago, he would have scoffed at her idea. But he had come to know Flick much better during the past few days. He had begun to admire her and, perhaps more relevant, to trust her judgment. There was a certain logic in her notion that Sir Simon Clowes had protected Dame Elspeth in death the way many others had apparently protected her in life.

English nobility—even minor nobility—takes care of its own.

He glanced sideways at Flick, who was browsing the pages of Philip Oxley's manuscript. What would she do if he agreed with her conclusion? She could be as unpredictable as a nutter at times, making downright lunatic decisions when she latched on to a duff notion. With a bit of encouragement, she might telephone Kent police or possibly even MI5.

But perhaps this was not such a duff notion after all?

"Assuming you have guessed right about the good doctor," he said guardedly, "what do you intend to do about it?"

"Talk to him. We should visit him this evening."

"Today? We?"

Nigel abruptly applied the brakes and steered left across the yellow line into a no-parking zone. The driver in the car behind honked in annoyance as she veered around the stopped BMW.

"Yes and yes," Flick said. "The faster I get Dr. Clowes to change his story, the better for everyone concerned. And it has to be 'we.' He'll agree to see you, but he might hang up the phone if I call him. Besides, you probably have his private number. I don't."

Nigel nodded. Six months ago, he had taken the trouble to store the private telephone number of every trustee in his cell phone. Without protest, he unclipped the phone from his belt and slipped it into the cradle attached to the BMW's dashboard. His mouth suddenly felt dry. He was about to run the risk of alienating an important trustee, but somehow that didn't seem as important as making Flick Adams happy.

Nigel moistened his lips with his tongue. "What should I say?"

"The truth. We need about fifteen minutes of his time later this evening."

Nigel nodded again. He switched the phone to speaker mode, found *S Clowes* in the number directory, and pressed TALK.

The doctor answered on the third ring.

"Yes?"

"Nigel Owen here, Sir Simon." He took a deep breath, then began again. "Here's the thing. I am with Felicity Adams.

We have to see you, preferably later today."

"About?"

"A museum-related issue. It would be inappropriate to discuss it over the telephone."

"A bit short notice for a business meeting, don't you think? In any case, my wife and I are entertaining dinner guests this evening."

Every fiber in Nigel's body wanted to yield, to apologize for disturbing a busy physician. Nonetheless, he pressed forward. "It is important that we meet with you today, Sir Simon, otherwise I wouldn't ask. We need only fifteen minutes. Possibly less."

Sir Simon made an unhappy grunt. "Do you know where my house is?"

"In Rusthall, on Manor Park."

"I plan to leave my surgery at five thirty. I will arrive home no later than six. You can have ten minutes."

He rang off without saying good-bye.

"That went reasonably well," Nigel said brightly, struggling to keep the foreboding he felt out of his voice. Sir Simon was merely irked at him now. He would be utterly furious when Flick finished presenting her latest conjecture.

You didn't really want a posh position in healthcare.

"It's almost four," Flick said. Nigel lifted his head and saw her nervously surveying the slow-moving afternoon traffic. She went on, "Can we make it to Tunbridge Wells by six?"

"We will make it—although I shall have to drive like Sterling Moss."

The thought straightaway cheered Nigel. There was nothing like sustained heavy-duty driving to take one's mind off everything else. "I think we will try a different route going back. Rusthall is west of Tunbridge Wells. I propose we make for Rusthall via East Grinstead."

"I'm game—even though I don't know where East Grinstead is."

On this leg of their trip, Nigel's optimism in his driving skills proved warranted. They passed through East Grinstead scarcely an hour later. Rusthall lay less than ten miles ahead. Nigel allowed himself to relax a notch. Although the sun had set, the rain had stopped and traffic was moving smartly.

He looked at Flick and said, "Do you realize that we are currently on the road to Tunbridge Wells?"

"Yep. Directly behind the 291 Metrobus. The exhaust fumes are making me sick."

"Actually, I had Nathalie Stubbings's words in mind. Specifically, her description of Desmond Hawker's late-in-life conversion to Christianity."

"Oh that."

He stopped talking to steer the BMW through a round-about and pass the bus, then he said, "Your tone signals that you don't believe Desmond had a genuine change of heart. Why are you so skeptical?"

Flick didn't reply, which surprised Nigel. She never had any difficulty stating—and arguing—her opinions. Yet he sensed an almost palpable reluctance to answer this question.

"Well, let me tell you what I think," he said. "I can't say whether the Holy Spirit refurbished his heart, but I am willing to accept that Desmond Hawker mellowed as he grew older. He seems to have done many good things in the latter years of his life, a fact that has set me thinking. My mother taught me to attend chiefly to what people do, not what they say. She often reinforced the principle with a line from scripture: 'By their fruit you will recognize them.' "

This time, Flick responded with an indifferent "I suppose so."

Nigel went on. "The simple truth is that Desmond Hawker turned into an astonishingly fruitful old man. He built a church, gave away half of his huge fortune to create a foundation to promote the betterment of humanity, and apparently helped a crowd of locals in Tunbridge Wells." He patted the top of Flick's right hand with his left hand. "If I am willing to give the old robber baron the benefit of the doubt, why are you disinclined?"

Nigel glanced routinely at the rearview mirror and realized that Flick had leaned to the right and was peering intently at his reflection.

"You're the businessperson in this car," she said. "Everything I know about commerce came from the handful of business courses I took back in graduate school. But I still remember what my management professor told us on the first day of class. 'The Japanese say that business is war. They are absolutely right.' He went on to explain that the language of business is full of military jargon. Businesspeople devise strategies, attack competitors, defend territories, dominate markets, wage competitive battles. One of our textbooks for the course was Sun Tzu's *The Art of War*, written in China about 500 BC. I can only recall one of Sun Tzu's tenets. 'All warfare is based on deception.' "

Flick leaned back against her seat. "Can anyone who lives with that kind of dog-eat-dog mind-set for forty years magically change his thinking? My problem is that I can't stop seeing Desmond asking, 'How do I come out on top?' and 'What's in it for me?' " She sighed. "Show me *one* businessperson who really changed his or her stripes and then maybe I'll believe that Desmond Hawker did it."

Nigel kept his eyes on the road, wondering for a moment if Flick had intended her last comment as an indirect slap in his face—a veiled criticism of his day-to-day ethics and be-havior. Probably not. She had stated the kind of sweeping generality that many people outside of commerce spout about businesspeople. He remembered a joke that had made the rounds in London a year earlier. *Question: How can one tell when a businessperson is lying? Answer: His or her lips are moving.*

Like all generalities, one could find some examples that proved the point and other examples that were completely contrary. During his early years in business, Desmond Hawker probably fell into the first category. Nigel hoped that his own career fell into the latter.

"I can't provide the proof you demand," he said. "I am not certain if anyone can. The changes you want to see are not ex-ternal like zebra stripes. If Desmond Hawker changed at all, it was on the inside. He experienced an epiphany that trans-formed his thinking forever."

"What caused this so-called epiphany?"

"Ah, that question we may be able to answer. One of us should browse among Desmond's papers in the museum's archives." Nigel eased his foot on the accelerator. "We've just passed Rusthall Road. To get to Sir Simon's house, we have to make a half-left turn onto Bishops Down Road and full-left turn onto Manor Park."

"Manor Park *what*?"

"It is a lane, although its name is simply Manor Park."

Flick shook her head sadly. "Whatever." She seemed to for-get about English street-naming conventions when Nigel steered into the driveway and parked behind a large Jaguar sedan.

"Wow! There must be big bucks in British cardiology," she said breathlessly. "That is one mean house. Kind of a story-book cottage on steroids. How many million pounds do you suppose it's worth?" She began to sing the vintage American song "You Gotta Have Heart."

Nigel chuckled at Flick's choice of words and music. Both seemed right on the mark. The large redbrick house was lit inside and outside to welcome the Clowesses' anticipated dinner guests. It was chiefly Queen Anne style, with a host of the usual quaint details, including white stucco on the ground floor bricks, intricate gables (Nigel counted at least four roof peaks), tile facings, a forest of chimneys, and windows broken into dozens of small panes.

Nigel checked his watch. Ten before six. "The Jag is Sir Simon's car," he said. "He made it home early."

They walked together to the front door. Nigel rang the bell. He heard the deep bark of a large dog somewhere inside. "Hope he's friendly," Flick said, voicing his thoughts.

A shadowed form approached the frosted glass-paneled front door. The door swung open and Sir Simon beckoned them inside.

"Welcome to you both," he said courteously but unenthusiastically. "We can talk in my study."

Nigel followed Flick inside into a well-appointed foyer with stone flooring, an ornate central lighting fixture, and a tall grandfather clock. Nigel heard the clink of dishes somewhere in the distance. The smell of food cooking reminded him that he was hungry.

A large, friendly golden retriever approached Nigel at a good clip, its toenails skittering on the stones. Sir Simon let the dog sniff Nigel and Flick—and accept a few head pats—before saying, "Elsie, go to the kitchen. Kitchen!" Elsie studied her master's face for a few seconds, decided he was serious, then trotted back the way she had come.

Sir Simon led them into a large front room that overlooked the driveway. Nigel thought the furnishings decidedly masculine: dark wood paneling, tall bookcases, a stuffed water buffalo head on one wall. Dr. Clowes gestured to a pair of leather-upholstered armchairs near a large stone fireplace that must have been responsible for the slightly smoky smell lingering in the air. Nigel let Flick choose her chair, then he sat down in its mate. Sir Simon turned a high-backed wooden chair around to face the twin armchairs.

"Now, what is so important that it could not wait until tomorrow?" he asked Nigel.

Flick spoke before Nigel could answer. "Not what. *Who.* We've come to talk about Elspeth Hawker."

Nigel winced at Flick's blunt tone; he had planned to begin with a more tactful opening statement. But Flick's lack of diplomacy seemed to have one useful effect: It startled Simon Clowes into quiet submission.

"Yes?" he said guardedly, his eyes suddenly wary. "What about Dame Elspeth?"

"Nigel and I learned this afternoon," Flick said, "about a near-catastrophic fire at Lion's Peak that injured Elspeth Hawker. She was five years old at the time."

Nigel saw Sir Simon stiffen at the word "fire."

"During the next two years," Flick continued, "Elspeth had five different operations—skin grafts of some sort, I presume."

Flick paused. Sir Simon said nothing. Flick went on. "We also saw a photo of Elspeth taken nine years after the fire. The setting is the seaside in Brighton on a sunny day. Elspeth has on a long-sleeved dress and stockings—a rather odd outfit for a day at the beach, especially since other young women in the background are wearing one-piece swimsuits, or bathing costumes, as the Brits say."

Sir Simon glared at Flick. "Does your fashion chronicle have a point?"

"A sad point. I believe that the fire at Lion's Peak left Elspeth with disfiguring scars. At least, she considered her scars disfiguring. And so she wore concealing clothing all her life, she never married, and she lived in self-imposed exile at Lion's Peak until she became a trustee of the Royal Tunbridge Wells Tea Museum. The scars were so distressing to Elspeth that her personal physician helped her to maintain her secret, even after she died a suspicious death."

Sir Simon seemed to shrink in his chair. His head dipped; his shoulders sagged. He gazed awhile at the antique Persian Kerman rug on his floor, then finally said, "You are a very clever woman, Dr. Adams." He sighed. "You have managed to deduce half of Elspeth's secret. She *was* cruelly burned in the fire. And she did obsess about her large, livid scars. As you surmise, her arms and legs suffered the worst damage. But there was nothing suspicious about her death."

"Dame Elspeth died of an overdose of barbiturates."

"Probably," he said, with a half nod. "Undoubtedly self-administered. I saw no need to burden the family or the museum with that painful fact."

Flick slid forward in her chair. "I don't believe Elspeth committed suicide. I considered the possibility—it made no sense to me."

"Of course, it didn't. You don't have all the facts." Sir Simon peered earnestly at Flick. "I know that you became Elspeth's friend, because she told me so. But her friendship with you did not alter her deeply secretive nature. I doubt she told you that she was dying."

Flick frowned, then gave a slight shake of her head.

"Elspeth's heart was failing," Sir Simon continued. "She knew there was a significant risk of a debilitating stroke from the medications she was taking. She greatly feared that possibility and also the absolute certainty that she would grow increasingly feeble as her illness progressed. On two separate occasions Elspeth asked me to prescribe a lethal dose of medication she could use 'if the need arose,' as she put it. Naturally, I refused. She evidently acquired the drugs elsewhere."

The clock in the hallway began to chime the hour. Sir Simon glanced at his watch, then rose from his chair. "I promised you ten minutes."

Nigel had listened patiently, waiting for the appropriate time to speak up. He cleared his throat and said, "I am afraid, Sir Simon, that *you* don't have all the facts, either. Two hours before Dame Elspeth died, she visited me and shared her intentions to reveal a systematic theft of antiquities to the trustees."

"Theft?" The doctor stared at Nigel in puzzlement. "From the museum?"

"Nineteen authentic antiquities worth approximately one half million pounds have been replaced by forgeries—apparently by one of the trustees." He added, "You, by the way, are not under suspicion."

The doctor's eyes widened. He sat down again slowly. "Marjorie Halifax told me that the story Dr. Adams told to the police was untrue. . . ." He let his words trail off.

"My story was quite true," Flick said.

Nigel held his breath, silently urging Flick not to gloat. Blessedly, she did nothing other than send a stealthy smile his way.

"There is more, Sir Simon," Nigel said. "Sometime after the impromptu trustee meeting that you were unable to attend, a tea canister in Felicity's office was contaminated with oleander leaves."

"Good heavens," he said hollowly. He frowned. "I have not heard of anyone being poisoned."

"We haven't told anyone other than you. . .*yet*."

Sir Simon turned to Flick. "What proof do you have of these allegations?"

Flick seemed to have anticipated the question. She counted off her four answers on her fingers. "We have persuasive evidence that Elspeth discovered the scheme to steal antiquities. We have the nineteen sham antiquities themselves. We have the tainted tea. And we have Nigel's observation of Elspeth's state of mind before the trustees' meeting—a woman about to reveal a crime is not likely to commit suicide before she gets the chance to speak."

The doctor stared at his hands, seemingly lost in thought. Slowly, the confusion on his face gave way to agonized resolve. He shook his head resolutely. "Not enough!" he said. "I need more. Present me with convincing evidence that one of my fellow trustees poisoned Elspeth and I will withdraw my original finding on cause of death. I will go to the Kent police immediately and recommend the exhumation of Elspeth's body for a postmortem examination."

"Thank you, Sir Simon," Flick said as she stood, in a voice without emotion. "The evidence that will convince you exists. We'll find it."

He looked up at her and responded with a vague wave. "Please show yourselves out. I need time to think before my guests arrive."

Nigel followed Flick to his car. Neither spoke until Nigel steered the BMW across Bishops Down and turned southeast on Major York's Road.

"I hope we can keep the promise you made," he said.

"The knot on the bag is beginning to untangle, Nigel. A few more tugs and the rest of the truth will spill out." She added in a somewhat sheepish tone, "Can you break free again tomorrow to go on another trek?"

"Sorry, but I am up to my hips in museum work. I have to talk the trustees into yet another special meeting. On Friday afternoon, they shall gather with Bleasdale and the Hawker heirs to finalize the acquisition of the Hawker collection."

Flick sighed. "Rats!"

"What do you have planned?"

"I am going to track down Philip Oxley this evening and make an appointment to see him in Oxford. Remember those sketchy details you mentioned? I'm hoping that he knows more about the relationship between Desmond Hawker and Neville Brackenbury than he wrote in his manuscript."

"You are welcome to borrow the BMW."

"No way! I haven't driven a car with a manual transmission in five years. I'm not going to start off with a hundred-mile trip halfway across England. I'll take the train."

Nigel laughed. "I thank you and so does my clutch."

"But you can do me a big favor," she said.

"Name it."

"Keep Cha-Cha for a second night. I don't want to leave him alone in my apartment all day."

The Shiba Inu gave a little yip at the sound of his name.

"With pleasure," Nigel said.

To his surprise, he really meant it.

Flick stood among the crowd of commuters at the Central Railway Station in Tunbridge Wells who were traveling to their jobs in London and wondered if she had lost any of her "visiting American" look during the past three months.

No one seemed to be gawking at her, even though she

was doing more than her share of gazing at different parts of the elaborate redbrick station that had been built in 1912.

Perhaps the sheer excitement of taking a *real* train journey showed on her face. Flick could count on two hands the number of train trips she had made in the United States. As she waited for the 06:57 to London, she totaled her various day trips from Baltimore to New York and one long round-trip from Baltimore to central Florida when she was a kid. Eight, possibly nine in all.

Flick had been surprised to learn that one couldn't travel directly from Tunbridge Wells to Oxford on England's celebrated rail network. The trip involved two different railroads—Tunbridge Wells to London on South Eastern Trains, then London to Oxford on Thames Trains—and was made even more interesting by the need to take a *tube* ride on the London Underground. The Tunbridge Wells train arrived in London Bridge Station; the Oxford train departed from Paddington Station.

She used the journey to read—and reread—the relevant chapters of Philip Oxley's manuscript. The evening before, she had found Oxley's telephone number on her first try at directory inquiry and reached him at home with her first call. Professor Oxley was delighted to talk with the chief curator of the Royal Tunbridge Wells Tea Museum. Flick had to pull the telephone away from her when he bellowed, "I am thunderstruck to learn that a copy of *Transformation in the Tea Trade* still exists and utterly bowled over that another scholar wants to talk about it." He immediately agreed to see Flick at ten thirty on Wednesday morning in his office at the History Faculty Building on Broad Street.

The 08:48 from London Paddington pulled into Oxford Railway Station two minutes late at 9:52. Oxley had predicted "a fifteen-to-twenty-minute walk from the station to Broad Street." The morning was crisp and Flick was in high spirits; she reached her ornate destination in less than thirteen minutes. Her guidebook explained that the History Faculty Building had been completed in 1896 as the Indian Institute, a place to foster and facilitate Indian studies and to showcase the languages, literature, and industries of India. "Well, that explains why the decorative carvings are Hindu gods and tiger heads," Flick muttered to herself, "and why the weather vane on top of the building is an elephant."

Dr. Philip Oxley—short, dark, plump, intense, in his midforties—welcomed Flick into a typically small professorial office that, also typically, seemed overwhelmed by books. He had set out tea and digestive biscuits on his desk.

"You know all about tea, right?" he said after he poured two cuppas. "What do you know about these things?" He held up the green box of biscuits and said, "Where does the dreadful name come from?"

Flick laughed. "Back in the States we call them whole wheat cookies. However, one of our exhibits at the museum presents a simple, plausible explanation of 'digestive biscuit.'"

"Good. You talk whilst I munch my cookie."

"Early in the nineteenth century, so the story goes, the need was seen to increase the amount of fiber in the everyday British diet to aid. . .uh. . .digestion. Someone invented a high-fiber biscuit made of whole wheat flour and other grains."

"Do you mean that this *cookie* is the precursor to the bran loaf?"

Another laugh. "An apt description."

"You have convinced me to visit your museum. I've heard of it, of course, but I have never made the trip south." Oxley leaned back in his chair and interlaced his fingers over his generous stomach. "Now, you told me you were conducting a research project about the relationship between Desmond Hawker and Neville Brackenbury."

It was a statement, but also an invitation for Flick to explain her evening phone call requesting an immediate appointment. Flick took a sip of tea and used the moment to collect her thoughts. Describing her search for more information as a "research project" hardly stretched the truth. She didn't want to lie to Oxley, but neither did she want to share the real reasons for her interest in Desmond and Neville.

"In many ways," Flick began, "the tea museum is a memorial to Desmond Hawker. However, I feel it's a mistake to sugarcoat his life in our exhibits. We owe our visitors the whole truth about Desmond, including his warts and shortcomings. His conduct probably wasn't any worse or better than those of his peers. He was ruthless in business, which many considered a virtue in the nineteenth century." She hesitated. This part of her "explanation" required a little white lie. "I'm in rather a hurry because we are planning our budget for next year. I need to decide quickly about any new exhibits."

Oxley's face filled with amusement. "I take it, Dr. Adams, that the recent death of Dame Elspeth Hawker has changed the rules at the museum. Let me assure you that the Hawkers I met—Mary and Elspeth—had no interest in airing Desmond's dirty linens." Oxley let his amusement break into a full smile. "The truth is, I accepted Mary Hawker Evans's commission to write a detailed history of the commodore's accomplishments for one reason only—I was a struggling postdoctoral fellow with a pregnant wife. I needed the Hawkers' money, and I fully understood that the Hawkers would not want the whole sordid story told. Alas, I naively assumed that the details of the vendetta—which fascinated me—wouldn't upset them."

"I'd love to hear the whole story, sordid or not."

Oxley gave a slight grunt. "If memory serves—the truth is, I looked at my old notes last night—the saga begins in 1860, when Desmond Hawker, age forty, a moderately successful businessman, joined forces with Neville Brackenbury and launched Brackenbury and Hawker, Tea Merchants. The business succeeded, and both men became modestly wealthy by nineteenth-century standards.

"In 1876, Neville Brackenbury left the partnership. The firm suddenly was renamed Hawker & Sons. With Desmond alone at the helm, the company prospered beyond his wildest dreams. He became one of the richest men in England. And then he got religion.

"It took me months of research to figure out what had happened to Neville Brackenbury. But the records are out there. Desmond seemed to have been serious about his Christianity; he became fairly open about his wrongdoing near the end of his life. I found much of his story captured in a ten-year correspondence he had with a lecturer in history at Balliol College, here in Oxford, toward the end of the nineteenth century."

Oxley reached for another digestive biscuit and said, "I prefer the chocolate-covered kind, but any port in a storm." He poured himself a fresh cup of tea.

"You Americans wax poetic about your Great Depression of the 1930s," he continued. "Well, England suffered through the Long Depression from 1873 to 1896. I'll save you the trouble of doing the arithmetic; our Long Depression lasted twenty-three years. Stocks plummeted. People lost fortunes. And, as it happens, Neville Brackenbury was forced into personal bankruptcy in 1876."

"I see."

"No. I am not sure that you do. To become a bankrupt in

Victorian England was considered a huge disgrace. Not too many years before Neville Brackenbury declared bankruptcy, similarly stricken people were sent to debtor's prison. Those awful places weren't abandoned until 1869. Much of Victorian literature deals with the tragedy of bankruptcy or the threat of it. At an earlier time in England, being declared a bankrupt was tantamount to a death sentence. Bankrupts were hanged."

Flick asked the obvious question. "Did the Brackenbury and Hawker partnership fall into dire straits?"

"Not quite. The disaster really started in another company— of all things, a firm in the midlands that made low-cost ceramic products, including teapots and teacups for the masses. It was called the Mansfield Manufactory, Ltd. Desmond and Neville both invested heavily in the company; Neville in particular overextended himself."

Flick watched a sly grin form on Oxley's face. She realized that he was about to get to the good part of his story.

"Desmond was unquestionably the smarter businessman of the two," Oxley said. "He decided to protect his investment by bribing one of Mansfield's bookkeepers. As a result, he received a wealth of insider information. He gauged a full year before it actually happened that Mansfield would go under. And so Desmond sold his shares in the Mansfield Manufactory for a hefty profit, but—"

Flick couldn't help interrupting. "But he neglected to warn his partner."

"Exactly! Desmond stood by as Neville lost nearly everything when Mansfield collapsed. He then proceeded to make his desperate friend an offer he couldn't refuse. Desmond bought out Neville's half of the partnership for pennies on the pound."

Flick nodded glumly. That was the sort of behavior she had

expected from Desmond Hawker in his early years of his company. A genuine robber baron saw nothing wrong with crushing friends along with foes. All that counted was his personal gain, his individual success. He made no concessions to such gooey concepts as morality or ethics or even friendship.

"That's appalling," she said. "Truly despicable."

"I agree. But Desmond's maliciousness doesn't stop there. Neville had built a superb collection of *objets d'art* related to tea. Paintings, ship models, maps, a bit of everything. The collection had considerable value. Brackenbury could have sold the items and paid off a large part of his debts, but Desmond never gave him the chance. He asserted that the collection was part of the partnership's assets. I assume that Desmond threatened to assert his rights to the objects by bringing an action in court and that Neville didn't have the money to pay the cost of an effective legal defense. In any case, Neville felt compelled to sell the collection to Desmond at a fraction of its worth." He added, "In his later years, Desmond considered this a fraudulent transaction, akin to actually stealing the objects from Neville."

With great effort, Flick kept her expression from revealing the colossal shock she felt. "You must be aware," she said evenly, "that the Hawker collection represents the lion's share of the antiquities on display in my museum."

"Of course." He offered a wry smile. "If my book had ever been published, I would have asked permission to include photographs from the museum's catalog of antiquities. One item in particular upset Neville Brackenbury above all others. He had commissioned a set of elegant tea caddies, decorated with wooden mosaics, that was destined to become an anniversary present for his wife, Lucinda. Desmond swept them up with everything else."

Flick gasped. *The "All the Teas in China" Tunbridge Ware tea caddies.* She covered her abrupt distress with a cough.

"Have some more tea," Oxley said. "These digestive biscuits are dry as desert sand."

Flick took two long sips, then said, "The picture you painted of Desmond Hawker makes him look irredeemably evil. And yet your book talks about his transformation into a fervent Christian." She recalled her discussion with Nigel as they drove to Tunbridge Wells. "Do you think Desmond really changed his stripes?"

Oxley spread his hands on his desk. "*Something* happened to Desmond Hawker. I can't say what was in his mind and heart, but he really did act a different person as he grew older. He died believing that God had forgiven his many sins."

"That seems remarkably generous of God, given the heartlessness of Desmond's transgressions."

Oxley laughed. "I made that very point to a minister when I was doing research. He said, 'Indeed, that is what God's grace is all about.'" The professor's face became somber. "Unfortunately, there were members of Neville Brackenbury's family who chose not to forgive Desmond Hawker."

"The fire at Lion's Peak," Flick said with a sigh. "'The Flying Scroll Vendetta.'"

"I have no proof," Oxley said, "but I feel that vengeance is the best explanation of what happened in 1925. It is a matter of public record that Neville died in 1883, although I never was able to track down the cause of his death. My theory is that he committed suicide, creating a pool of hatred that festered for fifty years among his survivors. Again, it is public record that Neville had two sons, twins, in fact. The best evidence I have suggests that Lucinda and the boys left England after Neville died in 1883 and immigrated to Canada.

I believe that one of the sons was responsible for the arson at Lion's Peak and accidentally died during the fire."

Flick watched Oxley's face as he spoke. She didn't see any sign of doubt, any hint of hesitation. He clearly believed everything he had alleged. She decided that his hypothesis made good sense to her, too. Then she saw him glance furtively at the digital clock atop his desk.

Time to leave.

Flick stood, brushed a few digestive biscuit crumbs from her skirt, and said, "I won't make any promises, but I will try to get the Hawker family's permission to place a copy of your book in our library, where it will be available to scholars."

Oxley stood, too. "I think of my manuscript as an incomplete work in progress—many loose strings remain to be tied up. But feel free to use my research in your new exhibit." He extended his hand. "Oh, please do let me know if you discover anything new about Desmond Hawker and family. I would like very much to learn how the Hawker saga ends."

"Badly!" she murmured under her breath.

Philip Oxley had mused about a pool of hatred that festered for fifty years and exploded in violence in 1925. But the murder of Elspeth Hawker—and the thefts of the Tunbridge Ware tea caddies—happened in the twenty-first century.

Could hatred continue to boil and bubble for more than 115 years?

Flick shivered as she considered the possibility.

FIFTEEN

Nigel's phone rang at 3:40 in the afternoon. He knew without looking at the caller-ID panel that it was Flick's cell phone, that she had just stepped off the 14:45 from London Charing Cross. He snatched up the receiver.

"Welcome back to Tunbridge Wells," he said. "How was your day in Oxford?"

"Productive," she said. The brief sound of her voice made Nigel realize how much he had missed seeing her today. But he also felt a stab of unease. He could hear something ominous in her tone. Anger? Disappointment?

He waited patiently without speaking for her to find the right words.

Flick began with a low moan. "The truth is, I learned too much about Desmond Hawker today. I feel like stripping his name off every exhibit in the museum. He was a bona fide, unreconstructed. . ."

Nigel drew in his breath, surprised at Flick's choice of

epithet. It was a ripe four-word expletive that he had never heard her use before. She started to say something else, when an announcement on a loudspeaker at Central Railway Station drowned out her voice.

"Hang on a sec!" she shouted. "I'm almost at the Mount Pleasant Road exit."

Nigel imagined Flick walking through the old station, the cell phone pressed to her ear. She probably had worn one of her trim business suits to visit the professor of history, perhaps the blue one that accentuated her abundant curves and made her look nothing like the usual museum curator.

Flick's voice returned. "I'm outside the station, approaching Vale Street. How did your day go?"

"I am over the moon with delight!" He tried to incorporate the right touch of sarcasm. "There is nothing I relish more than humbling myself before our charming trustees. I needed every minute of the morning to wheedle and whinge, but I finally convinced them all to show up at three o'clock on Friday afternoon. I swore on my mother's head that this would be our last meeting for at least a month."

Silence.

"Flick, are you there?"

"You may want to cancel the meeting," she said gravely.

"What?"

"Or at least postpone it a few days."

"Impossible!" Nigel struggled to regain a scintilla of self-control. "Why can't we hold a trustees' meeting on Friday?"

He heard Flick sigh. "Philip Oxley filled in many of the missing pieces. I am beginning to understand Elspeth's concerns about the provenance of our antiquities. She may have been right to worry."

"Worry about what? As you pointed out to me, the Hawker

family assembled the collection more than a hundred years ago."

"I don't know a thing about property law in the United Kingdom, but I think we have a problem—or rather that the Hawkers do." She added, "I should be at the museum in twenty minutes. I'll tell you the whole, miserable story."

"I can't wait."

"Put a kettle on. It's Wednesday, the Duchess of Bedford Tearoom is closed, and I am dying for a cuppa."

Nigel rang off and told himself not to speculate about the dimensions of their "problem." Soon enough, Flick would be there with the facts. Ownership of antiquities was fertile ground for conflict at museums throughout the world—why should the Royal Tunbridge Wells Tea Museum be exempt? The "Elgin Marbles" on display at the British Museum were the most notable examples: fifty-six sculpted friezes removed from the Parthenon in Athens in 1799 by Lord Elgin, the British ambassador to the Ottoman Empire. The modern nation of Greece demanded their return. And scores of famous art museums were embroiled in fights over treasures that the Nazis stole from lawful owners before and during World War II.

He took a yellow pad and began to make a list of resources that might be useful as Flick and he reviewed the provenance of the Hawker antiquities:

The binder full of computer-generated inventory logs that Flick had consulted when she showed him the objects on loan from the Hawker family.

A photographic catalog published by the museum that pictured the most important items in its collection.

The original loan agreements between Mary Hawker Evans and the museum.

Scholarly books about the Hawker antiquities written by art historians. Nigel had seen two in the bookcase in Flick's office.

Miscellany.

He underlined the last entry. Nigel's files were chock-full of magazines, white papers, and other publications written for museum directors. He would ask Polly Reid to look for anything relevant.

Nigel's phone rang again.

"I'm approaching the bottom of High Street," Flick said. "I wanted to make sure you've put a kettle on."

"Indeed I have," he fibbed. "By the way, let's meet in the boardroom. I am gathering every piece of information we have on the Hawker collection. We will need a big table to spread it all out."

The one item on his list that he could not find in his or Flick's office was the museum's photographic catalog. He decided to borrow one from the gift shop on the ground floor. He skipped down the stairs, waved to the security guard on duty in the Welcome Centre kiosk, and entered the one space in the museum he liked least. The gift shop stocked teapots, tea filters, teacups, tea mugs, teakettles, tea cozies, tea caddies, tea makers, tea infusers, tea bag holders, tea towels, Japanese tea ceremony sets, souvenir teaspoons, games about tea, and two hundred kinds of loose and bagged teas grown on five different continents.

He made his way past a shelf crowded with teddy bears drinking tea and dolls participating in tea parties, then skirted a long metal rack of postcards and photographs of the museum's most noted antiquities. Along the shop's back wall, a tall bookcase presented volumes on the history of tea and the serving of tea, cookbooks full of tea-related recipes, and a selection of novels set in tearooms, on tea plantations, or that involved tea-infatuated characters. He spotted several copies of the antiquities catalog on the top shelf—the shelf dedicated to slow-selling "professional" books—tucked next to a tome on tea tasting.

Nigel glanced around the gift shop, uttered a soft whimper of despair, and fled with the copy of the catalog that seemed the most shopworn.

He came face-to-face with Flick in the long ground-floor hallway. She looked a bit knackered from six hours of train travel, but the brisk walk from the station had given her complexion an astonishing rosy glow that took his breath away.

"Where's my cuppa?" she said.

"In the boardroom," he managed to say, "and I am equally pleased to see you, too."

Cha-Cha, who had enjoyed the run of the museum that day, had apparently spent the afternoon in discussions with Earl the Grey. Nigel caught a flash of red out of the corner of his eye as the Shiba Inu—who had somehow heard Flick's voice—clattered around the Welcome Centre kiosk and hurled himself at her legs.

Flick, who invariably smiled at the dog's antics, did not smile today.

"Beat it, Cha-Cha," she said gently. "I'm not in the mood."

An hour later, Nigel fully understood Flick's unhappy disposition. In fact, he had descended to her level of gloominess.

"I think we should review the bidding," he said.

"Be my guest."

"If we believe Philip Oxley—"

Flick interrupted. "And I do."

"As do I." Nigel raised both hands in a gesture of surrender. "*Because* we believe Philip Oxley, we must deal with the strong likelihood that Desmond Hawker fraudulently acquired the antiquities that we call the Hawker collection." He added, "In other words, the historical evidence suggests that he copped the lot from Neville Brackenbury."

"So does the evidence from a noted art expert." Flick dove into the papers, booklets, and documents scattered across the large boardroom table and retrieved a hefty textbook. She had used a yellow "sticky" as a bookmark. "This was written about the Hawker collection in 1965." She began to read aloud.

One of the more interesting aspects of the Hawker family's collection of tea-related antiquities is the relative mystery that surrounds its acquisition. The late 1800s was a time of enormous activity for wealthy collectors in England and America who scoured Europe and Asia in search of artistic masterpieces. Some collectors were art experts in their own right and made their own purchasing decisions; others hired agents to acquire the finest available artworks on their behalf. There are no indications that Desmond Hawker did either, although his one-time partner, Neville Brackenbury, is known to have commissioned the services of two agents in Europe and one renowned authority on objets d'art from India, China, and Japan. Most of the purchases attributed to these surrogate buyers seem to have made their way into the Hawker collection. The most likely explanation is that Mr. Hawker had, for some reason, tasked Mr. Brackenbury with the role of acquiring artworks for him.

Flick snapped the book shut. "Wrong!" she said. "The most likely explanation is that Desmond Hawker was a blasted thief." She lobbed the book at the pile of paperwork. Nigel rolled his chair backward as the heavy book skittered down the long conference table and sent smaller items flying in all directions.

"On the other hand," Nigel said as he pushed detritus

away from the edge of the table, "does any of this nineteenth-century intrigue amount to a hill of beans? Any wrongs done to Neville Brackenbury are ancient history. The collection has been in the Hawkers' possession for more than a hundred years, and we don't *really* know whether Desmond acted illegally. Who can possibly argue that the family does not own the antiquities in every legal sense?"

"Dame Elspeth Hawker can," Flick said sharply.

"And therein lies our dilemma," Nigel said. "Elspeth seems to have been spot-on in her other concerns. Is there a chance—even a wee chance—that the museum will make a serious mistake if we move ahead with our decision to buy the collection from the Hawker heirs?"

Flick raised her index finger. "The very same Hawker heirs who probably know all about the shaky provenance and would love to unload their dodgy collection on an unsuspecting tea museum."

Nigel grunted. "With the help of Barrington Bleasdale, their slick solicitor."

"We are caught between a rock and a hard place."

"Granted. But what do we tell the trustees? They will skin us alive if we simply *un*recommend our decision to go forward with the purchase. We need a substantial reason to veer from our announced course."

"Actually, we need some good legal advice."

"I could call Iona Saxby. She is a top-notch solicitor."

"And she likes you."

Nigel wrinkled his nose, then looked at his watch. "It's five thirty. She may still be in her office."

Nigel dialed Iona's business number. "No joy," he said. "Her voicemail picked up."

"Try her at home."

He dialed a second number and listened to the phone ring. He hung up when her personal answering machine invited him to leave a message. "Not there, either."

"Rats!"

Nigel nodded his agreement with Flick's frustration, although he felt relieved that he had not reached Iona. It made more sense for Flick and him to sort out the "problem" before they involved any of the museum's trustees.

"Do you know any other handy lawyers?" she asked.

"Now that you mention it, I do have an old friend in London." He reached for the phone once more.

A basso male voice answered, "Andrew here."

"Greetings, it's Nigel Owen."

"Nigel! Good man! Have you returned to civilization? Or are you still disgruntled in Tunbridge Wells?"

Nigel moved his finger to his lips, then pressed the speaker button so Flick could hear both sides of the conversation.

"My tenure at the tea museum has another five months to run."

"Poor blighter!"

Flick clapped her hand to her mouth and turned away. Nigel fought not to laugh along with her. He swallowed hard and said, "Andrew, I need a soupçon of free legal advice. After five years as a bureaucrat in London, do you still remember the law?"

"An adequate touché. Not bad for a provincial living so far from town. What do you want to know?"

"The museum intends to purchase a collection of antiquities that have been in the possession of a respected family for more than one hundred years. However, we recently received information that the founder of the family may have acquired the items in a fraudulent manner. We are concerned about issues of provenance."

"Provenance! The bane of every museum keeper. I get it—your issue pertains to the workings of England's celebrated Limitations Act of 1980. Think back to that omnibus course on business law you took at business school."

"As I recall, the Limitations Act takes away one's right to contest ownership of property after a reasonable number of years."

"Six years, in fact. Presuming that the property is acquired in good faith." Andrew sniggered. "However, if said family acquired said antiquities in bad faith—if they nicked them, for example—the six-year limit does not apply. The true owners could assert their ownership six *centuries* later."

"I see."

"Now, let us say that the tea museum purchases said items in good faith. After six years, the act would protect you against any claims. In theory, no one could contest your ownership." Andrew sniggered again. "Trouble is, laddie, you seem to be acting in bad faith because you have prior information that the goodies fell off the back of a truck. Consequently, the time limit might not apply to you, either."

Nigel watched Flick's eyes widen. He felt sure that his eyes had become even larger.

He thanked Andrew, promised to visit soon, and rang off.

"It's a muddle," Nigel said. "A blooming big muddle. And we are in the middle of it. Our chief problem is that we have to make assumptions about what Desmond Hawker did or didn't do more than a hundred years ago."

"Maybe we don't have to make assumptions. As you suggested yesterday, one of us should peruse Desmond's papers in the archives."

"A great idea. In fact, there's no time like the present."

Flick shook her head. "Count me out, Nigel. I'm disgusted.

I am thoroughly annoyed. Most of all, I'm pooped because I got up at five thirty to catch the early train to London." She spoke to Cha-Cha before Nigel had a chance to argue. "Come along, dog. You are going to spend the night with me."

After Flick left, Nigel tidied the boardroom and thought about the museum's archives. He had visited the basement before. The boxes and bins were neatly labeled. He did not need the chief curator holding his hand to poke through Desmond's personal papers.

More to the point, I won't sleep tonight if I don't at least begin the search.

The staircase that led down to the basement was next to the elevator on the ground floor. He descended and turned on all the overhead banks of fluorescent lights. The museum's architect had given the basement two purposes. The eastern half housed the traditional assortment of boilers, heaters, blowers, valves, pipes, electric panels, and other paraphernalia necessary to keep the museum comfortable and operational. The western half accommodated a small office suite for Conan Davies and his security staff and a much larger storage area designed for long-term warehousing of documents, artifacts, and antiquities. The storage area was cool, dry, and (Nigel had decided) remarkably un-basementlike, with a high ceiling, black-and-white asphalt tiles on the floor, brick-faced support columns, and smooth plastered walls painted a creamy off-white.

The Hawker archives filled three long ranks of metal shelves in the southern end of the storage area. The lion's share of Desmond's papers consisted of accounts and correspondence pertaining to his tea businesses. Nigel doubted that routine commercial records would shed any light on the antiquities. In any case, one would need a team of researchers to examine that much paper.

Nigel moved along the lines of shelves until he reached the last bay in the third rank. Here were twenty-odd file boxes full of the commodore's personal papers, the first labeled DESMOND HAWKER CORRESPONDENCE: 1860–1863.

That is too early. Think! What dates are important?

Nigel remembered that Flick had talked about the Long Depression and Neville Brackenbury's bankruptcy in 1876. Nigel scanned the boxes until he saw one labeled DESMOND HAWKER CORRESPONDENCE: 1875–1877. He heaved it down to the floor and unsnapped the lid. His heart sank.

There must be a thousand letters stuffed inside.

He plucked one free at random from the middle of the box and slowly made sense of the intricate cursive script. It was a copy of a complaint letter dated 18 May 1876, from Desmond to his tailor.

Blast! I would need a week to go through this one box.

Nigel replaced the letter and hoisted the box back on its shelf.

Perhaps this isn't such a grand idea after all.

And then a slightly battered file box sitting within easy reach on the bottom shelf caught his eye: MISCELLANEOUS HAWKER HOUSEHOLD RECORDS.

The word "miscellaneous" straightaway cheered Nigel. It implied a lack of structure and absence of discipline. Who knew what one might find in a box named *miscellaneous*?

He opened the lid and peered inside. As he had suspected, the box held a hodgepodge of loose papers. He fished one out and examined it: a baker's receipt dated 1904. Someone in the Hawker household had bought seven loaves of bread for a total price of fourteen pence—only tuppence a loaf.

The good old days.

Nigel reached in again: a receipt for coal from 1894. And

again: an order for bed linens placed in 1901.

His hand touched a large rectangle of folded paper. He unfolded it and discovered a neatly drawn floor plan for Lion's Peak—dated 1873 and signed by Decimus Burton.

"This belongs upstairs," he murmured. "Under glass."

Nigel felt a twinge of guilt. It was great fun to rummage around in Desmond's past, but he wasn't achieving anything useful.

Three more items, then I quit.

He reached inside the box and brought out a dunning letter from a solicitor to Basil Hawker, dated 1891, demanding immediate payment on a personal debt of seventy-six pounds and nine shillings that was in arrears for more than eight months.

Basil, you were a bad boy.

Nigel reached deeper into the box. His fingers touched the bottom, then brushed sideways against something thick and large. He lifted out a reusable interoffice envelope, the sort with a string clasp and many boxes to write the names of successive recipients. The same two names appeared again and again: Mary Evans Hawker and Mirabelle Hubbard. The last recipient—the only name not lined through in pencil or ink—was Mirabelle Hubbard.

Nigel squeezed the envelope. His fingers and brain recognized the object inside as a slender book. Nigel undid the clasp and turned the envelope on end. An old notebook with hard pasteboard covers slid into his hand. He opened the notebook and began to read.

Crikey! I hit the mother lode.

Her phone rang as Flick was preparing to step into a tub of

scrumptiously warm water laced with bergamot-scented bath salts.

"Hello," she said cautiously.

A barrage of short sentences came in reply. "It's Nigel. Are you still dressed? If you are not dressed, get dressed. We have to visit Mirabelle Hubbard. I just called her. She knows that we are coming. I stumbled upon what we were looking for. In the archives, all by myself. I am a blooming genius. I will pick you up in the BMW. Be ready in ten minutes."

Flick let herself groan. "This better be good, Nigel." Full of regret, she sniffed the pungent orangey aroma of bergamot that filled her flat. "You have no idea of the sacrifice you are asking me to make."

"*Good* is not the appropriate word. Try *spectacular*. Or *phenomenal*. I found answers to most of the questions we have about Desmond Hawker."

"Fifteen minutes."

"Twelve and a half." He hung up.

Flick exited her apartment eleven minutes later and saw Nigel's BMW waiting near the bottom of the Lower Walk. When she opened the passenger side door, her annoyance faded. Nigel's silly, boyish grin seemed to refresh her. She felt pleased—*surprisingly pleased*—to see him as she slipped into her seat.

There's no need for him to know that.

She slammed the door harder than necessary and said, "Where does Mirabelle live?"

"Good evening to you, too."

"Whatever!"

"We are going back to Rusthall. Mirabelle lives in a cottage near the High Street."

Flick noted that Nigel drove faster than usual inside

Tunbridge Wells. He sounded excited, he even looked excited—a decidedly unusual state of affairs for buttoned-down Nigel Owen. During his phone call, he had mumbled something about finding answers to their questions about Desmond Hawker. She tried to recall the rest of his words, but they seemed a blur. All except one short phrase: "I am a genius." Flick could no longer hold back her curiosity.

"Okay, give!" she said. "What does Mirabelle Hubbard have to do with any of this?"

"Mirabelle was Nathanial Swithin's secretary for many years."

"Tell me something I don't know."

"On occasion, she served as Mary Hawker Evans's secretary, in the same way that Polly provided part-time support for Elspeth."

"And?"

"All will be clear when we get to Mirabelle's cottage. I enjoy constructing surprises just as much as you do."

"Whatever—*squared!*"

When they reached the top of Major York's Road, Nigel swung left onto Langton Road, then right onto Rusthall Road. They parked in front of Mirabelle's small house on Rustwick Street.

The door opened before Nigel had a chance to ring the bell. Mirabelle must have been watching the street from inside the house. She beckoned them inside. The telly was on in the living room, but she quickly turned it off.

Flick glanced at Nigel and noticed that he was carrying an internal-mail envelope with something inside. Mirabelle also saw the envelope.

"Where did you find it?" she asked.

"In a box of miscellaneous household records," he replied.

She stared into space for a moment, then a smile exploded on her face. "Yes. . .that's right. I remember now. I hid it in that box twenty-five years ago, perhaps thirty years. In the very bottom, under a stack of litter."

"Why did you choose that particular box?"

Mirabelle colored. "Because it was the jumble box, full of odds and ends that weren't worth filing. I didn't think that Mrs. Evans would ever look inside." She gave a slight shrug. "It was also an easy box to reach, tucked in on the lowest shelf."

"The box is still sitting on the same shelf."

Flick's curiosity raged back at full intensity. What was "it"? Why did Mirabelle hide "it"? She had a dozen questions to ask but found herself restrained by the amiable smile on Nigel's face as he spoke to Mirabelle.

Don't interrupt. Let Nigel do his thing.

Mirabelle gestured for them to sit down. There was an overstuffed sofa and two matching reclining chairs, all positioned to face the telly. Nigel chose the sofa; Flick sat next to him.

"Do you think that I did the wrong thing?" Mirabelle asked.

"Not at all." Nigel punctuated his words with a firm shake of his head. "Mary Hawker Evans asked you to destroy the notebook, didn't she?"

Mirabelle nodded.

"But you decided to hide it back in the archives instead?"

Mirabelle nodded again.

"Why?"

"Because it didn't belong to Mrs. Evans anymore. She had donated all the commodore's papers to the museum. The notebook wasn't hers to destroy." She looked up with a pained expression. "Besides, I was the one who found it. Mrs. Evans didn't know that the commodore had written a personal journal before I showed it to her."

The words "personal journal" made Flick recoil against the back of the soft sofa. She looked at Nigel, who was grinning like a loon as he proudly presented the envelope to her.

"We finally have the story from the horse's mouth," he said. "Read the first few pages."

Flick resisted the urge to rip open the envelope. She fumbled clumsily with the string and finally managed to open the flap. Mirabelle had called the artifact a notebook, but it was actually a Victorian schoolchild's copybook—an inexpensive repository of all he or she learned at school. The coarse pages had turned brownish pink with age, but the twenty blue lines on each page were still visible. Flick found Desmond's tight and angular handwriting easy to read.

Lion's Peak
Maundy Thursday, 1904

I write these words, as my life draws to its close, to record a grievous wrong I have done, in the fervent hope that those who follow me will make proper amends for the damage I have caused to a man who trusted and believed in me.

Mr. Neville Brackenbury, of London, was for many years my faithful business partner. He was an honest and honourable gentleman with whom I could freely share any confidence. To his peril, Mr. Brackenbury foolishly believed that he could place an equal trust in me and that I would always act in his best interests.

I chose to betray Mr. Brackenbury when I could have helped him. I acted with malice, God forgive me, because destroying him seemed the best way to advance myself. I allowed Mr. Brackenbury to sink into the mire of bankruptcy.

And yet, while I bear a large share of the blame for his financial ruin, he also played an important role. His own greed led him to make foolish investments that sowed the seeds of his destruction. In this matter I feel remorse; I fear the wrath of God, but I do not see any way to offer recompense. There is no return from ruination.

My second betrayal of Mr. Brackenbury presents quite different circumstances. Here, I behaved like the thief portrayed in Holy Scripture, in the twenty-second chapter of Exodus. Here, I must make proper recompense.

Mr. Brackenbury purchased many objects that he valued far beyond their monetary value. I speak of his prized collection of paintings, decorative articles, goods made of Tunbridge Ware, maps, chinaware, and the like.

When it seemed clear that Mr. Brackenbury could not avoid financial disaster, he sold his collection to me for a miniscule sum of money, believing in my promise that I would safeguard his treasures and return them at a time when his financial conditions sufficiently improved.

When that time came, I refused to return the objects. I advised Mr. Brackenbury that I had purchased them legally and intended to keep them. Through that evil act, I who had been like the "neighbor" portrayed in Scripture also became the thief. My actions caused additional, dreadful harm to Neville Brackenbury, to his wife, Lucinda, and to his sons Geoffrey and Graham, who were only babes in arms at the time. For that I am truly sorry.

To make proper restitution, the thief must pay back double to Neville Brackenbury's lawful heirs. I have tried to find them, to no avail. The pages that follow present all that I have learned about the fate and whereabouts of Neville Brackenbury's kin.

Thus I request and beseech my beloved son, Basil, to vigorously search out the survivors of Neville Bracken-bury and return the collected objects to them, along with a sum of money equal to their value. I pray in the name of Jesus Christ our Savior that my son will have success where I have failed.

I chose not to make this request a provision of my Last Will and Testament because I do not want to bring public dishonour on the next generation of the Hawker family. The wicked sins I committed are my own. They do not belong to Basil or to his children.

(signed) *Desmond Hawker*

Very slowly, Flick looked up from the copybook. Her heart was thumping. She felt almost too giddy to consider the implications of what she held in her hands. A holographic document: a detailed explanation of Desmond's actions and motives, in his own handwriting, in his own words. Nigel had made an undreamed-of discovery, a window on the past that might somehow work to illuminate Elspeth Hawker's death.

"You *are* a genius," she said to him, her voice husky. "Although I'm still confused. Did Desmond steal the antiquities or not?"

"Morally yes, but legally no," he replied. "Professor Oxley got it wrong. Desmond Hawker did not defraud Neville Brackenbury. Neville made a valid transfer of his collection to Desmond in the belief that Desmond would return it after Neville's financial situation improved. Desmond didn't follow through." He gave a wry smile. "The bankruptcy judge certainly would have been upset had he found out that Brackenbury had conspired to hide valuable assets from the court, but

290

that doesn't change what happened. Desmond Hawker bought the collection. He owned it in 1876, and the family still does today."

"Okay. Second question: Why didn't Basil Hawker return the antiquities to the surviving Brackenburys after Desmond died in 1904?"

"I can answer that," Mirabelle said softly. "It was Mrs. Evans and I who sorted the commodore's papers and put them in the file boxes. You see, for many years, the papers simply sat higgledy-piggledy piled in wooden crates. When she donated them to the museum, the two of us tried to arrange them in an order that might be useful to scholars. I remember the day I came across the journal among a stack of paid bills. I gave it to Mrs. Evans; she stopped working to read it.

"She became very upset and said that her grandfather had made a request that her father did not respect. She told me that Sir Basil was not the sort of man to give away valuable property and large sums of money—even to honor a deathbed wish expressed by his own father. She knew for a fact that he had made no attempt to find the Brackenbury heirs."

"She also said that it was far too late to make amends. That is when she told me to burn the journal." Mirabelle sighed. "I could not bring myself to destroy it—not a book of writing that came from the commodore's heart. So I hid the journal in a box full of jumble. I even pushed the box all the way to the back of the shelf and put other boxes in front of it. I didn't want Mrs. Evans to find the journal again."

Nigel frowned. "The miscellaneous file box I found was all by itself on the bottom shelf," he said, "with the label easily visible to anyone standing nearby. I suppose that's why I decided to look inside."

Flick felt a tingle of insight that blossomed into a jolt of full-fledged understanding. "Elspeth Hawker spent months browsing through the archives. She found the journal before you did."

Flick stood up, unable to contain her excitement. "But she wasn't sure how to interpret the commodore's plea. Like me, she didn't know if he really had stolen the antiquities. So she asked Jeremy Strain for his opinion, and she decided to reread Philip Oxley's manuscript."

Flick flipped through the pages in the notebook. The additional information about the Brackenbury kin that Desmond Hawker had promised turned out to be three more pages of handwritten notes. Regrettably, the writing had become virtually illegible. Desmond had apparently used a different ink to write the additional pages—an ink that had faded over the years. Flick didn't try to make sense of these addendums. There was equipment in the Conservation Laboratory that could help decipher the writing, if necessary.

"I'm surprised," she said, "that Elspeth Hawker didn't encourage the museum to find Neville Brackenbury's surviving heirs. It's the sort of thing Elspeth might do."

Nigel, who had seemed to be lost in thought, raised his head. "Quite," he said, "although it may have happened the other way round. Perhaps Neville Brackenbury's heir found the museum first."

Flick experienced a new wave of giddiness. She sat back down on the sofa and stared at Nigel.

No words were necessary. They both knew he was right.

SIXTEEN

"Now what?" Flick snapped her seat belt shut. "It's eight thirty, I'm wide awake, and my mind is racing a thousand miles an hour."

"I feel the same way. I don't want to go home, either."

"I can't stop thinking about Desmond's ancient sins. Somehow they are linked to the recent thefts that Elspeth discovered."

"Somehow. . . ," Nigel echoed. He tugged on Flick's seat belt. "I know what I want to do."

"Tell me."

"I want to figure out the hard-to-read pages in Desmond's. . .what did you just call it? His copybook."

"Great idea. Let's go to the museum. I'll set up the equipment in the Conservation Laboratory and put on a teakettle and a coffeepot; you snag us some goodies from the tearoom."

"And we will work as a team to shut off the alarm system."

"Absolutely," Flick said. "I have my trainers on and I'm ready to run." She finished with a lilting giggle that sent a remarkable chill along Nigel's spine. He put the car in gear, sorry that their journey from Rusthall to the Royal Tunbridge Wells Tea Museum would be over in less than five minutes. He enjoyed having Flick a few inches away in the cocoonlike privacy of his BMW.

Someday soon you will have to tell her how you feel. Could there be a better time than now?

"I know that I will enjoy watching you run," he said softly.

Good grief! What a blithering thing to say.

Flick stared at him with a quizzical expression.

Of course, she is staring, you dunce! You sounded like a smitten, tongue-tied teenager.

He started the engine and gazed steadfastly at the road as he guided the BMW out of Rusthall. What on earth had prompted him to make such an inane comment? And what must Flick be thinking right now?

He risked a sideways glance at her. *What. . .she is smiling.*

He breathed in and out. Perhaps he had not done any lasting damage, after all.

"Nigel," she said.

"Yes?"

"I'm sure I'll enjoy watching you run, too."

He began to laugh. Flick joined in.

Nigel parked next to the side entrance. He unlocked the metal door, and they ran side-by-side down the hallway, laughing all the way to the kiosk. Nigel punched in the code to disarm the perimeter alarm; Flick used her index finger to turn off the motion detectors.

"Does milady crave a particular sort of goodie this evening?" he asked, with a stiff upper lip he thought would do a movie butler proud.

"I am easily satisfied with the best of everything," she

replied, in a credible Royal accent that raised his eyebrows.

"Well done! I will see you in the Conservation Lab after I raid the pantry."

Nigel found several day-old scones in the refrigerator, two probably older lemon curd tarts, a half-full jar of raspberry preserves, and a fresh bottle of clotted cream. He revived the scones in the microwave and filled two serving dishes with sufficient preserves and cream to feed a family of four.

Who knows how long we'll be working this evening.

In fact, Nigel and Flick needed more than an hour to transcribe Desmond's faded notes. They found that by illuminating the copybook with strong glancing light from the left side off the page—and carefully positioning a strong magnifying lens over the page—they were able to read a few words at a time. The story of Desmond Hawker's search for the Brackenburys emerged in fits and starts.

Dearest Basil,

In 1885, I commissioned the Marlborough Detective Agency in London to investigate several thefts from our dockside warehouse. The operatives routinely looked into all persons who had left the employ of the company, including Neville Brackenbury.

Thus it was that I learned for the first time that my old friend was dead, and worse, that he had taken his own life some two years earlier in 1883.

For reasons I did not fully understand at the time, the news of Mr. Brackenbury's suicide shocked me to the core. As good Christians are wont to say, the Holy Ghost worked in my heart to convict me of the wrong I had done.

My appreciation of my sins grew slowly. More out

of curiosity than anything else, I asked the Marlborough Agency to locate the rest of Mr. Brackenbury's family. They had no success. Mr. Brackenbury's widow and children had left London and seemingly vanished into the countryside. I tried again in 1887 and again in 1889. I commissioned wider investigations, in keeping with my growing faith and, I admit, my growing realization that I had misused the entire Brackenbury family.

In 1891, the agency had a bittersweet success. An operative discovered that Lucinda Brackenbury and her son Graham died during the same influenza epidemic that took our beloved wife and mother, Pamela Nelson Hawker. It seems that Mrs. Brackenbury and her children had been living with a distant relative in Wales. The public records of their deaths finally revealed their whereabouts.

Geoffrey Brackenbury was not taken ill during the epidemic. The agency made additional inquiries and found that soon after he buried his mother and brother, Master Geoffrey, age eighteen, immigrated to Nova Scotia, in Canada.

I immediately made application to an agency of detectives in that distant province. Alas, they were unsuccessful in finding him, as my further attempts also have been. It is my unshakable conviction, however, that Geoffrey Brackenbury, the heir of Neville Brackenbury, is alive today.

Nigel gave a soft whistle. "One must be impressed by Desmond's resolve. He was not the sort of man to take no for an answer. He never believed that Neville Brackenbury had no survivors—even though he knew that Geoffrey might be the last of the clan."

He expected Flick to agree with him, perhaps to append a pithy observation about Desmond Hawker's stubborn character. But she merely continued to stare at the copybook. He could see distress in her face, as if she found the very sight of the pages difficult to bear.

She finally looked up at him. "You want industrial-strength resolve," she said, "think of the depth of the hatred that Geoffrey Brackenbury—an eighteen-year-old kid—carried with him to Canada. He left England in 1890. The fire at Lion's Peak was in 1925. He brooded and seethed for thirty-five years. I didn't think that ill will could last that long."

"Alas, it can," Nigel replied. "Hatred based on the loss of family honor often spans centuries. It is the stuff of famous literature and infamous vendettas."

"Family honor. . . ," she repeated quietly. "I hadn't considered that, but, of course, you are right. Family honor explains the low profit margin on the thefts at the museum. This thievery isn't about money; it's to restore what was taken from the family." She turned pages in the copybook. "Desmond confessed to keeping objects that Brackenbury 'valued far beyond their monetary value.' The set of Tunbridge Ware tea caddies, purchased as an anniversary gift for Lucinda Brackenbury, must have held a preeminent place among the family's treasures."

"Why do you suppose that the Canadian detectives did not find Geoffrey?"

Flick shrugged. "Huge country. Zillions of places to hide."

"Perhaps. But I will wager that Geoffrey had sailed back across the pond, probably with a brand-new identity. Edwardian England was a much more likely place than the bucolic Dominion of Canada to brood ill will and breed a new generation of Hawker haters. He—*they*—would have seen the Hawker family living a pampered life that should have also belonged to the Brackenburys. And so—"

"The fire at Lion's Peak," she joined in.

"Intended to eliminate the Hawkers' ill-gotten gains in a single stroke." Nigel lifted his hands like a preacher offering a benediction. "The Lord Almighty declares I will destroy the house, both its timbers and its stones."

"Who do you think died in the blaze?" Flick asked.

"Geoffrey, if I had to guess. That must be why the attacks stopped after the fire." He picked up his coffee mug and discovered it was empty. "Only to be resumed eighty years later when a more recently hatched member of the Brackenbury family—say Neville's great-grandson—decided to start nicking Tunbridge Ware from us."

Flick's face darkened. "What about Elspeth's murder? Was that triggered by family honor, too?"

"I shouldn't think so. According to Elspeth's notes, the theft of the tea caddies spanned nine months. If one of the thief's objectives was to kill Elspeth Hawker, why delay so long? And while one is at it, why not also call down vengeance on Alfred Hawker and his penurious sister, Harriet?"

Flick lifted her gaze to meet Nigel's eyes. "You know, of all the Hawkers, it was Elspeth who suffered most for her grandfather's sins—first as a child caught in the fire at Lion's Peak, then later as a murder victim."

"Elspeth seems to have been the only good-hearted Hawker in the bunch."

"So good-hearted that she initially refused to believe the vendetta theory advanced by Philip Oxley." Flick picked up the copybook. "Only when she read Desmond's confession did she come to understand that a Brackenbury heir was responsible for the recent thefts. And why."

"What adds an element of Greek tragedy to the story is

that Desmond wanted to give the clobber back—to pay double, in fact."

"But Geoffrey Brackenbury never knew that," Flick said.

"True. But even if he had known, he probably would have doubted that Desmond turned over a new leaf." Nigel smiled at Flick. "Look how hard it is for you to accept the truth of his conversion."

A sheepish expression crossed her face as she looked down at the old copybook in her hands. "I have to admit that this is not a public exhibition of piety, like building a church. The Desmond Hawker revealed on these pages seems genuinely changed." She paused to choose her words carefully. "I may have to revise my. . .*opinion*. It certainly seems as if Desmond received a. . .*call*. And that the. . .*Holy Spirit* renewed his heart." She sighed. "That's another element of this tragedy. Desmond wanted to make amends but was never able to, no matter how much he tried. Despite the many good things he accomplished as a Christian, he couldn't find a way to do that."

Nigel walked to the coffee pot to refill his mug. Much like the Tea Tasting Room, the Conservation Laboratory had built-in waist-high cabinets with slate countertops flanking the windows. There were also five laboratory workstations arrayed along a line that bisected the narrow room. Flick had chosen the third workstation, close to the middle of the room, to examine the copybook. This, she explained, was to avoid disturbing Lapsang and Souchong, who had commandeered the first and fifth workstations as their own. There was one cat—Nigel still couldn't tell them apart—curled comfortably on the bottom shelf of each workstation. He might have completely forgotten their presence except for the faint aroma of slightly used cat litter that wafted throughout the laboratory.

Flick had set up the drip coffeemaker alongside the sink

in the corner of the laboratory that overlooked Eridge Road. Nigel poured, watched a large lorry roll toward Tunbridge Wells, and wondered what posterity would make of his checkered career. On occasion, he, too, had let his ambition run loose "at all costs." But he had not played the big-business game as well—or should the word be *badly*—as had Desmond Hawker.

Had he lied? At times. Had he deceived? Everyone at his old company did. Had he used confidential business information to get ahead of a business rival? Once or twice. Had he caused grievous harm to anyone? He didn't think so, but then neither had Desmond Hawker until many years later.

If there was a difference between Nigel Owen and Desmond Hawker, it was simply one of degree. Nigel had not coveted success enough to develop a true killer instinct. Probably that was why his company had declared him redundant while other higher-flying blokes in the organization were still at their jobs.

He would have a tough decision to make five months from now when his acting directorship came to an end. Did he really want another job in a building full of Desmond Hawker wannabes? There were decidedly pleasant aspects of his tenure at the museum, starting with the lack of a need to guard his back continuously. Oh, the trustees could be pains in the posterior, but Flick Adams was not after his job. His success did not imply her failure.

Another charming facet was the human scale of the museum. He could get his arms around the entire enterprise and take real pride when his management skills kept things running efficiently. And one might even argue that directing a museum promoted, in a modest way, the "betterment of humanity."

He sipped his coffee slowly. What if he didn't move back to London? What if he managed to find a full-time job along the lines of the one he had now? It certainly was worth pondering in the weeks ahead.

"Nigel."

"Yes," he replied hazily.

"Nigel!"

"Sorry!" He spun around to talk to Flick.

"It's my turn to be a genius," she said. "I've been thinking about our conclusion that our 'exceedingly clever thief' is a fourth-generation relative of Neville Brackenbury. Doesn't that change our list of suspects?"

Nigel had difficulty swallowing the coffee in his mouth. "Blimey! When did I become such a dunderhead? Of course, it changes the blooming list. Archibald Meicklejohn is the blue blood among our trustees. He has a pedigree that goes back six hundred years. I have seen portraits of his ancestors; he looks just like them. There isn't a chance in the world that he is kin to Neville Brackenbury. The same is true of Conan Davies, although his blood is plaid. Conan is indisputably Scottish through and through." He added, "Who is left on the list?"

"Marjorie Halifax, Dorothy McAndrews, Matthew Eaton, and Iona Saxby."

"A politician, an antiques expert, a landscape gardener, and an attorney." He waved his hand disparagingly. "I find it hard to picture any of that lot skulking into your office and sprinkling a lethal dose of oleander in your Assam tea. Even more difficult to accept is the notion that one of those duffers possesses the required electronic skills to defeat our security system."

Flick grimaced. "I keep remembering the alarm, then forgetting it again. We won't move forward until we can work out how the thief dealt with the motion detectors." She suddenly seemed energized with determination. "What time is it?"

"Twenty-two hundred hours. Ten o'clock."

"Five p.m. in Pennsylvania. I've been meaning to bounce the alarm question off my uncle Ted. He's probably still in his office." She reached for the telephone on the top of the workstation, switched on the speaker, and dialed.

A gruff voice came forth: "Homicide. Detective Adams."

"Hi, Uncle Ted, it's Flick."

"Speak of the devil. I yakked with your mother less than an hour ago. Half of our discussion was about you."

"I'm sure it was," she said quickly. "Anyway, we have an interesting. . .*issue* at the museum. We have experienced an after-hours theft or two, but we have a top-of-the-line security system."

"And you are confused as to how the perpetrator could get past your foolproof burglar alarm."

"Exactly."

"Simple. There's no such animal as a foolproof security system." He chuckled. "You've described a variation on the classic 'locked room' mystery. There's no way in or out of the room, except the thief managed to find one." Another chuckle. "There's *always* a way in and out." His voice became serious. "I assume you have the usual perimeter sensors and motion detectors?"

"We do."

"Then there are three likely explanations. One—it's an inside job. Namely, one of your own staffers is the perp. Two—you have a security breach. The perp learned how to disable the system. Three—the most likely answer. Your perp goes to work when the alarm is switched off."

"One or two may be possible, but not three. Our alarm is on whenever the museum is closed to the public."

"No, it isn't!" Ted said confidently. "If that were true, your cleaning people couldn't do their jobs. Think about it—security systems get turned off a lot."

"I will think about it. Thanks."

"By the way. . .expect a call from your mother. She is disturbed that you seem to have no love life these days. . . ." Flick yanked the receiver out of the cradle, which automatically turned off the speaker.

Nigel watched Flick blush. The wave of color sweeping along her cheeks seemed an extraordinary sight. He couldn't resist smiling at her momentary embarrassment.

Nigel went to pour himself another cup of coffee while she wrapped up her call to her uncle. He moaned softly when he found scarcely a quarter cup left in the pot.

"What do you think about the third explanation?" Flick asked.

"I think we had better talk to Conan Davies."

Nigel had Conan's home number on a laminated card in his wallet. He dialed and put the call on speaker.

"Davies," a gravelly, though sleepy, voice answered after six rings.

"Conan, I am sorry to disturb you so late, but I have a foolish question."

"There are no foolish questions, sir." Nigel heard a big yawn. "Just foolish hours of the day to ask them."

"Yes, well, is there a time when the museum is closed and our motion detectors are switched off?"

"As a matter of fact there is, sir. Two hours each day immediately after closing. That's when the cleaning crew and maintenance workers are in the museum."

Nigel and Flick both slapped palms against their foreheads in exaggerated why-didn't-we-think-of-that gestures.

Conan went on, "Of course, one of my guards is on duty in the kiosk on the ground floor. He inspects everything that is brought in or taken out of the building by after-hours personnel." He added, hopefully, "Is that all, sir?"

"Thank you, Conan."

"Good night, sir."

Flick pointed to the empty coffee pot. "Shall I brew some more?"

"Actually, I would rather try a cup of your Assam."

Her eyes became wide. "You want tea?"

"Indeed! In a teacup rather than a mug. And please put the milk in first."

"I have a weird idea, if you are game," Nigel said, peering at Flick over the top of his teacup. The boyish grin on his face made her wonder what he had in mind. There were all sorts of possibilities this late at night.

"How weird?" she asked warily.

"You be Elspeth for the next few minutes. Let's figure out how she spotted the thief taking pictures and swapping counterfeit antiquities."

Flick returned his grin with a big smile. "That's a great idea. Where do I begin?"

"In the Hawker Suite, I should think."

They walked down to the second floor. Flick stepped inside the Hawker Suite and swung the door ajar.

"Okay. I'm Elspeth Hawker and the museum has just closed."

"MMMMnnnnnn."

"What's that?" she shouted through the gap.

"The cleaning crew is vacuuming the second-floor lobby," he shouted back.

Nigel made the sound again, but it slowly faded away,

leaving her in almost total silence. Flick found it quite easy to picture Elspeth standing at this very door, waiting patiently for the cleaning crew to move to the third floor as they worked their way from bottom to top of the museum.

Flick listened at the door. The building wasn't completely silent, after all. She could hear cars going by on Eridge Road. And the tick of a clock somewhere nearby. And the wind whooshing around the corners of the building.

She opened the door. It creaked more than she had expected. The second-floor lobby was empty. She immediately understood the game that Nigel had invented. He would be an observer rather than a director. Her role was to think like Elspeth Hawker.

What did Elspeth know for certain? Only that one of the people on her list had engaged in systematic theft from the Tea Antiquities Gallery on the first floor.

What was Elspeth's goal? To identify the thief so that she could reveal him or her later.

What was Elspeth's first challenge? Get to the first floor as quietly as possible, in case the thief already was working inside the gallery.

Flick stepped outside the Hawker Suite. Elspeth would not have taken the elevator to the first floor; it was too noisy. Therefore, she must have used the staircase. Flick slipped off her trainers and tiptoed down in her stocking-covered feet. She was amazed by how little noise she made. The marble-sheathed steps didn't groan or creak, even when she moved quickly.

Flick paused at the bottom of the staircase. To her right was the Tea at Sea Gallery; to her left, the Tea Antiquities Gallery; around the corner behind her, the Tea Processing Salon and the Tea Tasting Room.

Now what?

Flick could hear herself breathing. She felt uneasy standing exposed in the first-floor lobby. Elspeth must have felt the same way. Uncomfortable. Out in the open. Painfully vulnerable.

A hiding place. That's what Elspeth would want.

Elspeth would have sought a secure vantage point—someplace she could watch the thief working inside the Tea Antiquities Gallery.

Elspeth would have taken her position before the thief arrived and then stayed put until after he or she had finished. Only then would Elspeth remount the stairs and spend a cozy night locked inside the Hawker Suite.

Flick slowly revolved on her shoeless heel.

The Tea at Sea Gallery was an open area with twenty low tables to display the various ship models and a dozen floor-to-ceiling exhibit panels standing close to the walls.

No place to hide.

The Tea Tasting Room seemed a more likely possibility. Its archway entrance provided a good view of the first-floor lobby area—and of anyone entering or leaving the Tea Antiquities Room. Flick padded into the Tea Tasting Room and stood silently in the corner next to the entrance.

No good. I would have to stick my nose around the archway to see anything.

And there was another weakness: The Tea Tasting Room was almost bare. With no available hiding places, Elspeth certainly would have felt nearly the same level of unease as in the first-floor lobby itself.

That left the Tea Processing Salon—a room full of machinery adjacent to the Tea Antiquities Room. Two wide archways in the shared wall connected the rooms.

Flick moved toward the Processing Salon, then changed her mind.

Do it the other way around. Begin in the Antiquities Room.

The rack that held the "All the Teas in China" Tunbridge Ware collection was set up in the northeast corner of the large gallery. Flick stood in front of the display and looked behind her into the Tea Processing Salon. She could see the gleaming pulleys of the cut, tear, and curl machine in the distance, but not much more. The big machine reminded Flick of an old printing press—a celebration of shafts, belts, and wheels. If Elspeth had positioned herself behind the iron frame, she would have been able to see through parts of the machine and easily observe the thief at work in the Tea Antiquities Gallery.

Without much fear of being seen herself.

There were also five freestanding display panels in the Processing Salon, any of which would provide a convenient hiding place. Flick could imagine Elspeth feeling secure and comfortable amid the various machines and exhibits as she watched the thief replace one of the tea caddies with a sham look-alike.

Comfort would be important, because she had to watch the Antiquities Gallery over several nights running to catch the thief at work. Elspeth could only guess when he or she would return to substitute another piece of counterfeit Tunbridge Ware.

Don't jump to conclusions!

The thief also replaced the *tansu* tea chest near the entranceway. What if Elspeth had been watching that evening?

Flick moved alongside the small chest. Its glass-panel doors glittered in the sharply focused beam of light from the fixture overhead. She was now much closer to the Tea Processing Salon, almost next to one of the connecting archways. When she looked toward the salon, she could see only one corner of the cut, tear, and curl machine.

No problem! It's still a good hiding place.

Flick looked back at the *tansu* chest—and froze. The shock wave of disbelief that coursed through her body made it difficult to catch her breath.

She could see Nigel's face!

Straight ahead was the reflection of the tea processing machine on the chest's glass panels, and there—to one side of a large metal linkage—was Nigel watching her, unaware that she could see him.

The same thing happened to Elspeth Hawker.

Images advanced like projected slides in Flick's mind.

Click. She saw the thief tugging the squat chest, making sure that the replacement was in exactly the same position as the original.

Click. The thief, stunned by Elspeth's reflected image, had to struggle mightily as Flick had just done so as not to give away the startling discovery.

Click. There was the thief leaving the Tea Antiquities Gallery, knowing that Elspeth Hawker fully understood how the thefts had been committed—wondering what would be the best way to silence her.

Click. Finally, Flick saw Elspeth emerge from her hiding place and return to the Hawker Suite, having no idea of her desperate peril.

Flick waved at the reflection on the glass. "I can see you, Nigel—just like the thief spotted Elspeth Hawker. Now we know why she was poisoned."

"Blast!" He stood up. "Should you ever decide that curating is not your cup of tea, you ought to apply for a crime-reconstruction post at the Kent police."

Flick slipped her trainers back on. "Thank you, kind sir." Nigel had delivered a tortuous compliment—certainly not the most gracious she had ever received—but a compliment nonetheless. To her surprise, it erased much of the gloom she had felt a moment before. She rewarded him with an amiable smile.

Unfortunately, Nigel didn't seem to notice. He was deep in thought, his eyes gazing intently into space. "The fact is," he said glumly, "we have only reconstructed bits and pieces of this crime. We understand how the thief got around the motion detectors. We have guessed where Elspeth hid and how the thief caught a glimpse of her. The next question is the biggie: How did the thief get in and out of the museum? I doubt that he or she marched nineteen antiquities past the security guard in the kiosk."

"Could there be a way into the building that we don't know about?"

"I doubt it. Conan Davies knows every nook and cranny of this museum. He certainly would have discovered a chink in our armor long before this."

"As Uncle Ted said, 'There's *always* a way in and out.' "

"If there is, we will find it."

"Tonight?"

He shook his head. "You are beginning to look knackered again. It is time to go home; you have done quite enough for one day. We will enlist Conan tomorrow morning. The three of us will tour the museum." He added with a grin, "Perhaps our building is riddled with clichéd sliding panels and hidden passages after all."

"Instead of an actual tour, let's do a brainstorming session with Conan," Flick said. "It's a more efficient way of picking his brain."

Nigel seemed to hesitate at first. Flick wasn't surprised; many people have misgivings about the hoary technique of brainstorming. But then, few of the doubters had tried her unconventional approach. He finally nodded. "Brainstorming it is. You are in charge."

They climbed together to the third floor. Nigel locked the old copybook in the small safe in his office. They descended to the ground floor, reset the security system, and left the museum through the side door.

Flick slid into the BMW and watched Nigel turn the key in the ignition. He seemed preoccupied, as if his mind had focused on another challenging problem. He wore much the same cheerful expression she had seen earlier that evening when he had made the bizarre comment about watching her run. She had been bewildered at first, then delighted that her snap decision to echo the comment back at Nigel had been the right thing to do. They had laughed about running for most of the short drive to the museum.

Brits have a strange sense of humor.

"I have been thinking about Desmond Hawker," Nigel said. Flick peered at him. Was this the start of another odd British joke?

Nigel continued. "We both agree that something changed him in midcourse, that he found peace during the second half of his life that he lacked during the first half."

"I agree that we agree."

"Yes, well, this Sunday. . .would you. . .*uh*. . .consider. . . *ah*. . .accompanying me to St. Stephen's?"

He's invited you to go to church with him.

"Oh?"

"If you are busy, I certainly understand."

"No."

"No?"

"No, I'm not busy," Flick said emphatically. "I think going

to church is a lovely idea."

"Ah."

She swallowed a sigh. She had sounded like a complete ditz. *He's probably sorry he asked.*

It was almost eleven thirty, late enough for Nigel to risk stopping his BMW on the no-parking side of the Lower Walk. Flick looked up at her apartment and wondered if it would be possible to revive the tub full of bath salts. She reached for the door handle.

"Hang on," Nigel said, "I will escort you to your front door." He leapt out of the driver's seat, came around the front of the car, and gallantly opened her door.

"It is only six thirty in Pennsylvania," he said, a soppy grin breaking across his face.

"That's true," Flick said, as evenly as she could. Her heart had begun to race. Nigel was up to something—but what?

"I suppose you will call your mother when you get upstairs?"

"If I don't, she will call me. It happens every time she talks to Uncle Ted."

"Well, if she should ask about your love life. . ."

Without warning, Nigel cupped her face in his hands and kissed her gently on the lips.

"Assure her that it is alive and well," he said.

"*O*–okay," Flick murmured, her heart now thumping. She looked up at Nigel. He still had the soppy grin on his face. She hoped that her smile looked just as silly to him.

Flick wasn't caught off guard when Nigel kissed her again.

A dog yapped somewhere overhead.

Nigel laughed. "Cha-Cha, your companion and chaperone, knows you are back."

"Okay," Flick said again, unable to think of anything else to say. She quickly let herself into her building. She drew several calming breaths and listened through the door as Nigel started the BMW and drove away.

"Wow!" she murmured and trudged up the long staircase to her apartment.

Cha-Cha raced around her feet as she let herself in. She walked into her parlor and sat down in her only armchair. The dog jumped up next to her and tried to lick her cheek.

"I just made a terrible mistake, didn't I, Cha-Cha?"

The dog replied to the sound of his name with a soft, squeaky bark.

"You are absolutely right. I did act dumb! I should have kissed him back."

SEVENTEEN

Nigel awoke in an emphatically jovial mood on Thursday morning. He stopped at the bakeshop on Mount Pleasant Road and bought a dozen French pastries for the museum's staff. When he arrived at his desk, he used his first twenty minutes to send cheerful e-mail notes to former colleagues throughout England. And by midmorning he had found a way to settle scores with Conan Davies.

Although Conan was chief of security, a management position, he chose to wear the same discreet uniform as his team of security guards: sharply creased gray trousers, a blue blazer adorned with the Royal Tunbridge Wells Tea Museum crest on the breast pocket, and comfortable black shoes—the sort with thick rubber soles that cushion the blows of walking and standing on marble floors.

Nigel applauded Conan's logic: The museum had a small security staff and Conan often had to pitch in and perform routine chores. This morning, for example, he stood on the museum's loading dock watching a food delivery lorry back slowly into the single concrete bay. The museum's security policy—written and enforced by Conan—ordained that a security guard monitor all transfers in or out of the museum. Nigel, however, felt personally aggrieved by the chief of security's shoes. They allowed Conan to move ghostlike through the museum and arrive silently behind Nigel in a wholly unpredictable manner. Conan shocked him to the core at least once each week. Today presented a golden opportunity to get even.

Nigel approached stealthily, the sound of his leather-soled footsteps entirely masked by the *beep, beep, beeping* of the lorry's reversing signal, and clapped Conan on the shoulder. The big man rose a foot off the loading dock and screeched an unfamiliar phrase that Nigel took as a mild Scottish oath.

Revenge is mine!

"Oh, it's you, sir," Conan said as he readjusted his dislocated eyeglasses.

"Sorry, Conan. I didn't mean to alarm you," Nigel said innocently. "Can we talk while you watch the driver unload? I have a remarkable story to tell you."

"Certainly." Conan gestured toward a pair of scruffy metal office chairs that overlooked the loading dock. They sat down as the driver rolled open the back of the lorry and began to move cardboard cartons to a low-slung trolley.

Conan listened stony-faced, from time to time murmuring, "Poor Dame Elspeth." He interrupted Nigel's narrative only once, when the lorry driver demanded that someone sign for the delivery. Conan scrawled his name on the driver's tablet computer and pushed the button that closed the loading dock's overhead door.

"Sorry, sir. You were telling me how Dame Elspeth first discovered the thefts."

Nigel could see Conan growing more and more upset as the balance of the sad story unfolded. The pained expression on his face proclaimed unmistakably how much he hated to learn about a problem on his patch from someone else—especially his boss. Conan was gripping his chair's armrests with sufficient strength to flex the metal tubing. Nigel wondered if the chair would survive their chat.

"And you say that my name was on her list of possible thieves, sir?" Conan asked when Nigel had finished.

"Yes, but only halfheartedly. You see, you are in the building so often that it was probably hard for Elspeth to eliminate you as a suspect." Nigel grinned. "We did it by reasons of your ancestry."

"*Thenk ye,*" Conan said in a thick burr.

"We need your help."

"You shall have it, sir."

"Felicity Adams has set up the Hawker Suite as our incident room. Let's join her."

Conan tipped his head toward the trolley full of cartons. "As soon as I push these provisions into the kitchen."

"You push; I'll pull."

When Nigel entered the Hawker Suite, he noted with some surprise that Flick had rearranged the furniture while he was gone. She had moved the sofa and armchair away from the back wall to create a large area of easily accessible surface. On one side she had taped public relations photographs, borrowed from Nigel's files, of the four remaining suspects. On the other side she had affixed floor plans of the museum's four levels.

Conan, who walked in right behind Nigel, said, "What's this all about, then?"

"A backward brainstorming session," Flick said. "We have

two questions on the table today. First, how can someone get in or out of this building without triggering the perimeter alarm? Second, what do we *really* know about these four people?" She tapped the page-sized color photos of Marjorie Halifax, Dorothy McAndrews, Matthew Eaton, and Iona Saxby.

Nigel could imagine what Conan, a man of action, must be thinking about the idea of doing detective work via brainstorming. The chief of security seemed disorientated by Flick's initial explanation, but he was clearly too good a soldier to express his doubts verbally. He sat down on the sofa—knees together, his hands resting in his lap—and awaited further orders. Nigel sat down in the armchair.

"What makes our brainstorming session backward," Flick continued, "is that Nigel and I are going to come up with intentionally silly ideas. As our expert on the museum, it will be your job to shoot them down with all the ferocity you can muster."

Conan's eyebrows rose. "You want me to *argue* with you, ma'am?"

"Tooth and nail. We need you to be merciless." Flick moved an easel with a large paper pad closer to the wall. She picked up a marker pen and unsnapped its cap. "I'll also be secretary and write down the interesting stuff that emerges as we talk." She glanced at Nigel. "If you please, Mr. Acting Director, tell us your silly idea for fooling our perimeter alarm."

Nigel worked to mask his own skepticism. He had had much the same reaction as Conan when Flick explained "my little game," as she called it, but her enthusiasm had won him over—not to mention her extraordinary smile. For some unfathomable reason, she looked more beautiful this morning than she had yesterday. He had agreed, albeit reluctantly, to give her approach a try.

In for a penny, in for a pound.

"Actually," Nigel said with a sniff, "I believe that I've come up with a rather brilliant idea. I enter the museum as a visitor during normal opening hours, but then find a convenient cubbyhole where I can hide until the museum closes that day. I now have the ability to skulk around to my heart's content, doing nefarious things, while the cleaning crew is working and the motion detectors are off." Nigel leaned forward conspiratorially. "Now here's the really clever bit. I open a window and use a rope to lower a real antiquity to my confederate waiting outside. Then use the same rope to haul up the fake. When the cleaning crew leaves, I return to my cubbyhole and spend the night. The next day, I join the new crowd of visitors and leave the museum— with no one the wiser."

Flick smiled at Conan. "Mr. Chief of Security, please explain to Nigel why that is an impossibly dumb idea."

"Well, sir, it is an *unworkable* idea for three reasons." Conan gazed down at his big hands, apparently unwilling to call his boss's idea *dumb*. "The first is that we count visitors entering and leaving the museum and compare the numbers. We would know if someone decided to spend the night inside. The second reason is that every window has a sensor. The security guard in the kiosk gets an immediate warning signal should anyone open a window. The third reason is that we don't have any cubbyholes big enough to hide a person. Every cubic inch of space in our building is accounted for, and most are protected by at least one motion detector. Even the loos and coat closets have them. The only area in the museum without a motion detector is the Hawker Suite." He glanced uncomfortably at Nigel. "Because the suite was rarely visited by Hawkers in the past, we presumed that locking the door would provide sufficient security. Dame Elspeth's. . .*unusual* use of the suite demonstrates that we were wrong. I will correct our oversight as soon as possible."

"Excellent!" Flick gestured triumphantly in the air with her marker pen. "Conan just provided three important facts about the museum that I certainly didn't know." She made three entries on the large pad: *We Count Visitors! Windows Protected! No Cubbyholes!* Flick turned from the easel and looked expectantly at Nigel. "See how my game works?"

Nigel laughed. "I do indeed. You take advantage of that most powerful of human drives—the primal craving to reveal that another person is wrong." He did not add that he, too, had not known about the process of counting visitors or that opening a window would signal the guard. There was no need for Conan—or Flick—to doubt that the acting director was aware of all operating procedures.

Mental note: Read Conan's security manual in its entirety.

"Now it's my turn to propose a silly idea." Flick took a moment to gather her thoughts. "I envision a member of the cleaning crew who decides to replace real antiquities with counterfeits. He constructs a garbage can with a false bottom— to smuggle fakes into the museum and real antiquities out. The security guards are so used to seeing him go in and out with his garbage can that they give it only a cursory inspection each evening and never spot the false bottom."

Nigel found himself thinking hard. Why was that a dumb idea? It seemed eminently possible. In fact, Flick may have come up with the answer to the mystery. He glanced at Conan in time to see the man's face quiver with despair. The man appeared almost distraught at the prospect of destroying Flick's hypothesis. Did she realize the angst her little game was causing the chief of security?

"Well, you see, ma'am. . ." Conan paused, then began again. "It's this way. The museum provides the trashcans to the cleaning crew, along with their other equipment. If we had a dishonest cleaner—I am sure we don't, because we do background checks on all staff—he wouldn't have the opportunity to do what you suggest. But even if he did, the tags would stop him."

"What tags?" Flick and Nigel asked in unison.

"Every item on display in the museum is tagged with a little gizmo the size of a one-pound coin. Our antitheft tags work in much the same way as the devices that discourage shoplifting in stores. We have sensors on the doors that detect the tags and sound an alarm should someone try to carry a protected object out of the museum. Unless one uses a special tool, it is impossible to remove the tag without damaging the antiquity." Another sigh. "We don't talk much about the antitheft tags. It is best not to share our security secrets with everyone."

Nigel swallowed hard. *I am not blithering "everyone." I am the acting director.*

Mental note: Order Conan to provide a detailed security brief.

"Rats!" Flick said as she wrote *Antitheft Tags!* on the pad. "The tags shoot down my next dumb idea before I can ask it. I was going to propose that Matthew Eaton smuggled the fakes in and the real objects out by hiding them in the pots of the plants his firm donates to the museum." She made a hazy gesture toward his picture on the wall. "You know—stash the Tunbridge Ware tea caddies beneath a sick ficus tree or a droopy philodendron."

Conan shook his head. "Sorry, ma'am. Every egress from the museum has an antitheft tag sensor."

"Including the loading dock?" Nigel asked.

"Well, the same as not to make any difference. The loading dock is really part of the greenhouse, sir; as such, it has its own alarm system. The last tag sensor is on the door that leads from the Duchess of Bedford Tearoom to the greenhouse. That door is the only way to travel from the museum to the loading dock. All of Mr. Eaton's plants enter or leave through that door."

Flick uncapped the marker pen and wrote *Tag Sensors on Every Door.*

"Another point to consider," Conan went on, "is that Mr. Eaton has been associated with the museum for the past twelve years, first as our horticulture consultant and then as a trustee. I have never known a man with larceny on his mind to demonstrate that much patience."

"A pity," Flick said. "A man who deals in plants would have ready access to oleander leaves. She added *Matthew Eaton = 12 Years!* to her growing list, then reached over and tapped Marjorie Halifax's photograph. "Nigel, you told me you had a silly idea involving our favorite local politician."

"I shall begin with the obvious," Nigel said. "Marjorie's last name is Halifax, and we know that Neville Brackenbury's son went off to Nova Scotia. That presents an extraordinary coincidence, don't you think? But even more relevant, Marjorie is well connected in local government. I assert that she was able to acquire copies of the museum's building plans on file with the authorities and consequently discover a secret tunnel"—he winked at Flick—"that leads into the building and completely bypasses our perimeter alarm system. The tunnel enables Marjorie to enter the museum whenever the motion detectors are disabled—and leave with any *objet d'art* she can carry."

"Highly improbable, sir," Conan said. Nigel noticed that the chief of security was now sitting tall on the sofa, that his hands moved with much animation, and that his voice had returned to its former gravelly splendor. Conan definitely had warmed to Flick's game and had shed his initial inhibitions about challenging his boss.

"If you reflect on your idea even a little bit, you will realize that this building was purpose-built as a museum. The design of the museum simply doesn't support secret tunnels. In fact, our foundations are unusually thick so that our basement can serve as a proper archive. And there are no nearby structures to provide a terminus for a tunnel, even if one wanted to create one."

Flick wrote *No Tunnels Possible!*

"And as for Mrs. Halifax's bona fides"—Nigel felt sure he could see a sneer on Conan's face—"you may not be aware, sir, that she was born a Griffiths, one of Kent's oldest families."

"You are sure of that, Conan?" he asked futilely.

"Completely, sir. I vet all new proposed trustees. Have done so for more than ten years."

Flick appended *Marjorie Halifax = Old Family!* and gazed at her easel.

Nigel watched Flick chewing on the end of her marker pen and felt a twinge of disappointment. She had fixed her mind on the brainstorming session; she seemed determined to make sense of her list. Why hadn't she mentioned their kiss this morning? His thoughts kept wandering back to the night before; why not hers? Perhaps she had found the kiss silly rather than romantic? Which led one to the inevitable question: How did she feel about him? He had made his feelings about her reasonably clear, but she had said nothing. Yes, she did agree to go to church with him on Sunday, but that hardly qualified as a proper date. Nigel let himself sigh.

So many important questions to answer, and Flick Adams is thinking about theft and murder.

Flick chewed on the marker pen and decided that her snap decision to suggest backward brainstorming had been a mistake.

The exercise wasn't going well. She had expected the technique to trigger an *Aha* moment for Conan Davies—a flash of insight that would immediately explain how the thief had been able to swap fake antiquities for real ones. Instead of simplifying the challenge, Conan had made it more difficult. Why hadn't Nigel known about the antitheft tags and the open-window warnings?

She peered at Nigel. He had glanced at her once or twice, then descended deep into thought about something. Nigel knew how to guard his emotions—it wasn't easy for her to read his expressions. But he looked vaguely worried. Maybe he regretted their kiss the night before. Nigel was a stickler for well-defined policy; he undoubtedly had written a whole set of rules that forbade relationships between people who worked together. She could imagine him brooding about the possible damage that he had done to his precious career by rashly kissing his chief curator.

Let's get this ridiculous session over with!

Flick rapped the marker pen against the easel to get Nigel's and Conan's attention. Both men looked up—neither with apparent enthusiasm.

"We are making significant progress," she said brightly. "Let's move on to Dorothy McAndrews. She is an antiques expert who would have little difficulty finding someone to manufacture counterfeit antiquities. She is also the trustee most concerned with the gift shop. My silly idea is that she bypassed our security system by the simple expedience of using the Royal Mail. Our gift shop ships many items each day to customers around the world. An extra parcel every week or so would hardly be noticed."

Conan answered immediately. "A bad idea for two reasons. She would require the connivance of a gift shop employee to succeed. Further, she would need to sneak the antiquities past the ground-floor kiosk to reach the gift shop. My security guard sits in it after hours, and Margo McKendrick is on duty when the museum is open."

"I have a third reason," Nigel chimed in. "It would seem a trifle challenging to post the Japanese *tansu* chest."

She wrote *Conspiracy Unlikely!* on the pad and fought back the urge to write off this session as a horrible mistake. "I agree that it is difficult to think of good bad ideas about Dorothy McAndrews—but that very fact makes her a likely suspect."

Nigel merely shrugged, but Conan gawked at her as if she had lost her mind.

Oh dear. Time to move on.

Flick pointed to the last photograph on the wall. "Nigel, do you have any scary thoughts about Iona Saxby?"

She gasped audibly. It was not what she had meant to say. Nigel's eyes went wide and he began to laugh. Flick started giggling; she felt herself begin to blush.

Conan abruptly surprised them both by saying, "I can give you a scary thought about Iona Saxby." He had spoken in such an ominous tone that Nigel instantly stopped laughing.

Flick looked at the chief of security. "Please—"

"Iona Saxby is a very wealthy woman. If she chose to try, she might be able to bribe one of my security guards. If that happened, Iona would be able to get into the museum any time the guard was willing to accompany her. He would have the codes to disarm the perimeter alarm and a proper finger image to disable the motion detectors. Working together, the pair could carry the largest antiquity in the building and move it right to the loading dock."

"The power of money," Nigel said softly.

Conan nodded. "Money is the one variable that must be

feared by anyone running a security operation. The most honest of people can be bent if the price is high enough."

"But you don't think that has happened—right?"

Conan's expression loosened. "No. I trust my staff. But that doesn't stop me from also doing periodic checks to find out if anyone is unexpectedly rolling in cash." He added, "It's a part of my security audit program."

Conan evidently saw the puzzled look on Flick's face. He spoke before she could frame a question. "Have you ever been to a magic show?"

"Sure."

"Well, one of the principles that a stage magician applies is to show his audience what they expect to see. That's a way to fool people. Seeing what one expects to see is a problem in security, too. Consequently, once each year I ask an independent security expert to review our operations. A new pair of eyes can recognize things that don't look right, that shouldn't be there."

Flick stared at Nigel, who was staring at her just as intently.

An image popped into Flick's mind. She felt sure that Nigel had also conjured up the same image.

"The pantry!" she screamed.

"It has to be!" he replied.

"What about the pantry?" Conan said.

"Follow us!" they shouted at the same time.

Flick stayed three steps ahead of Nigel. She charged down two flights of stairs, past a dozen bewildered visitors, lurched through the World of Tea Map Room, and flew past four people waiting to be seated in the Duchess of Bedford Tearoom. She made a sharp right turn into the kitchen and came face-to-face with Alain Rousseau, a tall, portly man with a well-trimmed beard and a short temper for trespassers in his bailiwick.

"Mademoiselle Adams," he said, then jumped in surprise as Nigel and Conan skidded to a halt behind her.

"Carry on, Alain!" Flick said. She raced down the steps into the pantry, turned right, and lunged for the wardrobe-sized gap in the shelving against the wall. She flung aprons, towels, and Alain's coat behind her.

"That was my face you just whapped," Nigel said. She ignored him and also the steady stream of pithy French spoken by Alain Rousseau from the pantry door.

She dropped to her knees and inspected the wall in the gap. "Does anyone have a flashlight?" She tossed her head in frustration at the differences in English spoken on both sides of the Atlantic Ocean. "I mean a *torch*."

"Try this one." Conan reached over her shoulder and offered a small, high-intensity pencil torch.

Flick used the bright beam to illuminate the paneling on the wall.

"I can see a very fine seam," she said. "I think there's a door here." She looked up at Conan. "What's on the other side?"

"A small storage room. It's part of the greenhouse." He added, "You both wait here. I will go to the other side."

"This would explain everything," Nigel said. "A door through this wall bypasses our perimeter security system." He ran his finger along the almost invisible seam. "I guess we do have a secret passage after all. Right into Matthew Eaton's private storeroom."

Flick heard metal rattling and glass clinking behind the paneling. Conan must have been shifting cans and bottles and whatever else was against the wall.

There was silence for several seconds, then a gentle wood-against-wood squeak. A square section of the wall—some four feet on each side—seemed to disappear in front of her eyes.

"It's a pop-out panel that fits perfectly in place," Conan said. "Beautiful workmanship. Almost impossible to see on the pantry side and hard to find on this side."

"What do we do now?" Nigel questioned.

"We call the police," Flick answered. "Have them arrest Matthew Eaton."

"On what basis?" Conan said. "Eaton will deny he knows anything about the panel. We have no evidence that he stole anything or poisoned anyone. Without proof, without a confession, there's no case against him."

Nigel suddenly sneezed.

"Bless you," Flick said.

"Thanks. I must be allergic to something on the other side of the wall." He found a handkerchief in his pocket and blew his nose. "I've just had an idea. A rather nasty idea—but I think Mr. Eaton deserves what's on offer."

"I hope it involves lots of oleander," Flick said.

"In a way, it does."

She couldn't imagine why Nigel was once again wearing his little-boy smile.

EIGHTEEN

Am I the only person ready to leap out of his skin? Nigel Owen asked himself as he watched the before-meeting chatter in the boardroom. A few feet to his left, Flick Adams was jawing merrily with Dorothy McAndrews about alternative methods of brewing tea. And across the room, Conan Davies had engaged Vicar de Rudd in a calm discussion about the fortés and failings of local golf courses.

How can they be so blasé about what is going to happen?

Nigel understood why his day had inched along. Because other people had done most of the work required to implement his idea, he had been left with too much free time on his plate. He had used it unproductively—to second-guess their preparations and worry about what might go wrong.

On three different occasions that morning, Nigel had checked the storeroom in the greenhouse to make certain that Conan had properly reinstalled the access panel and its camouflage of gardening chemicals. Would Matthew Eaton notice anything out of place if he arrived early for the trustees' meeting and decided to visit his storeroom? Had he arranged the cans and bottles in a specific way such that any variation would instantly signal that his secret passage had been discovered? Nigel finally decided that all he could do was hope for the best.

The best came to pass. Matthew arrived at quarter of four and happily spent the fifteen minutes before the meeting talking football with Archibald Meicklejohn.

He hasn't a clue that we found the panel, Nigel realized with much relief.

At four on the dot, Archibald took his seat at the head of the polished mahogany table. Nigel and the meeting's other participants followed the chairman's lead and found their seats. Long-standing tradition required that the senior management of the Royal Tunbridge Wells Tea Museum—acting director, chair of the trustees, and chief curator—be arrayed at one end of the conference table. And so Nigel sat at the corner of the table, to Archibald's left, while Flick took the opposite corner, to Archibald's right.

Flick offered an encouraging wink from across the table. It straightaway caused Nigel to remember the encouraging hug she had delivered before the meeting began. And then there had been the kiss after dinner the previous evening. . .

Keep your mind on the plan.

In theory, there were no seating customs for the other trustees. In practice, Marjorie Halifax always sat at the other end of the long table, facing Archibald. She did so today. The other participants selected their chairs on a first-come, first-served basis.

One seat near the middle of the table remained empty until five minutes after four, when Iona Saxby rushed through the door in a hat that, Nigel estimated, had a brim as wide as a full-sized Mexican sombrero. She sat down next to Dorothy McAndrews, who, fearing brim-whip or possible blinding, scooted her chair closer to Sir Simon Clowes.

"*Scusi*," Iona said to Nigel in badly accented Italian. "I am *tardi* because my train was a *locale*."

"Non importa," Nigel replied. *Iona must be getting ready for one of her periodic fortnights in Italy.*

"*Grazie!*" The happy look on her face went far beyond mere gratitude for his forgiveness of her minor transgression.

Crikey! She remembered my promise to have dinner with her.

"Well, now that we all are here," Archibald said, "we can begin. Nigel, this is your meeting—please take the lead."

Nigel put Iona out of his mind and drew a deep breath. "I want to thank the trustees for attending this special meeting of the trustees of the Royal Tunbridge Wells Tea Museum. As you see, we have several guests with us today.

"First, I am delighted to welcome Mrs. Harriet Hawker Peckham and Mr. Alfred Hawker, the soon-to-be-confirmed new owners of the Hawker antiquities. The gentleman sitting to the right of Mrs. Peckham is Mr. Barrington Bleasdale, the Hawkers' solicitor."

The Hawker heirs acknowledged their introduction with lackadaisical waves and feeble smiles, but Bleasdale bestowed a Cheshire cat grin on everyone at the table. Nigel instantly recognized the euphoric look of a man who expected to be much wealthier by the end of the day.

Don't count your chickens quite yet. . . .

Nigel finished the introductions. "All of the trustees know the gentleman on my left. Conan Davies is our chief of security. I asked him to join us today should we require his expertise on security matters pertaining to the collection. And sitting next to Conan is Mr. Marc Pennyman. I prevailed upon him to travel up from Maidstone to help me with any. . . legal issues that might emerge today."

Nigel paused for more smiles, nods, and waves, then said, "Vicar, please open us in prayer."

The vicar began with a invocation that asked, once again, for additional wisdom and discernment. Nigel listened carefully and offered his own silent postscript. *Lord, if You do happen to listen to the odd prayer coming from Tunbridge Wells on a Friday afternoon, I second the vicar's motion. The group gathered in this room today has need of a boatload of discernment.*

The first item on the agenda—the part of Nigel's plan designed to lull the trustees into believing that this special meeting was largely routine—was a longish slide presentation delivered by Flick. He asked her to project photos of the eighty most important Hawker antiquities and give a thirty-second description of each, ostensibly to bring everyone up to speed with the content of the collection. As before, her detailed knowledge captured the interest of the trustees. Even Nigel found himself paying attention. Her twenty-third photo was "Yunnan," one of the tea caddies from "All the Teas in China." He cast a sideways glance at Matthew Eaton. It was hard to read Eaton's expression in the near dark, but Nigel sensed a certain smugness around the man's mouth, a tinge of self-satisfaction.

We'll have that off your face in another hour.

Flick talked on, and Nigel had to fight back a yawn. Once again, the darkened boardroom became as warm as a tropical rain forest, with the drawn drapes blocking the windows and the heating system working passionately even though the outside temperature had reached sixty degrees Fahrenheit.

Flick finished speaking and received her accustomed accolades. Only Marjorie Halifax, who still seemed peeved at

Flick, was subdued in her praise. Nigel surveyed the conference table as Conan turned on lights and opened drapes.

Everyone is still alive!

Nigel cleared his throat. "By way of apologizing for the skimpy repast I served at our last meeting—and to compensate you for attending yet another unplanned trustee meeting—I have asked Alain Rousseau to provide the mother of all tea breaks this afternoon." Nigel nodded at Conan, who opened the door and helped Giselle wheel in two tea trolleys laden to overflowing with serving dishes, ceramic crocks, and silver tureens. "Quarter of five strikes me as an excellent time to enjoy our tea. *Bon appétit!*"

Nigel felt great satisfaction as he watched the trustees, the Hawker heirs, and Solicitor Bleasdale attack the tea trolleys from all sides. He recalled an image—perhaps from an old Jacques Cousteau movie—of a dozen sharks savaging a school of fish, each predator determined to get more than his or her fair share.

"I love prawns!" Dorothy squealed, as she shoveled savory prawns on her plate.

"Have as many as you want, Dr. McAndrews," Giselle said. "I brought more than enough for everyone to have a double helping."

"I've never seen scones this lovely golden color before," Marjorie cooed. "They are beautiful."

"I will relay your compliment to Chef Rousseau, Mrs. Eaton," Giselle said. "He tried a new recipe today."

"Add my congratulations for the superb lemon tart," Archibald said.

"May I suggest that you also try a spoonful of sorbet, Mr. Meicklejohn," Giselle said. "Tart and sorbet go very well together."

"This soufflé is magnificent!" Matthew Eaton gushed, a spoon still in his mouth.

"Have another," Nigel said. "I don't really care for Grande Marnier."

The feeding frenzy lasted a full fifteen minutes. Nigel exchanged occasional fleeting looks with Flick and Conan, both of whom had moved away from the tea trolleys and were sipping cups of tea. Marc Pennyman remained seated at the table, his face aglow with curiosity. Nigel watched him for a few moments. *Of course, the detective inspector is curious. He is wondering if we can pull it off.*

Getting Pennyman to attend had taken a good deal of "prevailing" when they called him early that morning. Fortunately, the DI knew Conan Davies by reputation. Although he doubted Nigel and entirely distrusted Flick, Pennyman finally had been won over by Conan's pleas and assurances.

He had arrived at ten but had nearly headed back to Maidstone five minutes later when Nigel explained his plan.

"That is daft as a brush," Pennyman said. "I will have no part of it."

Conan Davies patiently reviewed the accumulated evidence and showed Pennyman how the thefts had been committed. He also explained how the microphones on the conference table fed a voice-operated tape recorder in Polly Reid's office to capture everything said in the boardroom during a meeting.

"I see where you want to go with this," Pennyman said with the hint of a grin on his lips, "and I don't suppose that I will jeopardize my career by merely sitting through the first act of your farce and remaining in the immediate vicinity to see the final denouement, on the off chance you succeed." His face hardened. "However, it might be better for all concerned if a sworn officer of the Kent police does not attend the middle act."

"A very wise observation," Conan had said. "It is highly likely that Detective Inspector Pennyman will receive a telephone call at an appropriate time during the trustees' meeting."

At a few minutes past five o'clock, Nigel rapped the table with his knuckles. "Ladies and gentlemen, it is time to regroup at the table. I have a question for you: How did you enjoy the food today?"

The volley of enthusiastic applause from the hard-to-please trustees surprised Nigel. Alain Rousseau had more than met Nigel's challenge; he had clearly outdone himself.

"Now we can tell you the *whole* story," he said. "I am excited to reveal that our distinguished trustees and our honored guests have been the first to taste a new line of sweets and savories that Giselle plans to serve in the Duchess of Bedford Tearoom."

"Here! Here!" Archibald cried out.

"Three cheers for the chef!" Vicar de Rudd shouted even louder. Nigel hoped no one would actually begin hip-hip-hooraying. Providentially, no one did.

He went on. "What makes these new dishes especially noteworthy is that all of them are flavored with tea leaves."

"I don't believe it!" Dorothy said. "You can't mean that those scrumptious savory shrimp are made with tea."

"And certainly not the Grand Marnier soufflé," Matthew said.

"Or the scones," Marjorie put in.

"Well, if you don't believe me," Nigel said, with mock distress, "perhaps you will believe Giselle Logan." He added, "Giselle, please explain our concept to our doubting trustees."

Giselle gave a slight bow. "Let me start by saying that cooking with tea is quite common in Asia and has been for centuries. There are countless soups, sauces, marinades, entrees, and desserts that contain tea leaves—or tea oil, which is made by pressing the seeds of a tea plant. As you have just discovered, tea adds new flavors and smells to familiar dishes." She spread her hands. "Please do not feel bad if we fooled you. At first, many people do not recognize the presence of tea in cooked foods. However, we believe that visitors to our museum will be eager to try dishes made with tea."

"Are we going to publish a cookbook?" Marjorie asked.

"What a grand idea," Flick said. "That can be one of our first fund-raising ventures."

Nigel exchanged the faintest of smiles with Flick. Now Marjorie Halifax could take credit for an idea that Flick had mentioned to Augustus Hoskins more than a week earlier. The councilwoman had a jubilant look on her face and seemed to be viewing Flick from a much rosier perspective than previously.

Marjorie decided to ask another question. "What kinds of tea did Alain use in the treats we just enjoyed?"

Giselle spoke up first. "In fact, Alain used only one tea— a high-quality, estate-grown Assam. The idea is to feature a different tea every month and choose specific sweets and savories that make the best use of each one."

"Do you know which Assam Alain chose?" Iona asked.

"No. But Dr. Adams does. I believe she provided the tea."

Nigel locked his eyes on the yellow pad in front of him and began counting the lines. This was the question they had been waiting for, a perfect opportunity to set the hook. It was Flick's job to answer the question. She had to do it all by herself.

"It is one of my favorite teas," Flick said. "A bold, tippy tea from the Mangalam Estate. I ordered a full canister two weeks ago. I kept the canister tucked away in my office, on my credenza, just for this occasion. I didn't even brew a pot for myself, just to make certain that Alain would have enough for today."

Nigel risked a glance at Matthew. A few minutes earlier, his face had been a picture of contentment. Now he looked pensive, perhaps preoccupied with thoughts of canisters on Flick's credenza. Nigel could almost see thoughts forming in the landscaper's mind. *Does she have more than one canister? How full was the canister I found before I added the handful of crushed oleander leaves?*

Perfect! The fish is firmly on the line. Now to let him run a bit.

Nigel sat back in his chair. "The purpose of our meeting today is to review the terms of our purchase of the Hawker antiquities. Mr. Bleasdale has prepared a draft purchase agreement for the trustees' consideration. It is"—Nigel tipped his head toward the solicitor—"a quite straightforward document that sets down in writing a proposal that Mr. Bleasdale and I discussed some two weeks ago. Let us spend the next, oh, thirty minutes or so reviewing the provisions."

Nigel had been optimistic. It took nearly forty minutes to review the various provisions in the purchase agreement. The most important was the simplest: two independent appraisers—one chosen by the Hawkers, one by the museum—would value each antiquity. The museum would pay the average of the two estimates of worth, unless the difference between the two exceeded 10 percent of the low valuation. In that event, a third expert would reappraise the antiquity and the parties would conduct negotiations to establish a price satisfactory to both.

There was a knock on the door. It opened sufficiently for Polly Reid to poke her head into the boardroom and say, "Sorry, Mr. Owen. There is a call for Mr. Pennyman. Quite important, the gentleman says."

Pennyman stood and quietly made his way out of the room. He pulled the door shut behind him with a solid thump.

It had been Conan who decided that the "second act" was about to begin. He had keyed the TALK button on his cell phone and rung Polly's extension as a signal to summon Pennyman to his nonexistent telephone call. One look at Matthew Eaton's darting eyes and sweating brow convinced Nigel that Conan had chosen the perfect time.

Nigel tapped his copy of the draft with his pen. "Now that we all understand the terms of the agreement," he said, "I would like to open the floor to questions, comments, and suggestions from the trustees. I believe it is critical that we resolve any concerns today so that we can move ahead quickly with the appraisals."

Marjorie Halifax thrust her hand in the air, visibly keen to ask the first question.

"Yes, Marjorie," Nigel said amiably.

Before Marjorie could begin to talk, Matthew jumped in. "I am sorry to interrupt, Marjorie, but I just remembered that I have an engagement this evening. I think the agreement is brilliant, and I agree that we should move ahead with dispatch. Now, if you will excuse me. . ."

Matthew tried to stand up, but Conan had slipped silently behind his chair. A broad hand pushed Matthew back down in his seat.

"Are you mad?" Matthew turned his head to look at Conan.

"Not that I am aware of, sir."

The other trustees gaped at the sight of Conan restraining Matthew. Archibald was the first one to react. "Conan, please explain your actions immediately."

"It's quite simple, Mr. Meicklejohn. I am ensuring that Mr. Eaton remains in his seat."

Matthew was almost as tall as the chief of security, but not as strongly built. He tried to stand again, but Conan pushed him down with more force than before.

"Get out of my way, you fool!" Matthew shouted.

"No, Mr. Eaton," Conan said. "Anyone else can leave the boardroom whenever they want to, but not you, sir. Not for at least another two hours. Isn't that right, Dr. Adams?"

"Correct," Flick replied. "More than an hour has passed since the start of our tea break. A total of three will be more than sufficient—won't it, Matthew?"

Nigel glanced around the table. The other trustees appeared shocked by Conan's wholly untypical behavior. Their expressions ranged from simple perplexity to outright disbelief. The Hawker heirs were both slack-jawed with confusion. Bleasdale gazed at Matthew with unconcealed avarice—no other solicitor was better positioned to represent Matthew Eaton in his upcoming lawsuit against Conan Davies and Felicity Adams.

Matthew Eaton stared angrily at Flick. "I have no idea what you are talking about." He spit his words at her, but Nigel could readily see the fear blossoming in Matthew's mind.

"I'm afraid you're being disingenuous with us, Matthew." She shook her head in an exaggerated gesture of sadness. "You know exactly what I'm talking about. Did you notice how sweet Alain made the Grand Marnier soufflé? I'm sure you did. After all, you ate two full helpings."

Matthew stared at Flick, his eyes widening. "I don't believe you!"

"Turnabout is fair play. Don't you agree?"

"You wouldn't!" he said hoarsely. "Other people ate the soufflé, too."

"Perfectly true. But I didn't eat anything. Neither did Nigel or Conan."

Matthew whimpered. His face was pale, his mouth distorted in a terrified grimace.

Archibald spoke up again. "Nigel, please explain the meaning of this bizarre performance."

So far so good, Nigel thought. *It is time to reel in our big fish.*

Flick glared back at Matthew Eaton and resisted the urge to feel sorry for him. *Of course, the man is frightened. He knows that enough oleandrin will stop his heart. He's wondering when the initial symptoms will begin—a growing discomfort in his gut, a faint flutter of his heartbeat.*

She looked across the table when Nigel said, "It is my intention to explain everything, Archibald. Although I will need Matthew's help to tell the full story."

Nigel stood and moved around the table alongside Matthew's chair. His commanding presence, his obvious strength of character, made Flick wince at her earlier impression that he had the mind, heart, and imagination of a bean counter.

"Matthew," Nigel said evenly. "I believe that I can convince Conan to release you in far less than two hours if you tell us why you are so upset."

Matthew hesitated, then finally said, "We need help. We need to go to the hospital."

"Why do we need help, Matthew?"

Another hesitation. "We have all been poisoned. Those of us who ate the food during tea break."

Gasps came from all corners of the table. Nigel ignored them. "What kind of poison, Matthew?"

"Oleander leaves. In the tea Flick gave to our chef to prepare the food."

"Good night, man!" Sir Simon said softly.

The other participants reacted to the palpable concern in the doctor's voice. Flick could make out only a few snippets of the loud torrent: "What does he mean?" "Who's been poisoned?" "I don't feel sick." "I thought the scones tasted off." "Someone call an ambulance."

Archibald shouted, "Silence!"

"Thank you, Archibald," Nigel said. He turned back to Matthew. "Did you put oleander leaves in Flick's tea?"

Matthew let his head bob up and down.

"I can't hear you, Matthew," Nigel said.

"Yes, blast it! I put the oleander leaves in her tea." Matthew moaned. "It wasn't supposed to hurt anybody. Flick would have spotted the oleander before she drank the tea." He peered beseechingly at Flick, clearly wanting to convey that she had not been in any danger. She forced herself to disconnect from Matthew's frantic eyes and also to keep her expression neutral, free of the fury she felt.

"That seems an odd thing for you to do, doesn't it?" Nigel's voice was soft, almost comforting. "What was your purpose?"

"I wanted to frighten her," Matthew said, almost too quietly for Flick to hear.

"Ah. And why did you want to frighten her, Matthew?"

Flick held her breath. They were getting close. Matthew gazed hither and yon like a cornered animal.

"I had to," he said with a dry sob.

"Why?"

"Because she knew."

"What did she know?"

"About. . . ," he began. He abruptly gave a slight shake of his head.

"What did Flick know?" Nigel pressed.

Matthew drew a long breath and let it out slowly. "She knew what I did to Elspeth Hawker."

"Tell us about that, Matthew."

"I had no choice! None at all. Dame Elspeth saw me in the Tea Antiquities Gallery." Matthew's voice suddenly grew cold. The dam broke. He might have been talking about another person, in another time, as he recounted the details of how he had murdered Dame Elspeth. Flick found it hard to pay attention to his almost clinical recitation of his trip to Tonbridge to purchase a supply of Seconol from an illegal drug dealer. . .of his theft of a jar of lingonberry preserves from the pantry and a large jam pot from the kitchen. . .of the clever slight of hand he employed to place the lethal jam pot in front of Elspeth. . .of his knowledge of Elspeth's bad heart and his hope that her death might be seen as suicide.

"And you did all that only because Elspeth saw you replacing real antiquities with counterfeits?" Nigel said.

Matthew leapt to his feet. This time Conan did not return him to his chair. "The antiquities are all mine!" Matthew shouted. "The whole Hawker collection belongs to me. Desmond Hawker stole the lot from my ancestor Neville Brackenbury. I am his great-grandson, his legal heir. I planned to take only a few of them—the objects my grandfather cared about. Elspeth had no right to stop me."

Flick could not keep silent. "You don't get it, do you? Elspeth *wanted* you to have the antiquities your family claims. She spoke to Nigel about a thief having to pay double. In her mind, Desmond Hawker was the thief, not you. I'll bet that Elspeth saw you in the Tea Antiquities Gallery on several different occasions. She said nothing about your thefts of the Tunbridge Ware tea caddies. But she drew the line when you took an antiquity that hadn't been acquired by Neville Brackenbury.

Desmond Hawker bought the *tansu* chest long after Neville Brackenbury died. That's why Elspeth decided to put a stop to your thefts."

Matthew looked up at Flick, his eyes full of misery. "Everything I took. . .you will find in my basement. But this is no time to worry about Tunbridge Ware or *tansu* chests. I need a doctor. We all do."

"Actually, you don't." Nigel spoke without any triumph in his voice. He, too, seemed to feel pity for Matthew. "The canister of Assam tea that Flick gave to the chef was stored inside her credenza. The canister you tainted with oleander has been in the possession of Mr. Pennyman—correction, Detective Inspector Pennyman—since this morning."

Matthew Eaton seemed to collapse as Flick watched. His legs gave way beneath him and he slumped down into his chair without any help from Conan.

As if on cue, the door opened and Pennyman returned to the boardroom. "Quite an interesting third act you put on," Pennyman said. "However, there is still one aspect of this case that needs to be resolved." Pennyman turned to Sir Simon. "Dr. Clowes, you concluded that Dame Elspeth Hawker died a natural death." It was a simple statement, but also clearly a question.

Sir Simon frowned. "Yes, but upon reflection, I now withdraw my initial determination as. . .ah, premature."

Pennyman simply nodded. He and Conan Davies escorted Matthew Eaton out of the boardroom.

An embarrassed simper from Sir Simon Clowes wasn't much of an apology, Flick thought, but under the circumstances it was probably all she would ever get. The other trustees looked equally sheepish, but they, too, seemed unable to say eight simple words: "You were right, Flick, and we were wrong."

Well, at least they've stopped complaining about being poisoned.

"Moving right along. . . ," Nigel said as he sat down in his place at the table.

Several trustees gawked wide-eyed at him. Marjorie spoke first. "We can't possibly continue this meeting today. Not after what just happened."

"Oh, but we must keep going," Nigel said. "We have a serious issue to resolve. If Matthew Eaton is correct, his family has a prior claim to the so-called Hawker antiquities." Nigel looked squarely at the Hawkers. "Where does that leave our agreement?"

Had Harriet and Alfred been stone statues, they might have offered a livelier reaction to Nigel's question. The pair stared vacantly at the wall with pale horror-struck faces, apparently unable to move, or speak, or even breathe conspicuously.

Bleasdale, too, seemed to have been rendered immobile, but he had turned a bright shade of red, and Flick could sense that his mind was racing madly, trying to find an appropriate way out of this unforeseen—and thus unplanned for—morass.

Serves you right, you rotter. You tried to cheat us from day one.

She and Nigel had guessed right: Harriet, Alfred, and Bleasdale knew all about Elspeth's provenance concerns. Their solution had been simple: Sell the collection to the museum as fast as possible.

Pity that Elspeth never showed you Desmond Hawker's copybook. Then you would have known that the Hawker family owned the antiquities legally, if not morally.

Bleasdale snapped out of his catatonia: "If we do the deal quickly, I see absolutely no potential liability to the museum. You are buyers in good faith. The Limitations Law will protect you in the long run."

But what happens during the short run, before the six-year time limit cuts off claims?

The evening before, Flick and Nigel had discussed what to do in this very situation. "We do the right thing," Nigel had said. "We tell Bleasdale about the copybook, and we carry on with the purchase."

"I agree," Flick had said. "There has been too much treachery and deceit surrounding the Hawker antiquities. We don't need to add any more."

But there's no reason not to make Bleasdale sweat a little before we tell him.

"Gosh," Flick said, "all of this legal wrangling is a bit frightening to me. Do we really want to move ahead under these circumstances?"

Flick felt a twinge of guilt when Bleasdale looked stricken again and replied with a stammered "But. . .but. . .but. . ." Perhaps the time had come to fess up.

"Of course, you feel that way, Dr. Adams. Any nonattorney would."

It took Flick a brief instant to realize that Iona Saxby had chimed in. "Frankly," Iona went on, "it seems highly unlikely that Matthew Eaton will ever be able to prove that he is the rightful owner of the Hawker antiquities. Moreover, I believe that he forfeited any equitable rights to asset his claim when he murdered Elspeth Hawker. In short, I see no legal or moral reason not to proceed."

Unabashed joy crossed Barrington Bleasdale's face.

"Yes!" he shouted. "My thoughts exactly."

"However. . . ," Iona said. "Dr. Adams did make a cogent observation. The museum will have *some* additional risk, minimal though it may be. An appropriate change of terms definitely seems appropriate, don't you agree, Mr. Bleasdale?"

Bleasdale's eyes narrowed as lawyerly resolve replaced joy. "An appropriate change of terms. . . ," he echoed. "Well, I suppose that the owners might be willing to sell the antiquities at a discount compared to their appraised value—say 10 percent."

"Say 40 percent."

"Twenty-five percent."

"Done!" Iona said.

The talk of percentages revived Harriet Hawker Peckham as effectively as a vial of smelling salts. "We can't sell at a discount," she hissed at Bleasdale. "We won't have enough money to pay all the inheritance taxes."

"Dump Lion's Peak!" Bleasdale snapped at his client. "Neither of you wants the old eyesore anyway." He added in a more even tone, "The museum will buy all the old clobber at once. They have offered you a fair deal—take it!"

Flick held her breath. Should she have mentioned Desmond's copybook earlier? More to the point, should she mention it now? Probably not. If the Hawkers' solicitor thought they had a fair deal, why should she disagree?

"In that case, we have a deal," Iona said.

"In that case, let's celebrate," Archibald said, standing up. "I suggest we all adjourn to Hammond Bistro in the Pantiles and get our evening off to a proper start." He clapped a hand on Nigel's shoulder. "And should our discussion during dinner lag, we can chat about Nigel becoming the museum's permanent director when his contract as acting director is up."

"*What?*" Nigel seemed dumbfounded.

"It makes perfect sense, Nigel. You better than anyone else understand the work to be done in acquiring and paying for the Hawker antiquities. Why would we want to change horses in midstream?"

"I don't know. . . ," Nigel said without thinking.

"That was another rhetorical question, Nigel. You don't

have to answer it." Iona had immediately taken Archibald's vacated chair. She leaned so close to Nigel that Flick wondered if Iona had decided to climb into his pocket.

"Of course, we don't want to change horses," Iona cooed at Nigel. "Nor do we want to waste time on finding a replacement. You have found your ideal niche at the museum." She flashed a catlike smile that triggered a look of abject terror on Nigel's face. "Now, about this evening. I suspect that dinner will be over fairly early. . . ."

Flick crumpled up a sheet of paper and lobbed it at Nigel. Curiously, it also hit Iona. They both looked up at her.

"Nigel, you seem to have forgotten about our staff meeting. We have time for a quick dinner with everyone, but we'll have to get back to the museum promptly afterward."

"Staff meeting?" Iona said incredulously.

"Oh dear, yes. So much to do—in fact, we may be working most of the weekend. Could be all hours of the day and night."

"On what?" Iona said.

"On what?" Nigel repeated.

Flick managed to kick Nigel's ankle under the table.

"I meant to say, on *everything*!" he said quickly. "We have *thousands* of details to worry about now that we are acquiring the Hawker collection."

"In fact, I would like to press you into service in the Conservation Laboratory right now—just for a few minutes before we leave for dinner."

Nigel freed himself from Iona's near embrace.

"Indeed! A pressing matter. Well, then let's press on."

Flick led him out of the boardroom.

"About our staff meeting tonight. . . ," he said.

"What about it?"

"Do we have an agenda?"

"I don't know. Do you?"

"Oh yes!" Nigel slid his arm around Flick's waist and pulled her closer. "I definitely have an agenda."

They began to laugh and walked faster toward the Conservation Laboratory.

ABOUT THE AUTHORS

Ron Benrey is a highly experienced writer who has written more than a thousand bylined magazine articles, six published books on technical topics, and scores of major speeches for the CEOs of Fortune 100 companies. He holds a bachelor's degree from the Massachusetts Institute of Technology, a master's degree in management from Rensselaer Polytechnic Institute, and a juris doctor from the Duquesne University School of Law.

A native of Royal Tunbridge Wells in Kent, England, Janet Benrey has experience as a successful entrepreneur, a professional photographer, and an executive recruiter. Over the years, Janet has written magazine articles for consumer, business, and special interest publications before working in books. Janet earned her degree in Communication (Magna cum Laude) from the University of Pittsburgh. Together, they are the authors of three books in the Pippa Hunnechurch series, including *Little White Lies* and *The Second Mile*. Ron and Janet love to sail as much as they love to write, and they make their home in Maryland.